D1563289

THE
VALKYRIE'S
SHADOW

ALSO BY TIANA WARNER

SIGRID AND THE VALKYRIES SERIES

The Valkyrie's Daughter
The Valkyrie's Shadow

THE MERMAIDS OF ERIANA KWAI SERIES

Ice Massacre
Ice Crypt
Ice Kingdom

THE VALKYRIE'S SHADOW

TIANA WARNER

This book is a work of fiction. Names, characters, places, and incidents are the product of the author's imagination or are used fictitiously. Any resemblance to actual events, locales, or persons, living or dead, is coincidental.

Copyright © 2023 by Tiana Warner. All rights reserved, including the right to reproduce, distribute, or transmit in any form or by any means. For information regarding subsidiary rights, please contact the Publisher.

Entangled Publishing, LLC
644 Shrewsbury Commons Ave., STE 181
Shrewsbury, PA 17361
rights@entangledpublishing.com

Entangled Teen is an imprint of Entangled Publishing, LLC.

Visit our website at www.entangledpublishing.com.

Edited by Amy Acosta
Cover design by Bree Archer
Stock Art Credits Nerthuz/Gettyimages, stereohype/Gettyimages,
RedKoalaDesign/Gettyimages, Mykhailo Skop/Shutterstock,
Nanashiro/Shutterstock, and CGTrader/clayguy
Interior design by Toni Kerr

ISBN 978-1-64937-400-4
Ebook ISBN 978-1-64937-401-1

Manufactured in the United States of America
First Edition July 2023

10 9 8 7 6 5 4 3 2 1

To Adrianna, a little valkyrie in the making

At Entangled, we want our readers to be well-informed. If you would like to know if this book contains any elements that might be of concern for you, please check the book's webpage.

https://entangledpublishing.com/books/the-valkyries-shadow

CHAPTER ONE

A VEIL OF
NIGHTFALL

Standing on the brink of darkness, Sigrid tightened her grip on the reins, the leather digging through her riding gloves. The path into Svartalfheim was not so much an entrance as a wall of night. Life, light, and sound just seemed to…end.

An illusion.

An entire world existed beyond this veil.

Hestur snorted his displeasure and scraped a hoof against the grass.

Sigrid reached down from the saddle to stroke his neck, her insides churning. "I know, buddy. I don't like this, either."

The line between the realms of light and darkness was more abrupt than she'd expected. A few paces ahead, the lush grass and trees, the bright flowers, and the flocks of noisy birds thriving on the riverbank ceased, becoming a void that stretched infinitely upward and touched the horizon on either side.

The wall was like nothing she'd ever seen—opaque, shifting, *alive.* Flecks of night drifted off it, creeping toward her like ash, grazing her skin and inviting her closer.

It wasn't an invitation she wanted to accept, but she hadn't come all this way to turn around.

She also hadn't survived a trip to Helheim and back a month ago only to die today.

She reached back and unsheathed her spear.

Better to lose a spear than a limb.

Holding her breath, she threw it at the dark veil, then opened her palm to summon it back before it could disappear. As it turned around, tendrils of darkness clung to it like cobwebs, stretching far until they snapped and the spear returned.

The darkness roiled where the spear had touched it, ripples spreading out like she'd disturbed a pond.

Her stomach churned. "I *really* don't like this."

Hestur snorted in agreement.

But what choice did they have? They had to go in.

As the darkness settled, the hairs on the back of Sigrid's neck tingled. She twisted in the saddle to check the riverside.

The spring of Hvergelmir trickled past, connecting the nine worlds and missing one crucial piece—Ratatosk. The god would have been there to ferry travelers in his longship if the Night Elves hadn't captured him in an effort to control passage across the worlds.

The fate of the nine worlds depended on rescuing him, and so did her own.

After spending most of her sixteen years trying to join the valkyrie ranks, Sigrid was finally one of them—*a real valkyrie*—on her first mission. Succeeding today meant she would get to do more. She'd worked hard to earn this rank, and she was ready to do whatever it took to get Ratatosk back.

Even if, for now, that meant waiting in front of a wall while the valkyries flew the perimeter.

Sigrid faced the darkness once more, her nerves pushing her to take action while her orders were to stay. *Did the others get into trouble? Did the Night Elves shoot them down?*

"The valkyries are fine. They're the best warriors in the cosmos," she murmured, needing to hear a voice in the silence.

If only her friends were with her. She'd faced the unknown

enough times to learn that it was less daunting when she had them by her side. They had become a team, a force, conquering everything from here to Helheim.

It'd been weeks since they'd seen each other, and she missed them, especially Mariam. Sigrid's lips still tingled whenever she thought of that blissful goodbye in the woods. Had Mariam made it safely to her home world? Had she thought of Sigrid on the journey, or was she too busy to spare her a thought? She'd promised to return but failed to say when.

Should Sigrid expect to wait weeks, months, or years for her return? She already spent an embarrassing amount of time imagining all the ways their reunion could go, which always ended with them running to each other, limbs tangling, lips moving urgently as they tumbled into the grass...

A gust of wind blew loose strands of Sigrid's blond hair across her face. She looked around with a start, her spear raised and ready to defend herself against—

Hooves thumped like a hailstorm as the twenty-one junior valkyries touched down on their winged white mares.

Oops. So much for staying alert and attentive.

Sigrid sighed in relief at their return and sheathed her weapon.

Hestur nickered a greeting.

They looked majestic, even royal, in their white uniforms, winged helmets, and gold armor. Sigrid, by contrast, wore a hard leather vest over a red tunic. General Eira had bluntly informed her that there was no time to have real, expensive valkyrie armor made for her before they left. But Sigrid had fought in this vest in Helheim and survived, so she could do the same here. At least her helmet matched theirs.

"This is the spot," Ylva said, sitting tall with her usual swan-like poise even as her mare tossed her head and shuffled away from the immense sight before them. "We searched for miles in both directions. It's got to be here."

Upon arrival, they'd found a dock where Ratatosk would presumably moor when ferrying passengers to this world. The entrance to Svartalfheim should logically be here, but they'd all agreed it would be worth checking the area for other obvious entrances before plunging into the wrong spot and angering the Night Elves.

"All right." The flutter in Sigrid's chest grew stronger. "We'll want to stay on the path when they let us in. The darkness didn't exactly look like a warm bath when I poked it with my spear."

The valkyries eyed the dark wall, some skeptical, others fearful, and some doing a careful scan as if hunting for a snag in its fabric.

Sigrid shivered. What would it feel like to go in? Would it be cold, suffocating, painful? Would the cobweb-like strands stick to her skin like they'd done to her spear? "To be safe, we should—"

"Oda got a branch stuck in her tail, Sigrid," Gunni said, scrunching her pink face.

Sigrid exhaled hard and leaned to take a look. She clicked her tongue at the long bramble shoot clinging to the mare's white tail. "So she did."

"Sooo…" Gunni said expectantly, motioning to Oda's rear.

The urge to tell her to untangle it herself and shove it somewhere was strong, but they didn't have time for an argument. Swallowing the retort, Sigrid dismounted Hestur and went to pry loose the branch.

Ylva snickered.

Any friendliness Ylva and Gunni had shown on the journey back from Helheim had vanished. It was almost like they found comfort in knowing Sigrid was a mere stable hand and had been personally offended when she'd joined their ranks. And so the two of them had taken it upon themselves to make sure Sigrid remembered her place. Unfortunately, this request to remove a prickly branch from a mare's butt wasn't the worst they'd come up with during the journey.

"Come on, Gunni." Edith waved an arm, pausing her stretching ritual. "You couldn't have gotten that out yourself?"

Sigrid tried to convey her thanks with a glance. Small moments like this from the other valkyries were, at least, an improvement.

Gunni shot Edith a glare. "I'm busy."

"Oh, I forgot you can't breathe and do anything else at the same time—"

"Everyone ready, then?" Runa, ever the peacekeeper, asked over their bickering.

Sigrid mounted up and nodded, her stomach tightening into a nervous ball.

As General Eira had instructed before they left, Sigrid was to present herself to the king alone, because a lone girl on an ordinary brown horse was less threatening than a fleet of valkyries. And while trespassing on Svartalfheim, the last thing they wanted was for the king of this world to feel threatened.

"To be clear," Sigrid said, "when General Eira said *we could use you on the ground*, she didn't mean, like, a sacrifice, right?"

Runa gave a one-note laugh.

No one else answered, seeming oblivious that it was an honest question.

Sigrid was proud to serve Vanaheim—she'd become a guardian of the upper worlds, the highest class of warriors in the cosmos, and nothing could take away the glory that filled her chest at being given a critical role in this mission. But going in first?

Maybe a little overzealous for her first one.

"You know what to do." Ylva gathered her reins, and her mare began to prance.

Runa closed her eyes and murmured under her breath, maybe praying. The blood drained from her already pale face, and sweaty wisps of brown hair escaped from her helmet.

The sight wasn't helpful.

Edith gave a small nod, as composed as ever. Unlike the rest of them, not a hint of sweat dotted her flawless amber complexion. "We'll be ready when—if—things go sour."

The valkyries took flight, leaving Sigrid in a smothering silence.

Ahead, not a breath of wind or a murmur came out of the darkness.

"We've got this, right?" she asked Hestur as if he were the one who needed reassuring. "We've crossed worse barriers. Remember the gates of Hel?"

Hestur snorted as if to say, *Not helpful.*

Sigrid pulled down the brim of her helmet and adjusted her feet in the stirrups. She nudged Hestur sideways until she could touch the barrier between light and dark. Ashes of nightfall licked toward her, and when she stretched out her fingers, it seeped through her gloves like ice. Black tendrils clung to her like they had to her spear, and she fought the urge to pull her hand back and shake them off.

A *whoosh* came like a rush of water flowing away. According to Vala, the darkness would send the message that a guest was requesting entry. "*If you enter the land of night without permission, you'll sorely regret it,*" she'd said, yet glossed over the consequences. It'd sounded ominous enough that none of them considered *not* knocking.

Sigrid pulled her hand back, reached over her shoulder, and triple-checked her quiver. Her spear was secure. She poked a finger into her saddle bag to check her torch. Still there. She touched the flint rod clipped to her saddle. Ready.

The Night Elves would try to kill her the moment she wielded it, but she had no intention of fumbling through a dark void without an emergency measure in place.

Fisk had once told her, "*Darkness is the most flammable substance.*" He was the only Night Elf she knew, and he never removed his head-to-toe clothing while traveling through other worlds because even a hint of light exposure would burn him to death.

As long as the Svartalf King was reasonable, there would be no need to do something as gruesome as light up this world.

Her heart pulled at the thought of Fisk, who'd gone with Mariam. She missed him, too. If he were here, he would probably be standing loyally by her side in his massive dire wolf mask, ready to hurtle into danger while chattering endlessly along the way.

Get through this, and you're one day closer to seeing them again.

As long as things went well.

She swallowed hard.

At her clear intention, the darkness shifted.

Hestur raised his head, his every muscle tensing underneath her.

"Here we go," she murmured, tightening her grip on the reins.

A fissure appeared in the black veil. She held her breath as the darkness rippled, and then it split, opening a path into the land of night.

CHAPTER TWO

THE SVARTALF KING
SEEMS NICE

The chasm split the darkness like a river of daylight, revealing hard, gray ground. Sigrid waited a beat before nudging Hestur to walk on, taking the illuminated path into Svartalfheim.

A whisper of wind made her look back in time to see the dark veil sealing shut, leaving her and Hestur in a path of light that stretched onward, curving through the darkness. It was like riding along a path in the woods, but rather than trees at her sides, walls of night loomed.

Sigrid exhaled slowly and focused on the path. She resisted the urge to glance up to where the valkyries would have slipped into the opening with her to stay hidden above the clouds, hopefully undetected by Night Elves.

Past the surrounding walls of darkness, activity replaced the sounds of the riverbank. Murmurs, shouts, laughter, splashing water, clanking metal, even clip-clopping hooves passed by. She must have been riding through a village.

"Someone's here to see the king," a gruff voice said nearby. "Look."

"And she's got a nice, sturdy horse," another said. "Think we can keep him?"

Sigrid nudged Hestur into a trot, eager to get past the disembodied voices. His hooves clip-clopped loudly on the rocky ground, which was so barren that it appeared nothing had ever grown here, and nothing ever would.

Fisk aside, her experiences with Night Elves had not been good, and she had no intention of having another disastrous encounter right before meeting with their king.

"A girl!" someone shouted nearby. "Where do you think she's from?"

Hestur trotted faster without urging. Sigrid gripped tighter with her legs and resisted the urge to reach for her spear.

They wouldn't hurt us, right? Not if we're the king's guests.

Onward they rode, following a path that curved left. Though daylight surrounded them, the feel of total darkness lingered, as cold and damp as if they'd plunged into a river. A full-body shiver rocked Sigrid—two parts cold, one part fear—but she clenched her jaw and allowed Hestur to trot on.

They went far past the point where she could change her mind, far past fleeing to safety, far past the comforts of warmth and full sunshine. The chill rippling up her back and the way Hestur kept speeding up told her they weren't just being watched—they were being followed.

"I'm here to see the king," Sigrid called out, her voice bouncing with Hestur's stride. Maybe the note of fear in her voice would make her seem like less of a threat. "I've been sent from Vanaheim to discuss an urgent matter."

Laughter rose around her, making Hestur leap forward in fear. Sigrid nearly toppled out of the saddle, and she wrapped her hands in Hestur's mane to stay on.

"Shh, it's okay," she murmured, struggling to sound calm for his sake. But her breath quickened, and the hair on her arms and neck stood up.

A scrape of metal rang out. Then a loud clatter.

Sigrid tensed up as Hestur sprang into a canter. Her heart fluttered like a bird in a cage, just as desperate to escape whoever surrounded them. When Hestur pulled to go faster, Sigrid let him.

He erupted into a gallop.

She kept a firm hold on the reins and focused on the curves of the path. Without a long range of visibility, they could gallop straight over a cliff before she had a chance to react.

His hooves pounded over the stone, filling her ears.

Her breaths were sharp and cold.

This is a bad idea.

She should call the valkyries off. It wasn't too late to abandon this whole—

Around the next curve, the path abruptly ended at a towering stone wall.

Sigrid leaned back, her arms straining as she reined Hestur to a hard stop. "Whoa!"

He jerked to a halt, rearing in fright at what lay before them.

Sigrid regained her balance, gasping for breath. *Better a wall than a cliff.*

The relief was short-lived, and a new layer of fear coated her insides when the light surrounding them expanded, pushing back the night and forming a larger oval that placed her at the center. Like she'd been thrust into a fighting arena in front of an audience she couldn't see.

Except…

In the newly revealed area to her right, sitting on top of an earthy dais, was a huge throne made of gnarled black tree roots. The wood twisted and snaked, rising to twice her height and just as wide.

A Night Elf sat upon it, clad head to toe in leather and chainmail. His bear skull mask had long canines curving toward each other, and it was paired with huge deer antlers and a deadly looking iron crown. Calm poise radiated from him, unlike any of the others she'd met before.

Sigrid's heart pounded at the eerie sight of him, but she still nudged Hestur to move closer. *Please, let the valkyries be circling above me.*

When they stopped at the edge of the dais, she dipped her head in acknowledgment. "Greetings, Svartalf King."

The king raised a hand.

Sigrid almost raised her own hand, thinking it was a greeting of sorts, but it wasn't.

A group of elves in smaller antlered deer masks materialized out of the darkness and flanked the throne. At another signal, two came forward to meet her.

Hestur tried to back away.

"It's okay." She nudged him to stand still, though her heart raced faster.

His ears turned back to listen to her.

As much as she wanted to tell them not to come any closer, she had to be passive and agreeable. General Eira had been *very* clear about this.

One of the elves grabbed Hestur's reins. The other flung open her saddle bag.

Her heart jumped. "Hey!"

Hestur tossed his head and backed up, picking up on her tone. The elf at his head held tight, yanking the reins so Sigrid's hands jerked forward.

The elf at her side grabbed the torch out of her bag, wrenched the spear from the quiver on her back, and stepped away.

They'd known she would come prepared with fire. Of course they would. Why did she think they would let her walk in without searching her for weapons? More importantly, what in the nine worlds had she been thinking when she agreed to this?

The elf dipped his chin, giving the spear a long look. Three black stones were embedded in his mask's forehead, almost like a crown. "She's all clear."

The other elf let go of the reins, and they both backed off.

She held back her surprise. Did he not realize it was a valkyrie spear? If he were smart, he would've snapped it.

I still have a weapon.

Once the elves returned to their posts beside the gnarled throne, the Svartalf King spoke.

"Why have you come?" His deep voice was muffled beneath his mask.

Sigrid squared her shoulders, trying to let the saddle's height give her confidence. "I've been sent with a message from Vanaheim," she said, skirting the real answer.

The king tapped his fingers on the throne's armrests, his silence unsettling. The muted *tap, tap, tap* of leather on wood filled the still air. "I would have expected valkyries. Who are you?"

"Sigrid."

"Sigrid who?"

She paused. She'd spent her whole life without a surname, learning a fortnight ago that she was a Helenadottir—daughter of a lost valkyrie princess, of a royal who was now the queen of Helheim. Offering this name would do her no favors.

"Just…Sigrid," she said.

The king leaned back in his throne, which creaked and groaned beneath him. He moved slowly, with more dignity and grace than the horde of Night Elves she had the displeasure of meeting before.

"I see." Amusement constricted his voice. "Does King Óleifr think so low of me that he couldn't send more than an orphaned peasant girl?"

Words like these had been thrown at her as an insult enough times that they had no impact. She pressed her lips together, hoping it came off as a smile. "I've come to kindly request the return of Ratatosk."

There was a subtle, almost imperceptible shift. If she hadn't been waiting for a reaction, she would have missed it. But the

Svartalf King and those flanking him grew still, like a herd spotting a predator.

"We have no business with Ratatosk," the Svartalf King said, unmoving.

She held back a smirk at the non-answer. "King Óleifr has reason to believe he's here."

The *reason*, of course, was that Fisk had flat-out told Sigrid the Svartalf King put a bounty on Ratatosk—but she wasn't about to tell him that.

The king's sigh hissed inside his mask. "The way Vanaheim leans on the Eye of Hnitbjorg for knowledge is exhausting. You people have nothing but that lump of rock to give you status."

Sigrid narrowed her eyes. First, he'd assumed wrong—the Eye was *not* how they knew Svartalfheim had taken Ratatosk. Second, Vanaheim's status came from all kinds of magic and a noble line of Vanir gods, not just prophetic knowledge offered by the Eye. But the king wouldn't take kindly to being argued or corrected. Especially not by a peasant girl.

"Ratatosk's disappearance threatens the cosmic balance, Your Majesty," Sigrid said, a chill settling over her the longer she stood in this sunless world. "The spring isn't meant to be controlled by anyone but him."

The Svartalf King crossed one leg over the other, his leather and chainmail creaking in the silence. His antlers scraped against the tall throne, the sound filling the dead quiet. "Yggdrasil grows and changes, as does any tree." He waved a gloved hand. "Leaves grow, fruits ripen, and everything must ultimately fall back to the ground. Unfortunately, the rotten fruits of the world tree have far-reaching consequences. We have to do our part to nourish its trunk."

She furrowed her brow. Did he just call Vanaheim a rotten fruit?

"Your Majesty, if Ratatosk can't ferry anyone along its

branches, then the gods and valkyries can't do their part to nourish its trunk. Everyone will be stuck in their own…um, fruit." She was losing the metaphor. "You're preventing anyone from traveling," she finished bluntly.

"This does not sound like my problem to worry about."

A wave of hot anger flooded through Sigrid. How could he be so indifferent? "But traveling between worlds is dangerous and sometimes impossible without Ratatosk! This restricts Vanaheim from sending the valkyries to places that need them."

"You seem to be under the delusion that everyone cares where the valkyries go," the Svartalf King said, unmistakable mockery in his words.

"Of course they should care!" Sigrid exclaimed. How dare he suggest that the valkyries weren't revered. In Jotunheim, the seniors were risking their lives right now to help calm civil unrest. "Our job is to keep the worlds safe. If a war breaks out, we'll help stop it. If there's a natural disaster, we'll send aid—"

"*We? Our* job?" The king leaned forward. "Am I to understand that you consider yourself to be a valkyrie?"

Sigrid clenched her jaw. Never mind the slip-up, the taunt stung.

At her silence, the Svartalf King laughed, his voice booming. He shifted, becoming more animated. "We find ourselves in the presence of one of King Óleifr's fine valkyries. Where are your wings, orphan girl?"

The elves flanking him laughed, a muffled sound through their deer masks.

Hestur tossed his head, maybe in response to her fingers tightening over the reins. He snorted, no doubt as uneasy as she was in this strange, cold world.

She rested a soothing hand on his neck, clenching her teeth against a shiver. Her gloves couldn't keep her fingers warm anymore. Her helmet felt like ice atop her head. "Your Majesty,

Yggdrasil might crumble without Ratatosk to ferry anyone along the spring."

"Don't fret over Ratatosk, *valkyrie girl*. He's safe and comfortable among the worms. We have even given him light so he can feel more at home." He waved her away. "Trot back to Óleifr and tell him that."

Among the worms? That sounded like he was dead. But if he was safe and comfortable…

Underground.

Triumph surged through Sigrid. They had him imprisoned in a place where they could safely cast light. General Eira had suspected an underground prison. With her knowledge of Vanaheim's complicated history with Svartalfheim, she'd shared a few hunches as to where he could be. Her first guess had been the right one.

"I can't leave without him," Sigrid said, leaving no doubt that she meant it. But how were they supposed to search for him?

She scanned the guards, searching for a weakness, an escape, anything. The Night Elf who'd taken her spear took a few steps back, propping it against the wall behind the throne and resting a hand on his sword.

The fool had just made it even more accessible to her.

"Then I'm afraid we're at an impasse." The king heaved a sigh and rose from his gnarled throne, still moving in that slow, dignified way. His antlers curved impressively high, the tops cast into shadow. She could trace her gaze along each canine tooth, perfect except for one, which had a broken and jagged tip. "Unless you have something to offer me, it's time for you to leave."

What did that mean? Was he asking for a gift or a bribe?

No, these elves could make treasures as great as Thor's hammer. No material offer would please the Svartalf King— except maybe magic, and Vanaheim would never give that to a world as low as Svartalfheim.

There would be no reasoning with him, either, which meant they would have to use force.

Before she could think of a plan, the king spoke.

"Best of luck in the night," he said, his tone mocking. "Goodbye, *just Sigrid*." He swiped an arm as if slamming a door.

The deer-masked elves flanking him stepped forward, their swords raised like they expected Sigrid to charge.

Sigrid's heart jumped, and Hestur snorted, tensing. To either side, the walls of darkness advanced like a set of jaws moving to swallow them.

She wouldn't be able to find her way out in pitch dark!

You evil, rotten, heartless…

"Fine." Sigrid lifted her chin, letting defiance smother her fear. "You wanted to know where my wings are? Let me introduce you."

She whistled, and on cue, a blaze of fire opened the sky like lightning.

The king's mask jerked up toward the danger, and he let out a rage-filled cry. The others screamed, stepping back.

Sigrid's last glimpse of the king before the darkness swallowed everything was of him stumbling backward, pointing up at the *V* formation of winged mares.

"Valkyries!" he roared.

CHAPTER THREE

FIGHTING AMONG
THE WORMS

A waterfall of icy-cold darkness engulfed Sigrid and Hestur. It grabbed her like a thousand hands, smothering her, making it hard to stay in the saddle. She sucked in a breath of freezing air, spots popping in her vision in the sudden absence of light.

"Shoot them!" The king's roar filled the impenetrable night, disorienting.

Overhead, the twenty-one junior valkyries cut the darkness with torches in hand—and Sigrid's senses sharpened. The outlines of winged mares and riders barreled toward her in the sky, shouts and screams filled her ears, and Hestur's energy rose beneath her as he readied himself for a fight.

In the midst of darkness, anger at the arrogant king rose over Sigrid's panic.

"Down here! They have Ratatosk!" She opened her hand to summon her spear from where the elf had left it, ready to defend herself. She couldn't see the enemy, but she could hear them, and so could Hestur. When the spear clapped into her palm, she stayed quiet, letting his superior hearing do the work.

Hestur tensed, responding to movements she couldn't detect. Suddenly, he spun and kicked with both hind legs, nearly unseating her. There was a yelp when the hit connected and a clatter as bodies collided.

"Good job, bud—"

Hestur's neck thrust out like someone had yanked on the reins, pitching her forward in the saddle.

Sigrid held onto his mane just in time as he reared. Several shouts echoed from the darkness along with the sound of feet scrambling back.

When his hooves touched down, Sigrid took a chance and threw the spear toward the commotion.

"Oof!"

Satisfaction surged through her at the thump of a body hitting the ground.

She summoned the weapon back. The spear's golden hilt glinted as light passed over it, and she looked up to see the *V* formation of valkyries swoop low. Their torches illuminated their surroundings.

Sigrid looked around wildly, straining to see what was happening, and her heart dropped into her stomach. Light flickered over what must have been a hundred advancing Night Elves, all in armor and masks. Had guards been stationed beyond the veil? Of course they had. They might not have been expecting *this* attack, but their mistrust of outsiders was undeniable.

The guards moved like the elves she'd seen before, insubstantial shadows flitting across the ground like illusions.

She sucked in a breath and gripped the reins tighter.

We have to find the prison before they kill us all.

"Sigrid, catch!" Edith shouted.

The shadow of a torch fell from the sky.

"Yes," Sigrid said under her breath, nudging Hestur toward it. As he sprang forward, she sheathed the spear across her back and stretched out a hand to catch the torch. "Edith, he's underground! General Eira was right."

"On it!" she called back.

With a trembling hand, Sigrid flipped the torch and swiped it down the flint rod on her saddle. It erupted to life with a *whoosh*.

The fire lacerated the darkness like a spear opening a wound, its light pouring outward. It illuminated a set of antlers at Hestur's shoulder and a sword raised high.

With a gasp, she jabbed the flame toward the elf.

Though he was safely clothed, the ingrained fear of fire sent him stumbling backward with a yelp. She seized the weakness, swiping the torch like a sword to keep him back. It left an orange trail as it flew, illuminating more shadows advancing behind him.

With the other hand, Sigrid guided Hestur around and nudged him, desperate to get away from this horde.

"Go!"

He spun on his haunches and sprang into a gallop, taking her away from their attackers. If the illuminated path that guided her into Svartalfheim had left them with limited visibility, the torch had even less. But it was better than nothing. And with the valkyries flying by, torches in hand, at least she knew where to go.

Sigrid met up with a group of four valkyries, among them Ylva, who flew low along a dirt road, their mares' white tails whipping behind them. The girls expertly managed their spears, torches, and mares all at once, carrying a weapon in each hand and using their legs and voice commands to control their mounts. Sigrid did the same on Hestur, using one hand to light the ground so he wouldn't trip and the other to launch her spear at oncoming shadows.

"Any ideas where the prison is, Ylva?"

"A few others are searching the old keep over there," Ylva said, though Sigrid couldn't see where she pointed. "There's also a fortified tower up here we need to check."

Though Night Elves couldn't match the speed of a winged mare or Hestur, the flitting shadows multiplied, coming out of the darkness on all sides.

Cold dread trickled through her veins. *Was I a fool for not bringing Sleipnir?*

For the first time since leaving Vanaheim, her answer wavered. It was absurd that she'd chosen to ride her ordinary gelding instead of the eight-legged stallion trained for battle by Odin.

Peter, her big brother in all but blood, had gawked at her when she saddled up Hestur. "But Sleipnir was raised and trained for this! Hestur is—"

"First, I ride better on Hestur," Sigrid had snapped, cutting him off before he could insult her beloved gelding. "Second, if I take Sleipnir with me, it won't be a secret anymore that I kept him."

"You can't keep him a secret forever."

"I can and I will. No one needs to know Odin's steed is romping around Vanaheim."

She'd conveniently not mentioned the third point, and the biggest reason of all—the nagging feeling that Sleipnir made her evil. His chaotic power bled into her when she rode him, quickening her pulse, tensing her muscles, driving her to act on adrenaline. It was a cosmic force she couldn't understand, but she'd learned to recognize when it closed around her chest and left her short of breath.

The fear of being manipulated by this force had reaffirmed her decision. She'd chosen to ride Hestur to Svartalfheim because he didn't change who she was. She could think clearly, and she didn't need to doubt whether she was acting of her own volition or under the influence of the gods of war and death.

A mare swooped in front of Sigrid, then Runa and three other valkyries landed, the gust blowing Hestur's mane into her face and snapping her to the present trouble.

"They really don't want us in that tower," Runa shouted, spinning her mare around. "The upper levels are empty. The windows are too small to get in, but Gunni found an entrance."

"Let's go!" Sigrid turned Hestur to follow, racing with the

others down an alley. The buildings to either side were dismal stone and metal, not a whiff of vegetation to be found.

How did Fisk survive this place?

Ahead, a half-moon of valkyries kept a swarm of Night Elves back. Golden spears glinted in the firelight as they soared to their targets and back to their owners. Edith and Runa stayed low, helping Sigrid and Hestur gallop through the horde and into safety against the tower wall.

Once past the valkyries, she hurried over to where a few others convened at a nondescript wooden door.

Edith scanned the group and pointed back to the half-moon of valkyries with her spear. "Everyone should go help them except for a few of us. I'll stay here with Ylva, Gunni, Runa, and Sigrid."

"That's not—" Ylva began, then scanned the group. Too many of them crowded the door, leaving the rest of the valkyries severely outnumbered. "Yeah, okay. Go!"

While the others took off, Gunni cued her mare, Oda, to kick the wooden door. The mare's back hooves hit it with shattering force.

That's not going to be good for her legs.

Sigrid was about to suggest they let Hestur do it, whose legs were stronger, when the door broke open with a *bang*. The corridor beyond was a black hole barely high enough to avoid whacking their helmets on the ceiling. Instead of stairs leading up into the tower, the corridor led down into a tunnel.

"Ew." Ylva's lip curled in distaste. "No way will Roskva go in there."

Sure enough, her mare backed away, shaking her head in agitation.

Sigrid nudged Hestur forward.

Gunni cut her off on Oda. "We'll go. The rest of you stay here and keep the Night Elves back."

Oda trotted confidently forward, but the moment she stepped

inside the passage, she stopped, snorting in fright.

"Whoa!" Gunni grabbed the mare's mane to keep from tumbling off. "Hey, hey, calm down."

Oda's wings slapped into the tunnel walls as she backed away, frantic.

Edith, the next option, looked down at her stocky mare. If Oda couldn't fit, Mjöll would surely be too wide.

The mares weren't suited to go underground. After a lifetime of soaring through the sky, they were nervous of the enclosed space.

"Hestur and I will go," Sigrid said, adrenaline raising the volume of her voice. "All of you stay out here—"

A scream erupted behind her. Gunni toppled from the saddle and hit the hard ground, her armor clanking. Oda whinnied, staying close to her fallen rider.

"Oh gods, they got me!" Gunni shouted, panicking. "They got me! Help!"

An arrow stuck out of her thigh. The shaft glinted dully in the torch light.

Sigrid's mouth went dry, like she might vomit. *An iron arrow?*

Ylva leaped off her mare to help while the others spun to guard them.

"What is it doing to her skin?" Ylva shouted, recoiling. "Are those snakes?"

Black tendrils sprouted from the arrow, weaving across Gunni's thigh like a spiderweb.

Bile rose up Sigrid's throat. "It's the darkness. It looks like the veil when I touched it with my spear. It's trying to smother her or—"

Gunni screamed louder, kicking her legs. "Get it out of me!"

"Grab it, quick!" Sigrid shouted.

Ylva seized the arrow and wrenched it from Gunni's thigh. Gunni's roar of pain filled the air. The tendrils of darkness snapped, curling in on the arrow, and Gunni kicked free of the web on her thigh.

They all stared at the iron arrow in Ylva's hand, but the darkness didn't come out again.

In the distance, the rest of the valkyries still fended off the Night Elves, barely visible in the light coming from their torches. Had the arrow come from all the way over there? Whose aim was that good?

"Sigrid, you need to go in there. Now," Edith urged, panic constricting her voice as she scanned for the mysterious attacker. "We'll hold them off as long as we can."

Time was running out.

"Gather the ones searching the old keep, and be ready to fly as soon as I'm back." Sigrid pointed Hestur at the tunnel, and he bounded in without hesitating. With no wings to stretch out and a lean stature working to his advantage, he thought nothing of the small space. Besides, after facing a hellhound in a fiery cavern, this little tunnel enveloped them like a hug.

She trusted the valkyries to keep the Night Elves occupied. As long as they weren't mistaken to think Ratatosk was imprisoned here, they would be able to get out of this dark world.

They only had one chance at this rescue, and they'd better do it before anyone else got shot down. Would Gunni be okay? What sort of enchantment had been placed on that arrow? Not even Sigrid's darkest nightmares could have conjured something like this. Somehow, it had been made possible in the realm of night, where the most powerful and dangerous treasures in the worlds were forged.

But now was not the time to figure out the sinister arrows.

She had a job to do.

Hestur's hoofbeats echoed as they cantered through the cool, damp tunnel, sounding like she had a herd at her back. The clash of battle shrank away. Her torch illuminated a stride at a time, so she couldn't be sure what lay ahead.

The tunnel sloped downward, and Hestur slowed to a trot, taking her down a bouncy decline until the scent of soil and iron met her nose.

Open wooden doors lined the corridor. Empty cells.

As she continued on, her breath caught—slumped against the corridor walls, blood pooling, were several Night Elves. They must have been the guards of the underground prison. From the way their wounds gushed, they'd fought and lost not that long ago.

Which means whoever did this must still be in here...

Sigrid swallowed and reached back for her spear.

Flickering candlelight came from further in, but she was afraid to call out.

Who would have gone ahead of her, and why? It couldn't be a valkyrie, could it?

She nudged Hestur to keep going.

At the far end, one door remained closed. The faintest ray of light flickered through the crack between the wood and the dirt floor.

Her breaths came fast.

What if it's a trap?

A scrape behind her made her half jump out of her seat. She twisted in the saddle, ready to block the attack.

But the blow never came.

The elf with the black stones in his mask stood at the edge of her torch light, the long knives in his hands stained with the evidence of his kills.

A *Night Elf* had done this.

Why?

The elf dipped his chin, then slinked back into the shadows on silent footsteps before Sigrid could form words.

When Fisk had become an ally, he'd had his own reasons. She'd just never thought other Night Elves might disagree with the state of their world or the decisions of their king.

Far above, the screams and clanking weapons continued, barely audible. She had to hurry.

Back to facing the door at the end, Sigrid called out, "Sir, if you're in there, I need you to stand back." She spun Hestur around. "Kick!"

He struck out with his back hooves, rattling the door. She cued him again, and he struck it three more times before it broke off the hinges and slammed to the ground.

"Good boy."

Hestur snorted and danced on the spot, energized by his victory.

In the cell, an old man stood against the opposite wall, his hands splayed against it as though to flatten himself as much as possible.

His protuberant eyes, red hair poking out like a fringe over his ears, pale face with a pointed nose, and small mouth made him look like a squirrel. A red fur coat covered his shoulders, open to reveal a dirty, white tunic.

"Ratatosk?" Sigrid asked.

The squirrel-man stared at her, gaunt and waxy. The flame from her torch and the solitary candle inside the cell flickered, casting shadows over his wrinkled face. Almost imperceptibly, he nodded.

Her breath caught.

She'd done it.

She'd succeeded on her first mission as a valkyrie, and pride surged like sunlight in her chest.

Now they just had to escape. *Easy.*

Cueing Hestur to kneel so Ratatosk could climb on behind her, she extended a hand. "My name is Sigrid. I'm here to rescue you."

CHAPTER FOUR

GIFT FOR GIFT

Sigrid burst through the veil of darkness and onto the riverbank, the sudden brightness stinging. She raised an arm to cover her eyes, cursing under her breath, and let Hestur take her and Ratatosk to the water's edge.

The valkyries might buy them time by holding the elves back, but they had to hurry. The Svartalf King wouldn't let them go easily.

She dismounted Hestur and helped Ratatosk do the same. He hobbled forward until the waters of the spring of Hvergelmir lapped at his ankles.

"Whatever you need to do, sir, better do it fast. Please." They needed his ship. *Now*.

Through the trees, the veil of darkness was deceptively still, and Sigrid braced for the valkyries, armed Night Elves, or both to burst through at any moment. How fast would they catch up? Their horses were fast, but so were Night Elves, who moved like shadows.

Ratatosk slumped to his knees, and Sigrid gasped. "Sir!"

She hurried to help him up, but he held up a bony finger, and she paused.

He was alarmingly frail, especially for a god, but maybe being trapped in an underground cell for weeks would do that to anyone. Out in the daylight, his sallow skin looked like it was draped over his bones like an old tent.

Murmuring, Ratatosk dipped that same finger in the water. A ripple traveled away from them, as if a fish were going to fetch his ship.

A swift noise and muted thump had Sigrid reaching for her spear and facing the wall. A lance jutted out of the forest floor. Her breath caught. A second later, Ylva and her mare shot out of the veil, quickly followed by the others.

"Sigrid! They're right on our tail!" Edith yelled as she circled above.

They were out of time.

"Sir, we need to hurry." Sigrid turned back to Ratatosk, and he allowed her to help him up this time. "How long will it—" She snapped her gaze to something in her periphery.

Emerging from the misty waters, the wooden longship drifted toward them like a mare coming to her rider.

"Oh, thank the gods."

"Everyone aboard," Ratatosk said. Even his voice was brittle.

They needed no encouragement.

More weapons soared across the veil and thumped into the grass as the valkyries landed on deck. Sigrid took Ratatosk's elbow and helped him board, Hestur following closely.

Runa hurried to Sigrid's side and helped carry Ratatosk over to the helm.

Lances and axes hit the ship, glancing off and plunging into the water.

"Can we get going already?" Gunni yelled, trying to grab the reins to her agitated mare.

"We're going as fast as we can!" Sigrid snapped.

Ratatosk reached for the wheel.

With a *zing*, an iron arrow glanced off one of the handles, and Sigrid and Runa screamed. As it clattered to the deck, they pulled Ratatosk away, waiting for the black tendrils of night to erupt from it.

Nothing happened.

Do the arrows only unleash their magic if they hit a person?

Runa reached for the arrow, but Sigrid shouted at her to stop. "You might activate it. We'll bring it home wrapped in something."

Runa recoiled, wedging her hands under her armpits as if to protect them from what she'd been about to do.

At the veil, a handful of elves burst through, looking around wildly and pointing at the ship.

"Sigrid, hurry up!" someone yelled.

Ratatosk jumped into action, and they all stumbled as the ship lurched forward.

More weapons soared over and around the indestructible ship, and everyone ducked. None found targets, and soon, Svartalfheim's coast drifted out of sight.

Relief washed over Sigrid like a cool bath. She sucked in what felt like the first real breath in hours.

We did it. We're safe.

As they set sail through the dark forest, she leaned against the railing near Ratatosk in case he needed help. But he seemed to gain energy as he tugged ropes and hustled around by the helm like Fisk had done, as if being back at his post renewed his health.

The ship also seemed to have new life to it now that its captain had returned. It was as majestic as she remembered, and a welcome sight because it meant they wouldn't need to spend another nine days fighting their way home. She'd grown fond of it after spending so much time with it in recent weeks. The enormous blood-red sail billowed out like the throat pouch on a sea bird. The row of shields on each side, painted with the emblems of the nine worlds, could have been its folded wings. The serpent Jörmungandr curved up at each end, with expressive eyes and a fork-tongued mouth.

Ratatosk continued to putter about, tying knots and mumbling to himself.

Hestur left her side to march over to the food crate, obviously remembering it from last time. He ate an apple off the top, attracting the attention of the other horses, who came over to investigate the snack source.

The valkyries settled in for the journey, chatting and laughing. Gunni's thigh was bandaged, both iron arrows wrapped in a blanket beside her so nobody would touch them. They would need to bring them to the sorcerers to be studied. Sigrid's stomach turned as she recalled the way the first had nearly enveloped Gunni in darkness. It was clearly fused with dangerous magic, and the sooner they understood how to counter it, the better.

Sigrid turned her gaze back to the frail man. "Ratatosk, will you be okay? Once we leave, I mean." They'd left Svartalfheim in chaos, and she wasn't convinced he would be able to defend himself if the elves came after him again.

His small mouth pulled into a thin line. "Knowing now what the Night Elves are capable of, I will guard myself as Garmr does his cave. Don't fear for me."

Sigrid frowned. "The Svartalf King won't give up easily."

"A valid concern."

He said the words lightly, but Sigrid's chest tightened at having her main worry confirmed. After that ordeal, she had a hunch they hadn't seen the last of the Svartalf King or his troops. The Night Elves had captured Ratatosk for a reason. They would want him back—and they might also want revenge on the valkyries.

"Do you think Vanaheim is at risk of attack by the Night Elves now?" Sigrid asked.

"I'm afraid I don't know what the Night Elves will do next, but they will no longer have easy sailing to other worlds." He frowned, the deep lines of his face pinching inward.

His promise was a small comfort. After all, there were other ways to travel across the nine worlds.

Ratatosk said nothing more, leaving her frustrated and restless as she watched him tend the sail. The red fringes over his ears and his red fur coat blew chaotically in the wind, making it clear how fast they were going.

They'd succeeded in their mission, but at what cost? What would happen next? This couldn't be as simple as saving Ratatosk and sailing home. There would be consequences. Vanaheim would need to be ready.

As Ratatosk returned to the wheel to turn them left at a fork in the spring, an odd pang of sadness went through Sigrid's heart. It took her a moment to decipher it. Last time she was on this ship, Fisk and Mariam were with her, and Fisk had been the one captaining.

Gods, she missed them.

She chewed her lip, a nauseating thought occurring to her. Having Ratatosk back on his ship meant Mariam and Fisk no longer had it. They would need to travel a long and dangerous route to get back to Sigrid in Vanaheim—a route that would possibly involve angry Night Elves who were determined to take revenge on valkyries. Ratatosk charged an exorbitant amount of gold to travel the spring, and she would never be able to afford his fare.

Unless Mariam didn't have to pay…

Would he be kind enough to give Mariam a free ride to Vanaheim in thanks for being rescued? Would it be brazen to ask? Her stomach twisted at the prospect of asking a god for a favor, but this was urgent. She couldn't let Mariam and Fisk travel a dangerous route through the nine worlds.

Ratatosk clenched the wheel as if using it to stay upright, guiding them along the current at an abnormally quick pace. Rays of sun peeked through the trees and flickered across his tired face.

Sigrid cleared her throat. "How often do you go to Niflheim?"

Those protuberant eyes shifted from her to the valkyries and back. "You don't like to mingle with the others."

Sigrid paused, caught off guard, then shrugged. "I only recently became one of them. We aren't really…friends."

"Ah." The ship rocked, and he nudged the wheel. "The gods had much to say on the matter of friendship. *'Tis a bond built gift for gift, laughter for laughter; 'tis unwise to find friends in all who smile and flatter.* Would you agree?"

"What?"

"*The path to a foe is crooked and tough, even if they live nigh. But the path to a friend is easy and straight, no matter where they reside.*"

"Right," Sigrid said slowly. Whatever he was on about, she had yet to find an "easy and straight" path to anything in life. And she wasn't about to start buying the valkyries gifts.

Laughter erupted from the group. Edith and Runa tied their legs together with a horse bandage and hobbled across the deck in a three-legged race. From the railing, their mares watched with disdain.

They were obviously having fun, but Sigrid had spent the bulk of her sixteen years—soon to be seventeen—shoveling their mares' manure and oiling their saddles, and a number of them liked it that way. They liked that rank separation. This suited her fine.

Sigrid shook her head. It didn't matter now. She had important matters to discuss with the man they'd rescued. Ready to steer the conversation back to Mariam, she said, "Thank you for taking us back to Vanaheim."

"Gift for gift, Sigrid." He spun the wheel, and they emerged from the woods into a flat, rocky landscape. Their route wound through columns of steam that billowed into the sky. While Sigrid nearly gagged at the overpowering rotten egg smell, Ratatosk inhaled deeply through his squirrel-like nose, seeming to relish it.

Gift for gift. Would he give one more?

"I wondered if…if you'd be able to do one more trip for me." Her throat was tight. "There's a valkyrie in Niflheim who needs to get back to Vanaheim, and I wondered if you could…" She swallowed hard when his unblinking eyes scrutinized her.

"You want me to do another free trip to bring this valkyrie home."

Sigrid toed the deck, her face burning. "She belongs in Vanaheim."

Ratatosk paused. Sigrid's chest constricted, making it hard to breathe.

"I charge a fee for my services." He wasn't angry or stern, just factual.

Sigrid's heart sank. "I know, but I hoped that given…" She motioned vaguely back toward Svartalfheim.

"I am taking you home for free," Ratatosk said.

"I should hope so!" Sigrid exclaimed. Was Ratatosk really going to be stubborn with her after she'd rescued him?

He turned his beady gaze on her. "What can you offer me?"

"Other than your life?" she asked, then pursed her lips. Maybe it wasn't a good idea to be snarky to a god.

Ratatosk's eyes gleamed. The corner of his mouth might have twitched, but she couldn't be certain.

"It's a cart of gold for a trip like that," he said.

Sigrid's wages as a junior valkyrie would never be enough. She looked around desperately. What could she give him that would be as valuable as gold?

"The canvas on your ship," she said, struck with inspiration. "The Night Elves severed it. I'll find it and return it to you."

She was careful not to specify *when.* But finding and returning the canvas would benefit everybody in the nine worlds, and this was something she had a chance of doing.

Ratatosk looked at the torn remains of it, which was supposed to be there to protect the ship's passengers against monsters like Garmr. Again, the weapon used to break it was fused with magic Sigrid didn't understand—something that could destroy the indestructible. Night Elf magic was beyond anything they knew in Vanaheim.

As he considered, her heart thumped. If he didn't accept this offer, she didn't know what else to do.

"I can go to Niflheim's port," he said. "But if she isn't there, I won't get off the ship and search for her. She has to come to me."

Sigrid's breath caught. She nodded. From across the cosmos, this was the best she could do for Mariam. If Mariam was ready to come back, she would go to the spring, right? "Thank you."

He nodded once, then turned them sharply at a fork in the spring, his bushy red eyebrows pinched in concentration. Clattering hooves, screams, and giggles filled the air as everyone struggled for balance. Sigrid gripped the railing for support. Around them, the smelly columns of steam billowed more thickly.

Sigrid chewed her lip. More questions about the Night Elves sat uneasy in her gut, as turbulent as the spring beneath them. "Ratatosk, why didn't the other gods—Odin, Freyja, and the rest—stop the Night Elves from taking you?"

Not to speak ill of the gods, but for such a cosmic disaster, this seemed beyond the valkyries' job description.

Ratatosk dipped his chin. "A sharp observation, girl. When the gods neglected to stop my capture or ensure my release, it became clear that something was amiss. I have ferried gods and mortals along Yggdrasil's trunk and branches since time began. Odin decreed my role himself: *Ratatosk shall run on the ash tree, Yggdrasil.* So why did the gods not stop the Night Elves?" He paused, tapping his gnarled fingers on the wheel. "I intend to visit Asgard to find out."

The ship creaked beneath them, and horses snorted and stomped.

When he said nothing more, Sigrid asked, "Do you have any guesses?"

He glanced at her, twitching his small mouth as if debating whether to continue. "My suspicions tell me…that this is the work of Loki."

CHAPTER FIVE

EVIL IS RELATIVE

Sigrid flinched like he'd shouted the name. She'd heard stories about the god of mischief, but she'd always thought they were just that—stories. She never thought she would live through one of his tricks. "Are—are you sure?"

"*Loki is naught but mocking and sly, tainting the worlds with insults and lies,*" Ratatosk said. "The god of mischief is single-handedly responsible for all suffering in the nine worlds, Sigrid."

"So you think he's been communicating with the Night Elves?"

"It's possible—no, *probable*, I would say."

"But…" Sigrid furrowed her brow, trying to make sense of what little she knew about the gods. "Why do the other gods keep him around? Wouldn't the cosmic balance be easier to maintain if he couldn't act?"

Overhead, the red sail flapped, and the ship picked up speed. The rocky landscape became a blur, the columns of steam blending into thick fog. Sigrid kept holding the railing, ready for rapids.

"The answer is in the word *balance*." Ratatosk raised his voice over the wind. "It implies two sides. On one, you have goodness, order, nobility, and peace. On the other, you have evil, chaos, obscenity, and mischief. To achieve cosmic balance, both sides of the scale must coexist. I believe Loki felt that the scales had tipped too far into order. And so here we are, thrust the other way. I cringe to think what havoc he is wreaking in Asgard as we speak."

"That's grim." The idea of evil being necessary wasn't new, but it settled over her like a boulder. "Is there any way we can stop him?"

"Why would we? The fact that there will always be evil means there will always be good, too. Each of us must decide which side of the scale we want to be on. *If evil you see, then evil proclaim it, and make no friendship with foes. In evil, no joy should you know.*"

Sigrid rubbed the back of her neck, bewildered. "Who cares about *balance* when a world with only good is an option? We have to find Loki and stop him from whatever chaos he's unleashing." Her cheeks warmed as the words came out. She sounded naive. Who was she to stop a god? But if Loki was going to wreak havoc on the worlds like this, they couldn't sit by and let it happen. She was a valkyrie now, and this was part of her job.

The ship rocked as they serpentined through the dense white fog.

"A world with only good is impossible." Ratatosk swiped a hand over his nose in a helplessly squirrel-like manner. "All concepts are relative."

Sigrid squinted at him. "What do you mean?"

"How tall are you, Sigrid?"

"Um." In truth, she'd only gauged her height using a horse measuring stick, but she didn't feel like making a fool of herself by telling Ratatosk she was sixteen hands high. Anyway, what did this have to do with Loki?

"Are you tall or short?" he asked before she could respond.

"A bit short, I think."

"And when you were in Svartalfheim, were you tall or short?"

"Compared to elves, I guess I'm tall."

"And if you went to visit the giants in Muspelheim, then what?"

"I'd be short."

"See? Tall and short are relative concepts. So are rich and poor, dark and light. There is no such thing as one without the other. There is no *peace* without *war* as an option."

"Okay…" Sigrid tapped the wooden railing. "So you're saying there's no such thing as *good* without evil to compare it to."

Ratatosk's lips curved upward in a half-moon—possibly the strangest-looking smile she'd ever seen.

"I still think Loki is unnecessary," Sigrid said stubbornly.

"Sigrid, without the agent of chaos, there would never be progress. Suffering incites change. Look how the other worlds have abused and taken advantage of Svartalfheim. Now, Loki has goaded them into doing something about it. After so long, they want their turn in a position of power. And who can blame them? So we have war—but we are on the threshold of change. Chaos must come before balance can be restored."

Sigrid's heart jumped at the threat of war and chaos. She drew a breath and spread her feet wider to balance against the rocking ship. True, if there were no suffering, then nothing would ever improve. If she hadn't been unhappy with her role as a stable hand, she never would have sought out Sleipnir or tried to become a valkyrie. Was Loki somehow behind that decision, too? Was Loki behind every big change and tough decision?

It was hard to believe the Night Elves' rebellion was the beginning of necessary change. This was evil at work, and if Ratatosk was right that a war was coming, then the Night Elves had to be stopped.

Loki had to be stopped.

"I still think there could be a better way of going about this," Sigrid mumbled, glowering at the white fog obstructing their surroundings.

Ratatosk chuckled, a dry, wheezy sound. "The god of mischief has never been one for subtlety."

She could agree, given the stories.

She would have to bring up all of this to General Eira and Vala when they got home. There had to be something the valkyries could do to stop the cosmic balance from tipping.

Ratatosk did a double-take at something across the deck. "Smart horse you've got there."

"What? Oh." Hestur had lain down, probably because he remembered from the last journey on this ship that it was easier than trying to stay standing.

The fog thickened into an opaque wall, dampening her skin, carrying the pungent odor of hot springs.

"So you *do* think we'll be seeing more of the Night Elves," Sigrid said, the chill inside of her at odds with the warm mist.

Ratatosk took them around another sharp turn. "I think we must be prepared for more chaos in our fight to restore balance. If I am correct in thinking that Loki is responsible for the Night Elves' actions—and having been around as long as I have, I am probably correct—then we will have a great struggle on our hands."

Sigrid swallowed hard, a lot less confident about their victory than she was when they'd left the shores of Svartalfheim. A "struggle" must have been a light way of putting it. It sounded like they needed to get ready for the Svartalf King's next move.

Hunched against the sticky, smelly mist smothering them, she wondered how long she would be able to keep riding Hestur—or if she would soon need a fiercer, eight-legged weapon.

CHAPTER SIX

THE SECRET
CORRAL

By the time they said goodbye to Ratatosk at the edge of Vanaheim, rode through the trees and bushes of Myrkviðr, and came within sight of the Vanahalla's golden towers, it was mid-afternoon, and Sigrid was ready to sleep for days. The longship's wooden deck and musty furs hardly made for a restful night.

But rather than head to the stable with the others, she waved them on.

"Go ahead," she shouted as Edith circled back to check on her. "I'll catch up."

Edith was one of the few who'd been nice enough to slow down as Sigrid navigated the thick forest, occasionally dipping below the treetops to check that she was okay. Now, Sigrid wanted everyone to go ahead and leave her, because she had to check on Sleipnir before dealing with the aftermath of their mission. Relaying Ratatosk's theory about Loki goading the Night Elves into action could wait a few extra minutes. More important than any of that was making sure the best war horse in the nine worlds—the stallion ridden by the actual *Odin*—was safe and healthy.

The stallion who, by some odd twist of the cosmos, had ended up in Sigrid's hands.

And I might never understand why.

She waited until the formation of white mares landed on the other side of the stone wall encircling the hill. From here, the barns and outbuildings that made up the valkyrie stables looked like a village in itself.

Home.

Jittering with the anticipation of reuniting with the powerful and slightly terrifying stallion, Sigrid veered back into the woods and onto a narrow trail that guided her to the place where she'd been keeping Sleipnir in secret.

The trail narrowed until branches scraped her arms and the canopy blocked the sun.

Shouldn't Sleipnir be around here?

Was eleven days long enough that she'd forgotten where she hid him?

Hestur pushed through two ferns and stopped.

"Buddy, what's going… Wait." This was the spot. The tangle of wood and leaves that formed Sleipnir's fence had grown so dense that it was opaque, and so tall that she wouldn't even be able to reach the top on horseback. Fisk hadn't been joking when he said the fence would keep growing.

A grin pulled at Sigrid's cheeks as she dismounted. Fisk continued to surprise her with his craftiness. Why couldn't the other Night Elves—the Svartalf King, especially—be more like him? More like…whoever it was that helped her get Ratatosk?

But when she imagined Fisk on a throne, with all of his innocence and optimism, that settled that. People with those qualities didn't rule worlds.

She stretched her legs, aching from so many hours in the saddle, while Hestur set to work on a patch of grass.

"Hey, Sleipnir." Sigrid's voice bounced with a little nervousness.

Beyond the leafy wall, he snorted and stomped impatiently as she fumbled for the gate.

The wooden latch was so covered in vines that it blended

in. Her fingers closed around it, but before she could open it, a presence closed behind her. The ground crunched, jolting her senses awake.

Someone is here.

A warm breath raised the hairs on the back of her neck.

Sigrid gasped and spun around, her pulse spiking. She grabbed her attacker around the middle, throwing her weight so they toppled to the forest floor.

The person let out a sharp breath as they landed.

Sigrid clenched her fists, ready for a fight. "How did you find—*Mariam*?"

The valkyrie lay beneath her on the forest floor, a mischievous smile worthy of Loki playing at her lips. She was even more beautiful than Sigrid remembered, radiant and full of life since reuniting with her mare and healing her soul sickness. Her skin was smooth and tanned, the freckles across her nose more prominent than before, her black hair long and shiny. Her perfect smile accentuated the apples of her cheeks and reached her brown eyes, which were bright and playful.

Sigrid's heart gave a huge leap. She sat up, sitting on Mariam's thighs. "You're back!"

"What was that reaction?" Mariam's body shook as she dissolved into giggles.

Sigrid cracked a smile, her cheeks heating up in embarrassment. "I just came back from getting attacked by Night Elves in Svartalfheim!"

"You did? That's a story I can't wait to hear."

Mariam's returning smile was so beautiful that a warm, soothing sensation trickled over Sigrid, like lying in the sun. Then Mariam shifted beneath her, her hip bones digging into Sigrid's inner thighs—and Sigrid became excruciatingly aware of the position they were in.

She got quickly to her feet, stumbling for balance. "Sorry—

let me—" She cleared her throat and extended a hand to help Mariam up.

Mariam clasped her hand and rose to her feet. She'd regained strength since they'd parted, visible in her round face and the way her muscular body curved beneath her riding trousers and green tunic.

Inside the corral, an irregular clip-clop hit the forest floor as Sleipnir waited for Sigrid to come in. He nickered and snorted.

But Mariam snagged Sigrid's full attention as they stood nose-to-nose, their hands still clasped.

"Good to see you, stable girl," Mariam said, her sweet breath tickling Sigrid's lips.

I guess I didn't need to send Ratatosk to Niflheim.

"I—I didn't expect you for a while longer..." Her words trailed off, something about Mariam taking away her speech.

Kiss her. The time was finally here. She would be able to feel their bodies pressed together like she'd yearned for every night as she struggled to fall asleep.

A thump rose beside them, and they both flinched.

"We had Ratatosk's ship in our favor," Fisk said, emptying an overstuffed rucksack into a messy pile on the forest floor. "I think we should have left it to you, maybe. We felt awfully bad after taking it."

"Fisk!" Sigrid's frustration over the interrupted kiss gave way as she hugged her friend. The dire wolf skull on his head thumped painfully against her shoulder. "No, I'm glad you took the ship. We had it on the way home, anyway."

Aesa stood behind Fisk, cooling off by fanning her wings. All three of them seemed fine, but Fisk still moved his arm gingerly from the spear wound he'd gotten in Helheim, and his head-to-toe leather garb had been stitched up in places. Mariam's arms still had scars, too. Sigrid's heart squeezed at the memory of those injuries.

Sleipnir kicked the wall, demanding attention. The leaves and branches shook, raining down a few nuts and twigs.

"Coming!" Sigrid fumbled for the latch. All of the urgency of checking Sleipnir had somehow left her body when she'd landed on Mariam.

When she opened the gate, the stallion thrust his massive head at her, snorting in her face. She wiped the wetness from her cheeks with a grimace and pushed back a lock of sweaty blond hair, wishing she could have been a little less filthy before seeing Mariam again.

She motioned for them to follow her into the corral. "How long have you been back?"

"Couple days," Mariam said.

The three of them and Hestur stepped inside while Aesa migrated to a tree branch to eat the leaves. Sigrid shut the gate, looking around. Where there was once grass, there was now mud and dirt, and Sleipnir had obviously tried to eat the fence, too. He looked healthy and unharmed, to her relief, but she couldn't say the same for the inside of the corral.

When she turned around, her heart stumbled. Mariam was right there again, standing so close that her breath hit Sigrid's face.

Their gazes lingered, sending a tingling sensation through Sigrid's middle. She tried to convey without words how much she'd missed Mariam—and how much she'd been thinking about that kiss.

"Have you got any fruit, Sigrid?" Fisk asked. "I'm a little backed up. We've been surviving on bread and cheese since leaving Niflheim."

Sigrid pursed her lips. Silently cursing her dear friend for ruining what could have been a romantic reunion, she walked to Hestur to dig an apple out of her saddle bags. "Have you been staying with Sleipnir?" she asked, concerned for their comfort in this muddy paddock.

"Yeah," Mariam said, "but Fisk is going to start building us a proper shelter today because the sleep is awful. Also, we almost got found by two stable hands who came to feed Sleipnir at dawn."

"That'll be Peter. He might have gotten Roland to help." She trusted his judgment, and he obviously needed help with the unruly stallion.

Gods, it wasn't fair that Mariam and Fisk had to live in the bush. But Sigrid couldn't just bring them up to the stable and introduce "the girl from Niflheim who helped steal the Eye of Hnitbjorg and an actual Night Elf" to everyone. Was there any possible way of sneaking them up in the middle of the night? Could they live in one of the vacant barns until the senior valkyries returned?

She would have to give this some thought. Surely she could find a more comfortable home for them.

Fisk flitted to a corner and under a blanket so he could safely lift his dire wolf mask to eat his apple. The muffled crunching and subtly moving wool made him look like a kid who'd stolen a snack and was really bad at hiding it.

"I'm glad to see you so soon," Sigrid said to Mariam, stroking the stallion's steel gray coat. His abnormally hot temperature prickled her palm. "Weren't you going to stay with your mom for a while?" She tried to keep her tone casual so as not to convey how embarrassingly excited she was to be in Mariam's presence again.

The smile slid off Mariam's face. Her expression sank into a deep frown.

Sigrid's heart missed a beat. "Something happened to her?"

"No, she's fine. It's Niflheim. The world is… I don't know, Sigrid. Niflheim is in a state."

"More of a state than usual," Fisk added, muffled by the blanket and a mouthful of apple.

A chill crept over Sigrid like she'd gotten trapped in the rain.

"Why? What's going on?"

"Everything," Mariam said. "It's the whole world. It's like…"

"Chaos?" Sigrid said, her mouth dry.

Mariam met Sigrid's gaze, a hint of fear in her dark eyes. She nodded. "There have been earthquakes. Storms. Eruptions. Rivers of lava have opened up in the land. Niflheim has never been a beautiful place, but this is just…" She shook her head. "The people are out of control. There's always been looting and war, but this isn't normal."

Sigrid's stomach turned as Mariam confirmed her suspicions.

"The world is supposed to be ruled by Hel," Mariam went on, "but Sigrid, we *went* to Helheim, and where was she? Why was Princess Helena in the palace instead?"

Sigrid shook her head, chewing her lip. "I don't know. But this is all related. There's a chance Loki is behind everything that's going on."

Mariam gasped. Fisk's blanket grew still.

"Well, we're doomed," Mariam said flatly.

"Not yet. I'm going to tell *them*" — Sigrid pointed in the direction of Vanahalla's golden towers — "and we're going to stop all of this. Somehow."

The last word came out weaker than she intended. How were they supposed to stop Loki? Was that even possible, if evil was as unavoidable as Ratatosk had said?

There had to be a way. If anyone had a chance of going up against the god of mischief and everything he was unleashing, it was the valkyries, right?

"Sigrid, what happened in Svartalfheim?" Fisk asked from under the blanket, a note of nervousness in his voice.

"We found Ratatosk. The Night Elves had him in an underground cell."

"What?" Mariam cried.

There was a scuffle, and then Fisk whipped the blanket off so fast that his mask wobbled. "Golly, they kept him alive?"

"They did." Sigrid had meant to be quick in checking on Sleipnir so she could return to the stable with everyone else, but that suddenly seemed less urgent. She had to fill in her friends.

So while they groomed Sleipnir together, from his too-high-to-reach ears to his tree-trunk-size legs, she relayed everything that happened in Svartalfheim and everything Ratatosk had told her on the way home.

Her pulse quickened as she brushed him, which she tried to ignore. She couldn't explain the way her muscles tensed and her mind clouded when she was around him—this cosmic, possibly sinister feeling that lingered in her gut like spoiled food. But sooner or later, she would have to face it. She was Sleipnir's heir, and she had to figure out what that meant.

As she finished relaying what happened, Mariam stared wide-eyed. "I can't believe you faced all of that." A pair of creases appeared between her eyebrows, and Sigrid followed the lines down her nose and to her lips. They were turned down, parted slightly.

A piece of Sigrid hoped Mariam would fling her arms around her and praise her bravery. Instead, Mariam turned to Hestur.

"You were such a brave boy! Good Hestur. Good pony." She buried her face in his mane and kissed his neck.

Hestur perked his ears, looking pleased. Sigrid glowered at him.

With Sleipnir's gray coat glistening and his black mane and tail silky soft, Sigrid removed his halter. He immediately laid down and rolled, negating all of their brushing.

"The iron arrows sound interesting," Fisk said, tapping a finger to his mask's jaw. "I don't know what magic they used to create them, but it doesn't sound good."

"You haven't heard of a weapon like that before?" Sigrid asked, her insides hollowing out.

"Never. But give me some time to think about it and run some experiments."

"Thanks." Unease crept over Sigrid all over again. She crossed her fingers that Fisk would come up with something.

Abruptly, a deep, unnatural groan filled the air, making all three horses look up. It bounced off the trees, seeming to fill Sigrid's head with pressure. She held her breath, her brain working frantically to place the sound, before it faded.

The forest fell silent. Even the birds stopped chirping.

Mariam's eyes widened. "What was that?"

Sigrid let out her breath, her heart jumping into action. She'd heard that sound a couple of times in her life. "A horn," she said through numb lips. "From Vanahalla."

"Why?" Mariam asked in that curt way she did when she was trying to hide how worried she was.

All the blood seemed to rush out of Sigrid's limbs. "It means someone at Vanahalla has died."

CHAPTER SEVEN

TOO MANY
INTERRUPTIONS

The stable yard was dead quiet as Sigrid cantered Hestur to the open barn doors. She swung a leg over the saddle to dismount while Hestur was still trotting, and they burst into the barn in a scuffle of hooves and boots.

She blinked the dim aisle into focus, her vision taking a moment to adjust.

The stable hands and junior valkyries were all there, sitting, leaning on each other, their heads bowed.

Her breaths came fast as she scanned the faces, taking a headcount. Was anyone missing?

Wait, where was General Eira?

Peter strode toward her and stopped an arm's length away, his broad shoulders slumped as if carrying a weight. His pupils were dilated, a mix of surprise and sadness twisting his expression.

"Who was it?" Sigrid blurted, her words coming out strangled.

Peter swallowed hard. "King Óleifr."

Sigrid froze, her feet stuck to the barn floor.

The king…is dead?

The words stumbled through her brain, not quite fitting in place. She looked numbly past Peter, where the junior valkyries hugged each other and their mares, many of them crying. Those who weren't crying had blank, stunned expressions. A few stable hands untacked the mares slowly, like they weren't sure whether to keep working or to pause in memoriam.

"H-How…How did he—?" Maybe it sounded insensitive, but she had to know. Did his death have to do with the Night Elves? Was Vanaheim already at war?

"Illness." Peter ran a hand through his tightly curled hair. "Apparently he's been suffering for a while, but they thought he still had time."

She nodded, unsure whether to feel relief over the cause of death. If Loki was behind all evil and was stirring chaos, did he have something to do with this? Did it have some purpose in his scheme—and did this leave Vanaheim vulnerable to attack?

Her heart thumped faster. *I have to tell someone what Ratatosk said.*

She opened her mouth, saw Peter's distraught expression, and closed it, guilt burning in her throat. Maybe she should be crying, too, but she hadn't known King Óleifr personally. The tightening in her chest had more to do with what this meant for Vanaheim.

Roland came up beside them, his white hair in a high ponytail, his normally rosy cheeks colorless from shock. For once, he seemed lost for words.

"If there's to be a war with the Night Elves, who will lead us?" Sigrid asked, earning a sharp look at the word "war."

"Princess Kaia has taken the throne," Peter said slowly, as if he still couldn't believe it.

Roland nodded in agreement. "She's the only one left in the family. She'd better not kick it, or who knows what'll happen?"

Peter gave a familiar, thoughtful head tilt. "They'll have to go further along the family tree, I guess."

Sigrid's heart jumped with such ferocity that she had the urge to sit down. Óleifr hadn't married and had no heir, so what would happen to the throne? As the daughter of Princess Helena—the only living descendant of the royal family—where did this put

Sigrid? Did she even want the throne, if she had a claim?

No. Absolutely not. The thought sent her pulse racing. She'd vowed after returning from Helheim that she wanted nothing to do with royals. Her mother had given birth to her just to get Sleipnir, then lured her to Helheim sixteen years later to trick her into wielding his dangerous power—and those betrayals were forever branded on her heart. Never again would Sigrid let something like that happen. Just like Helena didn't want Sigrid, Sigrid didn't want anything to do with Helena or her bloody family.

Princess Kaia—or Queen Kaia, if that was her new title—needed to stay where she was on Vanaheim's throne, and Sigrid would stay in the stable.

"It'll be okay." Peter squeezed her shoulder as he apparently misread her panic. "Congratulations on rescuing Ratatosk, by the way. Your first valkyrie mission. How did it feel?"

"Yes… Fine," she said absently. What if she was *obligated* to step up and take her birthright?

Calm down. Nobody can even prove I'm Princess Helena's daughter.

The juniors knew it, and by extension, so did General Eira, but with Helena trapped in Helheim, Sigrid dared anyone to prove it. All she wanted was to continue being a stable hand and honorary valkyrie. The fact she had royal blood could die with her.

Peter touched her arm. "Hey, you good?"

She nodded, avoiding his gaze because he was too good at reading her expression.

Squaring her shoulders, she drew a steadying breath and returned her focus to the most pressing task. "Where's General Eira? I need to talk to her."

"After talking with the juniors, she flew off to Vanahalla to meet about King Óleifr."

Great, she'd missed the debrief. "Any idea when she'll—"

Metal jingled behind her, and Roland walked away with her saddle and bridle.

"What are you doing?" she asked.

"Untacking Hestur?"

She blinked, pulling her thoughts away from the Night Elves to meet his earnest gaze. "I can do it."

"But you're a valkyrie now."

He seemed genuinely confused, and she couldn't decide whether to be offended or pleased at his assumption. Either way, she liked caring for Hestur, so that didn't need to change.

"I'm still a stable hand. I'm just a stable hand with a side job."

A stable hand with no claim or interest whatsoever to the throne.

He shrugged and held out her tack. "I'm here if you need me."

"Thanks, potato sack."

He blew her a kiss and cast his most smoldering expression— at which she rolled her eyes—before going to help the other girls. They had spent their lives accustomed to having someone care for their mares.

Sigrid rubbed the back of her neck, her whole body heavy with exhaustion. The conversation with General Eira would have to wait until later.

"Sigrid—" Ylva stopped herself, huffed, then turned so her long braid swung. "Peter. Roskva is sweaty. Can you please hose her down?"

Peter obeyed without a word, taking the mare's lead rope.

"I never used to get a *please*," Sigrid mumbled.

It was nice not to have the valkyries bossing her around right now, but a boulder of guilt dropped into her stomach on seeing their demands diverted to her friends. Especially since she'd asked them to help with Sleipnir as well.

While the stable hands untacked the mares and the valkyries talked in low voices, she gave Peter a look and led Hestur to his stall, breathing deeply to try and loosen the tightness in her chest.

As she'd known he would, Peter fell into step beside her, bringing Roskva with him. "What is it?"

"Did everything go all right? With the spawn of chaos?"

Peter shook his head. "Nothing too bad. Hope you don't mind I recruited Roland to help while you were away. He hasn't told anyone."

"No problem." She trusted Roland, and admittedly, she'd been naive to think Peter could care for Sleipnir alone. "So…how'd it really go?"

"Well—" He tied Roskva outside the stall and came in, where Sigrid's hammock was set up at the back with everything she owned stacked beneath it. He reached behind the bins and emerged with what seemed to be a halter. "See this?"

Sigrid looked more closely. The nose piece was enclosed. *A muzzle.* She groaned.

"He tried to bite us every time we groomed him. This helped a little. Also, he broke four lead ropes, kicked a hole in his water trough, and ate three times as much hay as we thought." Peter shook his head. "We started supplementing with alfalfa cubes and beet pulp because someone was going to notice all the bales going missing."

She pursed her lips. "I'm so sorry."

He shrugged and, to her relief, smiled. "Can't say we didn't have fun. He's a change from the norm around here."

Though his tone was light, his words settled over her like the chill of nightfall.

A change…

The king's death and the new queen's appointment would inevitably change life as they knew it in Vanaheim. Even more, Sigrid's own life had just shifted a step closer to the royal responsibilities of being Helena's daughter.

And there was no turning back.

CHAPTER EIGHT

BATH HOUSE
BLATHERING

Once Hestur was comfortable and had enough hay to make a bed out of, Sigrid stretched her sore limbs—and cringed at the smell of sweat and mud.

Ew.

A hot bath followed by a much-needed sleep sounded like the greatest plan in the world. She gathered her soap, towel, and clean clothes, then made her way to the bath house behind the stable.

The place was spacious, with private tubs and trickling fountains shaped like the open-mouthed faces of Njord, Freyr, and Freyja. A couple of the tubs had their curtains drawn, and gentle splashes echoed off the walls.

Sigrid picked the tub at the furthest corner, shut the curtains around her, and turned the tap. The usual eggy smell met her nose, milder than the steam columns along the spring of Hvergelmir, as the tub filled with hot spring water. Finally, the chance to sink in and ease her aching muscles.

As the steam rose, she removed her clothes and made a mental list of all the things she had to do.

Tell someone what Ratatosk said about Loki.

Probably General Eira.

Ask someone if Mariam and Fisk could live in Vanaheim.

Again, General Eira.

Make sure Queen Kaia didn't find out she had a niece.

General Eira wouldn't care to tell her, right?

Crap, why did all of these things have to involve the short-tempered general? The woman once tried to take away Sigrid's riding privileges for stepping out of line and tended to treat her like a nugget of smushed horse poop stuck to the bottom of her boot.

Sigrid put a foot in the water, the hot tingle promising the most relaxation she'd had in weeks, and let out a breath as she submerged all the way up to her nose.

If there was a war coming, wouldn't it be in everyone's best interest if Mariam and Fisk lived and worked in Vanaheim? Mariam would be a valuable addition to the valkyrie ranks, and Fisk could be useful in any number of ways. Given his craftsmanship skills, he could make the valkyries better armor and weapons than they'd ever had.

Strong argument with plenty of good points. The problem was that last time Mariam had been in Vanaheim, she'd stolen the Eye of Hnitbjorg and then escaped the infirmary where she'd been held for questioning. And Fisk...well, there was no chance a Night Elf would be warmly welcomed here.

She blew bubbles across the water. It was hopeless. Her friends were doomed to live in hiding along with a high-maintenance stallion who liked to chew fences.

As for her secret? If any of the valkyries decided Queen Kaia should know Princess Helena had a daughter, she wouldn't be able to stop them from sharing it. It was out of her hands, and all she could do was pray nobody cared or believed it.

The bath house's door burst open, cutting off her morose train of thought.

"Gods, it's good to be back," Ylva said, her shrill voice like a punch to the eardrums.

"Love missions. Hate not being able to bathe," Gunni said with a sigh.

Sigrid rubbed hot water over her face. Bath time was never peaceful for long.

"I'm still wrapping my head around the king dying," Runa said, more subdued. "It's weird to think of someone else on the throne. Do you think anything will change?"

Sigrid leaned her head back to peek through a slit in her curtains. Runa padded away from Ylva and Gunni with a book and a towel.

Edith wasn't with them. She liked to bathe alone lately, even though her friends insisted she join them. Last year, Sigrid had been in this very tub when one of the older girls told Edith she should be using the boys' bath house. Sigrid hadn't been able to stop herself from telling the older girl to shut up and go bathe in the river if she cared so much. She couldn't tell if her words had helped—but maybe that had something to do with why Edith was nicer to her than the other juniors were.

"I think it'll be fun to have a queen for once," Ylva said.

"Wow," Runa said flatly. "He's barely dead and you're excited about his successor?"

"Come on, cheer up. Maybe you need to go back out there and take a look at the *hard-working* stable hands."

"That always cheers *me* up," Gunni said, and she and Ylva giggled.

Sigrid sank further into the tub, thankful for the invisibility offered by the curtains. Just once, she wanted to take a bath without overhearing something that made her taste bile.

Ylva sighed dreamily. "I swear his arms got bigger since we left."

"There's something to be said for lifting hay bales," Gunni said.

Ylva moaned. "Think he'd let me lick his biceps?"

Gunni laughed.

Sigrid made a face.

Poor Peter. He'd had valkyrie girls fawning over him for as long as she could remember. He handled it fine, but sometimes their advances clearly made him uncomfortable. Overhearing a comment like that would mortify him.

"You should invite him for dinner," Gunni said.

"Don't waste your efforts on Peter," Runa said, her voice much closer.

Sigrid had to agree. Peter was almost thirty, and aside from Ylva being way too young for him, she was nowhere near as kind and humble as he deserved.

"Why not?" Ylva asked, coming closer, too.

The bath house suddenly didn't seem spacious enough.

"I heard that while we were away, he and Roland kept disappearing into the forest together. *If* you get my drift."

The others gave dramatic gasps.

Sigrid's jaw slackened.

Ylva lowered her voice to a conspiratorial whisper. "Are you serious?"

"Mmhmm." Runa sounded pleased at being the bearer of such gossip.

Sigrid couldn't contain herself. She burst out laughing, almost choking on bath water and having to sit up.

"Who's that?" Gunni asked.

She regretted everything as bare feet patted over.

The curtains flung open, and Gunni's pink face scowled down at her. Ylva trotted up behind her. Both were wrapped in towels. Sigrid curled her knees up to hide some of her nakedness.

"Why are you laughing?" Despite Ylva's angry tone, her wide eyes and flared nostrils gave away her panic about being overheard. "If you tell Peter what I said, I swear, I'll…" She trailed off, seeming to fail to come up with a good enough threat.

"Peter and Roland aren't together." Sigrid had no interest

in gossiping about these girls' fleeting crushes, but the least she could do was spare her friends some embarrassing questions.

"How do you know?" Gunni snapped. "That's a mean thing to laugh about." She stood awkwardly, leaning to alleviate pressure on her injured leg. A thick bandage peeked out below her towel.

Behind them, Runa sank into her steaming tub, cracking open her book. She'd clearly lost interest in this conversation.

"Trust me. They're not." Sigrid would pat herself later for not rolling her eyes.

Ylva sniffed and looked away. "Okay, then... Do you know firsthand who Peter is into? Or maybe *Roland*?"

A moment passed before Sigrid processed the fact Ylva was asking if she was actually *involved* with one of them. "What? No! Peter is like a brother to me."

It was the wrong thing to say.

Gunni gave a dramatic gasp. "But not Roland? Oh! Sigrid is going out with Roland!"

The statement ricocheted off the bath house walls, amplifying like a thousand voices had said it. Runa giggled and turned her page.

Annoyance twisted in Sigrid's stomach. "We're not—"

"Don't even deny it." Gunni's lip curled venomously. "We've all seen him making you laugh and blowing you kisses."

"Oh, come on. That's just Roland being...Roland." Sigrid let them get their giggles out, then said flatly, "Can you please shut the curtains?"

Casting sly grins that made her want to splash them with dirty water, they tugged the curtains shut and left to take their own baths.

Great. One more thing to worry about—false rumors.

Gunni definitely still had a crush on Roland and would probably seize every opportunity to make Sigrid feel awkward and uncomfortable about her closeness to him.

Sigrid leaned back and closed her eyes, willing everyone to leave her alone for a few minutes. She let her mind drift, closing her ears to any more gossip or chatter coming from the nearby tubs.

What would they say if they knew about me and Mariam?

Her mind wandered out the door, down the hill, across the meadow, and into the woods, where Mariam would be spending the afternoon with Fisk. What was she doing right now? Was she thinking of Sigrid?

Beneath the water, she let her fingers roam, recalling the earlier feel of Mariam's sweet breath against her face. If they could get a few minutes alone so she could explore those soft lips and toned muscles, and maybe…

Someone knocked on the bath house door.

"Sigrid?" Peter said, muffled through the closed door.

Sigrid removed her hand and sat up with a splash, clutching the edges of the tub. Heat crowded her cheeks, and she frowned. What could he want?

"Come in," Ylva said, her voice husky. She and Gunni squealed and giggled, scrambling as they obviously rushed to clothe themselves—or not.

A click echoed.

"I have a letter for Sigrid?" Peter's voice came from afar, like he was trying to keep a respectful distance instead of moving in and searching for Sigrid.

"I'll give it to her," Gunni said. "Who's it from?"

"I don't— Is she here?"

Sigrid rose from the tub, cool air biting her skin, and wrapped her towel across her chest. "Coming!"

Lamenting the restful bath, she whipped open the curtain and trotted over.

Ylva and Gunni were also in towels. Unsurprisingly, Ylva's was wrapped in such a way that it barely covered her breasts.

She seemed to be pushing them up as she held the towel across her chest.

Outside, Peter held a scroll, his gaze averted to a distant field.

They all watched her take it from him. It was light, smooth, elegant.

"What is it?" she asked.

"A messenger just delivered it from Vanahalla. Didn't say who it was from. It has your name on it."

She turned it over, her damp fingers leaving marks. Sealing it shut was a spot of sky-blue wax imprinted with a boar's head—the emblem of Vanaheim. When she turned it over, her name was written in cursive on the side.

Sigrid Helenadottir.

Blood rushed out of her face so fast it left her light-headed.

Her secret had gotten to the royal hall. They had found out she was Princess Helena's daughter.

CHAPTER NINE

THE QUEEN'S
TERMS

Sigrid dismounted Hestur in front of Vanahalla's gold double doors, which were big enough for Ratatosk's ship to sail through. Her heart pounded hard, partly from the ride up the hill, but mostly from nerves.

After a lifetime of wondering what was inside the royal hall, the opportunity to find out had come—and she was no longer sure she wanted to know.

Drawing a steadying breath, she unfurled the letter with trembling hands and read it again.

Dear Sigrid,

First and foremost, I want to congratulate you on your role in helping to return Ratatosk to the spring of Hvergelmir. We were, at last, able to communicate with him again, and he is on his way to bring the senior valkyries back from Jotunheim. This is largely thanks to you and your magnificent Midgard horse. I understand his name is Hestur. Please give him an apple and a scratch on the wither from me.

I confess, I have seen you in the courtyard and among the stable hands since you were a child, and your resemblance to my sister always struck me. I am certain that others who knew Helena noticed, too. After learning what happened in Helheim,

I understand enough to cast aside any doubts: you are my niece, Sigrid!

It saddens me that we have spent our lives apart. If I knew, I would have contacted you sooner. Today, we find ourselves dwindled to a family of two, and I hope you agree that we shouldn't ignore this bond. I have much to tell you about our lineage, which I am sure you will find interesting.

Would you do me the honor of accompanying me for dinner tonight at seven o'clock?

All my love,
Queen Kaia

Sigrid studied the elegant cursive, feeling the words prickle beneath her skin. After spending sixteen years with no hint that she had parents at all, here was the handwriting of a woman who addressed her using words like "family," "bond," and "love." She'd noticed Sigrid before. She even knew Hestur's name.

Sigrid's heart ached for what the words promised—but as much as she wanted to believe the letter and its promise of belonging, the last time she trusted a family member, she'd been tricked, betrayed, and told that she was never wanted. Queen Kaia was Helena's sister, so trusting her wasn't an option.

Above all, Sigrid refused to reveal she was Sleipnir's heir. She had no desire to relive what happened in Helheim—her mother's betrayal, her mistake of nearly leading Hel's army into the land of the living. More than that, if she admitted she had him, she would be pressured into riding him, which meant wielding a dangerous power she didn't understand.

But despite her reservations, she'd accepted the invitation. Now that her secret was out, she had questions too important to ignore—about their lineage, about who she was and what her title meant.

Squaring her shoulders, Sigrid strode up to one of the six

guards flanking the doors. "Queen Kaia is expecting me."

Her voice came out frustratingly small and uncertain. She half expected the guard to laugh and shoo her away, but he nodded.

A boy Sigrid's age rushed over, his paddock boots and leather gloves indicating he was a royal stable hand. He took Hestur's reins with a little bow. "I'll take him to the stable, Your Highness."

Sigrid's heart flipped over at being addressed that way. "I-I'm not a Highness."

He bowed again, not meeting her eyes. "My apologies."

While he led Hestur away, Sigrid's feet seemed to have frozen to the stone walkway. *Why did he call me that? Does everyone in the palace know about me? What is Queen Kaia playing at?*

Without looking down at her white tunic and trousers, she brushed off the strands of Hestur's hair that she knew covered the fabric. She didn't own any gowns, and her decision to come in casual riding clothes had been purposeful.

Not so sure now.

At least she'd groomed herself better than she could ever remember. A thick braid hung down the right side of her head, which she'd redone at least ten times to get perfect, while the left side was freshly shaved. Roland had agreed to help her shave a pattern into it, and she now had Garmr's flames notched into her hair in intricate detail, a reminder of what she was capable of.

As the boy and Hestur disappeared around the corner to where the royal stable must be, two guards strode to the gold double doors and seized the massive handles. With a hollow *thunk* and a slow creak, the doors opened. A bright white interior glimmered through the gap.

Sigrid's breath caught.

An extravagant entrance hall greeted her like a marble-and-gold dagger in the eyes. Vast enough to fit an entire barn inside, it echoed as her boots hit the marble floor. The white floor and walls glistened, cleaner than anything she'd ever seen or stepped on, every gold handle and railing polished so it reflected like a mirror. At six places around the perimeter, staircases spiraled up several stories, no doubt leading to even more splendid rooms. Three gold thrones sat at the far end, as if the ghosts of royals were there to greet her.

It was impossible to see herself ever feeling comfortable in a place like this.

Though my idea of a nice throne is probably one made of hay bales.

The smirk fell from her face when Queen Kaia emerged from the right and strode toward her with a reverberating *click-clack* of wood-soled shoes on marble. Gold bands jangled on her forearms, and the subtle amber crown once worn by King Óleifr crossed her forehead. Her delicate, sky-blue robe flowed in a way that brought to mind flower petals shuddering in a breeze.

"Sigrid." The name left her lips in a breathless and emotional exhale as she stopped an arm's length away.

Sigrid wasn't sure what she had expected or wanted to see in the woman who was her aunt, but her shoulders relaxed a little at finding minimal resemblance to her mother. In fact, it was easy to see why she'd never suspected any relation to Kaia.

Queen Kaia was much younger, maybe in her late twenties, with straight, dark hair, large brown eyes, and a delicate air about her—far from Sigrid's blond hair, deep-set eyes that were so faint they were gray, and developed muscles from working in a barn her whole life. Their similarity ended at their round face shape and light skin tone.

The queen's gaze roved over Sigrid, as if searching for the same similarities that Sigrid had feared, before motioning behind her. "The dining hall is this way."

Sigrid followed her across the lobby, passing several potted plants with large, flat leaves that looked like no tree or bush she'd ever seen on Vanaheim. *Imported?*

Queen Kaia walked more short-stepped than Princess Helena, but just as regally. Her movements were contained so her straight hair and blue robe flowed gently behind her.

They entered a dining hall, which had a wooden table long enough to seat all of the junior valkyries. Two places were set across from each other at the far end. Along the walls, empty serving tables suggested this room was used for smörgåsbords. A closed door at the opposite end must have led to the kitchen—a lot of voices and clanking came from beyond it. To the left, a large window sat open, inviting a warm breeze and a lively hum from the courtyard.

It forced to mind when Sigrid had dined with her mother in Helheim. This hall was the opposite of that muddy palace—bright, warm, *alive*. Here, people moved beyond doors, birds sang outside, and voices talked and laughed in the distance.

Queen Kaia led Sigrid to the table. "Please, take a seat."

Her eyes were red around the edges.

Sigrid hesitated, unsure of what had made the queen cry. A twinge of guilt went through her chest. Should she apologize? But for what?

"You look just like I remember her." Queen Kaia raked her gaze over Sigrid. "Your eyes are the same color. I'm sorry…I tried to prepare myself, but the heart is hard to control."

Sigrid's insides squirmed. Maybe Princess Helena had been more poised and better groomed than Sigrid, but underneath Sigrid's barn clothes and the warrior-inspired haircut, their relation was undeniable.

Silence reigned as they sat. Sigrid refused to break it, unwilling to start this conversation by talking about her mother.

The kitchen door swung open, and four waitstaff emerged with trays.

"How was the journey home, Sigrid?" Queen Kaia asked, maybe understanding the hint and trying a more casual topic.

"It was fine. Why did you invite me here?" Sigrid asked, having no desire to talk about simple topics. Queen Kaia must want something from her, and Sigrid wanted the information she'd been promised about their lineage.

Queen Kaia waited as the staff loaded each of their plates with breaded herring, mashed potatoes, meatballs drenched in sauce, buttery carrots and yams, a dollop of lingonberries, and a steaming slice of rye bread. They finished by pouring each of them a small goblet of mead.

The smell was mouthwatering, but Sigrid kept her hands in her lap, not touching any of it.

The staff retreated, and Queen Kaia picked up her fork, the gold bands on her wrist jangling. The boar's head embroidered near her collar rippled. "You're my niece. The heir to the throne."

The heir. That word was getting tiresome.

Besides, what did that mean when Sigrid didn't even know how the ranking worked? Did Queen Kaia have the right to the throne, or did Sigrid have the right as the firstborn's firstborn?

Wait, should I be fearing for my life right now?

An icy rush surged through Sigrid's veins. She hadn't considered this possibility.

The window is open. I can jump through it.

"I don't want the throne," she said clear and loud while gauging the chances of escape.

Her aunt's lips twisted, almost a smile. "Nor do I. It feels strange to find myself here. I'm not sure I like it. I'm not used to the responsibility of making such impactful decisions."

She spoke softly compared to her sister, with a delicate, airy lilt. Her answers were…surprising.

Sigrid relaxed a little as it became clear the queen wasn't about to murder her. Could her aunt be a better person, or was her gentle air a front, and underneath she was bitter about her status as the youngest in the family?

Queen Kaia stabbed a carrot and let it cool on the end of her fork. It glistened in butter, steam rising. "Given your title, I hoped to tell you about your status as a royal."

"But I don't want to be—"

"I'm not going to put you on the throne, darling," she said, a touch of humor in her words. "But you are a royal. It's in your blood."

Darling. It echoed in her mind in her mother's voice and ignited something inside her.

"So what?" Sigrid snapped, allowing her anger to show through.

Queen Kaia furrowed her brow, seeming surprised by Sigrid's response. Did she expect Sigrid to be excited about being a royal? "No one can rule Vanaheim alone. I need you."

The idea of the queen *needing* her made her insides squirm. She didn't want to be tethered to this palace or the royal family. "Aren't there dozens of people living in this hall to help you? A council? The sorcerers?"

Anyone but me.

Queen Kaia set down her utensils. "It's not the same as having my family here."

"What do you want from me, then?" Sigrid's heart beat faster despite her aloof tone.

"I want you to live in Vanahalla with me," Queen Kaia said as if this were obvious. "I want you to accept your role as princess."

CHAPTER TEN

BLOOD RELATIVES

S igrid stared at the queen, empty of words. What was she supposed to say to an offer like that? Becoming a princess was one thing, but willingly returning to the family who'd abandoned her? The mere thought of letting her name become Princess Sigrid Helenadottir and living in this absurdly big hall where her mother used to walk filled her with white-hot rage.

"Sigrid, you're part of the royal family, and it's time to accept your destiny," Queen Kaia said into the silence, her tone calm and understanding.

As if she understood *anything* of what Sigrid felt.

Sigrid shook her head firmly. Whatever her destiny was, this wasn't it. "Family is what you make it. I know this well, growing up an orphan and all that."

Seeming to miss the accusation, Queen Kaia said lightly, "You're family by blood."

"So? Is that more important than family who sticks by your side?"

The queen searched Sigrid's face as if trying to decipher something. She picked up her utensils and cut into her food with soft, slender fingers. "It's important because we have a history, and you are part of it. I can tell you about our lineage, if you wish."

It was the reason Sigrid had considered this visit, because

after everything, she *was* curious about her blood family.

"Did you know my father?" It might have been an insult to ask about the one part of her family tree that wasn't royal, but she didn't care.

Queen Kaia swallowed her next bite hard. She shook her head almost imperceptibly. "I'm sorry, Sigrid."

The simple answer carved a hollowness in Sigrid's gut. *That's it? No?*

A silence stretched between them before her aunt cleared her throat. "Your food is getting cold."

Sigrid picked up her fork, admittedly hungry, and ate the most delicious meatball she'd ever tasted. She sipped her mead, using the goblet to mask her expression. Every tiny detail, down to a single meatball, was better than anything she'd ever had as a stable hand. Was this what being a royal promised?

Not that Sigrid cared. She wouldn't change her life at the stables to come live in excess with a stranger whose only link was blood and heritage.

"Is she happy?" the queen asked, breaking into Sigrid's thoughts.

An icy sensation engulfed her. There was no need to ask who "she" was.

Sigrid set her cup down and leaned back, ready to stand. "I didn't come here to talk about her."

"I just want to know—"

Sigrid pushed her chair back.

Queen Kaia reached a placating hand across the table. "I'm sorry. Please stay. We won't discuss her."

They stared at each other for a long, tense moment. Sigrid's jaw started to ache from how hard she was clenching. Queen Kaia motioned for her to sit, and after a pointed hesitation, Sigrid pulled the chair back in.

She refused to answer the question, not only because one

question invited more, but also because the answer was *no*. Helena was not happy. What would Queen Kaia think of Sigrid, the girl who'd left her own mother trapped in Helheim?

"Were…were you two close?" Sigrid asked, the words sticking on the way out. As much as she wanted to change the subject, she needed to know who she was dealing with.

"Lena and I had our disagreements, but overall, yes," Queen Kaia said carefully.

Lena. Helena had mentioned the nickname. Maybe she'd been truthful about how close the sisters were.

"As kids, she was my idol, and I wept for months when she disappeared." Queen Kaia shared a brittle smile before looking away. "I never knew how to relate to Óleifr…but my sister and I, we always had good laughs."

It wasn't the answer Sigrid would have liked—but then again, what was? Would she trust her aunt even if she said she hated Helena? Maybe. But did she realize what her sister had become since leaving Vanaheim? Clearly not.

Princess Helena might have been worth idolizing once, but not anymore.

Queen Kaia dabbed her eyes with her napkin. Locks of her dark hair fell forward, and she tucked it behind her ears with trembling fingers.

"I'm sorry you had to lose your family," Sigrid said, uneasy at seeing someone so poised crumbling before her. A piece of bread lodged in her throat, and she took a swig of mead to clear it.

"I've made peace with it. My sister disappeared a lifetime ago, and Óleifr was ill for years. It's just difficult seeing you, when you look so much like her." Her brown eyes traced over Sigrid, wide and watery. "I feel like I've stepped back in time."

Pity squeezed Sigrid's heart. Queen Kaia would have been a kid when she lost her sister. After all this time, the topic still reduced her to tears.

Sigrid didn't want to imagine how it would feel to lose any of her friends, the people who'd become family to her. She shoved a forkful of mashed potatoes in her mouth, considering that she might, possibly, feel sorry for—

No. Helena abandoned me as a baby. She used me to get Sleipnir and tried to use me again to get the throne.

Yet Kaia was not Helena, and there was a chance—a small one—that she was different.

"Will you tell me how we're related to the gods?" Sigrid asked, desperate to move this conversation away from her mother—and desperate to know how her connection to Odin had made her Sleipnir's heir.

"Of course," Queen Kaia said with a watery smile. "Have you read the great poems?"

"Only some. I never…" She shifted on the hard seat. "I'm a stable hand."

"What do you know of the different classes in the nine worlds?" her aunt asked, graciously skipping over this.

"Well, the gods are the highest class. Asgard has the Aesir gods, and Vanaheim was once home to the Vanir gods…" Sigrid tore apart the slice of rye bread, wishing more than ever that she'd gone to valkyrie school with the other girls her age. Her mother's words from not long ago came back with the correct lesson. *Elves of light and darkness, giants of fire and ice, humans of soil and sky…* "There are also the elves of Alfheim and Svartalfheim, the giants of Jotunheim and Muspelheim, and the humans of Midgard and Vanaheim."

"Good! You have a good grasp of how the worlds are divided. Never underestimate yourself, Sigrid." Queen Kaia's smile was bright and genuine, now that Sigrid had a chance to see it. "It's true the Vanir originally made their home in Vanaheim. Nowadays, the worlds have grown and mingled so our people come from all over—but as royals, you and I are descended from the Vanir. Njord is at the top of our family tree, followed by Freyja. Freyja was the original Seer and a valkyrie. Do you know who her husband was?"

"Odin," Sigrid said, remembering too late to pretend she didn't know she was descended from Odin. Revealing she was Sleipnir's heir was not in her plans today. She made her best shocked face. "Wait, does that mean Odin is in our family tree?"

The pause must have come across as a slow uptake, because Queen Kaia gave her an indulgent smile. But then she said, "I see something passing behind your eyes. Have you suspected this?"

Traitorous expressive eyes. Peter always told her how much they betrayed her feelings.

Sigrid lifted a shoulder. "I've always felt a connection to the gods."

"You see? We're different," Queen Kaia said, oblivious to the lie. "The power of the gods flows through our veins. Njord. Freyja. Odin."

Sigrid's pulse raced faster, as if in response to these words about everything that flowed through her veins. "Is our family tree recorded somewhere? Can I see it?"

As much as she wanted nothing to do with her family, curiosity rumbled inside her with every new piece of information. She wanted to hold a piece of her family in her hands and see the threads connecting her to Odin.

Queen Kaia waved a hand as if shooing the words. "Oh, it's somewhere. I have yet to discover everything in this indecently large hall."

Sigrid's lips quirked at the way she mentioned the excessiveness of this whole place. Was that contempt? Maybe she was a little different than her sister.

"How exactly does Odin fit into the tree?" Sigrid asked.

"Mother's mother's father's mother and onward. I don't know."

Sigrid waited, but Queen Kaia apparently had nothing more

to say about Odin. "What does having him in our lineage mean?" she asked, dancing around Sleipnir. For as long as she could remember, she'd wanted to know who she was, and more than ever since finding Sleipnir, she had to figure that out. *Why* was she Sleipnir's heir? What was her purpose on him?

Queen Kaia raised an eyebrow. "Vanaheim's place in Yggdrasil begins with the gods. They've given us relics, wealth, and magic that no other world possesses. The Eye of Hnitbjorg comes from the same mountain where Odin drank the mead of poetry."

"And?" Sigrid asked automatically.

Queen Kaia laughed, her whole demeanor brightening as her eyes crinkled at the corners. "You have high expectations, Sigrid."

Sigrid flushed and returned to her meal. She would have to find another way to dig into the secret of how she'd ended up with Sleipnir. She finished her plate, stuffed full to bursting. Food never tasted so good. Even the lingonberries had more flavor than usual.

Curse the appeal of this place.

As the staff returned to clear the dishes, she scowled at the open window with its warm breeze and chirping birds outside. The comforts of this hall were making it hard to remember why she refused to live here.

"Why should I accept my title?" Sigrid asked, curiosity buried beneath her skeptical tone. "So I can keep you company?"

"I hope you don't think my reasons are selfish."

Sigrid said nothing, letting the implication hang.

The queen shifted in the silence, biting the inside of her cheeks so her lips puckered. "I've inherited some…problems. I have a council, and we'll be better off once the seniors return home, but…"

A council! This was who she needed to tell about Ratatosk's warning—the valkyrie generals, sorcerers, and everyone else in charge of making decisions for Vanaheim.

"You mean Night Elves are the problem."

Queen Kaia nodded. "Now that we've openly taken Ratatosk from them, I don't know what we should expect. A retaliation, maybe? Not that any world would be so foolish as to attack the home of the *valkyries*, but…" She fidgeted with her gold bands, and then her crown, and then her robe, as if unable to still her hands.

It must be scary to be forced onto the throne with the worlds in this state. But why was she asking Sigrid specifically for help? Was their blood relation really that important to her?

No matter. At least Sigrid had knowledge they could use.

"Ratatosk thinks Loki is behind this," Sigrid said, feeling lighter as the words finally spilled from her lips. "He's tipping the balance of order and chaos, goading the Night Elves to fight for a higher position in the cosmos."

Queen Kaia raised an eyebrow, her lips parted as Sigrid's words hung in the room.

"I haven't been able to tell General Eira yet," Sigrid said. "But your council should know. We have to make sure Vanaheim is ready for whatever happens."

The queen nodded slowly. "To be frank, we have been discussing this sort of threat for some time. We need to prepare for war, Sigrid."

Sigrid's knee bounced under the table, and she picked up her mead for something to fidget with. A sense of importance battled with anxiety over what Queen Kaia would do with this information. After seeing Helena try to throw the worlds into further chaos by unleashing Hel's army, she hardly had faith in her family's decisions.

But if she listens to me…

"Sigrid." Queen Kaia cleared her throat, lacing her fingers on the table. "I know my sister was behind that attack from Helheim…"

Sigrid's heart thumped faster. It wasn't a question, but she still answered, "Yes."

"She also made you raise the army in Helheim to take over Vanaheim."

Sigrid's mouth was dry. This conversation was going in a dangerous direction. Her knee bounced harder under the table, and her fingernails tapped a rhythm on her goblet. "And other worlds. Yes."

"But you escaped Helheim alive," the queen whispered as the staff came back in, "and there's only one way to do that."

No, no, no…

A tense silence passed while the staff presented them with apple pie and ice cream. Sigrid's plate made a soft *clack* as it hit the table in front of her. The ice cream melted rapidly over the golden crust. The staff backed away, the kitchen door swung shut, and she was again alone with her aunt.

"Where is Sleipnir now, Sigrid?"

CHAPTER ELEVEN

BARGAINING
WITH SECRETS

The goblet slipped out of Sigrid's fingers and clattered to the table. The kitchen door swung open, and the staff swooped in to clean up the splatter. Sigrid murmured apologies as she tried to compose herself.

She knows. She knows I'm Sleipnir's heir.

It made sense. The junior valkyries would've told General Eira that she rode Sleipnir in Helheim, and then General Eira would've been bound to report it. They probably talked about it the whole time she'd been away in Svartalfheim.

She'd been so concerned with nobody finding out she was Helena's daughter that she forgot to worry about her other secrets.

Sigrid sat back in her chair, narrowing her eyes. She'd told the juniors she sent Sleipnir away with Mariam and Fisk, and that was the story she was sticking with.

Once the staff retreated, she said, "He isn't here."

"The word is that you sent him away," Queen Kaia said flatly, her eyebrows raised.

Sigrid hummed, a clear hint that she was done talking about this.

Queen Kaia either didn't get it or disregarded it.

"We need the best valkyries available if we hope to keep Vanaheim safe, not just from Night Elves, but from any other threat." The queen leaned forward as if trying to close the distance Sigrid put between them. "Sigrid, if you were to serve Vanaheim on Sleipnir, you would be our greatest line of defense. And you could live in Vanahalla with me and have everything you wanted—a private suite, a new wardrobe, tutors to catch you up on education, stalls in the royal stable for your horses—"

Sigrid shook her head, which swam from a combination of the mead and overflowing information. Riding Sleipnir meant succumbing to his power. Moving into the palace meant living with constant reminders of her mother. Nothing in the nine worlds was worth that torture. "I can't. I belong in the stable."

"We have a stable up here."

"I belong in the valkyrie stable."

Dimples appeared in Queen Kaia's round cheeks. "Sigrid, darling, what are you afraid of?"

Everything inside her tensed. "Don't call me that."

"What?"

"*Darling.* I don't like being called that."

Queen Kaia took a bite of apple pie, then dabbed at her lips with a hand cloth, as calm and unperturbed as ever. "All right."

Sigrid let out a breath and unclenched her fists in her lap. She hated feeling petty and argumentative against the queen's congeniality, but this conversation had gone in directions she hadn't expected. She couldn't lose control of this meeting.

"I like being a valkyrie and a stable hand," Sigrid said, trying to be less snappy. "My whole life is there. I don't want to sacrifice that for the sake of a fancy title and a big bed to sleep in— especially not when it's all because of *her*." She drew a breath, then shut her mouth before divulging that she didn't want to ride Sleipnir. Admitting she was scared of him was shameful after she'd gone to such lengths to get him. Plus, great riders weren't scared of their own horses.

Queen Kaia offered a small, kind smile, her eyes soft. "First of all, plenty of royals have also been valkyries. Freyja was one. Second, you can still visit the stable and your friends. But you can't live in a horse stall forever. You belong in your own home. With me. And third, you don't have to make this about *her*. This is about *you*." Queen Kaia held her gaze, then dug into her dessert. "Accepting your role as princess and lead defender of Vanaheim is just the start. You're destined for more, Sigrid. I suspect you already know that."

Sigrid's throat tightened. She'd always believed that, and she'd spent so long trying to prove it. She just never thought *"more"* would be so terrifying. Riding Sleipnir had never been easy or harmless.

The ice cream melted rapidly over the warm pie on her plate. She picked up her fork, her lips numb. "What would I need to do on Sleipnir?"

Queen Kaia's brown eyes seemed to spark, a nearly imperceptible glint. She chewed slowly and swallowed before speaking. "If war comes, you'd ride with the valkyries. Until then, you would be on standby, if that suits you. Your royal duties would fill your day-to-day life—engagements, correspondence, studying. You would have a say in important matters."

Sigrid was careful not to react. If accepting her princess title meant putting off riding Sleipnir until war came—if war came at all—then she might be able to do it. As for having royal duties? The smallest flutter of excitement went through her middle. She'd never studied before or had formal engagements.

If she ignored her mother's existence, and if she tamped down the fear holding her back, the idea of becoming a princess and helping to strategize against the Night Elves was incredible. She could work with the most powerful people in Vanaheim to help restore balance to the nine worlds.

The boulder of stubborn refusal shifted inside her.

She took a bite of pie to give herself time to think and

discovered the most blissful, cinnamon-sweet apple dessert in the worlds. What if she accepted her title? Her decision didn't need to be permanent. If she got the same impression from Queen Kaia as she did from her mother, then she would pack up and go right back to her stall in the valkyrie stable. It wasn't like they could force her to ride Sleipnir, either.

If she was going to do this, she had terms.

"If I agree to serve Vanaheim on Sleipnir, I don't care about a big bedroom or a new wardrobe, but there's something in particular I want in exchange," Sigrid said, determined to bargain for something that was actually important. Mariam and Fisk's freedom were reason enough to agree to this, even if it scared her.

"Anything." Queen Kaia's brow pinched, like she was afraid of what Sigrid would ask for.

Sigrid prodded her melting ice cream ball. "When I was in Helheim, I had help getting the Eye back."

"The junior valkyries, you mean?"

"From someone else. Two others."

Queen Kaia paused with her fork suspended, looking interested.

Sigrid cleared her throat. "Mariam's mother was a valkyrie. She—I don't know her name." She regretted not asking. "But she was banished to Niflheim for helping your sister. I just…I don't think it's fair to keep Mariam and her family banished for that. So I was hoping Mariam could live in Vanaheim, and maybe if you see how good she is, you'll let her join the ranks of the junior valkyries…and maybe her mother could come, too…" She drew a breath and shoved a forkful of pie in her mouth to stop the rambling. There was also Mariam's father, who must have been banished to Niflheim for a reason, but they would have to deal with one pardon at a time.

"Mariam helped you get the Eye of Hnitbjorg back?" Queen Kaia asked.

Sigrid nodded, swallowing hard. "She can be trusted."

The queen raised an eyebrow. "She's from Niflheim. A world of liars and thieves. Are you—"

"I trust her with my life," Sigrid said, leaving no room for argument.

Queen Kaia didn't meet Sigrid's eye for a long moment. She prodded at her dessert, her chest rising and falling evenly. Finally, she met Sigrid's eye with a little smile. "*A friend of a friend is a friend of mine.* The gods wrote it in the great poems. We'll start with Mariam, and if she proves herself, we can see about pardoning her mother."

Sigrid's heart beat faster. Before she lost momentum, she said, "And I had help from a Night Elf named Fisk. He can also be trusted. He didn't agree with what they did to Ratatosk. He's a master craftsman, same as all Night Elves, and he's willing to help us."

For the briefest moment, Queen Kaia's eyes widened in surprise. She tapped her fingernails on the table as she considered. "A Night Elf."

"I trust him, too. He's saved my life more than once."

He's also endangered it, but that's beside the point.

"I see." The queen's nails tapped faster. "I presume you have a means to contact both of them?"

Sigrid's breath caught. "Yes."

"All right, then please invite them to the valkyrie stable. They are both to be evaluated by General Eira. If she deems it appropriate, the Night Elf can be put to work, and the valkyrie can be considered for training."

Sigrid's head lightened, like she could have floated into the vaulted ceiling. Or maybe that was the mead. Her friends could stay! They didn't need to be kept hidden, a secret, constantly in danger of being discovered.

It would be fun to show Mariam around. They could ride

along Sigrid's favorite trails, go to the village to explore the market, maybe sneak into an empty barn or feed room when nobody was around…

Queen Kaia was talking, but she could hardly pay attention while dreaming of all the things she wanted to share with Mariam.

"—and we can find accommodations for your friends in the stables or in the village."

Sigrid snapped back into the conversation. "They're not staying in Vanahalla with me? With us?"

Queen Kaia winced. "I'm afraid that might be a security problem."

Sigrid pushed down the bubble of disappointment. It made sense that they wouldn't allow just anyone to live at Vanahalla.

"Do we have an agreement, then?" Queen Kaia's cheeks lifted as she tucked her hair behind her ears. "I'm looking forward to getting to know you, Sigrid. We have nearly seventeen years of catching up to do."

Sigrid chewed her lip. *Right. All of this depends on me agreeing to everything.*

Her mind turned like a cartwheel. If she accepted, she would live in Vanahalla and eat extravagant meals like this one every day. Her friends would be safe and comfortable instead of hiding in the woods like prey animals.

All she had to do was fetch Sleipnir and move into the hall.

It would hurt to move up to Vanahalla on the same day as Mariam moved into the stable. But if Sigrid had it her way, this wouldn't be permanent, and Mariam would one day live in the royal tower with her.

We could have fun in my own room…my own bed…

She dipped her chin toward her plate, hiding the flush in her cheeks. Admitting she and Mariam were more than friends was not information she was ready to share. Not with her aunt or anyone else.

She had to talk to her friends about this offer—Mariam, Fisk, Peter. Because as much as she had to gain, she'd learned the hard way that she also had everything to lose. She could make the biggest mistake of her life by trusting her aunt and bringing Sleipnir out of hiding.

"I'll consider your offer, Queen Kaia." She met her aunt's gaze. "I'll let you know of my answer soon."

Queen Kaia's face fell, like she wanted to argue further. But she nodded. "I'll expect a letter from you tomorrow. I'll be busy arranging my brother's funeral all day, but I would like to have you move up here in the evening."

Quicker than Sigrid would've liked, but she sensed her bargaining power was up. She'd already asked for too much by bringing Mariam and Fisk into the deal.

She nodded. The heavy weight of the decision she had to make settled in her chest.

By tomorrow, she would decide whether she was going to ride Sleipnir again, whether she would become Princess of Vanaheim, and what the future held for Mariam and Fisk.

CHAPTER TWELVE

WORTHY REASONS

Sigrid awoke before dawn so she could ride down to Sleipnir's corral before the other stable hands arrived. She'd barely slept, her mind whirling with images of Queen Kaia, Ratatosk, the Night Elves, and Loki. It would be a relief to talk to Mariam and Fisk about everything.

Plus, she had to bring Sleipnir breakfast.

In the hay room, she grabbed the wooden cart and rolled it closer. Guilt churned in her gut as she prepared to steal hay again. The proper thing would be to use her earnings from the Svartalfheim mission to buy her own feed for Sleipnir. No one had given her permission to use the valkyries' hay for a horse other than Hestur. Especially one who ate several times as much as a normal horse.

But if Sleipnir lives in the royal stable, I won't have to worry about this.

"Need help?"

Sigrid gasped and whirled around. A figure stood in the wide doorway, his head tilted as he appraised her.

"Peter!" She put a hand over her chest to calm her heart. "You're early."

He flashed a smile, coming into the hay room. "Now that Ratatosk is back in the spring and the senior valkyries can come home, we've got to prepare their stalls. I expect they'll be back in three or four days."

"Oh. Of course." After several months with the seniors away, the barn was about to become a lot busier.

Peter seemed happier than yesterday—and livelier than she'd seen him in months, really. Despite the news about the king, maybe their victory in Svartalfheim had lifted a bigger weight than she'd realized.

He grabbed a pair of gloves off the wall. "How many bales do you need?"

"Three."

"That's all?"

The implication hung between them—that Sleipnir wouldn't need more than today's meals.

Sigrid drew a breath and said in a rush, "Queen Kaia wants me to assume my role as princess. If I accept, I'll move to the palace tonight, and my horses will live in the royal stable."

He helped her load three bales onto the cart, silent, as if gathering his thoughts. "So you told her about our eight-legged friend?"

"She guessed it." Sigrid frowned. "With the reports of what happened in Helheim and the news about Princess Helena, she fit the pieces together. She wants me to serve Vanaheim as Sleipnir's heir."

"I see," Peter said calmly. He turned to face her. "Will you do it?"

Sigrid straightened out a bale, trying to organize all of her thoughts on the issue.

From the aisle, a mare whinnied and kicked her stall door, apparently hearing the rustling hay and demanding breakfast.

"What would you do?" Sigrid asked, tossing a rope over the bales to tie them down.

Peter grabbed the other end to help. "If someone told me I

was a prince, I'd be riding up to the hall right now with my stuff in a bag."

"Even if your royal mother was so awful that she tried to manipulate you into raising an army of the dead? Even if you would have to wield the most dangerous war horse in the cosmos?"

Peter's mouth twisted into a little smile. "You also have a lot to gain. Imagine the looks on Ylva and Gunni's faces when they find out they won't be allowed to push you around anymore."

Sigrid couldn't help cracking a smile. "That doesn't sound like a very worthy reason to accept my title."

"Then imagine the luxurious life that you, Hestur, and Sleipnir will get. You could probably ask for gold-plated feed buckets for them."

Sigrid laughed. "Neither does that."

These *were* semi-convincing points, but she couldn't let the promise of wealth and status cloud the more important factors—like whether Queen Kaia would betray her like her mother did, and whether she would be risking everyone's safety by agreeing to ride Sleipnir again.

"Okay," Peter said more seriously. "If you accept, and if you get to know your aunt, do you feel like she could help you understand yourself and your family? Do you think this would help answer the questions you've always wondered about?"

Sigrid lifted a shoulder. Could living with Queen Kaia give her the answers she'd been searching for? Sure, maybe. "The thing is, I've spent my life as an orphan stable hand. I was raised in a barn and knew how to groom a horse better than myself. Part of me thinks I'm better off leaving it that way."

"And you're an excellent stable hand. But this is a place of comfort, and comfort isn't always the best way forward." Peter crossed his arms and leaned against the cart. "You've got your family here in the barn, but what about the Sigrid who crossed the nine worlds in search of something greater?"

She exhaled hard. "She found something greater and didn't like it."

Before that journey, she'd been a frustrated stable hand, wishing to be more, to *do* more. Now, she was a frustrated princess with an eight-legged stallion hidden in the woods, wishing she could be less. She'd gotten her wish to be a valkyrie, but the burdens of her heritage and Sleipnir's dangerous power came stubbornly with it.

"Is it being a royal that you're afraid of, or being related to Princess Helena?" Peter asked. "Or is it the part about serving Vanaheim on Sleipnir?"

"I'm not—afraid—" Sigrid said, faltering.

Fine, she couldn't deny that all of those things made her pulse quicken. But she'd never been one to run away from things that scared her, so why start now? Should she face her fears?

If she wanted to stop the looming war and fix the chaos Loki was unleashing, this was her best chance. With a royal title, she could make decisions, and on Sleipnir, she could win any battle.

"What if you accept your title temporarily?" Peter brushed the hay clinging to the front of his tunic, a futile action. "Try living in Vanahalla for a month, and if you don't like it, Hestur's stall will always be ready for you to come back to. Do you think Queen Kaia would let you do that?"

"Maybe…" She'd had the same idea initially, but now she was doubtful. She picked up one of the cart's shafts, and Peter grabbed the other, and they rolled it outside so she could hook up Hestur.

He was right that she was living in comfort—and greatness didn't come to those who sat in comfort. She hadn't found greatness with her mother in Helheim, but maybe she could find it in Vanahalla.

It was as if she were straddling the spring of Hvergelmir, torn between two worlds. In one world, she would continue her simple life as a stable hand and honorary valkyrie—but she would always be tormented by curiosity. In the other world, she accepted Queen Kaia's offer and became Princess Sigrid Helenadottir. She would be in a position to help fix this cosmic imbalance and set the worlds right again.

She wanted both, and she wanted neither. She wanted nothing to do with royalty, but she wanted to know more about her family and her higher purpose as Sleipnir's heir.

The way Peter saw it, the benefits of living as a royal outweighed her worries. But it wasn't that simple. He hadn't seen the way Sleipnir affected her. He hadn't met Helena. And he didn't know Mariam and Fisk's future could be at risk if she changed her mind.

She had to talk to them.

After thanking Peter for the help, she headed down to Myrkviðr, ready to get a little more clarity from the friends who'd ridden with her to Helheim and back.

CHAPTER THIRTEEN

A COMFORTABLE HOUSE

"Absolutely not! No. Why would you even consider this?" Sigrid winced. She'd expected this reaction, but not the hateful fire in Mariam's gaze. It wasn't like she could blame her, either, not after the way Helena had manipulated Mariam.

Mariam crossed her arms. "Sigrid…the royals are horrible people. They banished my mother for being fooled by one of their own, for starters. And after everything your mother did to you?"

"That's what I thought." Sigrid sighed and went back to untying the rope securing the stolen hay bales. "I wanted to sever any connections to her. But I also wondered…what if Queen Kaia is different? What if this really is an opportunity?"

Mariam frowned, helping Sigrid unload the hay bales and bring one into Sleipnir's paddock. Fisk had apparently gone off to get breakfast for himself and Mariam.

"This feels like when your mother offered you a princess title in Helheim." Mariam let the bale go once they got it into place. She cocked one hip, looking pointedly at Sigrid.

Sigrid used a knife she'd borrowed to cut the twine, spilling the hay across the muddy ground. While Sleipnir dove in, she recalled the warmth of Vanahalla and the bustle of people around them. "It didn't feel the same."

"How?" Mariam asked, her gaze searching.

"She wants me to serve Vanaheim, which is a lot different from asking me to help on a personal conquest for the throne. In fact, she doesn't seem interested in all the palace splendor or the power of being queen."

They left Sleipnir's paddock and shut the door behind them. Mariam leaned against it, toying with her braid as she considered Sigrid's words. "What if this is all a ploy to steal Sleipnir?"

Sigrid's heart missed a beat. She hadn't considered that.

But no. That wouldn't make sense.

She shook her head. "Nobody has anything to gain by stealing Sleipnir from me. I'm his heir. Only I can bring out his full potential. Having me serve Vanaheim on him would be in everyone's best interest." She pointed at the fence he'd been working hard to destroy. "Besides, having him in the royal stable would actually be safer than having him continue to stay in this corral."

Mariam considered, her fingers winding around and around her braid. Finally, she nodded firmly, seeming satisfied. "And the condition is that you live in the royal hall with her, and I'd take your stall in the valkyrie stables?"

"Right." Sigrid's heart fluttered as Mariam seemed to soften to the idea. "I want you and Fisk to live better than this. You deserve more than a secret horse corral and smuggled food."

Mariam dropped her hand, her shoulders slumping. "Don't worry about us. We're doing fine."

"I *do* worry! You came all the way here for me. You can't live in a bush."

Mariam snorted and motioned for Sigrid to follow her. "We won't be. Come see the house."

Sigrid froze. "The *what* now?"

Mariam kept walking, so Sigrid hurried after her. Hestur followed, the empty hay cart bumping along behind him. They walked around to the other side of Sleipnir's paddock.

High above the ground, a wooden house sat on the branches of an oak tree, blending so seamlessly with the foliage that it was as if it had always been there. On first glance, Sigrid might have missed it, but the more she looked, the more of it she saw. Flower baskets even hung from a couple of open windows.

Her jaw slackened.

"Fisk made it," Mariam said.

Of course he did. He'd probably siphoned some sort of magic to make it blend in with the environment so well.

"It's huge." Sigrid shook her head. "How long did it take him?" Aesa even had a platform among the branches, where she stood munching on leaves, her wings fanning to keep her body cool.

"Most of the night. Isn't it great?" Mariam asked, her face alight. "You should see the bedroom."

Bedroom? Like, singular?

"I'm impressed." Sigrid walked closer and laid a palm on the rough bark of the oak tree, looking up at the house. There was a strange fizzle inside her, like disappointment. Because a home in the forest meant Mariam had less reason to move to the stables.

And if Mariam was fine living in hiding, then Sigrid had less reason to agree to Queen Kaia's offer.

What was this deflated feeling inside her? Was she disappointed Mariam wanted to stay in the woods—or had she secretly been hoping for a reason to accept her title?

Interesting. Maybe she'd gotten more attached to the idea of accepting Queen Kaia's offer than she'd thought.

Mariam's gaze traveled over Sigrid's face, then up to her hair. She bit her lip.

"What?" Sigrid touched the shaved side of her head with the pattern of flames, suddenly self-conscious.

Mariam flushed. "Nothing. I just—I like that. The look on you."

Sigrid's face heated up. "Oh. Thanks."

Mariam walked closer, a mischievous smile on her lips. She

reached up, brushing her fingers from Sigrid's temple to the back of her head.

Sigrid's breath hitched as the sensation of Mariam's fingers ran all the way down her body.

Why had they been wasting time talking about Queen Kaia? She was finally alone with Mariam, and she could finally kiss her again.

Her heart flipped over. The blazing way Mariam was looking at her was enough to weaken her knees.

"I've dreamt of you every night since you left," Sigrid said, barely a whisper.

Mariam cast Sigrid a devastatingly beautiful smile. "Same."

Sigrid reached out, sliding a hand around Mariam's waist. Her lips tingled. She could spend all day here, watching the way Mariam's cheeks rose when she smiled, memorizing each freckle dusting her nose.

She leaned in, eager for the feel of Mariam's body against hers, craving the taste of her again.

Something rustled in the woods. Hestur perked his ears and looked sharply through the trees, tensing.

Sigrid spun toward the sound, her heart skipping. *Someone found us.*

"Just me!" Fisk called out.

Sigrid relaxed her shoulders — and then immediately regretted not kissing Mariam when she had the chance. She cast Mariam a look that she hoped conveyed the absolute agony going on inside her right now.

Mariam sighed. "He came back faster than I expected," she whispered, and without wasting a second, she tugged Sigrid behind the oak tree and kissed her.

The suddenness caught Sigrid off guard, and her hands moved to Mariam's face before her brain caught up. She pressed closer and opened her lips, a rush of heat dancing through her body.

The kiss was urgent, the culmination of weeks of waiting. Mariam's lips were soft and plump, her taste as sweet as fruit. Her warm skin was as smooth as Sigrid remembered, her muscles strong beneath it.

There was a crunch, and twigs snapped on the other side of the tree, and Mariam let go as quickly as she'd grabbed her.

They broke apart, breathless. Sigrid's lips tingled and her belly fluttered like a winged mare was doing barrel rolls inside her.

Mariam stepped out from behind the tree. "Hey, Fisk."

"I managed a decent breakfast," Fisk said. "Oh, hi, Sigrid! Wow, I like your hair. Neat pattern."

"Hi." She forced her gaze away from Mariam's freshly kissed lips, blazing dark eyes, and tousled braid.

Fisk opened his rucksack and extracted two apples, two potatoes, and several eggs. "We decided to take food from a nearby farm. I know it's wrong, but we don't have much choice— oh, no." He looked into the bag, slumping. "One of the eggs broke."

"It's all right, Fisk." Mariam patted his back. "Sigrid has a proposal for us."

As they relayed Queen Kaia's offer to Fisk, his eye holes turned between them. Sigrid's head spun from the kiss, and Mariam had to help her finish her sentences. She seemed amused by this, much to Sigrid's embarrassment.

"She has to say no, right?" Mariam asked Fisk.

Fisk hummed. "Queen Kaia might be different from Sigrid's mother. She deserves a chance to show who she really is, don't you think?"

"Even if they're not the same, Sigrid owes that family nothing," Mariam said. "What have they done for her? They abandoned her. They left her an orphan, for gods' sake."

"Well, Princess Helena did, yes," Fisk said. "But it sounds like Queen Kaia wants to make up for all of that. Family is important, you know? My father always said—"

"That's for Sigrid to decide." Mariam spun to face her. "Do you think it's worth the risk?"

Sigrid blinked, taken aback by their heated debate over her life. Under the stares of Mariam's blazing eyes and Fisk's wolfy eye holes, she shifted her feet. "I'm…curious to spend time with Queen Kaia. I wonder if I can learn things about my family that my mother wouldn't tell me or that she lied to me about."

Her face burned like she'd admitted a shameful secret. She pretended to be interested in the way Hestur was eating the leaves Aesa dropped from the branches overhead.

"Sigrid," Mariam said, her tone constricted, "what if Queen Kaia knew about your mother's plan to take the throne? I don't want you to get betrayed again."

Was Mariam trying to protect her feelings? Sigrid's lips tugged into a smile—which became a grimace when she caught the meaning. True, her mother might have been close with Queen Kaia and confided in her about her plan to use Sigrid to get the throne. But given how closed-off her mother had been during her stay in Helheim, it seemed unlikely that she'd ever confided in anyone. She probably kept her plan to herself, not even trusting her sister with it.

"Golly, she's only going because it's in everyone's best interest," Fisk said. "She won't let her heart get invested. Won't you, Sigrid?"

"Not a chance," Sigrid promised.

Mariam huffed. "Fine, but what about the fact that she'll have to ride Sleipnir?"

Sigrid nodded grimly, looking to Fisk for his thoughts.

"True," Fisk said, "but that would be worth it if you get to help fix all of the imbalance happening in the worlds. Vanaheim needs your help, Sigrid. Look at what you did in Helheim!"

Kind of him to say, but what if they were all overestimating her abilities on Sleipnir? To save the worlds, she'd have to stop *Loki*.

"Besides, we won't be able to live in the forest forever, Mariam," Fisk said. "We'll have to be part of Vanaheim's society if we want to survive. This is our chance to be accepted here."

"But you worked so hard on the tree fort!" Mariam motioned to it.

"I know. I never got to finish my music room," he said sadly, his mask's nose drooping toward the forest floor. "But we have to think of our safety and not getting Sigrid into trouble. It wouldn't have been easy to live in secret, even with my camouflage enchantments. In time, someone would've stumbled on us or caught us stealing food."

Mariam looked like she wanted to argue, but she huffed and crossed her arms. "I guess."

The forest rustled around them, and the sounds of all three horses stomping and eating filled the silence.

Everything Mariam, Fisk, and Peter had said swirled in Sigrid's brain, assembling loosely into a plan. When she added her own feelings, the instincts tugging her in one particular direction, the plan solidified.

With all of the arguments laid out before her, Sigrid reached a decision.

"I'm doing it." Her heart backflipped as the words came out. "I want to accept my title, and I want to figure out my higher purpose as Sleipnir's heir. Maybe it's related to the cosmic balance, maybe not. But this is the way to find out. At the very least, I'll be doing my best to stop the war everyone thinks is coming."

The others stared at her.

Sigrid set her jaw, confident in her decision. She wouldn't be able to live with the alternative—giving into her fears, saying no to this cosmic path, backing down from what could be a life-changing opportunity for herself and her friends. She *had* to do this.

"Okay," Mariam said, breathless. "Then I suppose not living as outlaws would be nice. Also, it would…well, it'd be nice to explore the place where my mom grew up."

Of course. Before Mariam's mother was banished to Niflheim, she trained with the valkyries. Mariam would be able to experience what her mother's life had been like here.

"You could see all of it!" A feeling of lightness lifted Sigrid's shoulders. "The stables, the training field—I bet someone even knows which stall she kept her mare in."

Mariam smiled. A loose lock of hair fluttered across her eyes, and she lifted a hand to tuck it back, trapping Sigrid's gaze in the way she gently tucked it behind her ear.

"I'll live in the valkyrie stables," Mariam said. "Fisk?"

Fisk nodded so eagerly that his mask clattered. "If possible, I'd like to work with the sorcerers. I bet we can figure out what that iron arrow was all about."

Sigrid's pulse picked up. She had the sensation of floating up toward the tree fort. "We can still hang out here." She motioned around them. "It'll be our spot for when we want to get away from everyone else."

Fisk pushed out his chest. "I like that plan."

Mariam's face broke into a wide smile.

Oh, that smile.

Sigrid breathed out, her heart pounding faster in anticipation of what came next.

The plan was settled. It was time to write a letter to Queen Kaia.

CHAPTER FOURTEEN

GENERAL EIRA'S
DECISION

"You can't be serious." General Eira rubbed the well-worn crease between her eyebrows.

Sigrid stopped in the barn aisle, Mariam and Fisk flanking her. She held up the scroll with the reply from Queen Kaia. "The queen gave permission—"

"I am aware. I've just come from talking to her."

"Oh." Sigrid shifted on her feet as a wave of uncertainty rippled through her. What had Queen Kaia said, exactly? And why did Sigrid feel like she was about to get in more trouble than usual from General Eira?

The general swept her gaze over Mariam and Fisk, looking thunderous with pink splotches across her pale face and her dark hair unmoving in a painfully tight bun. She jerked her crisp white uniform straight. There was a slight chance she recognized Mariam from when she stole the Eye of Hnitbjorg—and from the infirmary, hours before Sigrid freed Mariam and they took off to Helheim together.

Yep, I'm in trouble.

A few junior valkyries stood behind the general, looking gleeful at her rage. Ylva and Gunni actually clutched each other in excitement.

General Eira stepped closer. "Where do I begin?"

Mariam lifted her chin, a flash of defiance in her expression. Since Sigrid had left the tree fort earlier, Mariam had bathed and gotten changed, and she looked as fierce and radiant as ever. She'd lined her eyes with dark makeup and wound her hair into a long, flawless braid. Her black tunic smelled like she'd washed it in rose water.

Fisk, on the other hand, stood behind her in his patched-up leathers, hunched as if trying to hide. His oversize dire wolf mask did a poor job of it.

"Should we discuss the part where you *quit* your job as a stable hand and offer me a *Night Elf*?" General Eira asked. "Or the part where I'm supposed to evaluate a new valkyrie, one who not only led Night Elves right to our doors barely a month ago, but also tried to steal the Eye? This is unheard of! All of it!"

Mariam sucked in a breath.

Sigrid cleared her throat. "General…" How was she supposed to navigate this conversation? The judgmental glares made it hard to speak. There were no sufficient words to explain to all of these girls, who'd bullied her since she could walk, that she was actually a princess and was going to live with her aunt Kaia in the royal hall. They would laugh in her face.

Sigrid can't be a princess! Her? Really?

A chicken clucked, emphasizing how silent the barn had become.

Sigrid swallowed. "Mariam helped us get the Eye back. She made a mistake, but—"

General Eira faced Mariam fully, fixing her with a cold gaze. "Queen Kaia explained it to me. Sofie's daughter wants to join Vanaheim's elite. Following your mother's footsteps?"

Betrayal. That was what the general was really asking. Mariam's mother had put her lot in with the wrong person and ended up betraying Vanaheim.

Sigrid held back a growl. If she had learned anything, it was that daughters should not be judged based on their mothers' actions.

Mariam's gaze didn't waver. Even as her hands clenched into fists at her side, her voice remained measured. "I follow my own path, General."

Sigrid's heart stuttered. She wanted to reach out, to slide her fingers into Mariam's. But she stayed still and waited.

After a tense moment, a small *tch* came from General Eira. "That's your mare outside, I take it."

Aesa waited at the hitching post outside the barn doors. Her rusty-brown spots set her apart from the other mares.

Mariam nodded, her shoulders tensing.

"I hope she's well trained." Doubt tainted General Eira's voice.

"She is."

"We will see."

Mariam's expression turned, her temper advancing in like a storm cloud, so Sigrid jumped back into the conversation. "Fisk here is ready to put his expert craftsman skills to work. You know how Night Elves are."

General Eira crossed her arms, glaring. "Do I ever."

Sigrid bit the inside of her cheek. *Okay. Wrong thing to say.*

"Pleased to meet you, General," Fisk said, muffled.

The general's gaze roved over his mask as if she weren't sure where to look or how to gauge his intentions when there was no expression to read.

The air between them strained like an overstuffed hay bag as the four of them stood appraising each other. Sigrid wanted to say something, *anything* that would help Mariam and Fisk get General Eira's approval. But her mind had blanked out.

Gods, I've never gotten her approval myself.

The silence was getting unbearable, until Ylva snickered.

General Eira whirled around to where the juniors were still

gawking and pointed out the barn doors. "Back to your tasks. All of you."

They obeyed, skittering away like startled rabbits.

"Roland, tack up Drifa," General Eira called out.

Roland rushed out of the hay room, where he'd possibly been eavesdropping. "Yes, General."

Pointing at Mariam, General Eira said, "Get your mare. We'll start with your valkyrie evaluation."

The moment the general disappeared inside the tack room, Mariam rounded on Sigrid. "You didn't tell me I was going to be *evaluated*!" she whispered.

Sigrid blinked. "I—I thought that was implied."

"No, it wasn't!" Mariam lifted her hands as if fighting the urge to seize Sigrid's shoulders.

"It really wasn't," Fisk said.

Sigrid glared at him.

He shrugged.

"When you said I'd live in your stall, I thought you meant I'd be taking your place as a stable hand," Mariam hissed.

Sigrid let out a breath of laughter. "Mariam, you're a valkyrie! Why would I have left you my job as a stable hand? This is a much better arrangement."

Mariam scowled, apparently disagreeing. "What if General Eira evaluates us and decides she doesn't want us? I'd have to go back to Niflheim."

"No way am I going back to Svartalfheim," Fisk said firmly, crossing his arms.

"She'll accept you," Sigrid said. "Mariam, once she sees how you fly—"

"But if she doesn't?"

Sigrid stepped closer and lowered her voice. "Then you can go back to living in the secret tree fort."

Mariam shook her head. "She won't just let us go free. She's going to have us escorted to the spring. We won't be allowed to stay in Vanaheim."

"That wouldn't happen," Sigrid said, though not entirely convinced. Had she risked too much by bringing Mariam and Fisk to the stable? What *would* happen if General Eira didn't want them here?

But the queen had ordered this evaluation, and that counted for something.

"You'll do fine. You're a great rider already." Sigrid gripped Mariam's shoulder. "Don't worry. Just imagine being inducted into the valkyries."

Mariam rubbed her hands down her face and said into her hands, "Sigrid, I'm not sure I want to join the ranks."

A chasm opened in Sigrid's stomach, and she let go of Mariam. "What?"

Mariam dropped her hands and frowned, not meeting her eye. "I never asked you to push for that for me."

"I thought it was a fair assumption." Sigrid's voice shook as she struggled against a spark of anger. After spending her whole life trying to convince General Eira to let her be a valkyrie, it was hard to believe anyone would turn down such an offer. "Do you not want to serve Vanaheim?"

She hesitated, glancing to where General Eira had disappeared. "The valkyries banished my mother."

"You don't know who, exactly, banished her," Sigrid said. "The valkyries were her friends. I bet a lot of them didn't want her to go."

Mariam tilted her head, considering. Her gaze darted between Sigrid, the far end of the barn, and the floor. She sighed. "Fine, but—I mean, I'm from *Niflheim*. I haven't spent my life in valkyrie training. I have no idea how to live here as a functioning person. I won't measure up to everything they expect of me."

Sigrid spluttered. "Yes, you will!"

Here she'd been born a non-valkyrie and had spent her life fighting to be one. Mariam had been born to be a valkyrie and was turning it down. Of the two of them, Mariam wasn't the one who should be afraid of not measuring up.

"Sigrid, I wouldn't make a very good valkyrie."

Sigrid stepped close again, until she could see each freckle dusting Mariam's nose. "You already are one. You were born one."

"There's more to joining Vanaheim's ranks than being bonded with a winged mare."

"What would you do, then?"

Sadness pulled down Mariam's features, from her eyebrows to her lips to her slumped shoulders. "I'm not sure. I do want to know where my mom grew up and what she did here, but I didn't plan on doing exactly as she did and becoming a valkyrie." Her jaw worked. "I also don't like the idea of being evaluated and shoved in with Vanaheim's most elite warriors."

Was Mariam so afraid of being rejected that she didn't want to try in the first place?

Softer, Sigrid said, "Mariam, you deserve the respect and nobility of a valkyrie. You deserve to earn proper wages and live a normal life—well, as normal as you can manage."

The apples of Mariam's cheeks lifted as she cracked a smile. "It means a lot to you that I try, doesn't it?"

Why does she have to be so painfully beautiful?

Sigrid toed the clay floor. "Well, yeah. I want you to like it here."

Mariam studied her, biting her lip, until Sigrid's face heated up again. What was she searching for?

Whatever it was, the way she was looking at Sigrid made her heart flutter.

"*I* like it here," Fisk said, stepping closer so his snout was basically between them.

They both turned to look at him.

Sigrid's insides deflated at the missed opportunity that hovered tantalizingly between her and Mariam.

"I do not have all day for this," General Eira barked from down the aisle.

They all jumped.

The general marched toward them, leaving Roland to hustle in her wake with her saddled-up mare. She held out a golden spear to Mariam. "Let's see how you handle weapons on the training field."

Mariam grabbed it.

"Elf," General Eira snapped.

"Y-yes, ma'am? General, ma'am?"

General Eira narrowed her eyes. "I have questions for you."

Fisk had no chance to say anything else as the general marched outside, and he hustled to catch up to her.

With a final, pleading glance at Sigrid, Mariam followed them out of the barn to start her evaluation. Her movements were graceful as she climbed on Aesa, spear in hand, and hurried after the general.

Sigrid's chest tightened as she watched them go.

Did I mess up?

What if General Eira failed Mariam? Was there any chance Mariam would still be allowed to live in the stable? She would be furious at Sigrid for pressuring her into this, and whatever was going on between them would be ruined.

As Roland walked past with Drifa, he raised his eyebrows at her in a *this-should-be-interesting* way, which did nothing for her nerves. She swallowed hard, unable to speak.

If General Eira didn't accept Mariam into the valkyrie ranks, Sigrid would never forgive herself.

CHAPTER FIFTEEN

MOVING OUT

A knot of anxiety tightened in Sigrid's gut as she packed up her stall. Her decision to move to Vanahalla was gaining momentum like Ratatosk's ship hurtling through worlds—boldly accelerating on its own, no turning back. Was she really about to become a princess? Had she really agreed to ride Sleipnir if war came?

I have to do this. We have to prepare for cosmic unrest, and Sleipnir won't be useful hidden in the woods.

Not ten minutes had passed when she snuck out of the barn to steal a glance at the training field. Aesa flew around the airborne golden hoops, but they were too far away to tell whether Mariam's spear hit its targets.

Please have a heart, General Eira…

"I can't believe she came back," Ylva said nearby, making Sigrid jump. She, Gunni, and Runa, and Edith leaned against the barn in a patch of shade, squinting toward the training field.

"She'll be sent home," Gunni said, scrunching her face.

"I don't know," Edith said a little more kindly, polishing her spear with a cloth. "She could easily become a junior. You saw how she flew in Helheim."

Ylva scoffed. "We can't just *recruit* valkyries from other worlds."

Edith lifted her spear to the light to examine it. "Why not?"

"If she's fit and skilled…" Runa said, hugging a book to her chest.

"She'll be kicked out. You just wait," Gunni said.

"Don't you have anything better to do than to eavesdrop and gossip?" Sigrid snapped.

The valkyries turned their gazes to her.

"What makes you think General Eira will want an *outsider* joining us?" Ylva demanded, narrowing her dark eyes and setting her lips with her usual swan-like poise. "This isn't open auditions. You might have been allowed to join us, but in the end you're still a—well, you're not even a stable hand anymore, are you? What made you think you can quit?"

Was Sigrid imagining the tremor in her voice and the widening in her eyes?

"She probably got a job offer in the village as a chimney sweep," Gunni said, but the note of laughter was forced, and she searched Sigrid's face closely for a reaction.

Runa and Edith's gazes flicked over her, curious.

Before they'd charged into Helheim together, Sigrid told them Princess Helena was her mother. With Sigrid joining their ranks and now moving out of the stables, of course they had to be wondering if she'd acquired a new title. A *royal* title.

Sigrid wouldn't indulge their silent questions. She had no desire to explore the answers and utter words like *"Princess Helena left me an orphan because she never wanted me"* and *"I'm Sleipnir's heir and it's my cosmic purpose to ride him, but I'm pretty sure riding him makes me evil."*

Ylva and Gunni weren't worth that conversation.

"Keep guessing." She rolled her eyes and left their glares behind, going to find a wheelbarrow. Yet Ylva's words lingered uneasily in her mind. *An outsider.* It was the truth. Why would General Eira risk letting outsiders join them, especially with the threat of war looming?

I should've told General Eira how amazing Mariam and Fisk are. I didn't do anything except push them onto her and leave.

As she passed a group of stable hands talking in low voices, she caught the word, "Svartalfheim."

When they saw her, they stopped talking, looking guilty.

"Oh, real nice," she said. "Clucking that gossip while the mares go unattended."

They bowed their heads in shame and dispersed.

Her stomach sank, partly the guilt of snapping at her brothers, and partly because even they were suspicious.

If Mariam and Fisk were allowed to stay, they'd still have to deal with all the whispers behind their backs. Maybe it wasn't such a bad idea for them to stay at the tree house in the forest.

Fighting the squirming feeling inside her, she got to work shoveling out Hestur's stall and cleaning his buckets.

Boots scuffed nearer, the steps too short to be General Eira's.

"Hey, Sig," Roland said. "I heard—whoa. You really are going." He leaned over her stall door, gaping at the disarray. His white hair was in a high bun, wisps coming loose as if a mare had gotten to it while he was tending her legs.

"Yep."

"Wanna talk about it?"

"Nope."

When he said nothing along the lines of *princess*, she let out a breath. "Not going to ask where I'm going?"

Roland tilted his head. "Do you want me to?"

"So you don't already know?"

"*Should* I know?"

Sigrid sighed. "You're annoying," she said, which only made him chuckle.

As she scooped up another shovelful of old shavings, Roland stepped into the stall. She paused. He'd never come into her stall before.

"Sigrid," he said seriously. "I want you to know that whatever new adventure you're going on, I support you. I'll always be with you. Right here." He hovered his palm over her chest—her heart, maybe?

"Thanks, Roland," she said, pursing her lips to keep a straight face.

"In fact…" He drew a breath, reached into his pocket, and bent on one knee. "I just heard from the valkyries that we're dating, and I would be honored if—"

Sigrid cuffed him on the head. "Oh, shut it!"

He toppled sideways, erupting into an impish laugh.

"You're such a turd," she said. "Did you make that out of baling twine?"

The "ring" in his hand was a loop of twine that looked suspiciously like something from the hay room.

"Homemade jewelry is romantic, I'll have you know," he said. "Any princess would love such a treasure, more so than gold and diamonds and…whatever else princesses love."

"So you *do* know!"

He gave a guilty half shrug.

She couldn't help laughing. His echoing laugh and the twinkle in his eyes said he'd done it all just to get that reaction from her. He had a way of making her forget her anxieties, even if in the most irritating way possible.

The moment was ruined when General Eira walked past. Alone.

Sigrid raced for the stall door so fast that she accidentally kneed Roland in the shoulder, making him fall back with a yelp.

"How'ditgo?" she called out.

The general stopped.

Sigrid's chest constricted, making it hard to breathe. Where were Mariam and Fisk?

Behind her, Roland stayed absolutely silent.

"She flies as recklessly as her mother," General Eira said, smoothing her jacket.

"You…knew her?"

"Sofie and I flew many successful missions together, and we spent two years at the highest rank before she…" She inhaled, her face losing a bit of her ever-present sternness. "I was devastated when I found out about her treason. I never expected it. Not of her."

Sigrid stared, her heart pounding.

"We never got the full story about why Sofie chose to follow Princess Helena. But who am I to make that judgment?"

A betrayal like that couldn't have been easy to live through. Sigrid knew that first hand. How must it have impacted the valkyries who knew her? Maybe this explained some of General Eira's personality—stern, closed off, unmovable.

General Eira shook her head. "Anyway, after all the missions she flew for Vanaheim, we owe it to her to accept her daughter into our ranks. She'll start training with the rest of you when sessions resume later this week."

"Nice!" Roland loud-whispered behind her, still on the floor, as if hiding from the general.

General Eira narrowed her eyes but otherwise ignored him.

Sigrid let out a chuckle and an exhale in the same breath, one she'd been holding all day. "Thank you. This is—"

"As for the elf," the general said sharply, "given what Svartalfheim is up to right now, I hope you understand that I cannot have a Night Elf in my stable."

Sigrid's insides deflated like a sail without wind. "What?"

"He might change his mind and turn on us, or he might already be a spy."

"No, that's not—"

"The risk is too high, Sigrid."

"He's different from those other Night Elves!" she exclaimed, her voice rising.

General Eira drew herself up, her nostrils flaring like a winded mare. "Save your breath on convincing me. He's gone, Sigrid. I already asked him to leave Vanaheim."

CHAPTER SIXTEEN

A PLACE FOR
A NIGHT ELF

Sigrid stampeded over the meadow, her ears full of the sound of Hestur's hooves and the steady blow of his nostrils. There'd been no time to put on the saddle or bridle, so she grabbed his mane for support as they bumped over the uneven ground.

The threat of losing Fisk put an ache in her chest. After all they'd been through together and all he'd done to help save the Eye of Hnitbjorg, she couldn't let General Eira send him away.

She had to find him and tell him to stay. She would sort this out with Queen Kaia. The queen would have the final word over the general, right? Surely *Sigrid* did, if she was a princess?

The uncertainty made her nauseous.

The daylight dimmed like a snuffed flame as they burst through the tree line into Myrkviðr. They jumped a log barring the trail and pushed through ferns. The woods closed around her, blocking her line of sight.

"Fisk!"

With the way he moved, swift and silent like a shadow, she might never find him in these vast woods.

She owed it to Fisk to protect him. When he'd decided to ally with her and Mariam long ago, that made him a traitor to Svartalfheim. What if he was no longer welcome there? If he wasn't welcome in Svartalfheim, and he wasn't welcome in

Vanaheim, where would he live?

Her heart squeezed for him.

"Fisk!" She slowed Hestur to a walk, catching her breath. Between the chirping birds, creaking branches, and hoofbeats, she had no chance of hearing her friend. But maybe Hestur could. "Help me find him, buddy."

His instincts had proven better than hers on many occasions.

She nudged him to a trot and let him pick his path, hoping he would take her to Fisk and not the nearest apple tree.

But he seemed confused, unsure where she wanted him to go.

Fisk had stored his belongings in the tree fort, so what if he'd gone there before leaving?

She urged Hestur in that direction, picking up speed.

As they approached the corral, Hestur raised his head.

"Fisk, are you here?" Sigrid asked, her heart leaping.

Her question was met with silence.

She rode a circle around the tree fort, trying to see inside.

The area was quiet.

He wasn't there.

Sigrid's breaths came fast, making her dizzy. She was too late. He could be anywhere by now. Should she gallop through the woods until she found him?

Branches rustled overhead, and a winged mare swooped down.

"Sigrid!" Mariam shouted, Aesa's wings stirring up a swirl of leaves as she landed. "Fisk—"

"I know!" Sigrid cried. "I can't find him."

Mariam pointed toward the stables with panic in her eyes. "Your friend, Peter, was talking to General Eira. I think he was trying to convince her to let him stay."

Sigrid's heart skipped. "He was?"

Mariam nodded.

Peter never disobeyed General Eira, and she respected him

as her top stable hand. But did she respect him enough to change her mind?

"But where's Fisk?" Sigrid asked.

"I don't know."

They looked around desperately, as if searching for a clue.

"Come on. Let's check the road." Sigrid nudged Hestur, and he sprang into a gallop.

With Mariam and Aesa at their tail, they raced for the dirt road.

As they emerged from the trees, Sigrid blinked, adjusting her eyes to the bright sunlight. To the right, the road led into the forest. Ahead, it led into the village. To the left, it snaked up to the valkyrie stables and Vanahalla. Hestur turned his head in that direction, hearing something before she did.

Peter strode toward them, talking to—

"Fisk!" Sigrid cried, the word coming out as a squeak.

"There you are," Peter said, as if Sigrid had been the one to disappear.

"I—General Eira said you'd left!" Sigrid stammered.

"I did," Fisk said glumly.

"And I caught up before he got too far," Peter said.

"You talked to General Eira?" Sigrid asked, breathless.

He nodded, his expression unreadable. "She doesn't want Fisk living in the stable, and she definitely doesn't want him working with the sorcerers up at Vanahalla—but she agreed that I could hire him as a stable hand and a smith. He'll be my apprentice."

There was a moment of shock, and then Sigrid and Mariam shrieked and wrestled Fisk into a hug. He made an indistinct groan of protest.

When they broke apart, he said, "I don't know. If the scary general lady doesn't like me, I'm not sure—"

"She doesn't like me, either," Sigrid said. "Don't worry."

Peter's mouth twisted into a little smile. "You don't need her to like you, Fisk. You'll be reporting to me, not her."

Fisk hesitated, then nodded.

Sigrid's heart lifted. She was as grateful as ever to have Peter in her life.

"Do you have somewhere to live, Fisk?" Peter asked. "If not, I can put the word out and find some lodging—"

"I do," Fisk said, presumably talking about the tree fort. He straightened his mask. "Thank you very much."

"How did you convince General Eira?" Sigrid asked Peter.

He waved a hand. "Don't worry about it."

She scrutinized him, not liking this secrecy. "But—"

"Your friends are allowed to stay. The hiccup getting them here is in the past, and we should move on." He grinned. "So these are Fisk and Mariam, hey? I've heard lots of good things about both of you."

Sigrid's cheeks warmed.

"Hi," Mariam said, distracted as she pulled a leaf out of her braid.

"I still think Fisk should be working with the sorcerers," Sigrid said, scowling. "We have amazing Night Elf talent right here, and the sorcerers are studying those dangerous iron arrows forged by Night Elves *right now*, and we're going to ask Fisk to shovel horse poop!"

"We'll put his skills to use." Peter nodded firmly, patting Fisk on the back. "Won't we?"

"Yes, sir," Fisk said, seeming bolstered by Peter's confidence in him.

"Thanks, Peter," Sigrid said, trying to convey with a look how much this meant to her.

He nodded, giving her an understanding wink. "Fisk, do you want to come with me? We can start with the feed room."

"Sure." He shuffled off after Peter, giving Sigrid a little wave.

As they walked back to the valkyrie stables, Peter said, "We have two types of hay. The alfalfa is fed once a day at dinner…"

Sigrid let out a big breath, and for the first time in hours, a real smile tugged at her cheeks. Both of her friends had jobs. They were allowed to stay in Vanaheim. And with them here, she would be able to conquer whatever waited for her in Vanahalla's towers.

CHAPTER SEVENTEEN

A SLIGHT
BEDROOM IMPROVEMENT

Sigrid and Mariam led their horses back to the stables on foot, seizing the moment alone.

"Congratulations, then," Sigrid said, relaxing into a real smile now that Fisk was safe.

Mariam blushed, a cute tinge of red in her round cheeks. "Thanks."

"I knew you'd be accepted. You're too good not to be."

Mariam said nothing, watching her feet. Was she nervous?

"You're going to be great, Mariam. Your mom raised you on real valkyrie training, so you're not behind. Not really."

"It's not that. I'm not nervous. It's—" She swallowed hard, looking like everything she said she wasn't, which made Sigrid smile. "I have to prove them wrong. The valkyries, the queen, everyone who voted to banish my mom. They shouldn't have done that, and they're going to see they've been missing out on some perfectly good warriors this whole time."

Sigrid nodded, taking Mariam's hand as understanding trickled through her. "You *will* prove them wrong. We're going bring your parents to Vanaheim. I feel it."

Mariam leaned over and kissed Sigrid's cheek with soft, full lips, keeping a hold of her hand as they made it back to the stables. Sigrid vowed to bring Mariam's family home one day, even if she had to petition Queen Kaia every single day until she agreed.

After they'd put their horses in a field and entered the barn, Mariam squeezed Sigrid's hand and said coyly, "Want to show me your room?"

The words nearly sent Sigrid through the rafters. Her stammering heart made it hard to reply.

"It's a bit of a mess—I'm emptying it—it's right here."

As she motioned to Hestur's stall, the reality of her *room* settled. It was a cube bounded by clay and wood, smelling like a horse. She'd definitely played it up too much when she told Mariam about it.

"We can check with General Eira, but you might take over this stall or an empty one nearby." She tried to sound casual as she watched for Mariam's reaction. "I have a hammock for you, and we'll get some bins for your stuff. You could also buy curtains and…decorations…"

"Oh, it's perfect!" Mariam walked around the space, studying the rings where the hammock would hang, the buckets for grain and water, and the metal bars separating the stall from the barn aisle. The dim light of the barn cast shadows over her body, drawing Sigrid's gaze to her strong shoulders, her arms, and the curve of her waist beneath her black tunic.

Mariam met Sigrid's gaze, and Sigrid blinked, realizing she was staring.

Mariam opened her mouth to speak but closed it when two stable hands walked by holding grain bags. "Not much privacy?"

"Well, it's pretty quiet at night," Sigrid said. "But the daytime can be busy."

Mariam's mouth twisted in a little smile, a glint in her dark eyes. "Too bad. With Fisk occupied, I was hoping we could find somewhere to be alone for a few minutes."

Sigrid had to grab the stall door to stay standing. "You're going to kill me."

Mariam stepped closer, pulling Sigrid into the bottomless pools of her eyes.

A lull came over the stable—no footsteps, no voices, all of the horses outside. Only chickens clucked in the aisle and birds chirped in the rafters.

"Once I'm settled in Vanahalla," Sigrid said, her heart pounding faster, "I'm going to ask again if you can live up there with me. I'll have a real bedroom and—um, a door that locks so we won't keep getting interrupted."

Her face heated up as the words came out. She'd never said anything like that before. Was this how flirting worked? Had she said the right thing? She wanted Mariam to know her feelings, but didn't want to come across too…Roland-ish.

To her relief, Mariam grinned. She caught Sigrid's hand and backed further into the stall. Their faces were close, Mariam's sweet breath tickling her lips as she whispered, "Sounds interesting. What would we do behind a bedroom door that locks?"

Sigrid's mind went wild with all of the possibilities—the places she wanted to kiss and touch Mariam, the things they could do on a real bed…

Footsteps came down the aisle.

Mariam's face reflected the agony twisting Sigrid's insides.

Go away, she wanted to shout.

Sigrid stepped back and said casually, "We can go get some empty bins from the supply shed."

Mariam snorted. "For all of my piles of belongings?"

"You'll earn a good wage as a valkyrie. You'll be able to afford things in no time."

Roland poked his head over the stall door. "Hey, Sig. Mariam, nice to meet you. Can you show me what your mare gets for food and supplements?"

Mariam's shoulder brushed Sigrid on her way past, definitely on purpose. "Sure."

Sigrid's insides danced with excitement, and she returned to the chore of packing with a burst of energy.

A world of possibilities had just opened up before her—a future with a girl she cared about, doing a job that was important, living in Vanahalla with her aunt. This was what she'd wanted when she went after Slcipnir. This was a purposeful life she could fight for.

She stuffed the last of her belongings into empty grain bags and fastened everything over Hestur's back like a pack mule. By the time she cinched the last rope and Mariam fetched her stuff from the tree fort, the sun began to set.

The junior valkyries left with suspicious glares and whispers among themselves.

"Do you think she's moving in with us?"

"General Eira would have told us."

"Maybe she rented a place in the village."

It obviously hadn't occurred to them that this was Sigrid's last day doing stable hand duties, and she wasn't about to correct them and invite a flood of questions.

As Mariam folded her clothes in her new home and Fisk left for Myrkviðr, Sigrid could no longer put off moving to Vanahalla.

Peter and Roland lingered, the only ones left.

"I'll still be here every day," Sigrid said, forcing the goodbye to be casual.

Peter pulled her into a hug anyway. "Of course."

She hugged him back, blinking away a weird burning in her eyes that had no reason to be there. This wasn't really a goodbye. It was just a change in accommodations.

"Remember, if you find yourself in need of a prince, Your Highness," Roland said, bowing, "I offer my services."

"Oh, shut it."

He scooted away, cackling, before she could smack him.

One day, she'd share that she and Mariam were together—

or trying to be. But keeping it between the two of them was so nice and so wonderfully *private*. The thought of the entire stable gossiping about her love life was mortifying. Besides, she'd worked so hard to let Mariam stay in Vanaheim. If everyone found out they were dating, they'd wonder about her motivations.

She shouted a quick goodbye to the other stable hands on her way out, desperate not to make an ordeal.

As she checked the ropes fastening her entire life on Hestur's back, she glanced at Mariam, who was in her new stall, stuffing her clothes into a bin while Aesa munched hay beside her. Was there any chance of kissing Mariam goodbye without everybody seeing?

Nope.

With the stable hands finishing the evening chores, they had no privacy.

She could ask Mariam to accompany her somewhere, but she didn't want to seem desperate. Plus, Mariam was so excited to set up her new home that she might see any distraction as an annoyance.

Sigrid stood outside her old stall and gave Mariam a little wave. "Um, see you tomorrow. I'll come down to see how your first day of training is going."

Mariam straightened up and wiped a lock of sweaty hair off her forehead. "Sweet dreams, Princess Sigrid."

Sigrid returned her smile — but with a twinge of dissatisfaction, like missing out on dessert. Dragging her feet away from the most beautiful girl in Vanaheim, she led Hestur up to Vanahalla.

CHAPTER EIGHTEEN

THAT GOOD
ROYAL LIFE

Sleipnir fought Sigrid the whole way up the hill, his energy rising like a brewing thunderstorm. She'd thought she could lead both horses at once, but he was so full of energy that she could barely hold onto his rope. Hestur pinned his ears as if to tell him to stop being so difficult.

"Stop—bucking!" she said through her teeth, letting go of Hestur's lead rope and holding onto the stallion's with both hands.

How had she ever managed to ride him? Was she making it worse by delaying the moment she got in the saddle?

Either way, she wasn't so sure about the promise she'd made to Queen Kaia if war came.

Dripping in sweat, she somehow made it up to Vanahalla, where everyone in the courtyard stared open-mouthed, pointing and whispering. More people came rushing outside as Sleipnir's snorts and clattering hooves ricocheted off the gold towers.

Sigrid's cheeks warmed. *Yes, this is the actual Sleipnir. Now finish gawking and go about your business.*

The stable hand from before stood out front of the royal stable along with two others. Their eyes were wide, a mixture of awe and fear in their expressions, as she put the muzzle on Sleipnir and handed over the lead rope.

"You'll thank me for the muzzle," she said, clutching her side as she struggled for breath.

The boys took Sleipnir and Hestur—who was being extra polite as if to show everyone how a good horse was supposed to behave—and led them through the barn's golden doors, where the polished white aisle was more pristine than a stable had any right to be.

Sigrid's insides fluttered. Calling a new barn home after nearly seventeen years in the valkyrie stables felt unreal.

Twilight darkened the sky, and when she entered the hall as before, lanterns cast a warm glow over the marble and gold.

Queen Kaia came to meet her with a smile in a shimmering blue gown. "Sigrid."

In the distance, there was a bang, a crack, and a whinny that was definitely Sleipnir.

Sigrid winced. "Uh, maybe I should help get the horses settled," she said, motioning back out the door.

Queen Kaia smiled and began crossing the vast lobby to one of the staircases. "You don't have to do anything. You've been promoted. Stable hands work for you now, and they'll take care of your horses and bring your belongings to your quarters."

Sigrid contemplated insisting she go anyway, but she was so tired after that long day and the trek up the hill that she couldn't find an argument. She ran to catch up. "Does this mean I won't have to clean stalls?"

Queen Kaia climbed a spiral staircase, one hand on the gold railing and the other holding her gown off the floor. "You'll never have to touch a pitchfork."

"Wow. I still want to brush Hestur myself, though."

"If you'd like."

No stable hand duties at all. Would it feel strange and empty? Or would it be a relief to have time for other things?

"Hestur and Sleipnir will settle in nicely," Queen Kaia said, and although *Sleipnir* and *settle* didn't fit in the same sentence,

Sigrid tried to be optimistic. "We'll put Hestur next to a sweet little mare named Disa."

"Is Disa yours?" Sigrid asked.

"No." Her aunt looked down as she climbed the stairs, a flush in her cheeks. "During a riding lesson when I was six, my pony tripped in a fox hole and fell. She was fine, but I hit the ground hard enough that I lost my nerve for riding. I haven't been on a horse since."

"Oh, I'm sorry to hear that," Sigrid said, sad to hear Queen Kaia had been scared away from horses. That was one of the first rules of riding: if you fall off, get right back in the saddle.

Something twisted in her gut. Was she doing just that with Sleipnir—sitting on the ground, too afraid to get up? Or did she have legitimate cause to be afraid of him?

Queen Kaia waved off the apology, her gold bands jangling. "I have no need to ride."

"You don't?" Sigrid asked, taken aback. "What about traveling? I thought princesses got to visit other worlds." The promise of traveling was one of the things that drew her to becoming a valkyrie.

Queen Kaia cast her a knowing smile. She seemed happier today, her expression soft and youthful. "You can travel if you wish. We'll talk about cosmic relations in time. We have a council and entire libraries for you to reference."

"Will you show me where the libraries are?" The sudden urgency to learn everything she could about Svartalfheim and Loki made her chest tight. Finally, she could catch up on the education she'd missed out on growing up as a stable hand, and so much more. "And will you show me where the sorcerers work? And seeing maps of the nine worlds would help—"

Queen Kaia laughed, taking Sigrid along a fifth-floor corridor. "You have the enthusiasm this hall needs, Sigrid. It's too late for all of that now, but I promise to give you a tour in the morning."

Sigrid didn't correct her that it was less enthusiasm and more worry about the future with the god of chaos on the loose.

It would be hard to sleep tonight, but a fresh start in the morning would be better to tackle her princess duties and figure out how to stop Loki.

Queen Kaia stopped at a closed door and motioned for her to go inside. "Your quarters."

Sigrid hesitated, excitement and nerves doing battle inside her. Who did these chambers belong to before? Whether it was her mother, the dead king, her dead grandparents, or someone else long passed, none of it was comforting.

"Whose—?" She couldn't finish the sentence.

"Óleifr's," Queen Kaia said, her eyebrows pulling down.

Sigrid's heart jumped while her mind unhelpfully shouted, *Did he die in here?*

But no, the room would have been cleaned and freshened for her. Wherever he'd died, there was nothing to be afraid of.

It was strange that her aunt had been so quick to clear out her brother's chambers. Unless it was easier to put her living niece in there than to face the empty room.

Queen Kaia searched her expression, dipping her chin to meet her eyes. "Is that all right?"

Sigrid nodded. Truthfully, this was better than being given Princess Helena's old room. At least Queen Kaia had enough sense not to try and do that. "Yes. Of course."

And without wasting another moment, she seized the massive gold doorknob and entered.

The view took the breath from her lungs.

King Óleifr's room had a natural, woodsy feel that Queen Kaia must have guessed Sigrid would like. The wooden walls, logs, and the abundance of plants all gave the impression of being deep in Myrkviðr. A cozy fireplace burned in the far wall. To the left, an open doorway led to what looked like a bathroom. To the right, another doorway opened to a study. Enormous paintings took up every wall, horses and gods looking down from every angle. The room's main feature was an outrageously large bed that could have fit Sleipnir.

Oh—my—gods.

After spending her life paying to sleep in a barn and being made to feel like an annoying pigeon who lived in the rafters, being given this luxurious room felt strange. It could not possibly have been more different from her old quarters.

It was more than she ever thought she would have…and it would be better if she could share it.

Guilt twisted inside her. Mariam was settling into her old stall a few minutes down the hill while Sigrid had a room big enough for both of them. The bed was certainly big enough.

The thought made her face burn as something new and exciting fluttered deep inside her.

She cleared her throat. "Thank you for letting my friends stay in Vanaheim, Queen Kaia. General Eira is accepting Mariam into the valkyrie ranks. She said she knew her mother."

"Did she? Well, we're lucky to have a new valkyrie in times like these," Queen Kaia said grimly.

"Mariam's wonderful. General Eira made the right decision."

Queen Kaia raised an eyebrow, and Sigrid's cheeks warmed. She was maybe-not-so-subtly trying to plant a seed for when she would ask if Mariam could live in the hall.

Before she could bring up Fisk, too, Queen Kaia said, "Call me Aunt. No need for formalities among family."

Sigrid tested the words *Aunt Kaia* in her head a few times. It didn't make her cringe.

She smiled tentatively. "Aunt Kaia."

With the words still on the air, the queen bid her good night and left, closing the door and plunging Sigrid into silence. There were no stomping hooves, swishing tails, or clucking chickens. Just the crackling fire.

She raced for the bed and threw herself onto it, a lot of feelings washing over her. Excitement. Loneliness. A hint of doubt over her decision to live here. Anticipation over what her new life would hold.

Vanahalla is my home.

The truth was too incredible to believe.

CHAPTER NINETEEN

VANAHALLA'S
ANCIENT ROOMS

Sigrid's first day at the palace began with sandwiches, cereal, and cakes spread across one of the biggest tables she'd ever seen. It was a more lavish breakfast than she could've ever imagined. Her usual fare consisted of whatever she could eat while she started chores—apples, bread, and sometimes eggs if she'd had time to boil them.

What are the chances I can smuggle half of this down to my friends?

"First thing we have to do is get you oriented," Aunt Kaia said, snapping her out of her breakfast-smuggling plans. "I'll show you the libraries and drawing rooms where you can study, the different wings and towers…and of course we'll introduce you to the sorcerers and staff later this week…"

The queen wore another blue robe today, apparently from an endless wardrobe of them, and her hair was woven back into a beautiful braid dotted with amber jewels. She thankfully had yet to tell Sigrid to wear anything other than her comfortable tunic and trousers.

Sigrid took a bite out of her sandwich. Oh yeah, she was definitely smuggling a few. "Remember I still have valkyrie training."

Aunt Kaia raised an eyebrow. "Not today. My brother's funeral is this afternoon."

Sigrid's cheeks warmed. With everything going on, she'd forgotten. "Right. Sorry."

The queen waved the apology away. "It's all right. But you should get used to missing a day of training here and there. You have other priorities now. General Eira will understand."

Sigrid's heart skipped a beat. *Miss* a day? No way. "I already missed sixteen years' worth of training. I can't skip any sessions."

Aunt Kaia's large eyes narrowed in scrutiny. She nodded. "We'll work around your training sessions, then."

Sigrid let out a breath, relieved by the answer. But as they ate breakfast, pressure built in her head, as if her list of responsibilities was ready to overflow. She might have been overextending herself, but she was determined to fit everything into her new life—including going to see her horses and riding down to see Mariam and Fisk later.

"Time for that tour I promised?" Aunt Kaia said, and Sigrid put down her goblet so fast that apple juice sloshed out.

They set off through the maze of corridors, passing kitchens full of cooks (who were too busy to notice them), dining rooms full of sorcerers (who looked too intimidating to talk to), chambers that used to be occupied by other royals (which Sigrid had no intention of exploring), libraries with floor-to-ceiling shelves (which she had every intention of spending hours in), gold statues and colorful paintings of gods and valkyries, and a lot of empty drawing rooms that could benefit from some ambient chicken clucks and hoof stomps. The vast hall felt far from home, but hopefully in time, this feeling of insignificance would fade.

There was so much mystery about Vanahalla—a crack in the floor that made her wonder how it got there, a door with no knob, a spiral staircase that led to nowhere. Maybe the most fascinating thing about it was the way it had obviously been built and expanded over centuries—some walls and floors were made of dark, old stones, while others were polished marble and gold.

Some windows had beautiful stained glass, while others were open rectangular slits in ancient stone, like the one she'd squeezed through that time she snuck into the Seer's Tower. As Vanaheim gained wealth and styles changed, the royal hall had expanded.

"What's the oldest part of the hall?" Sigrid asked.

Aunt Kaia hummed. "Probably the parts involving magic—the Seer's Tower, the Sorcerer's Tower…and one particular room I'll show you in a moment."

Sigrid quickened her step to follow her aunt's graceful strides as they headed down a long corridor connecting two towers. "Will you take me to the Seer's Tower?" It would be helpful to talk to Vala about what Ratatosk said. Maybe she would have wisdom from the Eye of Hnitbjorg.

Daylight flickered over the queen as they passed windows, illuminating and darkening her in turn. "I'm afraid entry is by Vala's invitation only. I suggest you don't knock unless you want to face her wrath."

"Ah." But Sigrid *had* visited her and hadn't faced any sort of wrath. Did Aunt Kaia not know she'd been into Vala's tower already? Maybe smashing down her door and climbing through her window had been more reckless than she'd thought. Or maybe Aunt Kaia's words were untrue. "You're not allowed to visit her whenever you want? I thought as a royal…"

"The Seer doesn't take visitors. It's not wise for her to mingle because it could affect her abilities. I've only been through once myself."

Sigrid had heard about Seers being reclusive, but whether or not Vala regularly took visitors, some things were too important not to discuss.

I guess I'll be sneaking in again if I go see her.

"Why did you go through that one time?" she asked her aunt.

Aunt Kaia slowed down as if debating whether to keep walking or to stop and face Sigrid. "I…I went to demand that she tell me what happened to my sister."

Sigrid wished she hadn't asked. A bubble of nausea rose inside her.

After a long pause, Aunt Kaia said, "She told me Lena took off to Helheim, and it was best that we leave her to her fate."

Vala, of course, had known a lot more than that. She'd seen a vision of Princess Helena giving birth to Sigrid and taking Sleipnir—the beginning of her plan to exploit an infant in order to get the throne.

Yes, I really shouldn't have brought this up.

"What about the Sorcerers' Tower?" Sigrid asked. "Will you show me that?"

"We're headed there right now," Aunt Kaia said, thankfully allowing the change of topic. "Can you feel it?"

The question seemed odd, but Sigrid nodded, running her hands over her prickling skin. The air seemed to shift, like static playing at the hairs on her arms.

They stopped at a dark wooden door, and Aunt Kaia motioned to it, her pale face half in shadow. "This is where magical research and development happens. Magic is a complex science. Phenomena appear, shift, and disappear before we can grasp what we've witnessed. Sometimes the sorcerers discover the root of some magic and harness it, but even then, the path forward can be difficult. What can we do with the force that makes a leaf change color, I wonder?"

"Make a cloak that changes color in the fall?" Sigrid said.

Aunt Kaia laughed, a glimmer in her eye. "Maybe. Though I'm sure the sorcerers have better uses of their time. Like creating new valkyrie spears."

Sigrid stepped closer to the door. "Can we go in?"

Aunt Kaia put out a hand to stop her, then pulled back as if regretting her sudden movement. "Sorry. No, we can't go in. Their work is dangerous, and for the eyes and hands of qualified sorcerers only."

This made Sigrid feel a little less terrible about Fisk not being allowed to work with the sorcerers. Still, she faced Aunt Kaia, ready to argue. "General Eira refused to let my Night Elf friend work with the sorcerers on studying the iron arrows. He's going to work with the head stable hand, but we're missing an opportunity by not letting him help us. He knows their craftsmanship tricks, so he could—"

"I trust General Eira's judgment, Sigrid," Aunt Kaia said, sounding unsurprised to hear about the general's decision. Did she already know? Did she agree?

Sigrid narrowed her eyes. "But Fisk can help us understand—"

"If the elf proves himself, we can see about letting him help with more important tasks," the queen said. "I hope you understand our trepidation when it comes to Night Elves."

"I thought under the threat of war, we would want to do everything we can."

Her aunt let out a breath. "There's no need to panic, Sigrid. Vanaheim won't be attacked. Nobody attacks the world that's home to the valkyries. We have time."

Sigrid said nothing, unconvinced.

Gods, Aunt Kaia had better be right about this. But she hadn't met the Svartalf King. She didn't know how scary he was. They'd rescued Ratatosk right out of the elves' grasp, and the king wasn't going to let them go so easily.

"You should be thankful he's allowed to stay," Aunt Kaia added sternly. "I'm trusting you, Sigrid."

Cold disappointment filled Sigrid's chest. They were wrong to make assumptions about Fisk, and they were going to regret not putting his skills and knowledge to use if they ran into more trouble with Svartalfheim.

She would have to work on everyone's perception of Fisk. He deserved better.

"Come on." Aunt Kaia turned down another corridor. "This is the room I told you about. Maybe the oldest room in Vanahalla."

Despite Sigrid's disappointment, she couldn't help the surge of curiosity.

They entered a room that looked more like the chambers she'd taken over from King Óleifr. Rough wood formed the walls, as if they'd stepped into a hollow tree. The humid air smelled like soil.

At the opposite end, leaves sprouted from the wall, twitching as if in a breeze. Aunt Kaia led her to it.

The leaves grew in a pattern shaped like an ash tree, sprouting up from the wood floor and stretching out an arm's length in either direction.

In an awed whisper, Sigrid could only utter one word. "Yggdrasil."

CHAPTER TWENTY

THE TIPPING
WORLD TREE

Yggdrasil, the tree that represented the universe, moved on the wall before Sigrid's eyes. The leaves twitched silently, and then an entire branch shrank into the wall and re-emerged in a different place, making everything around it shudder.

"Is it alive?" Sigrid whispered.

Aunt Kaia nodded. "Planted with magic when the hall was first built, enchanted to show a live representation of the worlds. See how unsettled it is?"

Sigrid took a step closer and studied it. Big gaps and off-kilter branches made the tree look sick. "What's it doing?"

"The branches are always in flux, but they usually take centuries to change. In the years since my sister's disappearance, they've moved more quickly. Now…" The queen traced her fingers over the twitching leaves, her brow furrowed.

One branch looked strong and healthy. At the highest point, perching over everything like an eagle, were the letters *Ásgarðr*. The realm of the gods was immovable, its leaves rooted firmly in the wood, intertwined like a thick canopy.

"This is what Ratatosk meant," Sigrid said. "Loki has tipped the scales too far into chaos. We'll have to face him if we want to restore cosmic balance."

"Loki is certainly responsible for all of this," Aunt Kaia

murmured. "When worlds tip too far into chaos, we get war, natural disasters, disease, people acting on anger and spite... Everything evil rears its head at once when Loki has his way."

Beneath her fingers, the leaves parted to reveal letters engraved in the wood.

Miðgarðr.

"Midgard," Sigrid said.

"Sinking lower. Civil strife and disease are ravaging their world. And Jotunheim..."

"Unrest," Sigrid said, thinking of the senior valkyries. She pushed back a cluster of leaves to reveal the letters *Múspellsheimr.* Was every world a victim of Loki's mischief? "Where's Vanaheim?"

Aunt Kaia reached down to a low branch. "Far out of place."

There, Vanaheim and Svartalfheim sat side-by-side, their leaves encroaching on each other's space.

Sigrid's insides sank at the sight of her world so low. One branch sat lower than this: Niflheim. Its branch was cracked, like a tree struck by lightning.

Mariam's words echoed in her mind. *"Niflheim is in a state... This isn't normal."*

Below it all, Helheim made up the roots. Sigrid didn't touch the two lowest realms ruled over by Hel. Or rather, they were *supposed* to be, but instead Helena had taken over.

Sigrid frowned. What had Princess Helena done to persuade Hel to allow her to rule? She regretted again not pressing her mother for answers.

She crossed her arms and studied the sick, imbalanced tree shuddering before them. "I don't understand. Are the worlds physically moving, like the leaves of this tree? Or is this like—" She waved a hand, trying to find the words. "Symbolic?"

"The physical positions of the worlds are fixed, but our relation to each other has fluctuated through the ages. You're seeing the relations on the wall. That is the cosmic imbalance we're talking about. The bonds between worlds form the fibers that hold up Yggdrasil. As those fibers bend and change, the tree weakens."

This made more sense than the worlds struggling to be physically higher up. The cosmic imbalance came from weakening connections between worlds. Strong bonds, like strong branches, could bear a lot of weight.

"So a low position in the cosmos isn't a bad thing," Sigrid said. "It's just about who everyone is connected to."

"No, it matters," Aunt Kaia said, something sharp in her voice. "Vanaheim belongs next to Asgard, given our history as the home of the Vanir gods. The elves are sorely mistaken to try and push us out—and I'm not just talking about Night Elves. Alfheim has tried to force their way closer than us, and I'm done being nice about it. What business does an elf have with a god?"

Not quite getting her aunt's point, Sigrid asked, "Can't more than one world be close to the gods? They can have more than one connection, can't they?"

"And what would that look like? If the branches become too clustered with all the worlds clamoring for the same spot, waging war, breaking their connections, the trunk will break." Aunt Kaia took a deep breath before continuing on a more reasonable tone. "This is where we have our problem, Sigrid. It's Vanaheim's responsibility to restore order, no matter the cost."

Her aunt's shift in mood hung heavily in the air, almost tangible.

Sigrid rubbed the goose bumps on her arms. "Are you okay?"

The queen stared at the tree, her brow furrowed, like she was afraid to look at Sigrid. She fidgeted with her amber crown as if trying to make it sit more comfortably. Her braid loosened, which made her look younger and less polished. It somehow suited her more when she looked this way—like a normal woman instead of the title she was supposed to uphold.

Jotunheim shuddered, its leaves retreating into the wall and reappearing in the same place.

"I received word last night that Ratatosk arrived in Jotunheim to fetch the senior valkyries," Aunt Kaia said, her delivery too even. "Three of them died in their efforts to restore balance over the last few weeks—and for what? We sent them to help with the civil unrest, but since they left, unrest has spread to every world. The upheaval in Jotunheim was a precursor to this." She flicked a hand at the wall, her lip curling in disgust. "It was a waste of our resources. I told Óleifr as much. I told him we shouldn't be concerned with the affairs of the other worlds. Valkyries should stay here where they can serve Vanaheim. Now we're down three, and the Ice Giants are out of control."

Sigrid's heart seemed to stop. Her mind spun, caught in a maelstrom. *Three valkyries, dead. Jotunheim, out of control.* "Does General Eira know?"

"All the right people have been informed," Aunt Kaia said. "But we'll all feel better once the valkyries are home. We'll have our defenses, and I'll have the generals back in my council."

Sigrid waited for her to go on—to share a plan, a decision, anything that would help make it better that they'd lost three lives.

The queen's eyes welled, and she turned her head as if pretending to be interested in the furthest end of the tree. "It's a lot, being queen. I didn't expect all of this."

A spark of disappointment ignited in Sigrid's belly. This wasn't the time to be upset and overwhelmed. They had to act. They had to figure out how to stop this cosmic imbalance before more lives were lost.

"We should send valkyries to guard the entrance to Vanaheim," Sigrid said, voicing her ideas since none were forthcoming from the queen. "We should try to meet with the Svartalf King, too. Not in his world—somewhere neutral. Anything to stop a fight before it happens."

Aunt Kaia nodded. "Yes, that's…that's a smart plan. I'll call a meeting and introduce you to my council. There may be more we can do. I…" She chewed her lip, deep in thought. "You should learn about runes, Sigrid."

Sigrid looked at her sharply. There were stories of curses placed on objects using runes. Nothing from her lifetime. The context was always some ancient war involving gods—but the state of Yggdrasil seemed dire enough for such measures.

Just one problem. "Aren't runes only used by sorcerers and Seers?"

"And royals," Aunt Kaia said with a pointed look. "They can be used to communicate with the gods. How do you think we're able to send messages to Ratatosk? How do you think the Seers receive guidance from the Norns, and our ancestors spoke to Odin? If we can open a conduit with Loki, we might be able to stop all of this."

Sigrid's pulse picked up. If her mastering runes increased their chances of stopping the chaos crashing over Yggdrasil, she was willing to learn.

Princess lessons were about to become much more interesting than she'd expected.

CHAPTER TWENTY-ONE

INSTEAD OF
MOURNING

A thousand people gathered in the courtyard outside Vanahalla, having come from all over Vanaheim to attend King Óleifr's funeral. Every gold statue and fountain had people perched on it, craning to see the dais where the casket would sit and grand speeches would be given.

Sigrid insisted on standing among the valkyries instead of on a throne next to her aunt, who agreed that a funeral wasn't the right time to introduce her to the court as the new princess.

Or we could just never introduce me at all? Sigrid thought desperately, wanting to avoid that awkwardness for as long as possible.

So while Aunt Kaia took her place on the dais, Sigrid wove through the crowd, searching for Mariam. What she'd seen in Yggdrasil churned in her mind like writhing eels. Her pulse raced as if she were being chased, and the somber atmosphere wasn't helping her calm down. She murmured apologies as she bumped against mourners and elicited indignant grumbles.

When the god of chaos was out there wreaking havoc and Vanaheim could be next on his list, nothing else should matter.

The king's death suddenly felt like the start of something bigger.

Finally spotting the junior valkyries near the back, Sigrid made a beeline for them. Her heart jumped in anticipation of seeing Mariam again. She'd listen and understand the gravity of it all.

But when she reached the group, Mariam wasn't among them. "Where's Mariam?"

Ylva and Gunni glared at her for interrupting their conversation.

"She didn't want to come," Runa said.

"Why not?"

"The stable hands weren't invited, and—"

"What?" Sigrid said loudly enough that the nearest mourners looked over.

Runa shrugged like this was obvious. "The elf wouldn't have been welcome here regardless. Mariam said she would rather stay with him."

"Where were *you*?" Ylva asked, studying Sigrid as if trying to find the answer pinned to her clothes.

Sigrid ignored her and walked away, fighting the urge to glare in Aunt Kaia's direction. Not inviting the stable hands was a punch to the gut, even if Sigrid wasn't a stable hand anymore. Why should they be excluded from paying their last respects to their king if they wanted?

Maybe as princess, she would be able to change the way stable hands were treated.

As she scanned the crowd and the empty space beyond it, a flutter of rebellion rose inside her. Would her aunt be furious if Sigrid missed the funeral?

Probably.

But right now, her friends were more important.

A man in a brown robe stood on the dais and held out his hands to hush the crowd—and Sigrid moved her feet in the opposite direction. She backed away until she reached the edge of the crowd and then turned and kept going, sneaking along the cobblestone path, across the courtyard, and down the hill. She picked up a run, wheezing for breath, wishing she could have ridden Hestur down instead of taking the long road on foot.

By the time she got to the valkyrie barn, beads of sweat trickled down her temples and beneath her tunic.

She spotted Mariam the moment she crossed the barn doors, as if she were a beam of sunlight in a dark forest. Emerging from the tack room, she wore a fitted brown training uniform, her hair soft and wavy, like she'd just let it loose from a braid. Sigrid's stomach did a wild swoop like it did the first time they'd locked eyes in the Seer's tower.

"Sigrid! Shouldn't you be at Uncle Óleifr's funeral?" Mariam said with a cheeky smile.

Sigrid shook her head. "The valkyries told me the stable hands weren't invited. So I took my cue." She stopped in front of Mariam, her breath catching high in her chest.

"Well, I'm glad you did," Mariam said, her smile growing.

Sigrid's heart thudded against her ribs. The barn was empty. *Finally.*

Mariam stepped closer, still wearing that grin, until Sigrid closed the distance to kiss it off her face. Their fingers interlocked. Between the feel of Mariam's fingers in hers, the feel of her full lips, and her sweet scent, Sigrid drifted into a haze.

"I thought I'd have a fun afternoon hanging out with the stable hands, getting to know them better," Mariam said between kisses, "but they've all been busy."

"Mm. Their loss." Sigrid pecked Mariam's lips one more time. "How's Fisk fitting in?"

Mariam stepped back, keeping their fingers entwined. "He's… attracting stares everywhere he goes."

Anger flared in Sigrid's chest. She could understand a little hesitation—after all, Night Elves had attacked not long ago and people had strong opinions about dwellers from lower worlds— but maybe it'd been naive to hope that he would be given a chance.

"Is he okay? What does Peter have him doing?"

"Mostly stable hand work, but a lot of people seem to think he's a spy or something. None of the girls want him touching their mares, and he's not allowed to help make weapons or armor, so…" Mariam shrugged.

Sigrid cursed under her breath. She would have to figure out how to help him. Maybe if they all hung out with Peter and Roland, the other stable hands would stop seeing Fisk as a threat.

They turned their heads as Fisk came around the corner, humming to himself.

Quickly, they let go of each other's hands. Mariam glanced down to where their hands had just been clasped with a flash of disappointment—like maybe she didn't want to let go.

Should I not have let go?

"Oh, hey, Sigrid!" Fisk carried a ball of gray wool big enough to be an actual sheep. "Happy birthday!"

"What?" Sigrid and Mariam asked in unison.

Fisk stopped. "Birth…day? Peter just told me…" He waved an arm behind him, maybe in the direction of Peter.

Sigrid blinked. It wasn't the first time she'd forgotten her birthday until Peter reminded her of it. To be fair, she'd been too busy saving Ratatosk and then dealing with the queen to note the days.

Sigrid tilted her head. It felt like years had passed since her last birthday. "I guess I'm…seventeen."

Mariam laughed. "Why do you look so surprised?"

"It's just…a birthday seems so normal, with everything going on." And how could she celebrate on the day of the king's funeral? On a day when Yggdrasil's branches were ready to crack?

Mariam gave her a concerned look, but before she could speak, Fisk said, "Here! I made you this."

From the end of the ball of wool, he held up something with two knitting needles poking out of it. "I'm almost done. It's a hat.

I siphoned magic from the hot springs so it'll stay warm in the winter."

Sigrid's throat tightened. A gift? She couldn't remember the last time she'd gotten a gift. The stable hands celebrated birthdays with desserts from the village, but gifts were never a thing because they were expensive to buy and time-consuming to make.

As good as it felt to have her friends celebrate her, her birthday had always been a complicated day since it was an annual reminder that her birth and her parents were a mystery.

Now, on her seventeenth, she finally knew the truth. Her "birthday" was the day that, out of greed for power, Princess Helena dumped her in the nursery and abandoned her.

But standing with her friends, Fisk holding up a gift he'd made himself, the usual anger and sadness stayed far away. Her heart filled, and a smile tugged at her lips.

"Thank you, Fisk," she said softly. "You didn't have to get me anything."

Mariam grinned. "Of course we do. Now, tell me. What do you want from me for your birthday?"

"Um—" Sigrid's brain went blank, but right that moment? *Another kiss?*

Mariam must have been thinking something along the same lines because her lips quirked.

Sigrid had to look away and pretend her cheeks weren't burning up.

"Anyway…" Fisk dragged out the word as if to point out the weird silence. "Peter asked me to oil everyone's tack, so I better…" He motioned toward the tack room.

"We'll help," Sigrid said. "I actually came to tell you about what I saw in Vanahalla. Yggdrasil and the nine worlds are… Well, it's not good."

Mariam's lips tightened, and Fisk gave a sharp nod.

They followed Fisk to the dimly lit tack room, where they

each grabbed a rag and oil and set to work on the saddles.

As she told them about the room with Yggdrasil on the walls and what she'd seen there, a chill settled in all over again. "There's a room that shows the state of all nine worlds. The cosmic unrest is...worse than we thought."

Lines appeared between Mariam's eyebrows. "How bad?"

Sigrid considered softening the truth to spare her friends the stress, but what would be the point? "It looks like the world tree is dying."

Mariam's eyes widened, a rare glimpse of fear. "Did it show you what's going on in each of the worlds?"

"It's not that specific, but we can make some guesses. Like, you said Niflheim is in a state of chaos, right?"

Mariam nodded.

"And we know Svartalfheim is trying to reach a higher status in the cosmos," Sigrid said. "Now that we've stopped them from controlling the spring of Hvergelmir, they'll be making a new plan."

"And the other worlds?"

Sigrid's stomach flipped. "In Jotunheim, the civil unrest is worse than anyone expected. The senior valkyries are on their way home, but three of them..." She shook her head, unable to say it.

Mariam gasped.

Fisk dropped the bridle he was working on. "Gone?" he whispered.

Sigrid nodded curtly. Whatever missions the valkyries went on, they'd always been able to help. To lose three valkyrie lives was unfathomable. "I keep going back to Helheim and Niflheim. They're supposed to be ruled by the goddess Hel, right? But my mother is on the throne. We have to find out where Hel is—and why she's fine with a woman from Vanaheim unleashing her army."

"Or why the gods haven't done anything to stop all the chaos."

Mariam placed a bridle back on its hook, rocking back and forth on her feet as if wanting to take action. "What are we supposed to do about all of this?"

Sigrid's heart beat faster. "Aunt Kaia wants me to learn about runes."

Mariam's lips parted in surprise. "Sorcerer runes? To cast curses?"

"I don't know." Sigrid tried to sound calm despite her jumping heart. "She said royals can use them to talk to the gods. If we can talk to Loki—"

"I don't like that." Mariam shook her head. "Communicating directly with the god of chaos sounds like a dangerous idea."

"It does," Fisk agreed.

"Then what do we do? If this ends in war…" Sigrid held Mariam's gaze, struggling to keep her breaths even.

"The purpose of the valkyries is to serve the worlds and protect the cosmic balance," Mariam said. "We'll fight if we have to, and you'll fight with us on Sleipnir. *That's* what we're supposed to do."

Sigrid's insides did such a wild flip that she felt nauseous. "Right."

Mariam must have seen something in her expression, because she said, "Sigrid, the cosmos meant for you to be a leader. It brought you to the royal hall for a reason."

"But I have no experience with anything except how to be a stable hand." To prove her point, she raised her hands. They were grimy and oily, and no amount of wiping on her trousers helped. "I have no political knowledge, no history knowledge… I can't even name the leaders of most worlds—"

"But you will," Mariam said fiercely. "It's why you moved to Vanahalla, isn't it? To learn everything you'll need to know to help the nine worlds?"

"You've already served Vanaheim more than once," Fisk said.

"So you're ready for this. You can advise the queen based on everything you've learned."

Sigrid studied her friends, the way they stood confidently in front of her, supportive no matter what. Her chest felt full, like her heart had expanded.

In a soft beam of daylight coming through the window, Sigrid could see the dusting of freckles across Mariam's nose and cheekbones. Something about those freckles was impossible not to love. She wanted to plant kisses across them.

Instead, she pursed her lips and nodded. "Thank you."

Mariam smiled.

Sigrid's heart skipped as the inevitable washed over her. She'd always wanted to serve Vanaheim—it was why she'd fought so hard to become a valkyrie. But since becoming a princess and since finding out she was Sleipnir's heir, serving Vanaheim had become a lot more complicated. It wasn't as simple as mounting up and riding out to fight.

Odin's stallion waited for her in the royal stables up the hill, trapped in a corral, a weapon ready to be wielded.

She wasn't ready, and she wasn't sure if she ever would be… but she didn't have much choice. If she wanted to protect her world from whatever precipice they were standing on the edge of, she had to accept the path the cosmos had made for her.

Tonight, she would have to start working with Sleipnir again.

CHAPTER TWENTY-TWO

THE BIGGEST, BEST,
AND UNRULIEST

Sigrid paused in the doorway of the royal stable, gaping at the pristine space. The vaulted ceiling, marble floor, and crystal accents made it look more like a palace that happened to have horses in it. It even had a special entrance from inside Vanahalla so Sigrid didn't have to walk outside to get to it.

At the far end, the golden barn doors leading outside were shut and barricaded with a drawbar. Above them hung a portrait of Thor soaring through a stormy sky in his goat-drawn chariot.

Awed and dazed that this gorgeous stable had existed all these years without her knowledge, she jumped at the loud *Maa!* that came from her left. Three actual goats with curved horns and long, white hair blinked at her from a large stall.

Sigrid blinked back at them. "Hello there."

At the sound of her voice, Hestur whinnied from the stall beside them.

"Hestur!" She beamed, going to greet him. "Are you all settled—whoa."

The stall was twice the size of his old one, as white and clean as the rooms of Vanahalla, with a banner of gold horseshoes along the perimeter. Opposite to the door, an opening led to a sand paddock big enough for him to gallop and buck. A stone wall on the other side separated the royal horses from the outside world, too high to see over. The moat would be beyond that.

"Well, I hope you realize how lucky you are."

He bobbed his head, looking smug.

Sigrid strode down the aisle, peering into each stall. Hestur's neighbor was a black mare with a voluptuous mane and a forelock that fell past her eyes—she must have been the mare Aunt Kaia had told her about, Disa. She was small and chunky, her wither coming to Sigrid's chest.

Past her, the stalls homed several more ponies with bushy manes.

And at the far end, stalled next to a chestnut gelding, was Sleipnir.

"Oh, gods." Sigrid groaned as she leaned over his door. Sleipnir had treated the walls, the door, and the fences in his paddock like they'd personally offended him and had chewed every edge down to splinters.

When he saw her, he thrust his head over the stall door and rubbed his forehead on her arm.

She stumbled back under the force of his boulder-like head. "Hey, Sleipnir."

A pang of guilt shot through her, more for the stallion than for the state of his enclosure. He was clearly bored in here. What was wrong with her, keeping the best war horse in the nine worlds like a finch in a cage? She was no better than her wretched mother, who'd kept him in the palace in Helheim where he didn't belong.

It was time to get over her fear and saddle him up.

Except the second I get on, all of this destructive energy will redirect to me.

She rubbed her arm, dissipating the heat that had spread from him into her skin.

"You're not making it very motivating for me to ride you, you know," she said firmly. "And I promised Aunt Kaia I would."

He flapped his lips and bobbed his head, a bratty look in his eye. Then he pulled a huge splinter off the wall and let it drop to the ground as if making a point.

Sigrid reached for the halter hanging on his stall door, a tremor in her hand. But when she reached for him, something inside her resisted. She wanted to believe Mariam was right and the cosmos meant for her to be a leader. Everything she'd discovered about herself supported it. But why did it have to be so scary?

Riding Sleipnir was the obvious way forward. He was her purpose in the royal family, in Vanaheim, and in the cosmos. Instead of fearing him, she had to work on controlling the overwhelming feelings he gave her.

The stallion stopped chewing his stall and held her gaze. She slowly slipped the halter over his nose, and when he didn't react, she let out a breath.

One tiny step at a time.

She rested a palm on his neck, the heat from his skin seeping into her skin like a live energy. Her heart skipped.

That's fine. It's just a sensation.

She patted him, running her hands down his neck, over his shoulder, along his back. He relaxed under her touch, dropping his head. In contrast, Sigrid's pulse quickened, and her breaths came faster.

Focus.

She listened to the chirping barn swallows overhead, the goats and horses shuffling around them, and Sleipnir's soft breaths. All of it seemed clearer than a moment ago—every sound sharpened, every hair and dust mote distinct in the light shining into the barn. Even the texture of his coat crackled like static against her palm.

"Am I overreacting?" she murmured. Sleipnir respected and liked her, and maybe knowing about the effect he had on her was enough to help her control it—like being prepared for a storm.

"This isn't so bad, right?" She kept patting him, her heart

thumping in her ears, while Sleipnir stayed calm. "What do you think? Can we ride into battle together?"

The stallion bobbed his head.

She scratched his wither, the heat from his body making her skin prickle all the way up her arm. Amazing how she'd never noticed the way each of his fine hairs moved under her fingers before. It was like her skin had suddenly awoken after seventeen years dormant.

Maybe she was attempting the impossible by trying to control and tame this feeling. She couldn't tame it, but what if she accepted it? What if she stopped fighting it? Did she trust Sleipnir's nature enough to let him in?

She chewed her lip.

If she relaxed a little, let the feeling in, a warm sensation filled her—and the tension in her head dissipated, blissful and *easy*.

A fly landed on the stallion's shoulder, and he twitched his skin to be rid of it, but not before Sigrid could count the insect's legs and memorize the veins in its wings.

She'd never noticed that before, either.

A smile tugged at her cheeks.

This must be the way to manage this feeling. Let it in.

Her senses kept sharpening, a blade swiping over a stone.

Embracing it meant bringing an unparalleled force to the fight against the Night Elves. On Sleipnir, she could destroy them, spilling their blood until there were no elves left. She had the power to make them regret trying to control the spring of Hvergelmir. They would regret listening to Loki.

I'm going to make them pay for what they've done to the nine worlds.

As for whoever killed those valkyries in Jotunheim? She would come for them next. She would get revenge on everyone involved until the land of the Ice Giants was stained red.

Sigrid wrapped a fist in the stallion's mane, her senses clearer than they'd ever been.

What had she been afraid of? This was her purpose. *War* was her purpose. She wasn't scared of fighting, of bloodshed, of killing.

And she *would* kill. She was ready to mount up right now and slaughter the Svartalf King, and anyone who stood in her way.

It was clearer than ever as she stood in Vanahalla's royal stable, the power of Odin's steed burning through her limbs, that she was meant to fight.

CHAPTER TWENTY-THREE

HARMLESS RUNES

Sigrid's confidence in figuring out how to work with Sleipnir started to run dry after a couple of days. The eight-legged stallion was a menace. Even with all the time and effort she put into training, the stallion kept terrorizing the stable hands, destroying his stall, and chewing on the repaired sections like the wood was made of applesauce.

Massive, hoof-shaped divots appeared in his paddock, meaning that even after hours with her, Sleipnir had been exercising himself by galloping laps. What he needed was a ride out through fields, his speed unchecked, until he tired.

But taking that step was a terrifying thought.

No matter how hard Sigrid tried to control the way he affected her, when she left the barn each night, her mind was clouded with thoughts that didn't feel like her own, and her senses were so overstimulated that she had to close her eyes and engulf her head with a pillow for a while.

The little progress was both frustrating and disappointing. If she couldn't figure it out, was it better to ride Sleipnir and risk losing control, or to leave him behind and risk losing in battle?

Maybe there was no right answer.

For now, she left him behind and continued to ride Hestur in training. She went down to the valkyrie stables as usual every morning and then returned to Vanahalla after lunch for private lessons in the royal hall.

"Valkyrie training first, princess training second," Mariam said teasingly on the first day, and Sigrid shot her a glare so fierce that she apologized.

Mariam wasn't wrong—after working to physical exhaustion in training, Sigrid worked to mental exhaustion in hours-long lessons.

Even as her life turned chaotic, the world remained oddly calm. Too calm. She couldn't shake the feeling that each day that passed had a false sense of normalcy. If war was coming, when would it happen? Shouldn't they be doing something else to prepare? There had been no visions from the Eye of Hnitbjorg, so did that mean no retaliation was coming?

The questions kept her on edge every day.

Even while waiting in one of the small libraries for her first lesson on runes, Sigrid couldn't sit still. Her pulse raced, and an ache developed in her temples. What would help her more in battle—runes or a valkyrie spear? She should be training, not sitting here learning about ancient symbols so she could attempt to talk to the gods. The gods had done absolutely nothing to help them so far, so what was the point in reaching out to them?

The library door groaned open, and a girl burst in.

Sigrid lowered her arm, pretending she'd been fixing her hair instead of grabbing her spear to fend off an attack.

"Sorry I'm late, Yer Highness. I had to locate a few things." She had an accent Sigrid had never heard before, suggesting she was from far away—maybe a farming town.

"It's—okay." Sigrid rubbed her eyes. The ache in her temples was becoming annoying. "Are you the person teaching me runes?"

"Oh, yes! I'm Tóra." She wobbled on her feet in something like a bow. "Nice to make yer acquaintance, Princess."

"Hi." Sigrid studied the girl. They were about the same age. But unlike Sigrid and everyone she'd grown up with, who had muscles from riding and working in a barn, this girl looked like she'd never lifted a pitchfork. Beneath an emerald green robe, her limbs were so long and frail that she moved like the blowing branches of a willow tree. She was fair and freckled, her curly red hair bunched in a thick knot at the crown of her head. Her most prominent feature was her nose, which was shaped like a raven's beak.

Tóra opened a huge rucksack and placed a few objects on the table, fumbling them and making a lot of clatter. "Vala told me about the Eye's recent visions," she said, casting Sigrid sidelong glances as she set up. "She told me how Princess Helena gave birth to ye 'cause she wanted Sleipnir, and how the Eye foretold of yer going to Helheim to claim him."

"Is that so?" It was hard not to sound bitter about all of it.

"She also told me I should trust you."

The tightness in Sigrid's chest loosened a little. "That was… very kind of her."

Tóra motioned to the array of objects. "There."

She'd set down a valkyrie spear, a magnifying glass, a veterinary device from the foaling barn, a block of wood, and the Eye of Hnitbjorg.

Sigrid's heart skipped at the sight of it. That lump of rock salt had changed her entire life. She and Mariam had met while fighting over it. When she traveled to Helheim to find her birthright, it was because of what it had shown her. Her mother's betrayal and their ultimate parting had all come down to it.

"Oh! We'll be needing…" Tóra dug into the rucksack for a fistful of crumpled parchment and two quills.

Sigrid had the urge to touch the Eye. Maybe it would show her a vision of what awaited. Or what she was meant to do with Sleipnir.

"We'll never get through all there is to know about runes," Tóra said, "but we'll see how far we get before—well, before ye need to use them."

The implication hung thickly between them—before war came.

Tóra cleared her throat and fidgeted with the valkyrie spear on the table. "So, the basics. Runes are used to communicate with the gods and cast curses. Seers use them to talk to the Norns, and people have talked to the gods this way since the beginning."

Sigrid nodded. "Aunt Kaia wants me to use runes to talk to Loki."

Tóra jumped a little in her seat. She moved on to fidgeting with the crumpled parchment, smoothing out each leaf. "Right. Well, one thing at a time, yeah?"

Sigrid pressed her lips together, feeling a little guilty for blurting out Loki's name. She'd forgotten not everyone was comfortable invoking it.

"Runes are also used for everyday enchantments." Tóra picked up the valkyrie spear, twirled it, and dropped it. She set it back on the table, blushing the same color as her hair, and picked up a quill instead. "Valkyrie spears are forged using gold enchanted by a rune. This rune."

She drew a complex shape on one of the crumpled sheets of parchment. It took her so long to draw that Sigrid began to wonder how long this lesson would last.

"You have that memorized?" Sigrid asked, impressed.

Tóra nodded. "I have about a thousand memorized. The head sorcerer, Harald? He's probably memorized twice as many. I'll get there one day, I hope."

Sigrid chewed her lip, not sure what Aunt Kaia expected of her. What if it took her decades to master the craft?

"Are ye all right, Yer Highness?" Tóra asked, watching her with a pinched brow.

Sigrid dropped her hand. She'd been absently rubbing her temple. "Headache."

Tóra brightened. "Oh, perfect."

"Excuse me?" Sigrid drew back at the odd excitement.

Tóra flipped over the parchment and drew three runes. "Trace over this. Here." She thrust a quill into Sigrid's hand and passed her the parchment.

Confused, Sigrid traced over the shapes Tóra had drawn. "What do these mean?"

"It's a prayer. We're asking the goddess Eir for good health."

Sigrid froze before she traced over the last line, meeting Tóra's eye. Tóra nodded enthusiastically, her freckled cheeks lifting in an encouraging half smile.

"I'm trusting that you're not making me ask to get trampled by a boar tomorrow," Sigrid said and finished tracing.

Tóra let out a few hiccup sounds, which might have been a giggle.

As Sigrid set down the quill, a light, tingling sensation traveled through her temples, like cool water washing away the pain.

"I...it really worked." She leaned back in her chair, gazing in awe at the shapes in front of her.

Tóra beamed. "Ready to learn more?"

Sigrid straightened up, renewed. "Yes!"

"Good. Now, do ye know what this is?" Tóra motioned to the device from the foaling barn.

"Uteroscope," Sigrid said, pleased she actually knew something in this lesson. "Used to detect pregnancy in the winged mares."

"Right. This is made by forging it with a fertility rune." Tóra drew another rune, and Sigrid nodded as if she would remember it later.

"What's the block of wood?"

Tóra passed her the valkyrie spear. "Stab it."

"What? Why?"

"Try to stab it."

Sigrid obeyed. She jabbed the spear into the block of wood. It glanced off without leaving a mark.

Looking satisfied, Tóra flipped the block of wood over to reveal a rune. "Impenetrability. It's near impossible to get perfect, but we use it where we can when creating armor."

Sigrid grinned. "That's amazing!"

Tóra smiled back, looking relieved that Sigrid was impressed.

"And the Eye of Hnitbjorg?" Sigrid asked.

"The Eye is enchanted with so many runes that nobody has ever been able to understand it."

Sigrid looked closely at the lump of rock salt. "Really?"

Tóra passed Sigrid the magnifying glass. "Look closely."

Sigrid leaned in and examined the stone.

"Closer." Tóra pushed her bony fingers into Sigrid's back until her nose was almost touching it.

The Eye was remarkable up close. The pink, semi-translucent texture was grainy, jagged, and—

Sigrid gasped. Tiny shapes covered the entire surface of the Eye of Hnitbjorg, ranging in complexity from a basic triangle to something even more complex than the one Tóra had drawn for the spear.

"Wow."

"That's what makes the Eye so special," Tóra said. "It's not just a rock from Mount Hnitbjorg. It's enchanted with the secrets of the Norns, and the looms that weave the past, present, and future."

Sigrid's heart beat faster. She'd always known the Eye was Vanaheim's most precious relic, but she'd never truly understood why. *This is incredible.*

That urge to touch the Eye came back. Would Tóra let her?

Tóra reached for the parchment, moving so quickly that a few of them fluttered off the table and fell to the floor.

Without pausing to consider, Sigrid leaned closer to the Eye under the pretense of studying it, letting her hand brush against it. She held it there for a moment, feeling its cool, rough texture, her heart pounding hard.

Nothing happened.

She slumped as no visions came to her, leaning back.

Tóra passed her a blank sheet of parchment. "I'll teach ye how runes are structured, and ye can start to memorize the most common ones. But there are millions of possibilities for writing runes by combining the basic shapes—so many that even the most experienced sorcerers can't learn them all."

"How do you read those ones, then?"

"For unfamiliar runes, ye have to make an educated guess. Ye interpret each one by studying its makeup and the context. That's why ye need to have the basic shapes memorized. It can take days to interpret a sequence of unfamiliar runes, even for those of us who have studied them for years."

Sigrid nodded, trying not to get overwhelmed.

Tóra motioned to the quill in front of Sigrid. "Let's get started."

CHAPTER TWENTY-FOUR

TOO MUCH
TRAINING

After several days of working with Sleipnir, learning runes with Tóra, and trying to keep up in valkyrie training, exhaustion took hold of Sigrid. All she wanted was a bed, a full night's sleep, and some uninterrupted time with her friends—but her new responsibilities didn't allow for that.

"Sigrid! You're out of place. *Again*," General Eira roared from the edge of the training field.

Sigrid jolted, nearly slipping out of the saddle. Somehow, she'd dozed off as Hestur carried her along at a trot beneath the *V* formation. She held back a groan, reining him into position.

Training was going horribly today. She'd been yelled at no fewer than six times for simple mistakes. The other valkyries were annoyed—and vocal about it—because every mess-up meant starting the drill over.

"Let's take a break," General Eira called out. "*Some* of you clearly need it."

Gunni groaned loudly.

Though she burned with shame for dragging everyone down, a mid-morning break sounded wonderful. Ideally, she'd go hide in the hay room and grab a quick nap, but at the risk of making the general explode, she sighed and followed Mariam to where the stable hands waited to check on the horses.

Fisk gave Aesa and Hestur juicy apples, then moved on to checking Mariam's tack the way Peter had shown him. The other mares looked over at the apples with jealousy, which made their riders scowl, and then Roland had to send a young stable hand sprinting back to the barn to get apples for all the mares.

Sigrid and Mariam exchanged a smile.

"Thanks for all your hard work, Fisk," Mariam said with a little extra volume.

The valkyries moved under the shade of nearby trees, while Sigrid, Mariam, and Fisk moved under the patchy cover of a slanted birch tree—their usual routine during training breaks. These short rests were the only time Sigrid got to spend with her friends, and they were mostly a chance for Mariam to squeeze in updates—news like "I figured out which stall belonged to my mom's mare" and "Runa said our moms were friends." But before they could ever get into a real conversation, they had to return to training, or else training ended and Sigrid had to go.

No chance to even sneak in a kiss.

Mariam nimbly hopped off Aesa, while Sigrid slid out of Hestur's saddle about as nimbly as a glob of honey dripping from a spoon. They sat in the grass, where she stretched and let out a yawn she'd been holding back. "Mmph. Tell me the stables are functioning normally and it's just my life that's a mess."

"Well, I don't know what normal valkyrie stables look like, so I'm afraid I can't answer," Fisk said, bending to check Hestur's legs. "But the stable hands sure do miss you."

"Really?" A warm tingle spread through Sigrid's chest. Then another layer of his words sank in. "Wait, are the stable hands finally talking to you?"

He straightened up and bounced on the balls of his feet. "They sure did yesterday! Peter suggested I knit hats and blankets for everyone, and even though they didn't want to take them at first, they couldn't refuse when it poured rain the other day. I was invited to sit with them at dinner last night."

"That was a great idea! Nice work." From her own experience, the stables got a bit chilly at night, especially on days it rained. It would be hard to say no to an offer of free elf-made clothing.

It was a brilliant idea to have Fisk win everyone over with his craftiness. Mariam had mentioned how a couple of new items had also appeared in the barn, including a self-propelling wheelbarrow and a grain dispenser, which made daily tasks easier for everyone.

Sigrid waited for Mariam to give an update, but after a pause, she poked Mariam's side. "And you?"

Mariam's lips quirked. She plucked a blade of grass and shredded it in her gloved fingers. "I'm fine. Training is fun. Everything's…good."

"More than good," Fisk said. "Golly, Sigrid, you should've heard what the scary general lady said earlier. Tell her, Mariam."

Mariam's face reddened. "It's nothing."

"It's not nothing!" he said.

"Fisk, don't—"

He turned to Sigrid. "She told Mariam she was better than half the juniors already without any training. Didn't she, Mariam?"

Mariam crossed her arms, then uncrossed them, looking everywhere but at Sigrid. "Something like that."

Sigrid's heart soared. "She did? That's amazing!"

Fisk did a little hop. "I'm not surprised, really. You've spent your life avoiding danger, practicing skills in the real world, and getting training from your mother, right? So of course you're good!"

Mariam looked at her boots, clearly not used to receiving praise.

Gods, Mariam looked cute when she was flustered.

Sigrid leaned over in the grass and threw her arms around her, held strong for a moment, then quickly pulled herself upright again. "See? You're proving them wrong already."

Mariam blushed and patted Sigrid's arm. "Thanks. It's been pretty great seeing the looks on everyone's faces. I just wish…"

Sigrid waited for her to go on. When she didn't, she asked, "What is it? Have you learned anything new about your mom?"

Mariam squinted across the field. "No." Another pause. Then she shook her head and directed a forced smile at Sigrid. "I'm sure I'll find out more eventually. But how's princess training?"

Sigrid bit the inside of her cheek, looking over at the rest of the valkyries under the nearby trees.

"Relax," Mariam said, "they're too far away to hear. And you know they'll find out eventually."

"I know. I just like it better when they ignore me." Sigrid stretched her sore fighting arm, not liking Mariam's stilted smiles and far-off looks. She could only hope Mariam would trust her enough to share what was going on at some point. "My lessons are…fine, I guess."

Mariam raised an eyebrow. "I thought you were so excited to learn things."

"I was. I am. But—well, I can barely understand the runes lessons, and the scholar teaching me history and cosmic relations is an old woman who is completely insensitive to my situation. Her first words to me were, *I used to teach your mother! You look so much like her.* And she keeps getting frustrated when I don't know things. Like, does she not realize I've spent my whole life shoveling poop? There wasn't much time to learn history between dumping wheelbarrows." Sigrid huffed, aware her voice was rising.

Mariam grimaced.

The lessons, too, were not as exciting as Sigrid had hoped, but she felt a little spoiled saying that aloud. She spent the long sessions with her gaze wandering out the window, wondering what Mariam was doing.

"What about the chance to advise?" Mariam asked. "Have

you talked about a plan?"

Sigrid's scowl deepened. "They're not interested in my opinions. I told Aunt Kaia we should meet with the leaders of the other worlds to discuss how to restore balance to Yggdrasil, and you know what her response was?"

Mariam shook her head.

"She *laughed*," Sigrid said. "Like it'd been a joke. But it's not a bad idea, right?"

Mariam shrugged. "It's *an* idea. Couldn't tell you how good or bad it is."

Hot embarrassment rushed back up her neck and into her cheeks, worse than when she'd made the suggestion. "Fisk, I'm still thinking of a way to get you up there to work with the sorcerers—or to bring one of the iron arrows to you. We have to figure out how they work."

Fisk rocked on his feet, his nose tipped downward. "You know I'd be happy to help, Sigrid…but I don't want to get into trouble if they don't want me there."

"We're not really wanted anywhere," Mariam murmured, watching the other valkyries mount up and get ready to resume training.

Sigrid studied the side of her face, a cold realization rushing through her. Was she keeping Mariam from the girls who could be her friends? "Hey, we should start taking our breaks with the others. Come on, let's go over—"

"No," Mariam said quickly, hopping to her feet. "I'll go warm up Aesa."

She swung a leg over the saddle and took flight, leaving Sigrid and Hestur at the edge of the field.

Sigrid chewed her lip, something twisting inside her.

As hard as she'd tried to get Mariam and Fisk accepted in Vanaheim, she couldn't help feeling like she'd fallen short. It wasn't hard to see that Mariam never talked to the others, and despite how good she was in her training drills, not a single valkyrie had bothered to approach her.

Sigrid was failing her friends, and with all of her new responsibilities, she had no time to help them.

She thanked Fisk and mounted Hestur, ready to get back to training.

But before she could join the others, General Eira walked over.

Sigrid straightened up in the saddle. "Ma'am, I apologize for my performance—"

The general waved her words away. "Your presence is needed at Vanahalla."

Sigrid froze. "But training isn't over."

"It's over for you," General Eira said. "Palace. Now."

Sigrid ground her teeth together, fighting the urge to say no. Aunt Kaia was breaking their agreement that Sigrid could continue valkyrie training.

But as she looked toward Vanahalla, a bubble of anxiety rose inside her. What could possibly be so important that it couldn't wait a couple more hours?

CHAPTER TWENTY-FIVE

THE RESPONSIBILITIES OF
A VALKYRIE PRINCESS

"She's waiting for you in your chambers, Your Highness," one of the royal stable hands told Sigrid the moment she got back. She thrust Hestur's reins into his hands and hurried inside.

Had news finally arrived about the Night Elves? Had Sleipnir done something in the royal stables? Or—wait—was Aunt Kaia about to insist on extra runes lessons instead of keeping up with valkyrie training? Because there was no way she would agree to that.

Sigrid pushed the door to her chambers a bit too hard as she stormed inside, ready for the worst.

Aunt Kaia stood in front of the full-length mirror holding a blue gown. Her critical frown melted into a smile when she noticed Sigrid in the reflection. "Just in time. The seamstress delivered these." She waved at the boxes full of fabrics lying open on the nearby table, all varying shades of blue.

Sigrid dropped her chin. "You pulled me out of valkyrie training to look at…clothing?"

"Yes. Oh, don't look at me like that. It's for an important reason." Aunt Kaia put down the dress and sat in an armchair by the fire, kicking off her wood-soled shoes and folding her legs under her. She wore a blue robe as always, with her shiny, dark hair fanning over her shoulders, gold bands decorating her wrists, and the amber crown crossing her forehead. "What do you think of Tóra?"

Reluctantly, Sigrid walked over to take the seat across from her. "She's nice. A little frantic. Why?"

"We have a ceremony today to make her our new Seer."

Sigrid almost missed the chair and fell on the floor. She gripped the armrests for support, her heart in her throat. "What's wrong with Vala?"

"What do you mean?"

"Why do we need a new Seer? What's wrong with the old one?"

"We aren't replacing Vala yet," Aunt Kaia said gently—though the word *yet* didn't put Sigrid at ease.

"Then why…?"

The queen straightened in her seat, placing her bare feet on the rug. "Tóra is going to be Vala's apprentice. You know as well as I that Vala is getting on in her age. It takes years, even decades, to train a Seer. She has to start now so Tóra is ready to take over when the time comes."

"Oh."

"I also…" Aunt Kaia ran her palms over the armrests, not meeting Sigrid's eye. "I thought this would be a good opportunity to have you sit next to me on the dais, Princess."

If Sigrid hadn't already been seated, she would've dropped to the floor.

Her aunt clearly saw her panicked expression and rolled her eyes. "Sigrid—"

"You don't think there are better uses of my time than a ceremony? I can stay here and keep studying." Or better yet, return to valkyrie training.

Lips quirking into a knowing smile, Aunt Kaia stood and stepped toward the boxes on the table. She was shorter in bare feet, maybe Sigrid's height. "As royals, it's important we show our united support for the people in our court. Tóra will be incredibly useful to Vanaheim. With her affinity for runes, we might be able to secure an advantage if the Night Elves wage war." She riffled through the materials in the first box. "It's in your best interest to not only learn all you can from her, but to also support her in this new role. You *are* the Princess of Vanaheim, after all."

Sigrid slumped back with a groan.

She had no counterargument.

And so, an hour later, after an intense debate over whether a tunic and riding trousers were a better option—which Sigrid lost—Aunt Kaia stuffed her into an azure gown. It was the least conspicuous of all her options.

"Isn't my comfort and happiness worth more than a prim appearance?" Sigrid's voice was muffled against the material. Her head came through the top, and she pulled the front, trying to make it sit right. Her skin was raw and her hair a mess after so much time spent pulling rough material on and off.

"No." Aunt Kaia tightened the laces. Sweat glistened on her forehead, and she'd clipped her hair back from her face, as if beautifying Sigrid had been very hard work.

Sigrid studied her reflection in the full-length mirror. The color made her pale eyes look blue instead of gray, but her fondness for the dress ended there. Floor length, covering her arms down to her wrists, and embroidered with silver thread, it weighed more than armor. No way could she do anything functional in this. Trying to run would end in tripping and eating dirt. Riding was completely out of the question.

Overall, the idea of the whole court seeing her in this was mortifying. She couldn't even think of the valkyries hearing about this without her stomach roiling. Everyone would compare her new appearance to her usual barn clothes and dirt and laugh themselves silly.

She fiddled with the gold pendant hanging from her neck, which was cold and rested uncomfortably between her breasts. It gave her a squirmy feeling to have it pressing against her sternum.

She tugged the gown again, feeling like it was twisted. "It doesn't fit right."

None of them did. Some didn't fit at all.

Aunt Kaia tugged the sleeves, frowning. They were tight around Sigrid's upper arms and would probably rip at the shoulder if she reached forward.

"Well, the seamstress doesn't have your measurements yet, and you're stronger than I am," Aunt Kaia said. "We'll have her make you some custom robes later. Would you like a lighter material, like this one?"

In the reflection, her aunt's cornflower blue robe flowed in the breeze coming through the window, as airy as silk.

"Yes, please. In red." It had always been her favorite color, and now it was a private joke with Mariam, who'd once pointed out that all of Sigrid's clothes seemed to be red.

"Blue is the preferred color for royals..." Aunt Kaia began, trailing off at Sigrid's scowl. "But you have the freedom to create your own style, if you wish."

"I do wish." The memory of her mother in a sky-blue robe flashed to the front of her mind, anger twisting the woman's expression, dirt and blood covering the delicate material as they fought for control of the Eye of Hnitbjorg.

"Then we'll find the richest red in Vanaheim," Aunt Kaia said, startling her out of the memory. "Now for the final touch." She opened a drawer and took something out.

Sigrid's breath caught in her chest. *A diadem.* Shimmering gold threads wove intricately through a cluster of amber gems, designed to rest feather-light on a princess's forehead.

She shook her head. "I'm not wearing that."

Aunt Kaia seemed unsurprised by her response. She stepped closer, the diadem resting lightly on her soft, delicate hands. "A princess needs to wear a crown. I've worn one in public my whole life. Your mother—" The word caught on her tongue. She cleared her throat. "It's part of being a royal, Sigrid."

"It's too much," she said, out of breath as if she'd run here from the bottom of the hill. "The gown is enough, isn't it? And the fact I'm seated next to you?"

This was more than a piece of jewelry. It was so much worse than appearing in public wearing an extravagant gown. If she wore the diadem in front of the court today, she was officially announcing her status and would forever be known as Princess Helena's daughter.

Aunt Kaia sighed, her eyebrows pulling downward. "We'll be introducing you with your princess title at the start of the ceremony. Really, the correct thing to do would be to have a whole crowning ceremony for you—"

Sigrid squeaked. "No!"

"—but I knew you would be like this, so I skipped it."

"I'm forever in your debt for that." She tugged her sleeves, trying to stop them from pressing into her armpits and making her sweat.

Aunt Kaia pushed the diadem into her chest. "Then repay me by putting this on. It's a formality. You can take it off as soon as the Seer's ceremony is over."

Sigrid took it. It sat delicately between her fingers, flimsy and breakable.

"If it helps, this one used to be mine," Aunt Kaia said, squeezing her shoulder.

"Thanks." At least she wasn't trying to put Sigrid into Helena's old crown, robe, and chambers.

I am a royal. Part of being a royal is dressing like one. As much as she repeated these thoughts, the facts wavered in her mind as precariously as the diadem on her head.

"How is training going?" Aunt Kaia asked, grabbing a comb from the table and returning to fuss over Sigrid's hair. "I've noticed you've not taken Sleipnir with you."

Sigrid's heart jumped at being caught. Avoiding her aunt's gaze, she said, "Yeah, I've been working with him privately. Ordinary valkyrie training isn't challenging enough for him. Should we head down to the courtyard?"

It was a thinly veiled change of topic, but Aunt Kaia seemed pleased that she'd stopped resisting the ceremony. "My staff will touch up our hair and faces, and then yes. You look lovely, Sigrid."

After a painful process involving combs and a mysterious array of face powders, Sigrid took one last look in the mirror. She was cleaner than ever, her hair smooth, her skin even, her legs hidden beneath a robe. She might look the part, but she didn't feel like any princess of Vanaheim. Before she could work herself into another storm of doubt, she followed Aunt Kaia.

They descended to the courtyard, where a dais was set up and decorated with blue flowers and gold draperies. Two of the marble-and-gold thrones from the entrance hall had been brought out and placed on the left. An enormous crowd had gathered. Too many people.

"I thought only the court was invited?" she panic-whispered to Aunt Kaia.

"A new Seer is a big change. Everyone should be witness."

Sigrid wanted to stop and run back into the palace. But it was too late now. She forced her feet to keep moving, squinting in the hot afternoon sun.

Then, as they walked over the cobblestones, shadows fell over the crowd, and the courtiers craned their necks.

Sigrid moaned. "No…"

The junior valkyries landed at the back with a clatter of hooves. All of them. Including Mariam.

I'm not ready for this.

A voice boomed over the crowd for all to hear. "Please rise for Queen Kaia and Princess Sigrid."

CHAPTER TWENTY-SIX

CATCHING THE EYE

Sigrid swallowed back her panic as everyone stood and her aunt began the long walk onto the dais. Her face burned as she followed, her insides growing cold and uncomfortably squirmy, making it hard to coordinate her legs. *Don't walk weird, don't walk weird…*

Was she supposed to hold her arms at her sides or swing them? Her diadem felt crooked. Would it look odd to hold it in place as she walked, or should she leave it like that? Was she smiling too wide? Why was it so hard to smile normally?

Oh, gods, I must look ridiculous.

An eternity later, they reached the dais. Sigrid tugged on her dress and sat on the throne next to her aunt. It was hard and uncomfortable. The idea of sitting still on this thing for the entire ceremony made her want to fake faint just to get out of it.

But that would draw even more attention.

Gods, what were the junior valkyries thinking as they saw her like this? Would Mariam think she was acting haughty and self-important? That Sigrid would rather play dress-up as a princess than spend time with her?

"Do we need to be *on* the dais?" Sigrid whispered, sweaty and forgetting how to breathe. The diadem wobbled on her head.

"We need to be part of the ceremony," Aunt Kaia whispered

back, somehow managing to uphold her smile. "There's no need to be nervous. All eyes will be on the new Seer, anyway."

"I highly doubt that," Sigrid muttered.

Everyone's gazes were already fixed on her, this mysterious girl seated next to the queen. Did any courtiers recognize her as "that stable hand," the unusual girl with the Midgard horse, or did they not bother with the goings-on of the valkyrie stables?

Maybe a formal announcement would have been better. It would have spared her the murmurs and speculation.

When Sigrid dared to look at the valkyries, Mariam caught her eye and sucked in a breath. Was that a look of horror?

I should run over and explain.

She must have subconsciously moved to do just that, because Aunt Kaia grabbed her arm. Her grip was surprisingly strong for her stature—maybe due to panic that Sigrid had been about to embarrass her. "Sit. It's about to start."

Sigrid's armpits dampened the ill-fitting gown, and a bead of sweat slid down the back of her neck. She should've insisted she stayed in her valkyrie uniform.

Risking another look at Mariam, Sigrid blinked at the bright smile aimed at her. It lit her up from the inside out, and for a moment, the rest of the world fell away.

Mariam mouthed the words, *"So pretty."*

Sigrid's heart did a wild flip in her chest.

Okay, maybe dressing up was worth it.

Standing beside General Eira on Drifa, who watched the proceedings seriously, Mariam and Aesa stood at the outer edge of the valkyries. She was a lot sweatier and dirtier than the rest, her fitted training outfit and Aesa more dust-colored than white. What drills had they run after Sigrid left this morning?

Now that Sigrid paid closer attention, Mariam looked overworked and miserable. She clearly wasn't sharing everything— and when Ylva backed up her mare so she not-so-accidentally bumped into Aesa, a flash of understanding washed over Sigrid. She clenched her fists until her nails cut into her palms.

Ylva and Gunni leaned their heads together and snickered in an all-too-familiar way.

I'll fight them for this.

No, first she would check on Mariam and make sure she was okay, and *then* she would fight Ylva and Gunni.

She glanced at her aunt and bounced her knee. It didn't matter what other priorities Aunt Kaia insisted she had. She would go as soon as this ceremony was over.

"The valkyries sure are fussing," Aunt Kaia said. "Do you think something happened in the stable?"

Beside Mariam, the juniors whispered and pointed openly at Sigrid. Most of them looked outraged.

"They're wondering why I'm sitting here," Sigrid said flatly, glaring at them. They could gossip all they wanted, but messing with Mariam was unacceptable.

Aunt Kaia looked at her sharply. "Sigrid, did…did you not tell anyone you're the princess?"

Sigrid tore her gaze away to address her aunt, fidgeting with the heavy pendant. "Um. They know I'm Princess Helena's daughter, and they knew I quit my job as a stable hand. But I didn't tell them I accepted my title and came to live with you."

Aunt Kaia stared at her for a long moment, her lips parted, before throwing back her head and letting out a hearty laugh.

Sigrid cracked a smile. "Was I supposed to?"

"Of course you were! I thought you would be shouting about it to everyone who would listen." She wiped a tear of laughter. "Oh, Sigrid. I can't think of anyone else who would keep such enormous news a secret."

Well, she'd told her friends, and that was the important part. She didn't care about telling most of the others.

The crowd stayed standing when the ceremony commenced.

Vala hobbled out, leaning on her walking stick. Sigrid had half expected to see her close to death and ready to hand off her Seer duties, but to her relief, the old woman looked the same as ever. Her white hair was thick and waist length, and her tawny-brown skin, while wrinkled and full of age spots, glowed with good health. She was wrapped in the usual excessive amount of wool and furs, pulling them tighter as she settled into a chair at the opposite end of the dais. She met Sigrid's eye and gave a tiny nod.

A man emerged after her, his arms outstretched. He was very tall, maybe part giant, wearing a simple brown robe that stretched over his protruding belly. He had short, dark gray hair and faint lines crossing his light brown skin like webs. He smiled broadly.

"Welcome!"

His voice was as much a presence as his stature, booming across the courtyard with such volume that a flock of pigeons took flight.

Sigrid leaned into Aunt Kaia. "Who's that?"

She answered without moving anything but her lips. "Harald, the head sorcerer. He oversees all enchantments."

Harald. Tóra had mentioned him in their first lesson. The rune expert.

"Why is he talking and not Vala?"

"Remember I told you Seers tend not to enjoy the company of others? Vala most certainly cringes at the thought of being in front of all these people."

She's not the only one, Sigrid thought, shifting on the hard throne.

"We're gathered here," Harald boomed, "to honor the greatest gift offered to us by Mount Hnitbjorg."

Either he'd used some kind of rune to amplify his voice, or else they'd asked him to speak because he had the loudest voice in all of Vanaheim.

He pulled a semi-translucent pink stone from a pocket of his robe and held it like an offering to the crowd, his massive hands making it look tiny. Its delicate chain slipped between his fingers and swung like a pendulum.

The Eye of Hnitbjorg.

"Since the beginning," Harald boomed, "Seers have held a role of great importance in the cosmos. Her weapon is not a spear, axe, or sword, but knowledge of the future! Odin himself consulted one in the early days, as written in the poem we now know as the Vǫluspá."

Sigrid leaned toward Aunt Kaia. "What's—?"

"It's the poem that depicts creation and Ragnarök," she whispered patiently.

Sigrid nodded. She might have heard parts of it before.

"Many sagas since then," Harald said, "have foretold critical moments in history. These are the documented triumphs of generations of Seers. Before Vala, we had greats like Heiðr and Gróa, who told us of the births, deaths, wars, and marriages that weave together to create the fabric of our history. Vala ranks among them. She has foretold events that have heightened our place in Yggdrasil and saved us from peril."

Sigrid's insides squirmed at the mention of births. Vala had seen the vision that Princess Helena would give birth to Sleipnir's heir, which prompted her to not only have Sigrid, but to abandon her and take Sleipnir for herself.

Vala admitted to keeping most visions a secret. What events had she seen that she refused to share?

"Today, we welcome Tóra into Vanahalla, where she will endeavor to glean all the wisdom passed down through generations of Seers."

While the crowd applauded, Vala used her walking stick to hobble over, and he handed her the Eye.

Tóra emerged between the flowers and draperies wearing

her emerald green robe, her curly red hair in a long, thick braid.

Sigrid narrowed her eyes. So, this girl would be Vala's replacement—the one responsible for receiving, interpreting, and sharing all of Vanaheim's knowledge of the future. Was she up for it? She'd been kind and humble to Sigrid, and she was definitely intelligent—but she was awfully young for a Seer's role.

Then again, wasn't Sigrid awfully young to be taking on royal duties?

Tóra's wide eyes showed a lot of white as she cast her gaze across the audience, bringing to mind a startled mare. Her chest heaved, like she struggled to breathe under the suffocating gazes.

As she took the stone from Vala, she gave a little, "Oh!" and fumbled it. The crowd emitted a collective gasp as the Eye nearly crashed to the ground before she bent to catch it. She straightened up, stone in hand, her face a deeper red than her hair.

"Tóra." Vala's voice quavered with the strain of speaking with enough volume. "Do you accept the responsibilities of—"

"TÓRA!" Harald echoed, booming across the crowd. "DO YOU ACCEPT THE RESPONSIBILITIES OF—"

"—being a Seer—"

"—BEING A SEER—"

"That won't be necessary, Harald," Vala said, and he fell quiet, dropping his chin in apology. She cleared her throat and continued. "Being a Seer, the sole link between Vanaheim and the Norns, Urðr, Verðandi, and Skuld, and to discern whether to transfer this knowledge to its subjects while interpreting it to the best of your abilities with the interests of Vanaheim and its people at heart?"

Tóra blinked. "What?"

"Say yes," Vala whispered.

"Sorry—yes," Tóra said, the redness in her cheeks deepening.

Vala clasped her hands around Tóra's, and a little pang of jealousy rose in Sigrid's chest. As the subject of more than one vision—and having been in the Seer's tower more than once—she'd thought she was special in Vala's eyes. But this new Seer was more than that. She was a student, a prodigy, someone Vala would willingly nurture, whereas Sigrid had forced her way into Vala's life by climbing through her window.

"A vision is simply a message," Vala said, her voice quavering. "The Norns sometimes allow us to see what fates they weave. You, Tóra, are the messenger who transfers knowledge between the Norns and the people of Vanaheim—"

Tóra let out a little scream, and Vala pulled her hands away.

"Sorry, I…" The girl's eyes widened, glazing over. Her hands trembled over the stone. With a cry, she let go, sending it crashing down with a thud that carried over the crowd.

"Tóra, what is it?" Vala asked sharply.

Sigrid's pulse raced. "She saw a vision," she said, a bit too loudly.

Aunt Kaia's gaze snapped to her in her periphery.

At the Seers' feet, the stone was so hot that the dais beneath it blackened, sending up a plume of smoke.

Tóra stepped back, shaking out her hands like they were in pain. She backed toward one of the extraordinary vases of flowers. "Vala, I saw—"

Sigrid jumped to her feet. "Look out!"

Tóra collided with the vase and, with a scream, flailed her arms for balance. As Harald leaped to catch her, she flung out a hand, and a burst of light erupted from her palm.

CHAPTER TWENTY-SEVEN

THE KING'S REVENGE

The world slowed and then stopped as Sigrid understood what'd happened. It was the way Tóra had dropped the Eye as if it were scalding hot, the blankness in her eyes, and the light that burst from her outstretched hand, opening a window of colors to another landscape.

Not again.

Sigrid had had enough ominous visions to last a lifetime — and based on the way Tóra's expression contorted in fear, this one was not good.

A buzz came from the crowd as the window into another landscape hovered over the dais. Like the visions Sigrid had seen before, its subjects moved at a time-slowed pace.

Night Elves in animal skull masks, leather, and chainmail marched along the edge of a cliff, which rose a terrifying distance above a river. Among them, the Svartalf King strode with purpose, a bow and quiver across his back, a gloved fist around an iron arrow—

The vision disappeared—the briefest flash with hardly enough time to take in everything it contained.

Sigrid blinked the world back into focus, frantically piecing together what she'd seen. Something nudged at the back of her mind. If she could just grasp it...

The crowd buzzed louder like a swarm of bees, the chatter rising and falling, everyone no doubt trying to make sense of what'd happened. Mariam disappeared in a swarm of white mares, who convened around General Eira.

It clicked, and Sigrid turned to the queen. "Aunt Kaia, I've seen that fjord before. I rode along that path going the other way when we went to Svartalfheim."

Aunt Kaia said nothing, a hand over her mouth, apparently lost for words.

"Calm down," Harald boomed. "Everyone quiet! Give us a moment to figure out…"

"V-Vala, they're coming *here*," Tóra said through gasps. Her voice was so low that only those nearest would have heard, but the news traveled like a gust of wind.

"Come on." Sigrid seized Aunt Kaia's hand and pulled her over to the two Seers, addressing all three of them. "Tóra's right. The army is taking the same route I traveled with the valkyries when we couldn't use Ratatosk's ship."

"But—o-on foot?" Aunt Kaia asked, stammering. Her face was ghostly pale beneath the layers of powder.

"Yes. The Svartalf King ruined his chances of traveling with Ratatosk ever again. It's their only option."

Vala nodded, a deep frown creasing her face. "Did you see more than that?" she asked Tóra.

"N-no." Tóra's skin turned waxy, like she was going to vomit. "It was too hot. I'm sorry I dropped it."

"The Eye can withstand being dropped." Vala touched Tóra's shoulder. "Are you all right?"

In contrast to that comforting touch, Aunt Kaia wrapped cold fingers over Sigrid's arm, making her flinch. "We need to gather the council."

Sigrid's attention jumped to the Eye, which cooled where it lay, the smoke dissipating in the still air. Beneath it, the charred wood looked in danger of crumbling.

The Eye burned hotter if a vision was going to happen sooner. This must be happening within minutes—seconds, even.

"Vala, is this happening as we speak?" Sigrid asked. "Are the elves at that fjord right now?"

Vala nodded. "Queen Kaia, will you address the crowd?"

Aunt Kaia's chest heaved, and surprisingly, her eyes filled with tears.

She confessed to being overwhelmed in her new role as queen. The gods were unfair to make her deal with a war at the same time as she was grieving over her brother.

"Harald should do it." Sigrid raised a hand to catch his attention. "Harald!"

Aunt Kaia let out a breath while he came over, and Sigrid nodded encouragingly to her. The queen seized the moment to square her shoulders and smooth her robe.

"Your Majesty," Harald said. He had a woman under his arm and a small boy and girl standing on his feet and clinging to his legs. "How might I help?"

"Please tell everyone to stay calm," Aunt Kaia said, her delicate voice drowned beneath the clamor.

Harald's family plugged their ears as he cupped his hands around his mouth. "PLEASE, EVERYONE STAY CALM!"

"We are not defenseless. We will prepare," she said, Harald echoing the words with volume, "and we will turn them around. Everyone, follow your assigned duties."

Sigrid put a supportive hand on her aunt's arm as they watched the crowd push away, their chatter still agitated, but at least following orders.

She craned her neck until she spotted Mariam, who listened obediently to General Eira. She was too busy to notice Sigrid's wave to get her attention. Then the valkyries took flight, arcing away from the crowd and back to the stables.

Cursing under her breath, Sigrid remained with the queen. Her blood cooled in her veins as the meaning of this vision sank in. The Svartalf King's army was coming for revenge—and the senior valkyries might not be home in time to help fend off the attack. They would be seriously outnumbered.

"We need to meet with the council in the hall," Aunt Kaia said, confidence returning to her tone and posture.

Sigrid hurried alongside her toward the large double doors, sweat prickling beneath her extravagant robe, her head tingling under the sharp points of the amber diadem. Her chest was tight, making her dizzy as she tried to gulp down air.

They'd run out of time to prepare for war. They weren't ready.

Mariam wasn't ready. She was supposed to have time to train with the juniors and become one of them before being sent off to fight. What if she was hurt in battle, or worse?

It would be my fault.

And what about Sigrid's new role as princess? She needed more time to study and learn—more time to figure out runes. She'd barely started her lessons, and she had no better idea of what to do than she had a few days ago.

As the courtyard spiraled into panic over an impending war, she had to admit that her new role as princess was off to a disastrous start.

CHAPTER TWENTY-EIGHT

MAGIC
WORTH STEALING

The doors of Vanahalla slammed behind Sigrid, muffling the panicked crowd.

"Queen Kaia, Princess Sigrid, this way." Two guards fell into step beside them, escorting them across the lobby, up one floor, and into a meeting room that housed a rectangular table with ten chairs. Gods glared down from paintings on the walls—Njord rising from a violent sea, Odin holding a goblet—and Sigrid frowned at them. Where were these gods now? Why were they letting chaos reign?

While the guards stood outside the door, Aunt Kaia faced Sigrid. "No one attacks Vanaheim knowing that the valkyries live here. The Night Elves must think they can win."

"Win what, exactly?" Sigrid asked. "What do they want?"

Aunt Kaia reset her crown, calmer now that they were away from the crowd. "Revenge will be part of it, but I have no doubt that Loki encouraged them to go after everything in these towers." She waved a hand upward, the gold bands on her arm jangling. "Magic, relics, gold, jewels. It's enough to put any world on top."

The door swung open. Harald stepped inside, followed by General Eira, and then Vala and Tóra. The young Seer rested a hand on Vala's back to support her as she hobbled into the room on her walking stick. Each of them bowed to the queen, and then to Sigrid. General Eira's bow to Sigrid was more like a spasm. She'd obviously not yet come to terms with the fact that the stable hand everyone had spent sixteen years stepping on was now a princess.

Aunt Kaia sat at the head of the table and motioned for the others to join. "Goodness, this feels like a small crowd with the other generals away and dear Óleifr gone."

Sigrid pulled out the chair beside her aunt, a familiar twist of shame and confusion surging back as she took her place among these important people. She was definitely out of place in this room. She fought the urge to fidget with her diadem.

Harald, General Eira, Vala, and Tóra took scattered seats. They must have had assigned places. Had Sigrid's seat been Aunt Kaia's days ago when King Óleifr's spot was at the head of the table?

"Tóra," Vala whispered, patting the place to her left.

"Oh." Tóra sprang to her feet from what was apparently the wrong chair, sending it clattering backward.

Sigrid reflexively stood to pick up the toppled chair, but Aunt Kaia put a hand on her arm to stop her. The meaning was clear—princesses didn't do that sort of thing.

While Tóra fixed it and moved to the correct seat, General Eira said, "Your Majesty, the Night Elves must know the senior valkyries are stuck in Jotunheim and our defenses are down."

"They also know not *all* the valkyries are there. The juniors bested them and escaped in Ratatosk's ship. Surely they can't—" Aunt Kaia inhaled deeply before continuing. "It doesn't matter. The seniors will dock in Vanaheim tonight, and it's only a few hours across Myrkviðr. What makes the elves so confident they can win against us?"

General Eira slid her chair closer to the table, as composed as ever. "The size of the army in that vision was…concerning. They must think it's big enough to overwhelm us."

"Is it?" Aunt Kaia asked. Though she lifted her chin, her throat tensed as she swallowed.

General Eira didn't answer, which was answer enough.

Sigrid tried to speak, but her nerves made it hard to produce any sound. Would anyone listen?

"I'm suspicious of what weapons they've got with them," Harald said, lacing his fingers on the table. He leaned forward, his chair groaning in protest. "We don't know what else they've been able to craft."

"The iron arrows are destructive enough. It's all they need," Sigrid said, the words coming out a little jumbled.

Aunt Kaia's brow pinched. "Are you sure that weapon was significant enough?"

"Yes!" Sigrid exclaimed. "It was the worst damage any of us had ever seen from a single weapon." She looked around the table for words of support. Nobody seemed to understand the severity—maybe because they hadn't seen how terrifying it was when the arrow had hit Gunni. But if they'd listened to Sigrid and let Fisk analyze it, he probably would have figured out the ones they'd brought back from Svartalfheim by now. They would be in a better position to counter that dark magic.

Harald hummed thoughtfully. "We haven't had a chance to discuss it, with all of the focus on our dear departed king." He cast a sympathetic gaze to the queen, who bowed her head. "We've been studying the arrows, but it isn't clear what the Night Elves siphoned to create it. The magic seemed to have dissipated when it hit its target, leaving behind inactive iron. It's clever, because it means we can't use the same weapon back at them. But we should be worried about how many of these they've made."

"Any ideas about how to block them?" Aunt Kaia asked.

Harald shook his head. A glint of sweat broke across his brow, which he dabbed with the sleeve of his brown robe. "The Night Elves keep the details of their craft a secret."

Sigrid cleared her throat, and to her surprise, everyone turned to listen to her again.

This is new. She couldn't recall a time when people stopped talking to listen to her instead of interrupting and speaking over her.

"We have a Night Elf ally working in the stable, Harald," she said without looking at General Eira or Aunt Kaia. "He's more than willing to help us figure this out. You can talk to him if you'd like."

It was bold, even defiant—and in the silence that followed, Sigrid's heart seemed to stop beating.

"Good!" Harald boomed. "Very good. I have questions he might be able to answer. Will you bring him up here?"

"Yes," Sigrid said, breathless.

Everyone's gazes lingered on her. General Eira and Aunt Kaia exchanged a look, and she swore she caught a flash of anger in their expressions. But they stayed quiet, and a rush of victory surged through her chest.

Finally.

"But *why* are they attacking?" Aunt Kaia asked the room. "What do they want from us? Are they just looking to destroy, or…?"

The unasked question hung heavily over their heads—were Aunt Kaia and Sigrid in danger of being assassinated?

"If I may," Harald said. A frown cut deep lines into his face as he met everyone's gaze, his words reverberating. "There is celestial magic in this hall that would help them turn Vanaheim into a second realm of night. We've feared it for some time, but… they might be on a conquest for a dark empire."

An intake of breath passed around the table.

Vala nodded, confirming his words.

Goose bumps rippled up Sigrid's arms. What happened to Gunni's leg would happen on a massive scale. If the Night Elves shrouded Vanaheim in darkness, like Svartalfheim, everything in this world would die. From the lush forests to all of the creatures who lived in it, this entire beautiful world would be ruined.

"How long do we have?" Aunt Kaia asked sharply. She grew pale again, a sheen on her face and chest.

"We passed that fjord on the way to Svartalfheim," Sigrid said. "It was…a day or so from here on horseback." Her cheeks warmed as she wished she had a better time estimate.

"We can safely assume thirty-six hours," Tóra said. "That's Gatafjord, which passes Alfheim. I–I studied maps." Her last words trailed off, like she noticed the number of eyes on her and lost confidence.

"Good," Vala said, patting the young Seer's hand. "Thank you, Tóra."

"So we don't have long," General Eira said matter-of-factly. "We'll gather every reserve and retired valkyrie until the seniors return. I'll station them here to protect Vanahalla and take the juniors to meet the attack at the spring of Hvergelmir."

Sigrid's heart pounded. Every valkyrie in Vanaheim would come fight, including those who hadn't fought a battle in years and those who were supposed to be taking time to rest. The junior valkyries would be fighting alongside their mothers.

Thirty-six hours.

"If the senior valkyries dock in Vanaheim tonight," Sigrid said, finding a little more power in her voice, "then by the time they cross Myrkviðr and get to us, we'll have to turn them around and send them right back to the spring. Can we get a message to them that they should wait for us at the spring of Hvergelmir instead of coming all the way here? This would save their energy and a lot of hours of travel time."

General Eira didn't even meet Sigrid's gaze. "Absurd. We can't do that to them. They've been away for weeks and will want to see home before we send them to fight again."

"Of course they do. But is that best?" Sigrid challenged. "It's worse to make them ride seven hours here and seven hours back to the same place. We'll exhaust them."

"It's not that far."

"It is! You've forgotten because you haven't left Vanaheim in—" Sigrid let the end of the sentence die when General Eira's eyes met hers, widening dangerously. She'd been about to mention how long it'd been since the general was in active service.

"Princess Sigrid is right," Aunt Kaia said, which made General Eira look murderous. "We can't sap the senior valkyries' energy. They'll already be drained from Jotunheim. Harald, can you send a message straight away?"

"Will do, Your Majesty!" he boomed.

"And do we think the valkyries will be able to stop that army from entering Vanaheim?" Vala asked. Though her voice was barely a whisper, her words filled the room.

There was a heavy silence.

The elves would try to cross the spring of Hvergelmir, the wide, deep river flowing across the entrance to Vanaheim.

"I don't think they can swim," Sigrid said. Fisk told her how he almost drowned once. Something about the weight of their masks. "But they must have a plan to get across the river."

"Masters of craftsmanship," Aunt Kaia said. "We have to be prepared for anything."

Sigrid nodded, chewing her lip. When rescuing Ratatosk, she and Hestur had the advantage when none of the winged mares were willing to go underground to get him—so wasn't there something she could do in this invasion that the valkyries wouldn't be able to?

She caught herself fidgeting with her diadem and dropped her hand. "The stable hands should come. While you're fighting, we—they—can build fortifications along the riverbank and fight on the ground if needed. We'll block them from the air, land, and water."

She flushed at the blunder of accidentally referring to herself as a stable hand, but Aunt Kaia nodded.

General Eira raised an eyebrow. "Fortifications? With what?"

"We'll bring supplies from here and borrow from the village. We'll cart it through the forest and can even chop more wood when we get there. We'll build a wall to help stop them from crossing the river."

The others looked at her intently.

General Eira tapped her fingers on the table. "That…might be a good idea. We have to assume the elves have a plan for crossing the river, so we should prepare to have another means of blocking them from getting past us."

Although it was far from a compliment, Sigrid couldn't hold back the burst of pride.

"I'll have the sorcerers prepare some curses," Harald said. "We've not battled in a while, but we'll help hold them back in any way we can."

Tóra nodded enthusiastically.

"And if they get past us," Aunt Kaia said, "we should plan to send divisions to protect the villages near the spring. Based on what we know about the Night Elves in past wars, we have to assume they intend to ransack everywhere they can."

The words "*based on what we know*" put a twist in Sigrid's gut, reminding her that she was the least educated person in the room. But she'd contributed to this meeting, hadn't she? She still had experience that could make her helpful.

The plan gave Aunt Kaia life like water on a wilted flower, and she looked as regal as before the vision interrupted the ceremony. Sigrid, too, savored the renewed energy, ready to introduce Harald to Fisk and find out more about those iron arrows.

Maybe…possibly…Aunt Kaia and I could work well together.

"We'll take this afternoon to prepare," Aunt Kaia said, her chin high. As calmness returned to her, she looked more regal, more in control, and that energy seemed to bleed through the room. "The juniors and stable hands will depart tomorrow to meet the seniors at the spring. We'll send any sorcerers we can spare, too. That should give them several hours to set up a fortification before the Night Elves arrive. Are we in agreement?"

Vala and Tóra nodded.

"Brilliant!" Harald shouted.

"Will Sigrid be joining everyone, or does she have different duties now?" General Eira asked. Her tone was flat, but she issued a challenge in her refusal to use Sigrid's title.

Sigrid ground her teeth, trying to ignore her.

Aunt Kaia tapped her nails on the table, chewing her lip. "I would like to suggest something. I ask you to keep in mind that I've spent my life studying politics, cosmic affairs, and history. Do you trust my opinions?"

General Eira, Vala, and Tóra nodded.

"Without doubt!" Harald shouted.

It wasn't clear how much of this automatic trust was because of her status as queen and how much was genuine.

Sigrid had seen no reason not to trust Aunt Kaia, but she said nothing, unwilling to answer that question.

"Princess Sigrid has proven herself in so many ways." Aunt Kaia gripped Sigrid's shoulder and leaned in. "As a child, you jumped into a role as a stable hand, watching the other girls your age go on to serve the nine worlds. You went to Helheim and back, passing Garmr twice. Then you joined the valkyries on a mission in Svartalfheim and played a crucial role in rescuing Ratatosk. You're a young woman of remarkable skill."

Sigrid's face burned hotter than the Eye had after Tóra dropped it. "Th-thank you."

This sounded over the top, but the facts weren't untrue. She hadn't even included using Sleipnir to raise Hel's army—not that Sigrid would volunteer those shameful details.

General Eira raised her eyebrows, like she wasn't sure where the queen was going with this.

Neither was Sigrid, whose heart beat faster.

"I want you to work with General Eira to lead the valkyries," Aunt Kaia said.

CHAPTER TWENTY-NINE

QUESTIONABLY PROMOTED

A sharp breath left Sigrid as she hit the back of her chair. *What?*

"Ah! A royal leading the valkyries," Harald exclaimed, rubbing his hands together. "We haven't seen this since Princess Brunhild. Good of you to jump on this opportunity, Your Majesty."

General Eira's lips flattened into a thin line, and the crease between her eyebrows went deeper than ever. It was the expression she always wore right before she yelled at Sigrid—but in this company, under these circumstances, she stayed quiet.

"How do you feel about being a general?" Aunt Kaia asked Sigrid.

"A general of what?" Sigrid exclaimed.

Far from being proud or flattered, she worried over the outrage this would cause among valkyries who'd spent their lives training and serving. It wasn't fair of her to swoop in and claim a high rank when she'd only been on one mission.

Aunt Kaia's smile was calm, confident—and oblivious. "We can have you work that out with General Eira."

General Eira's nostrils flared. Her knuckles were deathly white where she laced her fingers together on the table.

"Experience is best balanced with fresh talent," Aunt Kaia said. "Look at Vala and Tóra."

Yes, but Vala doesn't want to murder Tóra in her sleep.

The two Seers sat motionless, looking down, as if trying not to be dragged into this.

Sigrid shook her head. "I can't."

"Why not?"

"General Eira has the experience we need," Sigrid said. "I don't. In Vala and Tóra's case, Tóra is born a Seer. In my case, I'm born a—stable hand." Her insides plummeted, because she was technically *not* born a stable hand. Royalty was in her blood.

Aunt Kaia must have seen this pass over her face because her smile widened. "You were born *a royal*. You were made for this. Experience is only part of it, and what Vanaheim needs right now is our princess leading our defenses. We need a direct connection to the troops."

Sigrid shook her head and stared at the table, panic blurring her vision. Making decisions in battle was way over her head. She didn't know the first thing about directing troops, especially ones who would resent her. And the valkyries already followed and respected General Eira.

"Aunt Kaia, I'm seventeen," she whispered, wishing they could talk in private.

"And?"

She held her aunt's gaze intently, willing her to understand. "And I'm not even a real valkyrie."

Aunt Kaia winked, as if this argument was all in fun. She placed a soft, cool hand over Sigrid's. "This is about your lack of confidence. You have an amazing amount of talent. Don't underestimate your ability to lead an army."

Except I sort of did lead Hel's army, and I also sort of led the junior valkyries against them, and on both occasions, I had no idea what I was doing.

In the silence, General Eira cleared her throat. "Perhaps there's a different leadership role that Princess Sigrid could accept."

Aunt Kaia tilted her head thoughtfully. "What about a lieutenant? Would you consider that?"

This also sounded like too much. She couldn't name all the battle formations and had no idea what tactics would be effective against the Night Elves. But it was a better option than trying to work alongside General Eira as an equal.

She drew a deep breath. Harald's warning that the Night Elves might be after celestial magic—something to turn Vanaheim into a realm of darkness—lit a fire in her. She could never let that happen to her home. Endless love and joy were tied to the sun that rose every day, bathing the world in warmth and light, nourishing the forests, the towns, and the fields she galloped through on Hestur. She would die before letting the elves take this world from her.

If protecting Vanaheim meant riding Sleipnir and working with General Eira to become a lieutenant, then that was what she would do. She would work her hardest to come up with plans to defeat the Night Elves.

"Yes. I can do that," she said firmly.

Aunt Kaia let out a breath, her shoulders relaxing. "Wonderful. General Eira, what do you say?"

"Lovely," General Eira said through her teeth. It seemed to cause her pain to watch Sigrid nearly get promoted to the same rank as her—with good reason.

"Lovely!" Harald boomed.

Vala and Tóra were still motionless, their gazes flicking back and forth as if watching a valkyrie training drill.

Work with General Eira, Aunt Kaia had said, like this wasn't the equivalent of asking her to poke a dire wolf in the eye.

Sigrid would do it despite the risk of being bitten. She would find a way to become the leader that Aunt Kaia wanted her to be, that *she* wanted to be, and that the cosmos apparently destined her to be—although this seemed to involve a lot of humiliation and feelings of incompetence.

Her gaze caught on a painting on the wall behind General Eira—a *V* formation of valkyries soaring through the clouds. Below it, a gold plate read, *"Freyja leading the valkyries in the Aesir-Vanir war."*

It sounded familiar, but she still had so much to learn.

Perhaps she'd get the chance to earn her own painting one day, leading a valkyrie charge on Sleipnir as elves, giants, humans, and beasts fought against the tipping cosmic balance.

If I can ever face a real battle on Sleipnir.

The training sessions on Hestur and her experience in Helheim had given her skills, but were they enough?

Tomorrow, she would find out. The time had come to do what she was destined for, whether she was ready or not.

As the meeting ended, Sigrid pulled Aunt Kaia aside. "I need to tell you something," she whispered before she could change her mind. "I made you a promise to ride Sleipnir into battle, but I'm not sure what will happen when I do. The power of Odin and Loki are in him, and he has that over me. He's really hard to…control." She trailed off, not sure how to elaborate without making her aunt worry about the mental state of her new lieutenant.

"Of course it's scary riding Odin's stallion, Sigrid." Aunt Kaia rested a hand on her shoulder. "But it's just power you're feeling, nothing sinister. You should be proud of what you've accomplished on him."

Some pride might have been in there, but so was shame, and so was fear. Sleipnir brought forth all of those things and more.

Aunt Kaia's dark eyes searched her face. "You've ridden Sleipnir a few times, have you not?"

Sigrid's pulse quickened as if reacting to the memory of riding him. "I have. All through Helheim and all the way home."

"Then you know you can ride him."

Sigrid shifted. It wasn't that simple, but how could she explain?

"Sigrid, I know I have no right to talk about what it's like to fight a war as a valkyrie, but I will say this. Vanaheim needs you on Sleipnir. He is the greatest war horse in the nine worlds, and you are his heir. You *are* meant to do great things with him."

"I know. I'm just so…" Sigrid huffed, struggling to get the words out.

Aunt Kaia held her gaze. "You need to decide whether to let fear block you from achieving your potential or fire you into action."

Sigrid swallowed hard. Aunt Kaia was right. Regret would haunt her days if she surrendered to fear now. She was the only person in the cosmos destined to ride Sleipnir, and what a waste it would be to refuse such a fate.

A path formed in front of her, tentative, a little overgrown, but clearer than before.

She was a princess, a lieutenant, a valkyrie.

She would ride Sleipnir into battle, no matter how much it scared her.

CHAPTER THIRTY

POKING A DIRE
WOLF IN THE EYE

Nerves rampaged through Sigrid as she struggled out of the robe, into her riding clothes, and saddled up Hestur. The sun continued its relentless pursuit for the horizon, moving too quickly for all they had to accomplish before leaving at noon tomorrow.

As for her? Not only would she have to ride Sleipnir, but she would also have to figure out how to be a lieutenant by then.

Hestur mirrored her energy, frisky as she galloped down the hill to the valkyrie stables. Good thing she put on the saddle, or else she might have popped off his back like a cork from a bottle.

All she could do was focus on the things she knew how to achieve. Right now, she had to bring Fisk to Harald, as well as gather the stable hands and catch them up on their role in defending Vanaheim. Also, she desperately needed to check on Mariam, because she couldn't get the image out of her mind of Mariam looking miserable and caked in dirt earlier.

As she dismounted at the open barn doors, the buzz inside didn't help calm her. The words "vision," "Vala," and unfortunately her own name drifted toward her from the chattering stable hands and valkyries.

She tried to slip in unnoticed, but Hestur whinnied to his mare friends and announced her presence to the whole barn.

"Hey, Sig," Roland said, pushing a wheelbarrow past her. "The valkyries filled us in. Not a great start to your new job, huh?"

"Yeah…" she said weakly. "Hey, have you seen Fisk?"

Roland shook his head. "Sorry. Haven't seen him since this morning."

"Okay." She looked around, moving to the next item on her list. "Can you round up the stable hands? We're riding out to the spring of Hvergelmir to meet the Night Elves tomorrow, and you're all coming. We need provisions and supplies to build fortifications."

Roland's eyes widened. "Really? We're coming?"

Sigrid nodded, her heart skipping as she suddenly doubted her ability to give orders.

Roland's breath caught, and he drew himself up, seeming to grow several inches taller. "Wow. Okay, I'll let them know. We'll gather as many carts as we can. Maybe we can borrow some horses and carts from the village to haul everything."

"Great idea. Thanks, Roland."

Sigrid let out a breath as she watched him go. If only the valkyries respected her the same way.

Now, where are Mariam and Fisk?

She made it two more steps when Gunni emerged from the tack room and smiled wryly. "So, is being a valkyrie not good enough? You have to weasel your way into the royal hall?"

Sigrid suppressed a groan. *Not now.*

She lowered her voice so only Gunni could hear. "I didn't *weasel—*"

"Oh, we know," Ylva said, stepping out of the tack room behind her. "Your boyfriend filled us in."

Sigrid clipped Hestur into cross-ties. So, *that* rumor hadn't died.

Peter walked by at that moment. He stopped, raising an eyebrow.

As Ylva and Gunni giggled and continued down the barn aisle, Sigrid shouted after them, "We're leaving for battle tomorrow. General Eira will be down here to brief you in a minute."

That shut them up.

"You're riding out to meet the elves, then?" Peter asked Sigrid once the girls were out of earshot. "Also, boyfriend?"

"They think Roland and I are dating," Sigrid said flatly. "At least, they're pretending they think that. And yes. The stable hands—"

Footsteps stopped beside them. "What's this about you dating someone?"

Sigrid's heart flipped at the sound.

Mariam was coated in grime, her white training outfit dusty and damp. Behind her, Aesa looked freshly bathed.

Heat rose in Sigrid's cheeks beneath the stares of too many eyes. She wanted to shout at the whole barn to stay out of her love life.

"I'll dry off Aesa," Peter said, stepping forward to do his job. "You rest."

Mariam held onto the lead rope for a moment before letting Peter take it, as if considering refusing his offer. But she seemed to wilt with exhaustion as she wiped a dirty sleeve over her forehead.

"Get in some extra practice today?" Sigrid asked bracingly.

"I've got a bit of catching up to do." Mariam's voice was clipped. She removed her helmet and gloves with jerky movements.

"Is everything—?"

"Mariam," Ylva said in sing-song, "are you enjoying your little vacation to Vanaheim? I'd start packing my bags for home, if I were you."

Mariam rounded on her. "Maybe if you spent more time paying attention in practice and less time being jealous of me, you'd actually hit a target once in a while. You know the spears are actually supposed to go *through* the hoops?"

Ylva looked affronted as Mariam stomped into the tack room. Sigrid darted in after her.

"How dare you talk to m—" Ylva's words were cut off as Mariam slammed the door.

Sigrid's stomach churned. Ylva and Gunni had probably made life a nightmare for her—and now she had to leave for battle with a team who didn't want her.

And I pushed her to do this.

The tack room smelled of leather and horse sweat, and the open window brought in the warm outside air and sunlight. Normally, such sights and smells would cheer Sigrid up.

She blinked back the prickling in her eyes. "How long have they been bothering you?"

Mariam let out a breath. "I'm handling it."

"I'm sorry I've not been around more. I should've—"

"So, that vision." Mariam roughly put away her gear. "That was the kind of thing you saw before? It was a real vision that Seer girl showed everyone?"

"Mariam…"

Mariam turned back with scowl.

Yep, she's mad at me. She'd probably spent all week remembering she was suffering through spiteful taunts and attacks because of Sigrid's bold assumption that she would want to be a valkyrie. That fact lingered between them like sticky sap oozing from a tree.

"Yeah, it was real," Sigrid said. "I've seen that kind of thing before from the Eye of Hnitbjorg."

"Hm. I wondered—hoped—it was false." She shook loose her braid, letting her hair cascade over her shoulders. "I mean, that new Seer seems a little green."

"The Night Elves are really on their way right now. We're going to the spring to stop them, and the stable hands are coming to help."

They held each other's gaze as the many conversations beyond the walls of the tack room blended together. Sigrid wanted to ask more questions and find out how much of Ylva and Gunni's awfulness Mariam had had to deal with, but Mariam seemed likely to bite her head off if she brought it up.

Had she honestly expected Mariam's stay here to be perfect? Of course it would be hard to join the valkyries as an outsider. Of course prejudiced people would doubt the abilities, dedication, and loyalty of a girl from Niflheim. But this was better than being forced to live in the woods like an animal or, worse, being sent back to that bleak world—wasn't it?

Mariam let out a loud breath. "I'm fine, Sigrid. They're exhausting to deal with, but I'm fine." She eyed Sigrid up and down. "You looked good in that dress. What are you doing down here, anyway? Shouldn't you be in the hall?"

Sigrid swallowed, uneasy both at the compliment and the snappy questions that followed. "Queen Kaia made me a lieutenant."

Mariam raised an eyebrow. "Like, to give the valkyries orders?"

"I know. Help."

Mariam smirked, and the rest of the tension between them melted. She glanced to the door, as if checking for listening ears, then stepped closer. Her lips were parted, the room's shadows making her skin irresistibly smooth and her eyes as dark as bottomless pools.

Sigrid's insides fluttered as they stood close enough to kiss. Would they ever have time to be properly alone?

"Which horse will you ride when the attack comes?"

Sigrid's heart jumped at having Sleipnir brought up. "I've been working with Sleipnir, trying to get a hold of his power."

"That's good." Mariam nodded. "I was worried you were going to leave a war horse in the barn when we ride off to battle."

Sigrid frowned. "It's not that simple. You know I'm…"

"What?" Mariam's brown eyes bore into hers.

Sigrid shook her head. "Nothing."

Mariam sighed, placing her palm against Sigrid's and moving their fingers so they all lined up. "You're good at keeping secrets, Sigrid. I just wonder how many of them you have."

Beyond the door, the valkyries' voices mingled loudly. Was she referring to keeping their relationship a secret or something else? Keeping the two of them a secret was in their best interest. Right?

"What's that supposed to mean?" Sigrid asked.

"Tell me what you're thinking. Why are you afraid of getting on Sleipnir?"

Sigrid's mouth went dry. She studied their hands, grinding her teeth. Finally, without looking at Mariam, she said, "I'm afraid of who I become when I'm on him."

"You're afraid you'll end up like your mother," Mariam said, and the words came so easily that Sigrid wondered if she'd already known the reason.

The words struck so close to Sigrid's heart that tears sprang to her eyes. She averted her gaze to a tangle of spare reins hanging on the wall.

Mariam stepped closer until her breath tickled Sigrid's lips. "Sigrid, you aren't at all like her."

"You know that's not true. You can't look at my eyes, my face, even the shade of my hair, and tell me I'm nothing like her."

"I mean inside." Mariam placed a hand on Sigrid's neck. "You're a much better person."

At this gentle touch, Sigrid's heart thrummed so strongly that she was sure Mariam would feel her racing pulse. A pleasant shiver ran through her and settled in her belly.

"Thanks."

Mariam's fingers lingered on her skin, leaving hot trails along her neck, ear, and cheek.

Sigrid clasped her hand around Mariam's and brought it to her lips, vaguely aware that Mariam was asking her something. "Hm?" she murmured into her palm.

Mariam let out a breathy laugh. "I said, how are your bed chambers?"

"Huge. And you should see where Hestur gets to stay. It opens up to a huge paddock—"

Mariam's raised eyebrow and smirk told her she'd completely missed the implication.

"O-Oh. I mean...you should see them. Sometime." Sigrid swallowed. "Soon?"

Mariam tilted her head playfully, but whatever reply she'd been about to share was interrupted when the door creaked open. They quickly stepped apart.

"I'd like you to lead the Borthorpe division—" General Eira stopped dead and glared at Sigrid like she was a Night Elf skipping into Vanaheim.

Ylva, who'd been following, bumped into her. "Oops. Sorry, General."

Mariam let out an annoyed huff. Yeah, Ylva had done this on purpose.

Sigrid tried to speak, but no sound came. Should she acknowledge the meeting they'd both come from? How was she supposed to work with General Eira, exactly? How was she even supposed to begin this conversation?

Hey, General, want to discuss battle plans with me?

"We've been graced with a visit from our princess!" Ylva dipped into a mocking bow. "Welcome, Your Highness. Or is it Lieutenant?"

"I think it's Lieutenant Princess Sigrid Helenadottir," Gunni said from the aisle beyond them, her voice shaking with suppressed laughter.

General Eira shushed them. "Sigrid, we need to prepare you for tomorrow. You have a lot to learn in a day if you want to avoid leading our troops to death."

She might not have sounded as spiteful as Ylva or Gunni, but her choice of words made Sigrid clench her fists. "I need to bring Fisk to Harald," she said firmly. "The sooner they figure out the arrows—"

"That can wait. Come on."

"But—"

"*Now*." The general spun on her heel, parting Ylva and Gunni, leaving Sigrid to look pleadingly at Mariam.

"It's fine. I need to take a bath." Mariam motioned to her dusty training uniform. "See you first thing?"

The question lifted Sigrid's spirits a little—especially when Mariam's gaze flicked to her lips.

"Definitely," Sigrid said.

"Good." Mariam gave a little wave. "I'll ask Peter to tend Hestur. See you later, Lieutenant."

And with that unsatisfying, distant goodbye that left Sigrid's insides twisting with want, she ran after General Eira.

CHAPTER THIRTY-ONE

FIGHTING POWER

The generals' strategy room was attached to the veterinary barn. Sigrid had never been allowed inside before, though she'd peeked at it years ago. A round table dominated the room, big enough to seat a dozen, with a few sheets of parchment strewn across it. Lines and scribbles outlined what must have been battle formations. General Eira collected these into a pile and motioned for Sigrid to sit, her expression unreadable.

Sigrid pulled out a chair, the legs scraping over the clay floor, and they sat across from each other, silent.

"We need to prepare to be hit by a violent attack." General Eira leaned back in the chair, one hand resting on the table. The setting sun beaming through the window highlighted every spot, wrinkle, and scar on the aging woman's skin. "The Night Elves have always relied on brute force and big weapons. They've never ventured into advanced tactics and trickery, which means we can gain an advantage by being strategic."

Sigrid nodded. She had firsthand experience in Night Elf attacks, but she tended to end the fight by escaping, not confronting and besting them. "How should we do that?"

"The spring of Hvergelmir acts as a natural moat, so the goal is to stop them as they're trying to cross it. The other generals and I will direct the valkyries to cut off their advance."

"And if they get past?"

General Eira searched Sigrid's face, her thin lips curved into a frown. "We can't lose control of them. We'll keep their army tight, and if they try to go for a village, we'll use our advantages—our knowledge of where cliffs and valleys are, our ability to cut off their access to food and water. And a vantage point from the sky. The sky has always been our strength and will continue to be."

"What about the Svartalf King?" Sigrid asked. "We have to talk to him—figure out what he wants and how we can come to an agreement."

The general scoffed. "He wants to decimate us. I don't think we'll discover anything more interesting by attempting a civilized talk while they invade our world."

"Even if he can't be reasoned with, we need to learn his plans."

"Explain." General Eira crossed her arms, making her muscles strain against her uniform—a reminder that she was still as ready to fight as ever.

Sigrid took a deep breath and organized her thoughts. "Kidnapping Ratatosk, invading Vanaheim… It's all for a reason. The worlds are in chaos. Even Aunt—Queen Kaia knows a shift has happened. There's something deeper going on, and we should try to find out what it is."

General Eira considered, then nodded. "Very well. But only if we can find a way to safely meet with him."

Sigrid sat taller, surprised to find General Eira considering her words. "How are we organizing the troops?"

General Eira narrowed her eyes, her lips puckering as if tasting something sour. Maybe using the word "*we*" had been too bold. "I've already decided who will go where if we need to protect the towns near the spring, and everyone knows their positions."

When she didn't elaborate, Sigrid asked, "Have you planned who is going to each town?"

"Let me worry about that, Sigrid."

"You should avoid sending Ylva to Micklhol, since Roskva can be skittish. I'd also keep Gunni in the sky, unless you want Oda to hurt her legs a few hours in. And I hope you assigned Edith to Steinholm, knowing the way Mjöll is with grass—"

"I don't need you telling me how to organize my troops," General Eira snapped, that familiar crease appearing between her eyebrows. "You know the mares and their riders, yes. But you don't know war. Don't overextend yourself into a role you aren't qualified for."

Sigrid narrowed her eyes. "I'm not overextending—I'm trying to help!"

General Eira sighed, leaning forward across the table. "I'm not insulting you, Sigrid. I'm stating a fact. You have no leadership experience, and a war with Svartalfheim is not the moment to practice."

"I led the valkyries in Helheim. And maybe that doesn't amount to years of experience, but it should count for something. I'm not helpless." Her pulse spiked as she entered dangerous territory. She'd never spoken to the general in this tone, but if it was the only way to make her understand, so be it.

The crease between General Eira's eyebrows softened. She studied Sigrid as if trying to decipher her. "And how exactly will you help?"

Sigrid sat back in her chair, trying not to fidget. "I'm going to ride Sleipnir into battle."

A hungry gleam sparked in General Eira's eyes, an expression not unlike a mare being presented with a bucket of oats. "You have Odin's stallion with you again?"

Huh. Maybe Aunt Kaia and General Eira didn't talk as much as Sigrid had assumed.

"He never left."

General Eira huffed out a breath, either in exasperation or

acknowledgment that Sigrid had successfully gotten that one past her.

It also seemed that Sigrid riding the best war horse in the cosmos changed the general's opinion.

The gleam vanished as the general broke eye contact. "You'll still be riding on the ground as planned."

"Last I checked, he had extra legs, but no wings," Sigrid said flatly.

The corner of General Eira's mouth twitched.

A glimmer of an idea took form. Sigrid was destined for the ground, and her place was among the stable hands. It always had been. She respected them, and they respected her. And if they were coming to battle, they would need a leader to keep them organized. Sigrid could do that from the ground—her own division of the army, albeit an unconventional one.

"When we depart tomorrow," Sigrid said, "you and the junior valkyries will want to fly ahead and meet the seniors at the spring as quickly as possible, right? That leaves the caravan of stable hands, sorcerers, and provisions unguided and unprotected. I can lead them through Myrkviðr and guide them through building fortifications. The stable hands and sorcerers will be my ground troops."

General Eira sat back, considering her, her expression less taut than it'd been minutes ago.

When she didn't argue, Sigrid's heart skipped in excitement.

"All right," the general said finally. "Everyone on foot will be your ground troops. I'll trust you with the fortifications, Sigrid."

Sigrid nodded.

So did General Eira.

We have an agreement.

Sigrid bit her tongue to stop from smiling.

CHAPTER THIRTY-TWO

NIGHT ELF
ALLIANCES

At dawn, Sigrid arrived in the stable yard on Hestur to find a lot of shouting and bustling around. Stable hands pushed wheelbarrows stacked with crates, loaded them onto carts, and argued about how much to bring. The valkyries ran around making preparations—Runa sprinted past with only one boot on—and their mares picked up on the energy, stomping and snorting in their stalls.

"We need enough medical bags for all the senior valkyries," Peter shouted, snappier than usual. "Take away some of the tools if you need to. Their health is the priority, got it?"

A young stable hand named Durinn nodded, alarmed, and dropped a wooden post to dart inside the veterinary building.

Sigrid's stomach twisted, but there wasn't time to deal with any nervousness or doubt. In a few hours, everyone here would be riding through Myrkviðr to meet the invasion. They were about to face Night Elves armed with enchanted iron arrows.

To her frustration, she never found Fisk last night after her long lesson with the general, and she *really* had to get him to Harald before they left so the sorcerers could keep working while they were gone. The sooner they could figure out the secret to those iron arrows, the safer they would all be.

Leaving Hestur at a hitching post, she entered the main barn to look for her friends.

Ylva's voice floated down the aisle. "She's just so intense. Like, has anyone seen her laugh? Or even smile or relax?"

"I feel like she doesn't know how to be normal," someone said.

They'd better be talking about General Eira.

"She asked if my mom knew hers," Gunni said, "and then had the gall to sound offended when I brought up treason. Like, she knows people don't get banished for no reason, right?"

"I'd be hiding in shame if I were her," Ylva said.

Several girls laughed.

Sigrid's insides erupted like a volcano. *No.*

She marched forward, and they fell silent at her footsteps. Fists clenched, she stepped around the corner. Several junior valkyries stood leaning against the wall, helmets in hand.

"You know what?" Sigrid said, mildly satisfied by their startled expressions. They'd obviously not expected her to be in the barn. "I've spent my life listening to you be horrid to me, but I'm not going to let you do the same to Mariam. She came all the way here from Niflheim to join our ranks and serve Vanaheim. She's as loyal as any other valkyrie. The least you could do is welcome her."

Stunned silence met her words. Gunni opened her mouth as if to say something, but nothing came out, and a blotchy red tinge rose in her cheeks.

Good. They deserve to feel embarrassed.

She left them, feeling sick. This wasn't fair. Mariam never had friends in Niflheim, while these girls had grown up in the nicest of worlds and had been automatic friends since birth.

Murmurs rose behind her, no doubt the gossip continuing at a lower volume.

As she neared the end of the barn, a clip-clop approached from outside, and Mariam rounded the corner with Aesa in tow. Once Sigrid's insides finished doing a flip at the sight of her, she noticed the familiar linen bag draped over the saddle.

"Took her long enough," Ylva said, her voice ringing. "I'm starved."

Mariam tossed the bag on the ground without a word, letting the cloth-wrapped sandwiches spill across the clay floor. The juniors appeared from all directions to have breakfast, scoffing and glaring at her.

"What's up?" she asked Sigrid, impervious to their attitudes. "You look ready to spit fire like Garmr."

"They're just being cats. Nothing new. It's fine."

Except *fine* was her biggest lie of the day. She was so far from fine. Mariam had been handed Sigrid's former duties and become the new target of everyone's bullying. Sigrid hadn't improved her life by bringing her up here to join the valkyrie ranks. She'd made it worse. Mariam might have been better off living a peaceful, secret existence in Myrkviðr with Fisk.

"I'm handling those idiots," Mariam said, not bothering to lower her voice.

"It's not that—it's—" She couldn't let Mariam feel like an outcast. She'd done enough damage. "It was about me."

"Oh, okay," Mariam said with no indication of whether or not she believed it.

One sandwich remained on the floor, and the chickens made a beeline for it. Mariam scooped it up before they made it there, receiving an indignant *"ba-GAW!"* from the nearest hen.

"It's roast chicken, you cannibals," Mariam said, waving the sandwich at them.

"Is Fisk around?" Sigrid asked.

Mariam took a big bite and said something inaudible through it. "…shtable handsh."

"What?"

Mariam swallowed. "Behind the manure pile building carts with the other stable hands."

Carts?

Whatever he was doing, it was a relief that someone had finally seen him.

"Thanks. I just have to…" Sigrid hesitated, but Mariam waved her off and turned to Aesa.

Wishing she could be in several places at once, Sigrid jogged to find Fisk. He was kneeling beside a half-made cart with a few other stable hands—and behind it were three more brand-new carts.

"Pass me the tooth-turner," he said to a boy, who rushed to hand him a tool Sigrid had never seen before.

When Sigrid stopped beside them, Fisk raised his head and fixed her with his eye holes. "Hey, Sigrid!"

"I've been trying to…" She blinked, her thoughts veering off. "Did you make all of these?"

Fisk nodded and motioned to the stable hands. "We did together."

"Wow. These look better than the ones we already have."

"They should be. I siphoned magic—"

"Of course you did."

"—from the hot springs so the steam will help it keep moving."

Sigrid shook her head in disbelief. "That's really smart."

He kept working, the tool making a *click-clack* as he put the fourth wheel onto the cart.

"Fisk, remember how you said you'd be willing to help figure out…" She hesitated.

Click-clack click-clack.

She turned to the boys. "Can you please give us a minute?"

They seemed relieved to be dismissed and left quickly for the shade of the barns.

When they were out of earshot, Sigrid continued. "…help us figure out the iron arrows we brought back from Svartalfheim?"

He tightened a bolt and gave the wheel a spin. "Oh yes! I've been trying to think of how they siphoned darkness like that, but…"

The wheel spun and spun, giving no signs of slowing.

When he added nothing more, Sigrid said, "The head sorcerer in Vanahalla is interested in talking to you about them."

Fisk froze. His mask made it hard to tell what he was thinking. Sigrid was going to prompt him when he said, "I'll finish this for Peter, and then I can talk to him."

Sigrid exhaled into a smile. "Thanks."

Anyone who was avoiding him and saying nasty things about him—anyone who was convinced he was a spy about to betray them—was about to be proven seriously wrong.

She crossed her arms, watching him work.

Spies…

Maybe there was more he could do. Maybe he *could* be a spy—but for them, not the Night Elves. Nobody from his world knew that he'd upgraded to a dire wolf mask, so they wouldn't recognize him. He should be safe. And if he succeeded, it would also make him win favor with everybody here.

She couldn't ask him to sneak into the enemy ranks and into the line of valkyrie fire, but what if he could slip in for just long enough to talk to a few elves—and maybe get allies? The memory of the lone elf who'd dispatched the guards at Ratatosk's prison came to mind. He was proof that Fisk might not be the only one willing to break away from the brutalities of his world.

"Fisk, do you think you'd be able to have a conversation with any of the Night Elves? Form an alliance, even?"

He grabbed the wheel, stopping it from spinning. "You want me to talk to them and see if they'll agree to turn traitor like I did?"

"Um. Something like that." *When he puts it like that, it sounds like a horrible thing to ask.*

She was about to backtrack when he said, "Do you remember how I used to wear a different mask than this one?"

"Vividly."

"See, the way things work in Svartalfheim is that the lowest ranks have herbivore-type masks, or else easy-to-kill beasts like jerffs. That's me, right? The runt. And I think…well, golly, if I was unhappy and willing to turn traitor, I bet others will be, too."

"Yes!" Sigrid's excitement burst from her lips. "That's brilliant. You think we can grab some of them and win them over as allies?"

"It sure is worth a try." He tinkered with something on the wheel, then faced her again, like he was about to say more. A silence passed. "Sigrid, who's in charge of designing the fortifications we're going to build?"

Sigrid froze. She hadn't thought about a design, but they couldn't just slam posts in to the ground at random. Since she was the one in charge of the ground troops, it fell on her to direct and assign people, so she'd better pick someone to come up with a plan. Peter was the one with most experience, so maybe he would know who to…

And then it hit her. Why hadn't she asked an actual *master of craftsmanship*, the elf responsible for building the best tree fort she'd ever seen, to help with building a wall to fend off the Svartalf King's army?

"Are you interested? Do you have any ideas?"

Fisk looked around the stable yard as if taking inventory. He mumbled and tapped a finger to his mask. "We can build a palisade. We'll sharpen the tops and angle them outward, you know? It'll stop them from climbing over."

Sigrid grinned. "I love it."

"We can also funnel the army toward us to make sure they're contained." Fisk made a *V* with his arms to demonstrate. "I'll work on a diagram."

Sigrid nodded enthusiastically. "Thanks, Fisk."

She let out a breath. His help would be crucial against the Night Elves, and she was looking forward to proving everybody wrong about him. In fact, between the new carts, the fortifications, the promise to get allies, and working with Harald, Fisk had the most crucial role out of everyone in this battle against Svartalfheim.

When he declared the cart finished and Sigrid helped him wheel it over to the others he'd made, they went to get Hestur. The sun moved rapidly higher in the sky, bringing them closer to noon when they would have to depart for the spring.

They mounted up, Fisk behind Sigrid—and for what might have been the first time in history, a valkyrie brought a Night Elf up to Vanahalla.

CHAPTER THIRTY-THREE

FIRE WITH FIRE

After leaving Fisk with Harald outside the Sorcerers' Tower, Sigrid raced to her chambers, where she put on her brand new, crisp white valkyrie uniform. She turned back and forth in the mirror, studying its effect on her body. It fit tighter than she was used to, but it made sense to avoid loose material in battle. She ran her hands down her arms and stomach, admiring how strong it made her look.

But nerves raged inside her.

She drew a shaky breath, holding her own gaze through the mirror. Between her light skin, blond hair, and gray eyes, she looked colorless enough to vanish on a snowy day. She patted her cheeks, trying to get some blood into her face so she wouldn't look like she was about to drop dead.

Mariam would've been given a proper uniform, too. She probably looked amazing in it. Was she putting it on right now? Was she also nervous about riding to the spring for a real battle as a valkyrie?

Aunt Kaia entered looking pale and sunken, her hair up in a tight bun reminiscent of General Eira. Her crown and robe remained as extravagant as ever. In her outstretched arms was a pile of beautiful, golden armor. "Fresh from the kiln."

Sigrid put on the breastplate and greaves, doing her best to look confident. The armor was sturdy and light, unlike anything she'd worn.

This, to her pleasure, completed the picture.

She was a *valkyrie*.

"You look ready for vengeance—like Víðarr ready to take on Fenrir," Aunt Kaia said.

Sigrid tried to place the myth her aunt was referring to but couldn't remember it. Her brain had been endlessly overflowing since moving to the hall. "I don't feel ready."

Aunt Kaia pulled her into a hug. "You'll be fantastic. I'm so proud of you."

Sigrid stiffened in her aunt's arms, hugging her back tentatively. Although the words didn't spark the same anger as when her mother had used the word *proud* weeks ago, she had yet to take down the invisible shield between them.

When they broke apart, Aunt Kaia smoothed Sigrid's braid. It was a loving, motherly gesture that made Sigrid's insides twist.

"Will you be okay here?" Sigrid asked.

"The reserve valkyries are on their way from Vindabek. Don't worry about me."

Sigrid checked her reflection one last time, hoping to find a confidence boost.

"Sigrid." Aunt Kaia paced the room, her shoes clacking softly, her gaze fixed on the wooden floor. "When I was a little girl, there was a general named Annhilde. She was effective but cruel. She would enact physical punishments on the valkyries during training, and she used psychological means to manipulate situations to her liking. When General Eira came up for a promotion, things got nasty. General Annhilde tried to trick General Eira in battle, and her plan backfired. She met her demise by her own hand."

Aunt Kaia paused, facing Sigrid. "What I mean to say is, General Eira had to fight hard to get where she is, and she's no stranger to a fierce power struggle. If she seems resistant to surrendering some power—well, that's why. It's nothing to do with you. General Eira might have years of experience, but you have *recent* experience, along with natural skills that any valkyrie would envy. Let your talent and sense of leadership shine through, Sigrid. Don't let anyone try to stop you."

Sigrid nodded, thankful for the encouraging words. "Do you think the fight will turn ugly, Aunt Kaia?"

"I have confidence in the valkyries, but I'm afraid of what we don't know about the Night Elves. We can surmise what'll happen based on past wars and our limited knowledge from trade agreements and cosmic relations…but do we *know* Svartalfheim? No. I don't think we do. And failing to know the enemy can be detrimental." She fussed over a lock of hair that'd come loose from her bun, staring at her reflection. Carefully, she said, "We ought to take a *fire-with-fire* approach. Óleifr wouldn't have been a fan of this angle, but he was nonconfrontational to a fault."

"Was he?" Sigrid asked, surprised to hear anything less than perfect about the late king.

Aunt Kaia's large eyes narrowed. A muscle tensed in her jaw. "A lot of Vanaheim's wealth comes from selling visions to other worlds. Prophetic knowledge is more valuable than gold. Óleifr got into the habit of giving them away for free in order to appease the foreign leaders."

"He gave away visions?" Sigrid hadn't even known about Vanaheim selling visions. Probably not common knowledge, but did the council know? And agree? "That seems a little…"

"Foolish? Frivolous? The actions of a boy with no backbone?" Aunt Kaia huffed at her reflection, squaring her shoulders and lifting her chin. "I loved my brother, but sometimes, he was not the leader Vanaheim needed."

Maybe Sigrid shouldn't be surprised to find out King Óleifr was less perfect than she'd believed. There was no such thing as perfection, after all.

The queen turned away from the mirror to scowl at the wall. Were her feelings about her brother a mix of good and bad, like her feelings about Helena? Which sibling did she like better?

"What's the *fire-with-fire* approach you want to try?" Sigrid turned to face her aunt instead of looking at each other through the mirror.

"I want to capture some of the Night Elves and take their weapons." Aunt Kaia crossed her arms. "If they're as great at craftsmanship as they're supposed to be, we can force them to build more and use their own weapons against them." She said this with a question behind her eyes, like she was afraid of how Sigrid would react.

Sigrid nodded. It was a bold plan, but maybe an effective one. "Fisk is helping Harald with the iron arrows. They're looking for a way to block the enchantment, so that's a start."

Aunt Kaia tilted her head, seeming less averse to the idea now that Harald approved of it. "Have you also asked that stable hand who looks like he's part elf?"

Sigrid furrowed her brow. "Oh, Roland? He's a Light Elf."

"Same thing." She waved a dismissive hand. "Can he help us?"

Sigrid blinked, the words taking a moment to absorb. "They're not the same," she said slowly.

"Elf is in the name. Human subclass, underground dweller roots. If we want an elf's help, we should look to Alfheim. At least they're an upper world."

A subclass?

Her aunt was obviously upset about what the Night Elves were doing, but anger sparked in Sigrid's gut at the comment. Where did that come from?

This didn't seem so different from the way the stable hands regarded Fisk. Maybe they'd lived through Night Elf attacks and had reason to fear them, but calling all elves a subclass was wrong. Roland couldn't be more different from the Svartalf King, and nor could Fisk.

"I disagree that elves are a subclass," Sigrid said, surprised by the sharpness in her tone. "Our war is against the Svartalf King and the army he's amassed—not all elves."

Aunt Kaia met her gaze, a brief widening in her eyes. There was a pause. "Yes. That's true. I shouldn't have said that."

They stood an arm's length apart, staring at each other, the threat of Vanaheim's ruin stretching taut between them.

Deep lines were etched into Aunt Kaia's face, bags weighed down her normally bright eyes, and sweat glistened on her smooth forehead. She wrung her hands, failing to mask the way they trembled. Dealing with the loss of her brother, becoming queen, and now an invasion had all taken its toll on her.

"Do you feel ready?" Aunt Kaia asked, the words catching.

The right thing would be to reassure her that Sleipnir would help them win. They needed to fight the Night Elves with their best weapons, and Sigrid had the best one of all. But she couldn't get the words out. Would her limited training and education be enough? She was nervous—terrified, even—to find out.

She nodded anyway, not confessing her fear, because fear was the last thing anyone needed right now.

Her heart galloped at a frantic pace to match Sleipnir's eight-beat stride.

Time to saddle up.

CHAPTER THIRTY-FOUR

A FAMILIAR SENSATION

Standing outside of Sleipnir's stall, it was hard to tell if Sigrid's frantic heartbeat was from her own nervousness or the stallion's strange power already reaching for her.

I can do this. I've controlled him before, and I can do it again.

As she unlatched the door with steady hands, he watched her closely, head high, nostrils flaring. The stable hands had thoroughly groomed him until he glistened like silver. A new black saddle accented his black mane and tail, along with a freshly polished steel breastplate and fur-lined boots around his eight legs.

He tossed his head impatiently.

Is he waiting for me to untie him so he can explode out of the barn?

Sigrid took a deep breath and let it out, putting on her helmet. Her mind was clear, her hands steady. *Now if I could just stay this way.*

Sleipnir behaved as she removed the muzzle and smoothed the hair on his face. His abnormal heat seeped through her gloves, making her pulse quicken to match his. He pawed a front hoof as she put on the crystal-studded bridle. She would have laughed it off if it were Hestur, but the stallion's bottled-up energy wound her nerves tighter.

Leading him from the barn and into the courtyard went

smoothly. She tossed the reins over his head, her heart pounding faster and faster.

"Good boy," she said, grateful he was cooperating.

So far, so good. Nothing left to do but get on.

With the golden barn doors at her back and an empty stretch of courtyard in front of her, she led him alongside the carved stump used to help riders mount up and put her foot in the stirrup.

Her heart pounded faster and faster, making her breaths come quickly.

Do it. If he acts up, I can jump off.

Holding her breath, she swung her leg over his back.

The moment her legs closed over his ribs, a familiar awareness surged through her. Sleipnir tensed, his ears turned back to listen, ready to do whatever she asked.

The last time this sensation overtook her, she'd been leading the valkyries over a landscape of red, lava-flecked sand. That adrenaline had been like nothing she'd experienced, coming out in a roar as they burst through the gates of Hel on what could have been a one-way journey. Now, the ghost of it trickled back.

Sleipnir tossed his head and pawed the cobblestones. She breathed into his anticipation, the sensation dousing her like a hot bath.

This stallion was created by the gods and trained to win any fight. He'd known lifetimes of victory under Odin and had spent the time since then wandering the nine worlds, waiting for his heir. All of that power and purpose pulsed through him, rising into Sigrid's legs, abdomen, and chest. There, it swelled in time with his pulse.

Ba-bump. Ba-bump.

Pressure built inside her, crimson, warm, like blood flowed in and had nowhere to go.

Sigrid vibrated, as ready as the war horse beneath her—ready for charging, fighting, *leading*.

Her senses sharpened, the chirping barn swallows behind her growing louder and clearer, every particle of the dust swirling under the bright, mid-day sunlight coming to her attention. She rolled her neck, letting out a slow breath.

Sleipnir coiled like a spring, responding to the pressure building between them.

Ba-bump. Ba-bump.

Their pulses quickened, synchronizing.

Sigrid squared her shoulders and tightened her grip on the reins. A little smile tugged the corner of her mouth. Had the feeling of riding Sleipnir been this intense before, or was their connection growing stronger?

I can handle it. Maybe she'd been afraid and uncertain before, but now, confidence flowed through her veins.

Far from terrifying, the sensation was *wonderful*.

"Let's go—"

The barest of nudges had him breaking into a gallop and stampeding over the cobblestones. They surged past the statues, fountains, and golden towers. Courtiers shouted and leaped out of the way, their words lost as she whipped by as fast as a lightning strike.

Sigrid whooped and wrapped her fingers in Sleipnir's mane, moving with his strides as they galloped over the bridge and down the grassy hill toward the valkyrie stables.

This stallion was completely unrivaled. Why had she been so afraid of getting on? Why had she ever been stressed about riding to meet the Night Elves? On Sleipnir, she would win against them. They could do *anything* together.

His eight-beat stride ate up the ground, the swaying grass blurring beneath them. Wind howled in her ears and stung her eyes. The stable grew nearer before she was ready for it. She wanted to keep galloping, to revel in this feeling for longer.

Valkyries and stable hands alike froze as she trotted into the yard.

At least a dozen carts had been loaded with supplies in the time she'd been gone, and several horses she'd never seen were hitched up and ready to go. The goats from the royal stable had also been brought down to help pull and were trying to eat each other's harnesses while they stood waiting.

Peter and Roland paused in the process of backing Hestur toward another cart. Hestur whinnied, looking as small and wispy as a pony from this height.

Roland raised both hands. "Finally!"

Peter smiled so widely that he seemed about to laugh. "There's a nice sight!"

Sleipnir tossed his head and snorted as if to announce his presence.

"Great work, everyone," Sigrid shouted. "We're leaving in twenty minutes."

The stable hands reacted at once, rushing into the barn to fetch the winged mares. The valkyries were slower to respond, whispering among themselves. Hisses followed her across the yard, rising above Sleipnir's eight-beat walk.

"I told you she didn't get rid of him."

"Where's she been keeping him?"

Sigrid scanned for Mariam, swallowing a bubble of disappointment when she didn't see her. Instead, she found General Eira striding from the barn with the stern expression of someone about to demand what the commotion was about.

The general froze, staring with her lips parted. Ylva sprinted out of the barn behind her, her dark hair flying loose like she'd been about to braid it, and stopped with a gasp. Gunni limped out a moment later, half of her golden armor on her body and half of it in her hands.

They cast Sigrid glares that were probably meant to be

haughty, but their awe betrayed them as they lingered on Sleipnir.

Sigrid turned away. Where was Mariam? They needed to talk before they left for battle.

From the meadow, a girl trotted up on a little black horse.

"Tóra?" Sigrid exclaimed, her stomach sinking. *Don't tell me there's been another horrible vision.*

The young Seer wore a black robe instead of riding trousers and had chosen a poor-fitting helmet. Her large, freckled nose extended past the brim, which sat crooked across her forehead. She tipped forward as Disa came to a halt, then folded awkwardly to dismount, nearly meeting the dirt with her face.

Sigrid moved to dismount. "Are you okay? Is everything—"

Tóra waved for her to stop. "Fine, fine. I'm glad I made it. We're leaving in a few, yeah?"

"*We*? Wait, are you coming with us?" Even with little experience, Sigrid knew it wasn't the smartest move to send the young Seer to the frontlines. "Is that…wise?"

"I'm yer messenger." Tóra put a hand proudly on her chest. "Since it's too dangerous to bring the Eye of Hnitbjorg to battle, Vala stayed behind to watch it. And I'll be here to receive any urgent messages from her."

Though not entirely convinced it was the safest place for Tóra to be, Sigrid had to appreciate her presence. "That'll be helpful."

"Vala also said I might be able to open a conduit with the Norns from the edge of the world. Magic runs strong near the spring, so the visions would be clearer."

"You can do that?" That could give them an incredible advantage. "Will the Eye or the Norns tell us how we can win the battle?"

Tóra shook her head, which made her helmet slip over her eyes. She pushed it back up. "Ye can never tell a god what to do. But if we're lucky, they might show us the outcome. Then we can change our path if we don't like it."

Tóra's gaze fell to Sleipnir's legs, and Sigrid swore she could see her silently counting to eight.

"Sigrid!" Fisk shouted, making them both turn. A large backpack bounced on his shoulders as he skidded to a stop at their horses' noses. Sticking out of the top was the indestructible wooden sword he'd crafted several weeks ago. Out of breath, he held up a piece of paper with diagrams all over it in red-and-black ink. "I made…some plans, and I think…if we can build the palisade like…" He braced himself with his hands on his knees, wheezing for breath, and held up a finger to motion for her to wait.

Tóra giggled.

Fisk straightened up, turning his mask toward her. "H-hello."

"You must be Fisk. I've heard about ye and watched ye in the Eye—oh, that sounds odd, doesn't it?"

There was a long pause, which Disa broke by snorting.

"I'm flattered to have been watched by a beautiful lady like yourself," Fisk said with such an air of formality that Sigrid squinted to make sure it was really him speaking.

Tóra ducked her head and fiddled with the buckle on the end of Disa's reins, failing to hide her blushing cheeks.

Choosing to ignore whatever was going on there, Sigrid prompted, "You already finished with Harald, then? Did you figure out the iron arrows?"

"Not yet." He lifted one shoulder. "I shared all I knew, and Harald said they would relay any discoveries to us."

Sigrid pursed her lips, disappointed.

"In the meantime, I brought you this." He waved the papers again. "Plans for the palisade. I think if we build it following these designs, we'll be able to do it as quickly as possible while making sure it's effective. It's about balance between speed and strength, you know? Plus, if we build it on the riverbank, the water will make it near impossible for them to climb over it."

Sigrid beamed. "Brilliant."

"Thank you." He performed a full bow, which almost made him fall over with the weight of his pack.

Sigrid fought back a smile. "We can fill everyone in on the journey. Do we have the tools we need to make this happen?"

He nodded.

"You're really smart, Fisk," Tóra said, breathless.

Fisk's nose tilted down, and he dug a toe into the dirt. He seemed not to know what to do with his hands before he settled on clasping them behind his back. "Thank you, my lady."

"It's time to leave," Sigrid said, getting fidgety in the saddle. "Are you ready to go, Fisk?"

He nodded, jabbing a thumb over his shoulder to indicate the backpack. "I'm all set!"

Sigrid scanned the gathering crowd, noting the way Sleipnir did the same. Synchronized and in control, her connection to him was so strong it was like an extra layer of armor.

The yard became a jumble of valkyries, carts, horses, and stable hands. Dust rose as wings flapped and hooves stomped. People shouted over each other, fetching forgotten items and adjusting tack. Horses whinnied as they sought their stable mates.

All of it came to Sigrid in rushes of sounds and colors, her senses sharper than ever. From the nearest stable hand to the furthest horse and cart, she tracked all of it.

At the far end of the rapidly forming caravan, Mariam was on foot, checking Aesa's girth and bridle. She adjusted her helmet and gathered her reins to mount up. As expected, she'd been given a new white uniform—and she looked stunning in it.

Sigrid's belly gave a pleasant swoop. She jumped off Sleipnir and handed the reins to Fisk. "One minute. Mariam!"

Mariam turned, her brow furrowed, as Sigrid ran over and stopped in front of her.

"Are you okay?" Sigrid asked, panting.

"Why wouldn't I be?"

She stepped closer. "I'm sorry I haven't been around. I brought you here, and then I left you, and now we're going to war—"

"You've had other priorities, Sigrid. I get that."

Sigrid searched her dark eyes, finding the faintest glint of fear. "What's going on? Are they being awful to you again?"

"No, that's… It's not just them." She let out a breath. "I guess I was naive about what I would find here. I thought I'd be able to get all of this evidence that my mom shouldn't have been banished and that my parents would be able to get on Ratatosk's next ride to Vanaheim. But it's obviously not that simple. Some people aren't sorry to see a traitor get what she deserves."

"Those people are idiots," Sigrid said firmly. "Anyone who knew your mom probably knows they didn't get the whole story. Even General Eira thinks so."

"Gunni said my mom had a reputation for skipping practice," Mariam said, the words seeming to flood out. She blinked rapidly, her eyes glossy. "She said she hung out with the wrong crowd and nobody was surprised when she was sent off. So I'm not even sure what I'm doing here, and what I'm trying to prove, because everyone's already made up their minds—"

"Don't listen to her or anyone else. You know your mom is a good person, and Helena probably manipulated her the same way she did me. If people hate you, hate *us*, for being daughters of traitors, it's their problem. We know the truth better than anyone."

Mariam nodded, her lips pressed together in an attempt at a smile. Her cheeks lifted, but her eyes stayed sad.

"Plus, even if your mom did skip practice once in a while, who cares? Nobody's perfect." Sigrid moved closer and grabbed Mariam's hands, rubbing her thumbs over them until Mariam looked up. "Vanaheim is lucky to have you fighting for us. In this battle, you're going to prove it. You're an amazing valkyrie, and I bet your mom is, too, and they're going to realize how much they lost by not having you two around all these years."

Mariam held her gaze, and then her lips twisted into a tiny smile. "Time to prove them all wrong, I guess."

"Let's fight our hardest." Sigrid squeezed her hands, committing the feeling to memory. Why couldn't they have had time together before the Night Elves came? This was all too soon.

Remembering why she came looking for Mariam, she stepped closer. "Look, I don't know what's going to happen after we leave, and how long we have before we run into the Night Elves, but before we go…" She drew a breath. "I never wanted to keep us a secret. I just *really* liked the privacy."

Mariam let out a breath of laughter, glancing sideways to a few lingering stares. "I know what you mean."

"I liked that nobody was gossiping about us or wondering why I fought so hard to keep you here. But the thing is…I don't want to waste another day keeping us a secret. Not when I feel…" Sigrid swallowed hard as she ran out of words, and there was only one thing left to do.

She leaned in and kissed Mariam.

After a brief, surprised pause, Mariam kissed her back, her soft hand sliding behind Sigrid's neck and sending a ripple of goose bumps where she touched. For a blissful minute, their lips moved against each other, their breaths hitching, their bodies pressing closer, and heat roared through Sigrid's middle.

Nearby, someone gasped, and a couple of whistles and calls broke out.

Let them.

Sigrid grinned into the kiss, causing their teeth to clack, and Mariam pulled back with a full laugh. If anyone stood around whispering about them, Sigrid was too busy drowning in the dark pools of Mariam's eyes to notice or care. She was proud to be with Mariam, and the valkyries could talk all they wanted about it.

"Let's go fight some Night Elves, princess," Mariam said with a wink.

Sigrid bit her lip, breathless. "See you in Myrkviðr."

As she wove through the winged mares and returned to Sleipnir, her heart took flight. Was it fair to call Mariam her girlfriend, or was it too soon for that word?

Not the time. Focus on the upcoming battle.

All of the pieces of her life were coming together into a slice of perfection beyond anything she'd dreamed of, and she was ready to fight her hardest to protect it.

She hurried over to Sleipnir, her pulse synchronizing with his the moment she grabbed the reins and her knuckles brushed his neck. She mounted up quickly, relieved when the strength returned.

A grin pulled at her lips. *Unstoppable.*

She was a valkyrie princess about to lead her own division through Myrkviðr on the most powerful steed in the nine worlds. She wouldn't go into this battle reluctantly and driven by fear— she would charge in, ready to show the worlds everything she was meant to be.

CHAPTER THIRTY-FIVE

VISIONS OF BEARS

At the edge of Vanaheim, the forest ended in a vast meadow with the spring of Hvergelmir cutting through. The wide, deep river flowed from left to right, curving away from Vanaheim. Sigrid scanned the swaying grass for threats—the place where she and Mariam had been kidnapped the day they met Fisk—but there were no signs that anyone or anything had passed through the area recently.

Sleipnir tossed his head impatiently.

Sigrid agreed. All this waiting for battle was making her antsy. "Let's go!" she shouted to the stable hands. "Bring the carts to the riverbank. Start setting up the palisade. We have to set up before the Night Elves arrive."

The caravan of stable hands and the borrowed horses pulling carts flattened the meadow on their way to the spring, exhaustion making them quiet. Hestur marched among them, as energetic as ever after the seven-hour trek.

Among the group were the two sorcerers Harald had sent, Mabil and Ragnarr, who wore the same style of plain brown robes and had such a height difference that it was like looking at Disa next to Sleipnir. The pair had introduced themselves earlier in short bursts—happy to serve, experienced in battle, old enough to be your parents—before retreating to themselves on the journey, talking and planning in low voices.

Sigrid didn't know what to make of them, but as long as they helped win the war, they could be as odd as they wanted.

As the ground troops settled into their duties, Sigrid studied the landscape that would become their battleground. Bisected by the spring, the meadow was wide and open on their side. On the opposite bank, it faded into the misty space between worlds. *The elves will come from there.* This was the only place they could enter Vanaheim—and they were about to be stopped in their tracks.

The sky was empty. The junior valkyries, including Mariam, would have flown into the mist earlier to find the senior valkyries, which left Sigrid and her ground troops alone.

Would the valkyries get back in time for the Night Elf attack? What if they didn't and it was up to Sigrid and the stable hands to defend Vanaheim? Or what if the valkyries ran into the Night Elves out there and Sigrid was here with the stable hands with no idea that they needed help?

A squirming, fidgety sensation rose from the saddle and into her, filling her with the need to move. She huffed and urged Sleipnir into a trot, checking on everyone as they positioned the carts along the riverbank.

"Fisk," Sigrid shouted, and Fisk straightened up from amid the stable hands, his mask making him stand out. "We're relying on your diagram for the palisade, okay? Tell everyone what to do. Peter? Make sure they listen?"

Peter nodded, his jaw tight. He kept checking over his shoulder toward the mist, like a compulsion.

Sigrid continued through the area as they started unloading wood from the carts, but by the time she returned, they were still at it. Her pulse thumped in her ears. Why weren't they moving faster? Did no one understand *urgency*? Did they not realize that failing to set up the palisade in time meant risking a disastrous attack?

She dismounted to help. When her feet hit the ground, she stretched her arms, discovering her whole body was wound up tighter than if she'd wrapped herself in stable bandages. Everything seemed muted, dull, and a couple of steps had the world tilting at the edges. She rubbed her forehead beneath her helmet, taking a moment to breathe.

Why am I so faint?

Small hooves pit-patted up beside her. Tóra smiled at her from Disa's back. Beneath her ill-fitting helmet, which was tipped back so the brim pointed skyward, her pale cheeks had a pink tinge from the ride.

"Hi—oh." Her smile fell.

"What? Have you seen a vision?" Sigrid asked.

"No, it's… Are ye okay, Yer Highness?"

"I'm fine," Sigrid said shortly. She didn't want word to get back to General Eira that she couldn't even handle herself before the battle.

She led Sleipnir over to Hestur's cart to help the stable hands, and Tóra followed. Disa's hooves made a delicate *pit-pat-pit-pat*, while Sleipnir's made a rattling eight-beat *thumpa-thumpa-thumpa-thumpa*.

"Ye looked about ready to faint, Yer Highness."

Sigrid ignored her words, opting for a distraction. "Tóra, after all of our lessons together, I'm offended that you're still calling me *Your Highness*."

Tóra flushed. "Sigrid, then. Do ye need a rune for energy? Pain reduction, maybe?"

"No. Thanks." The last thing she needed was more energy. Her heart might explode.

She checked over Hestur, who was happily eating grass, then left Sleipnir beside him and grabbed a hammer. "Tell me, what do you need from me in order to open a conduit with the Norns?"

She dragged a post over to where Roland was busy

hammering another one into the ground.

Tóra dismounted and followed with Disa in tow. "Ye should focus on fighting. I'll come to ye if I see any visions. Vala is working with the Eye back home, too, and she'll send me messages with anything she learns."

"I see." All of this rune and magic stuff was complicated. "And what about…the reason for my lessons? Loki. Should I try to talk to—"

Tóra's eyes widened, and she shook her head vigorously. "Ye aren't ready for that. Definitely not. And to think if we open a conduit with Loki during a *battle*…" She shuddered.

Sigrid nodded, a little bit of relief trickling through her. Maybe Aunt Kaia would be disappointed with that answer, but oddly enough, Sigrid trusted Tóra, even if she didn't know her very well. Her kind smile and tilted helmet made it hard to see in her anything but an earnest desire to help.

After planting the post along the curving shoreline, angling its sharp tip toward the enemy so they couldn't climb over, she swung the hammer down on it. *Thwap.* It sank a couple of inches.

Away from Sleipnir, Sigrid could focus better on the people around her, and she glanced back at Tóra. "Where did you study runes, by the way?"

"Nowhere special. My mom and dad bought me a lot of books when we realized I was a Seer. I'm from Appletoft. Have ye heard of it?"

"Oh! I actually have." *Thwap.* She'd read the name for the first time in one of Aunt Kaia's books the other night while studying Vanaheim's maps. This explained her accent. *Thwap.* "Farming town, right?"

"That's right. Few hours that way." She pointed left, back toward the forest. "When I started showing Seer traits as a kid, my parents were beside themselves. They sent a letter to Vanahalla straight away, and Vala kept in touch as I grew older. I'm the only known Seer born this generation. The whole town made a big fuss about me going to Vanahalla. My parents would've come for the ceremony, but they had to tend the farm."

"How did you know you were a Seer?" Sigrid asked, going to get another post. It was a nice distraction talking to Tóra—and an important one if she was to figure out who was replacing Vala one day.

"My parents told me I started saying odd stuff when I was a toddler. Once, my mom was going to feed some breakfast scraps to the chickens and I said, 'Bring Sköll.' Sköll was our dog. And she wasn't going to, but I threw a fit 'til she did. 'Bring Sköll! You need Sköll!' And you know what happened?"

Sigrid shook her head.

"A bear came, growling and everything. He wanted the food my mom had. Sköll chased it away and she ran inside screaming. Bring Sköll, I'd insisted." Tóra drew a breath and let it out in a big huff. "Things like that kept happening. Foresight. I saved them from another bear not two months later, same thing. That was how they knew."

"Lucky for your mother." Sigrid paused before raising her hammer. "Do all of your early visions involve bears?"

Tóra considered. "Well, we lived beside a river that had a lot of fish in it."

Sigrid laughed. "Your home sounds…wonderful." With loving and supportive parents, a fun childhood, and a cosmic calling everyone had celebrated, her life was everything Sigrid dreamed of. Instead of jealousy, Sigrid was glad Tóra hadn't had to go through all she had.

Tóra gave another hiccupy laugh, then gasped softly.

Sigrid looked back to find Fisk headed their way.

"We'll be able to get the palisade built in two hours at this rate." He flitted up to their sides, panting. "And I'm going to get you allies. I promise. I'll sneak around with the stable hands and grab a few runts from the back of the army."

"Excellent," Sigrid said, a lot lighter at the prospect of getting some Night Elf allies. They could help figure out the iron arrows *and* how to defeat their king.

The palisade was coming along now. The rows were angled to funnel the elves to a point, making them easier to kill. Between the wide, deep river, the palisade, and the valkyries, the elves didn't stand a chance. They were blocked by water, land, and air, just like Sigrid had planned.

Only a fool would attack Vanaheim.

"I was thinking, Fisk," Tóra said, seeming to like the sound of his name, "you're like, a *secret defender* of Vanaheim."

Fisk puffed out his chest. "In a way, I suppose."

"Vanaheim is so lucky to have you as an ally," Tóra said, her face turning a tomato-like shade.

"Not as lucky as they are to have you as a Seer, my lady."

Sigrid pressed her lips together. *Am I this awkward toward Mariam?*

Shouts rose around them.

All three of them started.

An enormous shadow came toward them out of the mist— nearly a hundred winged mares and riders descending from the sky.

CHAPTER THIRTY-SIX

VANAHEIM'S DEFENSES

"They're back!" Peter shouted, abandoning the palisade to follow the shadows of the winged mares coming to land. His excitement echoed in the faces of many, and the atmosphere around them changed like a beam of sunlight in this otherwise stormy day.

Sigrid let out a breath of relief, immediately scanning for Mariam. She hadn't seen this many mares in one place since before the seniors departed months ago.

Mares landed, their hooves sounding like a hailstorm—and in the midst of all the greetings, someone shouted, "Peter!"

In the cluster of people and horses, Peter and a valkyrie launched at each other in a desperate hug. They grabbed each other's faces and kissed, stumbling sideways.

"Um—" *What?* Shock cascaded over Sigrid, followed by embarrassment for watching this private moment.

Since when was Peter dating someone? Why hadn't he mentioned it? And had his girlfriend's absence secretly weighed on him all these months?

As they finished kissing and peeled away from each other, Sigrid could finally see who it was—Leah, a willowy senior valkyrie in her late twenties.

A little wave of relief hit her. Not that Sigrid had any right to tell Peter who to date, but she was glad to see him with someone nice, as opposed to one of the many valkyries who went out of their way to treat her like a barn rat.

Tears glistened on Leah's cheeks, but even with stress making her look years older, she stood tall and strong. She'd been fighting for weeks—her dark, curly hair was shockingly longer than when they'd departed, and her white uniform was tattered and stained with dirt and blood—but she was ready to fight again. Her winged mare stood coolly behind her, surveying the scene.

Her heart ached for them, separated for so long, and now that they were finally reunited...

Sigrid set off, searching for Mariam before she could think about it. But she was unable to pick her out among all the matching gold armor, white uniforms, and winged white mares. Her heartbeat stumbled, and she pushed her way through the crowd, breaths coming faster.

Where are you?

When she finally spotted Aesa, distinct by the red markings on her shoulder and haunches, a squeak of relief passed her lips. "Mariam!"

Mariam looked up, a smile spreading across her face.

All of the tension left Sigrid's body at the sight. *How will I be able to focus on the battle if I'm worrying like this?*

"Bit of an improvement from the last time we hung out in this meadow," Mariam said as they walked to meet each other. "Stuck in a pig cage, waiting for Fisk to set us free..."

"I'll take this any day," Sigrid said, remembering their lucky escape. "Though I wouldn't mind being stuck in close quarters with you again."

Mariam pulled Sigrid in, pressing their bodies together with clear intent. Sigrid's heart skipped as their lips met. She slid a hand around Mariam's waist and held her tighter.

"Ahem."

They stepped apart quickly, Mariam giving a little gasp.

Sigrid's lips tingled and her face burned when she recognized the incredibly tall and muscular valkyrie standing nearby. The winged mare at her back was close to Sleipnir's height and just as thick.

"G-General Ulfhilda!" Sigrid stood at attention. She swallowed to try and get rid of the tremor in her voice. "It's good to see you."

Ugh, was she standing there the whole time we were kissing?

Sigrid looked at Mariam, who awkwardly jabbed her thumb over her shoulder in an *I'll-be-over-here* gesture.

"Glad to be back in Vanaheim," General Ulfhilda said in her deep, gravely tone. "We received the letter from Queen Kaia, and she explained about you and Sleipnir. I wanted to congratulate you on securing Odin's steed, Princess Sigrid."

She extended a meaty hand, and Sigrid was so stunned that it took her a moment to reach out and take it. "Th-thank you, General."

They shook hands, and Sigrid blinked back tears as the woman crushed her fingers. *Gods, she's strong.*

"Are you leading the junior division, Princess?"

"No," Sigrid said quickly, glancing at General Eira and praying she hadn't overheard. "I'm leading the, um, ground troops."

"Ground...?" General Ulfhilda scanned the stable hands, who swiftly built the palisade from Fisk's designs. "I see. Very good."

Sigrid suppressed a smile. That was one more valkyrie, an active duty general no less, who thought she'd had a good idea. "Did Queen Kaia's letter explain the elves' new weapons?"

The general's scowl was fierce. "Yes. The iron arrows. Any new information on them?"

"The sorcerers are still studying what they're made of and if there's any way of stopping their imbued magic. We have an elf ally who gave them valuable information." Sigrid shifted on her feet, wishing she could offer more. "I just wanted to make sure you knew. Until there's a way of stopping them, we need to be extremely careful."

General Ulfhilda nodded. "Not much we can do except hope they don't hit us, I'm afraid."

This plan provided zero comfort, but it was true. They would have to fight to defend Vanaheim and protect its people, even with the risk of getting hit.

A valkyrie's ultimate purpose.

A few senior valkyries in General Ulfhilda's division caught Sigrid's eye and nodded. They would be fighting this war together, differences in age and station set aside to defend their world.

"Let's convene while we have the chance," General Ulfhilda said, drawing up to her full and impressive height. "Valkyries! Gather around. We might not have long."

Mariam returned to Sigrid's side, smiling in a way that told her she'd overheard that whole conversation. They held hands while the valkyries, mares, stable hands, and sorcerers all clustered before the generals.

"Valkyries," General Ulfhilda shouted from the towering height of her winged mare. "Guardians of the upper worlds. Your gods-given purpose is to protect and defend the vulnerable. Today, our world and our people need us."

Only the muted sounds of shifting leather and armor were heard as the crowd remained silent, hanging on every word she spoke. The skin on Sigrid's arms pebbled over, and she shivered.

"This fight is not only for your home, but for the home of everybody you know and love. The Night Elves have come to rob us of our world's joy, its light, its beauty. Together, sisters, we will push the Night Elves back. And if they won't go"—the general let the words hang for a moment—"we will kill every single one who steps foot onto our soil."

Mariam squeezed Sigrid's hand tighter. Around them, it was

like a current moved across the crowd, everyone standing taller and nodding.

"The fight will be hard, and they will outnumber us—but nobody in the nine worlds can beat the valkyries. Remember that. Remember you own the skies. You will feel tired and afraid, but you will continue to *own the skies*."

A few senior valkyries cheered and whooped, their energy spreading like a wildfire. Sigrid's pulse picked up and her senses sharpened as her body prepared her for the inevitable.

The general nodded as she paced her mare and gazed upon her troops. "You're going to be tested, and there will be times when you feel overwhelmed by fear and exhaustion, but know that this is what it means to be one of the mighty valkyries. Use those feelings to fuel you, and we will prevail for Vanaheim!"

General Ulfhilda thrust her fist in the air, and a chorus of voices rose to echo her.

"For Vanaheim!"

Sigrid's breath caught at the powerful display as the generals began barking orders to their divisions, commanding some valkyries to patrol the sky while others stayed back. She, Mariam, and the stable hands were the only ones who hadn't echoed the cry—the only ones who hadn't experienced a battle like this before.

She exchanged a look with Mariam, hoping for reassurance. Mariam's eyes were wide—a bit of fear, a bit of exhilaration.

Oh, gods.

If Sigrid hadn't known what to expect in the battle preparations, how was she supposed to handle the battle itself?

They held each other's hand for another second of safety before parting ways.

"Keep building the palisade," Sigrid told her ground troops, willing her heart to stop hammering so hard against her ribs. "Move quickly. We don't know how much time we have."

It didn't take long to locate Mabil and Ragnarr. They were already standing at the built section of palisade with their hands pressed to the posts.

As Sigrid drew closer, she noticed a couple of runes carved into the wood. "Anything I can do?"

"Nothing, Your Highness," Mabil said. "We work best like this."

And they really did. While Ragnarr carved a rune at his height, shorter Mabil worked on the second rune below it.

"We'll be as quick as we can to make this impenetrable," Mabil said.

Ragnarr simply grunted.

Sigrid nodded, satisfaction surging as all of the pieces of their defense came together. "Perfect."

She ran back to the unfinished section and grabbed a post and a hammer. Roland hurried over, gave her an exhilarated grin, and set to work at her side. They might not finish in time, but she was going to give it her all.

Yet she hadn't even finished pounding it into the ground when six valkyries descended from the sky, shouting frantically. "They're coming! Just over there!"

Sigrid's heart jumped into her throat, her limbs growing cold as an icy sensation flooded her veins.

They were out of time.

The Night Elves were here.

CHAPTER THIRTY-SEVEN

A FLOOD
OF DARKNESS

Sigrid dropped her hammer on Roland's foot, who cursed loudly.

The Night Elves? Already?

Shouts broke out across the meadow. Everyone looked into the distance, waiting for whatever nightmare would come out of the mist. The generals reacted first, snapping quick orders that had the valkyries vaulting up onto their mares and launching into the air, the long grass swaying in their wakes. They spread across the sky in five *V* formations.

"Keep building!" Sigrid shouted, jolting the stable hands back into action. "It doesn't have to be perfect. Just get the posts up."

Even an unfinished palisade would impede the Night Elves.

While the stable hands hammered posts into the ground as fast as they could and the sorcerers reinforced the wood with runes, the Night Elves emerged through the mist on the other side of the river.

Sigrid couldn't help freezing in place as they rolled over the land like a blanket of darkness, moving like flitting shadows. Her pulse pounded in her ears as something primal overtook her, telling her to *run*—run away from that chilling, otherworldly force coming toward them.

But she couldn't back away.

She was a valkyrie, ready to meet enemies with strength and bravery.

Even if her legs trembled while doing so.

Overhead, shadows swept across the meadow and river as the valkyries flew to meet them. War cries filled the air.

General Ulfhilda's shout spread across the sky like thunder. "Fire!"

Sigrid stared in awe as hundreds of spears rained down and punctured the army like a popped bubble. The shadows scattered and swirled like a disturbed pond, and their retaliating arrows shot up toward the valkyries—none of them able to hit the mares. They either fell short or missed their target completely, the mares too far and too fast.

"Yes!" Sigrid whispered, a jolt of victory shooting through her veins.

Regaining feeling in her limbs, she raced for Sleipnir, weaving through half-erected posts and carts, leaping over tools. She might not be in the sky, but she could throw a spear from the ground while the stable hands continued to build.

"Split, circle narrow, weave thrice!" General Ulfhilda's orders faded in and out as she flew over the field, directing her troops.

In short glances, Sigrid saw how the valkyries split down the middle and looped back, making a criss-cross pattern like a weaving loom. Flashes of Mariam and Aesa darted in and out, keeping pace with the others.

Within seconds, they reaped the benefits of being in the sky. Even with an army a thousand strong, the elves couldn't retaliate against the valkyries so high overhead. They broke apart as they tried to fend off the zig-zagging white mares working to keep them contained.

Fools…

Sigrid grabbed Sleipnir and mounted up, sucking in a sharp breath at the surge of power in their connection. His energy bled into her like water from the hot springs biting her skin, and she had to draw a steadying breath, channeling the power, letting it become a part of her.

Her pulse quickened.

Ba-bump. Ba-bump.

She adjusted her legs and shortened the reins.

Channel it.

Sleipnir's height brought her above the palisade, leaving a clear view of the army, whose focus was on the swirling valkyries keeping them on the edge of the mist between worlds. They were too far away for Sigrid to fire at—but she twirled her spear, ready to use it if they came closer.

While keeping an eye on the battle, she nudged Sleipnir into pacing along the open section of the palisade. Questions shot through her mind as her senses sharpened, taking in the swarm of masks and armor across the way. Where was the Svartalf King? With the way the elves all blended and their weapons swung through the air, his antlers and iron crown would be impossible to spot. Even more baffling—how long had he been preparing for this invasion? Given the size of the army, he must have planned it for years, and yet none of them knew this was coming.

Aunt Kaia's words haunted her. They knew so little about Svartalfheim, and their relationship with the darkest world was next to nothing. What else had they overlooked?

The stable hands must have noticed the size of the army, too, because tight expressions and a heavy silence surrounded her as they continued to work on the palisade.

"Good job, everyone," she shouted, determined not to let fear plague her division. "As long as we keep them from crossing the spring, we're winning. Our part is just as important as the valkyries. We have just as crucial a role in keeping the Night Elves out of Vanaheim."

"Yeah!" Roland shouted, swinging his hammer down on a post.

Peter gave a battle cry, sweat streaming as he timed his swings with Roland's. The stable hands followed their example, quickening their pace. Shouts, battle cries, and words of encouragement rang across the meadow.

Sigrid's heart skipped. They could do this. She was leading the ground team the same way the generals overhead directed their troops into the most effective attack formations.

"Halfway there!" Peter shouted.

A quick scan of the palisade had her insides hollowing out. Now that she studied the space and the size of the invading army, halfway wasn't enough. They wouldn't stop the elves with a wall like this. It was erected in patches, with several gaps big enough to let the enemy pour through.

Across the river, the distance between the shadowy army and the opposite bank looked a lot narrower than it had a moment ago.

Sigrid gripped her spear tighter.

The ground troops would have to join the fight soon.

"Juniors, split left-heed! Pause to aim!" General Eira shouted, and her division split in the middle, the right launching spears while the left slowed and lifted in unison. Mariam was among the right. Edith shouted to her, pointing, and Mariam swooped in behind to stay in formation.

Sigrid's pulse pounded in her ears at the thought of Mariam trying to learn the maneuvers, use her weapon, and stay safe all at once. Gratitude toward Edith rushed through her, because if even one valkyrie helped her, that was enough.

The valkyrie divisions had split up to try and keep the enemy contained, but shadows kept pouring out to the left and right as they approached the river, as if the valkyries were trying to contain liquid. And although a lot of Night Elves lay sprawled in the grass across the river, their armor made them hard to kill, and the valkyries' spears were more likely to knock them over than to finish them off if they didn't aim perfectly.

While the elves still hadn't managed to send a single arrow or spear high enough to hit a valkyrie, they held strong, and the impossibility of stopping a thousand elves closed around Sigrid, making her chest tighten until she felt like she was suffocating.

How are we supposed to win?

The Night Elf army was almost at the opposite bank.

Every shout, whoosh of a spear, and swinging hammer competed for attention in Sigrid's ears, her heightened senses overwhelming her ability to think. She exhaled slowly. Channeling the strength of the stallion beneath her, she lifted her arm. She aimed—and hesitated.

It took her a moment to understand why her arm refused to move.

Wherever her spear landed, she would be aiming to kill. She hadn't really thought about how it would feel to stand across from an enemy and know it wasn't about disarming or knocking them out to escape—she had plenty of experience with that—but about eliminating the threat completely.

She would be making a lot of kills today. But so would the other valkyries. They'd all ridden here to defend their home from invaders, and they would do whatever was necessary.

Jaw set, she launched her spear into the swirling shadows across the bank.

It drove hard into a Night Elf's chest, knocking him back so he took out several more with him.

Sigrid let out a battle cry that was echoed by the stable hands.

And with that same breath and surge of triumph, Sleipnir's power overtook her with the same totality that water overtakes a drowning swimmer. It poured into her body, unstoppable, making her want to fight with everything she had. The tiny part of her that feared it was extinguished.

"Keep building!" she roared. "Bring the carts closer. Use them as an extra barricade."

The nearest stable hands cast her startled looks.

Sleipnir reared, erupting from their combined energy. When he touched down, they galloped along the riverbank, scanning for places where the army pushed too far ahead. There, she threw her spear, trying to push back the flood of shadows. The stallion responded like they were of one mind, agile on his hooves, exploding into a gallop and stopping abruptly as she reined him in.

A knot of frustration tightened in her gut as she was forced to stay on this side of the bank when the battle was across the way. But she fought as best she could—an opponent on the ground that the elves didn't consider as they all looked skyward.

"Your Highness!" Mabil appeared on Sigrid's left. "There's a water curse I'd like to try. It won't hold in such a powerful spring, but it will help keep them back."

"Do whatever you have to." Sigrid didn't take her eyes off her targets. "Anything to stop them from setting foot on this side of the water."

Mabil slipped through a gap in the palisade and ran for the river, where she crouched on the bank.

Suddenly, a shriek split the sky, and a shadow fell over them.

Sigrid reined Sleipnir to a halt, a gasp escaping her lips.

A senior valkyrie broke formation and spiraled toward the ground.

Sigrid's heart plummeted with the mare. Gasps rose around her.

The mare neared the ground like a leaf in the fall, her wings beating erratically. In the saddle, General Marta, who led one of the senior divisions, had an iron arrow sticking out of her side, tendrils of darkness snaking over her white uniform.

CHAPTER THIRTY-EIGHT

TARGETS

General Marta's mare whinnied as darkness erupted from the arrow and crept over her rider like ivy around a tree. It stretched out, unstoppable, engulfing the white feathers of her wings. She landed hard among the stable hands, folding her wings over her back in an effort to protect her rider.

"Pull the arrow out!" Sigrid cried, nudging Sleipnir into a gallop.

Peter looked from Sigrid to the arrow. "What if—"

"She's a goner if that darkness overtakes her!"

Gritting his teeth, he lunged forward and yanked it out of General Marta's side. The webs of darkness snapped and clung to him as if scrambling for something to hold onto. He shook his arm and brushed them off until they dissipated.

The valkyrie slumped forward onto her mare's neck, gasping and coughing. The tear in her shirt looked singed at the edges, the skin beneath it bloody and mangled. She slumped, semi-conscious, as the stable hands pulled her from the mare's back.

Sigrid swore. *We can't afford to lose a general.*

"Grab the medical bag," Peter shouted. "Clear off Hestur's cart. We'll use it as a bed. Roland, help me carry her over."

Everyone leaped into action. Ragnarr abandoned the palisade to sprint over and help.

"Flank turn, left-left!" General Ulfhilda boomed.

Overhead, the valkyries redoubled their efforts with rage fueling them. Mariam swooped through the sky with the juniors, the golden spear flying from her hand and returning on command.

The army was a blur of shadows intent on crossing over. Pinpointing the source of the arrow was impossible, which meant anyone could be in danger of being hit next.

Sigrid's breaths came fast, anger burning under her skin. As soon as she found the Svartalf King, she would set to work strangling him.

"Sigrid!" Tóra ran up to them, stopping in her tracks when Sleipnir snorted and tossed his head.

"Have you been able to—" Sigrid waved a hand, struggling to understand how the Eye and the Norns worked. "Connect to the Norns or whatever?"

Tóra shook her head, teary. "They won't answer me. I don't know what's going on. I can open a conduit, but they don't want to show me anything. Vala said the Eye hasn't received any visions, either."

It must have taken a lot of effort, because her face shone with sweat and her curly red hair was impressively frizzy.

"Keep trying until you get them to answer." Sigrid barely kept her frustration in check. Was Tóra the problem or was something else going on? This would be a really good time for the Norns to show them a vision of the battle's outcome.

She spun Sleipnir around. "Go! And stay out of the way."

While Tóra skittered backward, Sigrid fired more shots across the river, and the valkyries did the same from overhead. Sleipnir fought her for control, wanting to go where the fighting was thickest. Sigrid allowed him to take her there.

Elf after elf dropped to the ground, some winded from a hit to their chainmail, others injured or killed from a hit to a weak spot in their leather. Sigrid aimed for the eye holes in their masks, piercing whatever semblance of a face lived inside.

The army teetered on the opposite bank, blocked by the water, which grew more turbulent by the minute.

Mabil was still at the shore, dangerously exposed, the source of the turbulence. The water roiled and steamed while waves grew steadily larger. Where they hit the opposite bank, they hissed and spat, and elves jumped out of the way.

But it wasn't enough.

They surged forward in a shadowy mass, their armor protecting them, and formed a line at the water's edge. The king had to be near—she'd never seen Night Elves this organized.

What are they doing now?

"Bridge!" Fisk shouted, pointing with his wooden sword. "They're going to build a bridge!"

"With what?" Sigrid exclaimed—but as the words came out, she saw it.

The elves carried a log forward and dumped it in the water with a splash. Another log followed close behind, and then another. They moved with precise coordination, placing the logs, tying them together, and pushing them out, forming a floating bridge across the narrowest part of the river.

"Ground troops, hurry up!" Sigrid yelled. "If they get across, this palisade is the only thing stopping them."

The water splashed up and over the logs, its heat burning the wood, but they kept on building—working faster than anything the valkyries could disrupt with their attacks.

An arrow shot toward Mabil and missed her by inches. She fell back, and the river instantly became less turbulent.

"Mabil, get back to safety!" Losing their sorcerers would be disastrous. Sigrid nudged Sleipnir into a gallop and headed toward the bridge. "Valkyries, shoot the ones building! Kill them!"

The bridge was a bottleneck. If they hurried, they could still stop them from getting across.

While Mabil ran, General Eira led the juniors lower, firing rapidly to keep the elves back. Edith barrel rolled to avoid an arrow. Ylva swerved to avoid another.

Mariam hadn't been fired at, but Sigrid still wanted to scream at General Eira for putting her at risk. *Not so close!*

The valkyries moved in to attack again, the mares swooping over top of the ground troops as they fired at the elves building the bridge. The elves retaliated, their arrows and lances missing and falling short—except for one.

General Eira roared and broke formation, plummeting with an iron arrow in her side. Her mare, Drifa, whinnied, tossing her head as she lost forward momentum.

"No!" Sigrid screamed, one shout among many.

Drifa splashed into the river, sending high waves that soaked the bank. With a blast of air, she resurfaced, blowing her nostrils. She paddled for shore, using her wings to help, while General Eira coughed up water from the saddle. The arrow stuck out of her side, precisely through the gap in her armor. Darkness spread over her, covering her side, her legs, her arms.

The valkyries assembled to block the elves' view of the general while Drifa swam. Cries rose as the juniors shouted to her. Sigrid threw her spear as well, helping them along.

Darkness consumed the general, enveloping her in a web of nightfall while she shouted and struggled against it. She got a hand around the arrow and pulled hard, letting out a stifled shout.

The stable hands raced forward with medical supplies and led her to safety. There, near Hestur and the other cart horses and goats, General Marta lay with her waist bleeding. Her mare was still at her side, which meant she was alive—but would she survive that terrible hit?

Sigrid's body was a kettle, bubbling with so much anger she trembled. "Protect the generals!"

Overhead, a mare swooped lower, and Mariam shouted, "What?"

"They're saving the iron for the generals!"

Mariam cursed. "I'll tell everyone."

As she flew off to rejoin the formation, Sigrid asked Sleipnir to jump over a pile of wooden posts lying across a gap in the palisade. From the closer position, she fired another shot, relishing the moment when her spear pierced an elf's abdomen.

Where were the iron arrows coming from? In the swirl of shadows, she couldn't distinguish who wielded bows and arrows. Many of them had lances, clubs, and short swords, but where were their archers?

Elves splashed into the water under the shower of valkyrie spears, but enough were able to keep working. Even in this crude construction, their legendary craftsmanship was evident as the logs stacked neatly against one another as if tied by magic.

Sigrid urged Sleipnir to descend the bank toward the water, his eight legs keeping them well balanced. Their new position gave her a clear shot at the elves already crossing the bridge. She took out elf after elf, until her arm burned with the repeated throwing motion.

But still they kept building. The logs floated closer and closer as they were pushed across the spring. What had seemed like a great distance between shores now showed to be nothing but a short ride across. Then the logs touched land…

They'd finished the bridge.

Bile crept up Sigrid's throat at the rushing mass of Night Elves, who gained momentum to reach the shores of Vanaheim right where the palisade remained unfinished.

She cursed and reined Sleipnir around. "Stable hands, defend! Use whatever you have as a weapon."

At their quick response, a burst of pride swelled in her chest. Those who weren't tending to the fallen generals obeyed, grabbing hammers and axes. Staying behind the palisade, they raced to where the Night Elves poured across the river.

General Ulfhilda shouted more orders overhead. "Merge in! Circle tight!"

The valkyries' collective shadow eclipsed everything as they bombarded the elves, swirling so tightly that there was hardly a gap of empty sky between them. Three divisions convened over the floating bridge while the other two hovered over the closest gaps in the palisade to help stop the elves from getting past.

Sigrid ground her teeth, wanting to shout her own orders to them, because as hard as everyone fought, the elves were proving unstoppable. They'd crossed the river, and now the only barrier between them and Vanaheim was an unfinished wall of wooden posts.

Sleipnir's hooves splashed as she pushed him back to the water's edge, keeping close to their targets.

Ragnarr ran past her and knelt on the riverbank, where he began tracing shapes in the dirt. The ground trembled and cracked beneath him, startling the nearest horses. A fissure went right under Sleipnir and toward the elves, the quake knocking them off their feet.

"Nice work!" Sigrid shouted, throwing her spear and taking down another elf.

A whoosh of wings blew dirt into her face and whipped Sleipnir's mane across his neck. Ylva swooped down beside her. "Get back with the stable hands!"

"You need help," Sigrid said, proving her point by knocking a Night Elf into the water.

"General Eira told you to stay—"

Abruptly, all the breath left Sigrid's lungs and she jerked backward. Pain exploded through her body as everything became a blur of movement and shouts.

Sleipnir reared and she tipped back, leaning...falling...the ground rushing toward her...

Sigrid slammed into the riverbank, shoulder first. A sickening *thump* filled her head as her helmet hit next, her pain-filled cry cut short as a frozen fist closed around her chest.

Black lingered at the bottom of her vision — darkness reaching for her face.

She'd been shot with an iron arrow. Maybe the elves were targeting more than just generals — they were also targeting her.

I'll kill The Svartalf King...

Darkness.

Closing in over her.

CHAPTER THIRTY-NINE

TAKING CAPTIVES

Sigrid couldn't breathe.

Everything in her screamed for air.

A terrifying noise escaped her when she rolled over, like the moan of someone struggling for their last breath.

Cold. Colder than she'd ever been, the darkness aching worse than if she'd plunged into glacier water.

I'm dying.

Chest spasming, she clawed at her breastplate, trying to make it stop. Tendrils of darkness squeezed her tighter, wrapping around her ribs and arms.

A scream, hollow and distant.

Sigrid closed her fingers around the iron, dread surging when it wouldn't come out. The arrow stuck out of her chest below her right collar bone. The tip had broken in and pressed against her skin.

Any harder and it would have fully pierced through.

Her mind clouded over, spiraling into black nothingness.

Deep down, the need to remove the iron arrow grew stronger, forcing her to keep moving. Summoning her last drop of strength, she roared and yanked the arrow.

It popped free, and she drew a shuddering gasp as the icy tendrils loosened their hold. She brushed them off with shaking hands, warmth rushing back to her limbs.

The sounds of battle returned, along with her name being shouted by several people.

"Sigrid!"

"Sig, are you okay?"

Stable hands rushed to help her up and grab Sleipnir, who'd ended up a few strides away. They pulled her up the riverbank and behind an upturned cart.

"Where'd it get you?" Peter asked, checking her over.

"Breastplate." The sound barely came out. "Just a scratch."

Gods, this hurts.

"Too close." Peter pulled her into a careful hug.

Part of her wanted to stay there, safe in his arms, the same way she'd done many times growing up. Then Sleipnir drew close and nosed at her hair, and whatever emotion had overcome her evaporated.

Sigrid trembled, anger building until she was ready to erupt like a steam column. "I'm going to kill every single one of them," she snarled.

Peter let go, watching her with wide eyes. "Sigrid?"

The volume of the fight rose even more, the air full of roars, screams, weapons hitting targets, and the rumble from Ragnarr's quake.

"Are you sure you're okay?" Peter asked, holding up a hand to motion for others to stay back.

"No." The word came as a bark. She took Sleipnir's reins and got back on, shaking from a combination of pain and anger. Sleipnir snorted, his ears flat to his head, gnashing the bit.

She'd lost valuable time. The elves were up against the palisade, slashing at the wood with axes, while the valkyries struggled to stop them from getting to the unfinished gaps. Many stable hands backed away nervously—like it was a dam about to crack.

"Where's Fisk?" He would know how to reinforce the palisade before their last defense broke.

Peter looked around. "He disappeared a while ago. I don't know—"

"Probably betraying us right now," Durinn, the young stable hand, said behind him. "I told you we should be careful—"

"I don't want to hear it," Sigrid snapped. When a few others glanced over nervously, she waved a hand. "Go find him! Tell him to fix this mess."

They skittered away like nervous horses at the fury in her voice. Even Roland cast her a terrified look before running after them.

Sigrid rubbed her temple where her pulse thumped hard enough to be annoying. Sleipnir tossed his head, his front four hooves lifting off the ground. "I know. We'll get to fight closer soon."

While she studied the field, she fired more shots at the Night Elves, stopping them from breaking through the places that hadn't been reinforced with runes.

A shadow darted through her periphery, and she spun with her spear raised before realizing it was Fisk.

"Sigrid, I left a gap in the palisade big enough for me to squeeze through over there," he pointed with his sword. "It looks like it's solid because I siphoned the reflectivity of the water. I can go through and get a Night Elf or two, but we have to be—"

"Good," Sigrid said, a thrill going through her. Grabbing some Night Elves took priority over fortifying the palisade. "Capture three of them. We'll start there."

He stopped in his tracks. "But Sigrid, we risk—"

"We don't have time to talk about it!" Sigrid shouted, keeping Sleipnir moving so she wouldn't get hit again. She launched her spear over the palisade, hitting a Night Elf so hard that he knocked down several behind him, and they all toppled down the bank and into the water.

"Sigrid," Peter said, "before we capture Night Elves, we should—"

"Stop arguing with me!" Why were they pausing to discuss things? Didn't they want to win? "Somebody get me some Night Elf captives, now!"

Fisk, Peter, and Roland exchanged a look. Then Fisk sheathed his sword and ran for the place he'd pointed to in the palisade. He slipped through it—seeming to pass right through the wooden posts.

Over the spiked tops, Sigrid saw him merge with the army unnoticed.

Perfect.

"Stand ready." Her spear dug into her hand as she gripped it.

On the other side, Fisk grabbed a Night Elf in a bovine mask by the elbow, pointing frantically at the gap he'd slipped through. The elf obliged, no doubt thinking Fisk was an ally who discovered a way in.

Peter and Roland ran over to grab the elf as they came back through. The elf struggled and kicked, realizing it was a trap, but the boys were strong enough to force the elf to the ground.

"Sigrid!" someone roared. "What are you doing?"

Sigrid turned in the saddle.

General Eira was on her feet, holding a bloody clump of cotton against her side, ghostly pale. "You're putting all of us at risk."

Webs of nightfall clung to her hands and her ripped, bloodied uniform, looking chilling and unnatural. Around her, the stable hands stood with fresh cotton and cleaning solutions, ready to keep tending her injury but hesitating as she shouted at Sigrid.

General Marta lay on a cart behind her, clinging to life, with more stable hands tending the wound in her side.

"I have a plan that goes beyond throwing spears at targets," Sigrid snapped. Sleipnir danced, ready to burst, and she held the reins tighter.

General Eira pointed a trembling finger at Fisk. "Stop and think, girl. If you jeopardize this whole fight—"

"We tried it your way, General," Sigrid yelled. "Now we try mine."

General Eira straightened up, wincing. "Sigrid, if they break through because of your poorly planned, poorly executed, miserable excuse of a strategy—"

"Sigrid!" Roland shouted, cutting them off.

As Fisk pulled a second elf in a deer mask through the gap, several other elves saw this happen—and they began to follow.

An icy feeling plunged into Sigrid's gut.

They were about to lose their last barrier.

CHAPTER FORTY

FALLEN VALKYRIE

"Keep the others back!" Sigrid kicked Sleipnir forward to meet the elves before they poured through the gap. She cued him to rear, and he lifted his four front legs and thrashed, striking fatal blows. While the valkyries threw their spears from overhead, Sleipnir's front hooves knocked out more elves than all of them combined.

Each hit reverberated in her bones, a pulse of energy from Sleipnir to her and back. Was this what Odin felt when he'd gone to war with other worlds?

A spear whooshed past Sigrid's head, and she flinched.

General Eira had jumped back onto Drifa despite looking weak enough to pass out. "Juniors, with me!" she shouted, her face twisted in anger.

Overhead, the juniors broke away from the other valkyries, and every warrior in the sky took a position to stop the elves from pushing through the unfinished parts of the palisade.

"Don't lose our captives, Fisk!" Sigrid threw and recalled her spear quickly, determined to make her plan worth it. She didn't regret telling him to go get those Night Elves. War involved taking risks. Sometimes, people had to get hurt.

"Ragnarr," she shouted, cueing Sleipnir to rear again. The quaking had stopped, but where was he? And where was Mabil?

She'd lost sight of them in the scramble.

Sigrid cursed. "Ground troops, come on! Seal the breach!"

While Peter and Roland restrained the two captives, Fisk and the other stable hands rushed forward with posts and hammers.

Once the elves could no longer get through, Sigrid backed up Sleipnir. "Good," she said between gasps, nodding to the stable hands. "Get to work on the other sections before the enemy reaches those, too."

A couple of groans met her instruction, but she stared them down until they ran off to find more posts to hammer in place.

Behind her, Peter had the more fiery of the two captives in a headlock.

The elf wearing a bovine mask grunted and flailed. "Get—off—me!" he said gruffly. "I've got a bad back and this is—not—helping!"

Fisk and Roland flanked the one in the deer mask, who calmly observed their setup. "I admire how you were able to pull together this palisade so quickly," she said in a motherly voice. "Was this your design, dear? It's quite the feat."

Fisk nodded, puffing out his chest. "Thank you, ma'am."

Over the field, General Eira roared directions and the juniors sent up a cloud of dirt as they swooped lower to push back the army.

Sigrid wanted to get back out there again, to feel the thrill of destroying their enemies. "Get information out of these elves," she told them. "Use any means possible."

Every gaze snapped to her.

Fisk started. "Golly, I thought the plan was to—you know?" He flapped his hands and then linked his fingers together as if miming something.

"What?" she asked shortly. "The plan was to capture them so we can get information about their plans, weapons, anything."

"By gaining allies!" Fisk threw his arms up. "What is going

on with you?"

A hot flame ignited in her chest at his challenging tone. "I want to win, Fisk! I want to find the enemies' weakness and then eliminate them. Is that so wrong?"

Sigrid stared them all down. Peter stared back with a strange, almost sad expression, while Roland's mouth pulled into a grimace and Fisk kept a defiant stance.

A yell of frustration crawled out of her throat, Sleipnir echoing it with a guttural sound. "Elves are storming our wall— which, by the way, is unfinished because we were too slow to build it. If they break through, this world is lost." She took a breath and tried for a more reasonable tone. "We *need* information. Where is the Svartalf King? Who is firing those arrows? What magic are they enchanted with? I need you to find that out for me."

Fisk crossed his arms, for once looking as fierce as any other Night Elf in his dire wolf mask. "I am not torturing my own people for information."

"Thank you, dear," said the elf in the deer mask.

"I have to agree!" said the elf in the bovine mask, who'd given up fighting Peter's headlock and hung limply under his arm.

Sigrid stretched her shoulders, her whole body winding tighter and tighter. "I'll do it myself, then."

Her mind and senses were more focused than ever, the pain in her chest reducing to an afterthought. Since getting on Sleipnir, she'd unlocked something within herself.

"Sigrid," Peter said with the air of someone trying not to provoke a feral cat, "is this really what you—"

Shouts rose from the junior valkyries.

A scream that sounded like Mariam's made Sigrid look up, sucking in a breath.

A rider had separated from her mare, falling, falling.

In the long seconds before she hit the ground, a collective gasp rose from the juniors and stable hands.

It was General Eira.

Drifa whinnied, diving to meet her fallen rider.

Roland rushed over, shouting for others to come help.

Sigrid clenched her jaw as everything—sensation, sounds, thoughts—stormed too fast for her. *It's too much. Too much.*

A resounding crack filled the air, making her jump. Even with runes holding it together, the palisade fell apart faster than it had been put up. With a chilling roar, Night Elves flooded through like a dam had broken.

Sleipnir reared, snapping her mind back into focus.

Sigrid tightened her grip on the reins. "All hands to the break in the wall! Push them back!"

She fired her spear at the first elf she laid eyes on, her heart racing as she worked desperately to stop the flood. If the elves got to the woods, it would be easy for them to scatter and hide among the dark trees.

With a roar, she nudged Sleipnir forward, and he plowed through the flood of Night Elves. Weapons splintered on his breastplate and under his massive hooves as he charged into a group of shadows. He bit one Night Elf on the back of the head and threw him aside, then kicked out his back legs, taking out several at once. Nothing could stop him.

"Good, Sleipnir!" Bolstered by his power, Sigrid threw her spear hard, hitting one in the back of the neck and piercing the leather. She summoned it back and threw again and again, driving Sleipnir over top of the bodies to ensure they were finished.

In all the nine worlds, no other horse could move and fight like this. He didn't need wings. He had all the power he needed.

"General Eira, stay awake," Peter shouted, his voice coming from somewhere distant.

A knot built in Sigrid's throat. She fought harder, ignoring the emotion building up behind her rage. The clarity she'd been so sure of waned, like fog obscuring her mind.

They wouldn't lose General Eira. They couldn't.

Sigrid's muscles burned, but she kept fighting. She threw and recalled her spear more quickly than ever, letting instinct guide her actions, her breaths roaring from her lungs.

A ruckus behind her made her turn.

Drifa shoved through Peter and the stable hands who'd gathered around General Eira, forcing them all back. Her ears were pinned and her teeth exposed, like a mare defending her foal. Sigrid had never seen anything like it. Even after a lifetime of working with horses, the stable hands scrambled away from Drifa.

The mare stood over General Eira, bending her long, white neck to examine her. Then she folded her legs and lay down, curling beside her rider. A long, majestic wing stretched out to cover General Eira's body.

Her white feathers rustled gently in a breeze.

The mare laid her head down, her neck outstretched, and closed her eyes. She and General Eira grew still.

CHAPTER FORTY-ONE

LOSING CONTROL

A cold, empty sensation surged through Sigrid's chest, extending to her body and leaving her numb. Mariam once told her about the cruel winters in Niflheim—of how no matter how many layers you wore, your skin felt frozen and all you wanted to do was lie down and never wake. *Is this how it feels?*

A chorus of cries and screams rose above the din of battle. The juniors lost momentum, all of them watching Drifa and General Eira.

"No!" Edith yelled, her voice distinct over everything. She made a reckless landing, jumping off Mjöll and running to the general. Roland stopped her, hugging her close as she cried harder.

Sigrid had to look away. She found Mariam in the air with the others, but she was too far away to read.

More pieces of wall cracked and fell, with more and more Night Elves surging forward. The senior valkyries tried their best to push them back, but they lost ground fast.

We can't stop. If we stop, we die.

Sigrid raised her spear, gasping at the explosion of pain below her right collar bone. She couldn't focus. Her pulse beat out of line with Sleipnir's, like they'd lost their connection. Had he kept the pain away?

The world tilted, and she swayed in the saddle.

Valkyries weren't supposed to die today.

This should never have happened. This fight was supposed to be a sure victory. The plan was to fight and defend, and maybe injuries would happen, but nothing so absolute as death.

She sucked in deep breaths, struggling to get enough air. As if triggered by General Eira's death, images of all the kills she'd made during this battle flashed across her mind, their masked bodies closing around her, suffocating.

I've killed today. A valkyrie is dead. Mariam could be next—

"No," she said hoarsely, shrugging out of the panic closing around her.

A shadow flitted at the corner of her eye. A Night Elf broke away from his group and headed toward the junior valkyries, who hovered above General Eira.

He raised his weapon and aimed.

"Runa, look out!" Sigrid jumped into motion and threw her spear at the elf, clipping his arm but failing to knock him over. His javelin missed Runa and Tobia by inches.

Runa cried out and took her mare higher in the sky. The others scattered, breaking formation.

"Juniors, don't lose focus!" Sigrid shouted, the words coming automatically. "We need you."

General Ulfhilda swooped down next to her, and Sigrid lost her breath in the mare's powerful wing gusts. "Princess Sigrid, we've lost control."

Sigrid's heart plummeted as the general voiced her fear. All the blood seemed to drain from her, taking every drop of strength and determination. Her hand shook as she opened her palm to summon her weapon back, but she gritted her teeth. "We haven't. We can't think like that."

"We can't lose track of any elves," General Ulfhilda said, ignoring her vain optimism. "Can your division be ready to go to Borthorpe with the juniors?"

"Yes—but I thought—" The village sat less than an hour south of the forest. There was no time to warn them that Night Elves were coming their way. She swallowed hard. "Yes."

She'd been about to point out that General Eira made a plan for which valkyries were to go to where, but given the situation, it was time to abandon any previous plans. She trusted General Ulfhilda's judgment.

"Be careful," Sigrid said. "I probably don't need to point out that they're targeting generals with those arrows."

"And royals," she corrected with a glance to Sigrid's dented breastplate. "But yes, I will stay farther back than I otherwise would have."

She soared higher, calling out commands to her troops.

Focus. It wasn't the time or place to fall apart. She had a bigger role to play, with people depending on her.

Desperate to get her confidence back, Sigrid pulled off a glove and touched her bare palm to Sleipnir's neck. His heat seeped through her skin.

Steady, quick, with the cadence of a trot, their pulses beat in time.

Cool, refreshing air filled her lungs.

I am a valkyrie. I have Sleipnir. I can stop the elves.

Strength returned to her muscles, and her pain eased to nothingness. She rolled her neck, inhaling deeply.

The elves raced for Myrkviðr, some dropping under a shower of spears but most slipping through unharmed. The canopy protected them from the valkyries as they flitted through the trees.

Sigrid growled, yanking her glove back on.

"Junior division, to Borthorpe with Sigrid!" General Ulfhilda's voice carried like a thunderclap. "Marta's division, to Steinholm. The rest of you, stay here with me."

Sigrid raised an arm to get the stable hands' attention. "Grab whatever supplies you need and leave the rest behind. Split up to support each division." To Fisk, who stood paces away with the two captives, she said, "Bring them as well."

While the stable hands sprang into action, the juniors broke apart in the air upon receiving the order to follow Sigrid. Indistinct shouts drifted toward her.

She gritted her teeth. Now wasn't the time for questions and defiance.

Mariam broke away from the group to fly to her. After a moment, others followed, until the minority had no choice but to come along.

"Go!" Sigrid shouted to the juniors, waving them onward. "Stop them before they get to Borthorpe."

While the stable hands grabbed the cart horses and got ready, Sigrid nudged Sleipnir into a gallop and they plunged into Myrkviðr. She had to follow. They couldn't lose track of a single Night Elf.

An unnamed emotion threatened to overtake her—something raw and weak—but she pushed it away, shedding her gloves and tangling her bare hands into Sleipnir's mane. His strength was all she had—the only thread of hope keeping her going.

CHAPTER FORTY-TWO

THE FATE
OF BORTHORPE

Any sliver of advantage they had in chasing the enemy in familiar territory vanished under nightfall. The Night Elves became shadows darker than the night, rolling into Borthorpe like a sudden summer storm, just as fast and unstoppable.

Screams erupted, animals brayed, and crashes echoed through the night as the elves ravaged the little village. They overtook it within minutes, sending its hundred or so people rushing out of their homes to fight and flee.

Sigrid squinted in the darkness, trying to distinguish elves and villagers in all the chaos. Sleipnir lashed out and sank his teeth into a passing shadow. The elf screamed before being tossed aside and stomped on. At least she could trust Sleipnir's instincts and let him guide her.

When he next lunged at something unseen, she threw her spear in that direction. A thump and a sharp exhale answered back.

"Finish him!"

Sleipnir galloped on, a bump beneath him telling her they'd eliminated the enemy.

One down, hundreds to go.

Somewhere, in the distant edges of her mind, she knew that she and Sleipnir should be exhausted after all the fighting and the long gallop through the woods. But they were alert, angry, ready for more. Although her chest seized up when she thought of General Eira, the tired winged mares and riders overhead, and her friends, white-hot fury smothered it.

She fired another shot, but a hollow *thwap* told her it hit a house instead of an elf.

Growling in frustration, she held back her next shot.

Nightfall was making this impossible. Above, the valkyries also struggled. Gunni and Runa crashed into each other trying to aim, and the rest barely held formation.

"Find torches! It's impossible like this," Sigrid instructed.

They were losing this battle fast.

Bodies kept dropping in the streets.

She had to save them, no matter what. She had to—

A shadow darted past, and without pausing to consider, she jumped off Sleipnir to finish off the elf from the ground. Their shared energy lessened, but not enough to weaken her.

The elf must have sensed her because he grabbed the arm of a woman fleeing past the other way, yanking her between him and Sigrid. "Come any closer and the woman dies," he shouted, pointing his dagger between Sigrid and the woman's neck.

The woman screamed, not daring to move.

Sigrid barked out a laugh, raising her spear. "You think I won't?"

The elf stepped back, holding the woman firmly in front of him, the dagger against her neck. She whimpered.

"Tell me where your king is," Sigrid said, "and I might let you live." She had no intention of doing that, but she had to find the Svartalf King and finish him off.

"Please, save me," the woman pleaded, tears glinting on her cheeks in the flickering light from nearby torches.

The elf pushed the blade harder into the woman's throat, making her sob.

Sigrid raised her spear, ready to throw it. Hopefully, her aim was good enough.

But before she could pull her arm back, someone crashed into her from the side, knocking her off-balance so she nearly fell to the ground. She shrieked, rounding on her attacker with her spear up.

It was Mariam.

"Sigrid, stop it!" She grabbed hold of the spear and Sigrid. "You're going to get an innocent person killed."

The elf laughed, backing up with the woman still held in front of him.

"What are you doing?" Sigrid shook her arm free of Mariam's grip. "Get off me!"

Mariam grabbed her again, forcing her back a step. Behind her, Runa swooped low, and Tobia's hooves knocked the elf's mask with an echoing *crack*.

The woman he was holding fell forward, gasping for air.

"Grab everyone you can and get away from this village!" Runa shouted to her. "We can't hold them off."

The woman did what she was told and ran.

Sigrid struggled against Mariam, furious at her interruption. Sleipnir snorted and pawed at the ground, equally agitated. *How dare she get between me and my kill?*

"Sigrid, look at me." Mariam grabbed Sigrid's chin and forced her to turn her gaze.

Sigrid heaved for breath, her whole body jittering. Her vision was so fuzzy that Mariam's face took a moment to appear through the darkness. Then Mariam's bright eyes found hers, and the fog dissipated.

She stopped struggling. *What am I doing?*

Behind her, Sleipnir grunted, shaking his head.

Suddenly she couldn't get enough air. She was cold. Heavy. Exhausted.

"You with me?" Mariam asked in a low voice.

She nodded, drawing a slow breath, and Mariam let go.

"Come on. Let's get out of here," Mariam said. "We're going to get someone killed if we keep fighting when we're this tired."

Sigrid hesitated. They couldn't just retreat and abandon the village. They had their orders. But risking the lives of more valkyries for a village that was already lost…

Indecision twisted her insides as she held Sleipnir's reins. Maybe there were no clear choices in war. There were only lesser evils.

She cupped a hand to her mouth and shouted skyward. "Valkyries, hold fire! Meet in Myrkviðr."

"We can't just leave them!" Ylva said, her high-pitched voice cutting like a knife.

Sigrid mounted up. "This isn't working. We need a plan."

"But the village—" Edith said.

"It's done for," Sigrid went on, louder, "and judging by everyone's sloppiness, we need a rest. We'll monitor the elves overnight and surround and invade in the morning. But we can't do anything more now without someone getting killed."

Nobody else argued.

As Mariam and the valkyries fell into formation behind her, the villagers' screams faded like the final drops of a rainstorm. Borthorpe had no hope. Night Elves left no life behind.

Fighting against the suffocating tightness in her chest, Sigrid led the junior division away from Borthorpe. Sleipnir's stride and the gentle whoosh of wings replaced the screams and crashes.

CHAPTER FORTY-THREE

OUT OF
THE SADDLE

Sigrid halted Sleipnir at the edge of Myrkviðr, taking cover under the ancient trees. For a quiet second, branches creaked in the breeze and a creek burbled past, and then the valkyries landed in a hailstorm of hooves, wheezing for breath and coughing.

Whispers drifted through the muffled woods.

"Those poor villagers…"

"This is awful…"

"We failed…"

The sun was long gone, the forest lit by glowing insects that looked like embers from a dying fire. Under the moonlight, the pure white mares were the brightest part of their dark surroundings. The blood marking on Aesa's shoulder snagged Sigrid's gaze, and she watched Mariam dismount heavily.

Sigrid pushed her fingers under her helmet to rub her forehead. "Everyone, let's stay—oh." She trembled, the fight leaving her. Sleipnir's energy still crackled inside her, but her body couldn't take any more.

Am I going to pass out?

Dismounting proved to be the wrong move. Her leg muscles failed, and she sank to her knees, more exhausted than she'd ever been in her life.

"S-stay here," Sigrid said to the valkyries, each word an effort.

"We'll take turns watching the village o-overnight."

She rubbed her eyes, everything seeming muted as her senses returned to normal.

"Are you okay?" Edith's voice came as if from underwater.

Sigrid's chest seared, the bruise from the iron arrow agonizing without Sleipnir's connection numbing it. It filled her body, mixing with fatigue. She shivered, cold and feverish like she had the flu. She should have been ready to collapse hours ago, but Sleipnir had kept her going. Yet no valkyrie could fight or ride for so long without consequence.

Warm hands closed over her arms. Through the darkness, Mariam's face appeared, her eyes wide.

"Sigrid."

All the stress and fear Sigrid had pushed down bubbled over, threatening to come out in tears.

Mariam had valiantly fought this battle like she'd trained for years, staying in formation and doing her part to fend off the Night Elves. Was she okay? Through the darkness, it was hard to tell if she was injured. Why hadn't Sigrid paid more attention?

"I'm fine," Mariam said, apparently noticing Sigrid checking her over.

"Are you sure?" Sigrid asked, the words barely coming out.

Mariam cupped a gentle hand over her cheek. "It's you I'm worried about."

Without thinking, Sigrid leaned forward, relieved when Mariam met her lips. Her sweet taste tingled through Sigrid's insides like a tonic, dulling the pain and exhaustion. Under the privacy of nightfall, the kiss lingered, Sigrid's skin dancing as their lips brushed. From this close, she heard every tiny hitch in Mariam's breath, which sent a tingle down her arms and legs. There weren't enough words to express how grateful she was that they were both here, safe and together.

Around them, the valkyries dismounted and sank to the

ground—some flopped on their backs, others curled to rest their heads on their knees. No one spoke above a whisper. The mares and Sleipnir set to work eating grass and leaves, and everyone, horses and riders, guzzled water from the stream trickling past.

Oddly, a few valkyries eyed Sleipnir with an air of fear, like the stallion was Jörmungandr, the world serpent about to swallow them whole.

"I heard you were shot." Mariam's voice caught on the last word as her fingers hovered over Sigrid's collarbone.

Sigrid reached up and squeezed her hand. "I'm okay. Promise."

In truth, the bruise hurt worse than any she'd ever had in her life, and she was afraid to look at it. The place where the darkness had tried to overtake her burned, feeling frostbitten. But given what happened to the generals who were hit with the same weapons, she had no right to complain.

She adjusted her legs with a groan, and Mariam sat beside her, each leaning into the other for support. The soft dirt and moss beneath them were a more welcoming bed than even the one waiting for Sigrid back in Vanahalla.

"On the bright side," Mariam said, "the Night Elves deemed you as high value as the generals, which is pretty impressive."

Sigrid exhaled. "Pretty sure I can thank the king for that."

With a grim half smile, Mariam rested her palm on Sigrid's thigh. Her soft touch numbed the pain for a blissful moment. "Sounds like you did leave a bad impression with him." She chewed her lip, her brow furrowed, and the moonlight revealed an indiscernible glint in her dark eyes. "How's Sleipnir?"

There was something odd about her tone that Sigrid couldn't identify. "I can feel his power in me. It sharpens me like a blade, makes me a better warrior."

"But?"

She sighed. "But we're still figuring each other out."

Mariam's jaw worked. She searched Sigrid's face, frowning,

as if waiting for her to say more. "You don't feel like his power is taking you over?"

Taking over? Interesting way of putting it. Was that how Mariam felt? Sigrid shook her head firmly, needing her to understand. "We share a connection, but I know how to work with it instead of against it. I wouldn't have been able to do half the things I did today without him."

Mariam's eyebrows pulled down, and Sigrid averted her gaze to the babbling stream.

True, there'd been moments where her mind clouded over or she'd taken an action that didn't quite *feel* like her. The memories were murky, like she'd had too much wine during the battle, but a little knot of guilt formed as they trickled back—shouting at Fisk and the stable hands, turning away from the fallen generals with more rage than sadness, killing as easily as if practicing on wooden targets… Fury had overtaken her, as if the gods of war had guided her actions.

But amid all of that, she'd been able to destroy the Night Elves without hesitating. She'd killed more than she could count, commanded her division, taken captives, and galloped and fought harder than she ever would have done without the stallion's influence. Sleipnir's power unlocked her potential for leadership and battle, which meant doing things she'd never done before. He made her into the warrior Vanaheim desperately needed. Even if he made her hot-headed, she would be a fool to step back from that. This was war. *Kill or be killed.*

Sigrid frowned. *Sounds like something Helena would say…*

Mariam let out a slow breath. "You know you can tell me anything, right?"

Sigrid nodded. "I know. Thank you for worrying. It was an intense battle, but I'm still me. Someone smart once told me nothing can *make* someone evil." She pecked Mariam's cheek, hoping to ease whatever worries plagued her.

Mariam studied her for another moment, then nodded.

"Water?" Sigrid asked, motioning toward the stream. They hauled themselves closer, groaning with the effort of it. Sigrid knelt and splashed her face and the back of her neck, letting out a sigh. She cupped her hand and drank for a long minute, parched.

A short distance away, Runa sniffed. "I can't believe she's gone."

Edith wrapped her in a hug. "I know."

They were both crying.

Now that Sigrid paused to look, every valkyrie was crying or sniffling and fighting back tears. Guilt churned her insides. General Eira, who she'd known her whole life, was dead. Drifa, who she'd spent her life caring for, had gone with her.

I should be crying with them.

She splashed water over her face again, fighting the part of her that threatened to snap. It wasn't the time to think about death and loss and regrets—not when she had to lead this division.

But Peter, Roland, Hestur, and everyone else they'd left behind forced their way to the front of her mind, making it hard to breathe.

They'll be okay. They have to be.

Mariam was talking to her. She stood and forced her attention back, wobbly on her feet.

"…keep thinking about the iron arrows," Mariam said. She rubbed Aesa's wings, giving the mare a well-deserved massage. "Their supply must be limited—otherwise they'd be throwing them all over the place, right? And if that's the case, they're probably only trusting their leaders to call the shots, not the common grunts. So if we can find their leaders…"

"Maybe we can get the iron arrows," Sigrid finished, trying to rub the shooting pains out of the back of her neck. "Yeah. That's a good plan. I'm also hoping to find the Svartalf King." A truce seemed more impossible than ever, but maybe they could figure out some other agreement that didn't involve bloodshed. "How do we tell which elves are leaders?"

"Fisk said the most dangerous creature skulls were higher ranked. So, we just…" Mariam shrugged. "We take a look and see who is scarier?"

Sigrid couldn't stop the smile tugging her lips. "Scarier?"

Mariam snorted. "Shut up. I'm tired."

Sigrid stepped closer. "But I like the way you're thinking. Very cunning."

"Well, I like the way…" Mariam stepped closer until their lips brushed. "You shoot down my ideas and then try to distract me like this."

Sigrid grazed her lips over Mariam's, her sweet taste everything she needed. Mariam teased her back, nipping at her lower lip.

"We do have to figure something out, though." With great effort, Sigrid forced herself to step back. Frustration bubbled inside her, the urgency of everything making her rock back and forth on her feet. "We shouldn't have had to retreat."

Between valkyries, sorcerers, and Seers, none of it had been enough to hold off Svartalfheim's massive army. That was the chilling thing. How many more elves were there, and how were they supposed to fend them all off?

Most concerning was that Tóra and Vala hadn't been able to reach the Norns. Sigrid had assumed Vanaheim's Seers could have easily received insight to the battle's outcome. But they'd gotten nothing. Not even a whisper.

First, the gods hadn't responded to Ratatosk's capture, and now, the Norns weren't responding to Vanaheim's pleas for help. Whatever was going on, one thing was certain—Loki was behind it all.

But why? Was he truly after creating chaos and nothing more?

She pulled her mind away from the gods to find Mariam staring. But before she could voice her thoughts, Aesa spun around, nearly knocking them over.

Every horse turned, alert to something coming from the depths of the forest.

Sigrid and Mariam drew their spears from their sheaths.

"Just us!" Peter shouted, emerging from the darkness of the surrounding woods. Others followed, their footsteps slow and heavy. From further back, Hestur whinnied.

Sigrid let out a breath. *They made it.*

Roland, Tóra and Disa, a few other stable hands, and the two sorcerers came into view, too.

"We brought as much food as we could," Peter said, shrugging out of a rucksack.

Sigrid ran to meet them. She punched Peter's shoulder and then threw her arms around Hestur's neck, kissing him repeatedly. "You did so good, Hestur. So brave."

He nickered softly, his lips flapping on her hair.

Peter snorted. "Never change, Sigrid."

Once she finished showering Hestur with affection, she walked over to where Peter handed out fruit and cheese to the seated valkyries. "What happened at the shore?"

Peter's mouth turned down. Sweat shone on his skin, and he wiped an arm over his forehead. "Another Night Elf battalion arrived, same size as the first. We couldn't hold them off."

A chill rippled through Sigrid. Gasps passed over the group.

"Is everyone okay?" Edith asked.

Peter swallowed hard. He shook his head. "General Marta is in bad shape, and they had a few close calls. The valkyries signaled a full retreat."

CHAPTER FORTY-FOUR

NOT A
PHYSICAL MESSAGE

Sigrid cursed, walking a circle. She waved away the pear Peter offered her, too nauseous to eat.

A second battalion. Could the Svartalf King be among them?

"What about the other villages? Are they okay?" Runa asked, brown locks flying loose from her topknot as if Tobia had been trying to eat it as usual.

Peter shook his head. "There aren't enough of us to protect them all."

"Gods," Gunni moaned, sinking down onto a boulder. "And we couldn't even defend one."

Peter looked toward Borthorpe. "The elves are in there?"

"Yeah," Sigrid said bitterly. "We had to pull back to make a plan."

He looked around at the collapsed valkyries. "Probably good to take a rest."

"We'll storm the village at dawn," Sigrid said, unease churning inside her. "Can we send a message back to Vanahalla? Mabil or Ragnarr?"

The sorcerers nodded stiffly. They were covered in blood and dirt—the fight had not been kind to them.

Everyone passed around the food the stable hands had brought and drank from the stream. Sigrid stayed standing. They couldn't let their guard down with the elves so close—they would have to keep a close watch on the village.

She rocked on her feet. This was where they could benefit from knowing what the elves planned to do next. They needed allies—or spies.

She found Fisk at the edge of camp, sitting on a boulder looking slumped and defeated as he watched his two Night Elf captives. They were tied at the wrists and didn't seem to have a problem with it. Maybe he'd already made progress with them.

She had to ask them for information. Maybe they knew where the Svartalf King was.

But first...

Sigrid walked over to the boulder, her throat tightening as she remembered how she'd shouted at Fisk. He didn't acknowledge her as she sat down beside him. "I'm sorry I yelled at you."

He sniffled, his eye holes turned downward.

Oh, no. Was he crying? Was everyone at this bloody camp crying?

She draped an arm across his shoulders. "I'm really sorry, Fisk. I didn't mean to. It was the heat of battle, I...I got desperate." *And taken over by forces stronger than me.* She swallowed. "I shouldn't have yelled at you for things out of your control. It's not your fault we failed."

Fisk tilted his mask toward her. "I should have come up with a plan to build the palisade more quickly. Or make it stronger somehow," he said miserably.

"No, you shouldn't have. Your plan was perfect. We got there late, and the Svartalf King's army got there early, and it's not your fault."

He hesitated, then nodded.

"I also shouldn't have tried to force you into going against your own people." She waved a hand at the two captives, who waved back awkwardly. "That was...insensitive of me. I'm truly sorry."

Fisk nodded again, finally relaxing into Sigrid's half hug. "You know, I don't have many friends in this or in any other world. Let's not fight again, okay?"

"Deal." Sigrid put her fist up, and they bumped them side by side.

With a glance at the captives, she motioned for Fisk to step back with her, and they took three careful steps away.

"Have they said anything?" she whispered.

Fisk shook his head. "They won't say much. I don't think they like the Svartalf King, but they still don't want to be traitors. I'll keep trying to gain their trust."

A scuff rose behind them, and she checked over her shoulder. "Okay. Thanks for all your work, Fisk," she said. "I'll leave you to rest."

She clapped him on the arm and stepped back, letting Tóra take her place.

The Seer, whose robe was torn and whose arms were full of cuts, appeared to be okay otherwise. She cast Sigrid a sheepish smile before shuffling over to Fisk.

"Hello," they said at the same time.

Sigrid's lips pulled into a little smile as she left them to sit on the boulder. *This should cheer him up.*

She went to Peter next, sitting with him on a mossy patch of forest floor. "Did Leah make it okay?"

He nodded. "Thanks for asking."

There was a pause.

Peter's mouth quirked into a guilty smile. "If it makes you feel better…if I was going to tell anyone, you would've been first."

"It does feel better," she said, making them both chuckle. She ran her hands across the moss, feeling the soothing tickle on her palms. "Why was it a secret, though?"

He shrugged. "Things were going so well between the two of us. You know how people can be. We thought gossip might mess it up."

"I get it." Valkyries and gossip could be like birds and songs. She drew a breath. "I'm happy for you. She's nice. I've always liked her."

He pulled her into a hug. As they broke apart, he said, "But to be fair, you never told me about Mariam."

"Same reason as you. Also, we're kinda…"

"New?"

"Very new." She huffed, chipping a hole in the dirt with her heel for something to do. "I don't even know if she—we've only known each other—we haven't talked about—"

Peter let out a short laugh. "Yeah. When Leah and I started seeing each other, I wasn't sure if what we had was a summer thing or something more. I wanted more, but I was afraid of her not feeling the same."

"What did you do?"

"I walked up to her and told her how I felt."

"Just like that?" Sigrid exhaled. "That's brave."

"Actually, I'm about to do another brave thing and tell you something I've been a bit afraid to share." Peter cleared his throat. "Remember how I convinced General Eira to keep Fisk as a stable hand? Well…I'm quitting my job when Leah and I get married. That leaves a vacancy."

Sigrid sat up straighter in a rush, everything seeming to tilt. "Leaving? But—to where?"

"Just down the hill." Peter smiled. "I've lined up a job as a smith in the village. If I'm going to support a family, I need better pay."

"But—but the stable will crumble without you!" Sigrid said, high-pitched.

Peter shushed her. "Hey, it'll be fine. Roland is taking charge. And before you say anything, I know he can do a good job. Even with his antics."

Sigrid couldn't even find the humor in that statement, caught up imagining a valkyrie stable with no Peter in it.

"I guess we're all moving up, aren't we?" Peter said. "You in Vanahalla, me as a full-time smith—we're both moving onto bigger things. But remember a job is just a job. No matter where fate takes us, you'll always be my little sister."

Peter pulled her into a side-hug, and she was glad it was dark out because her eyes were embarrassingly full of tears. Maybe his were, too, because a silence passed where he sniffled a few times.

"You'll always be my big brother," she said, the words mangled. Now that she'd let herself feel this one thing, it was like she felt everything. Deep down, she was happy for him, but the only thing she could feel right now was bittersweet sadness.

I'm being selfish. I moved up to Vanahalla, so why shouldn't he move on, too?

It was just nice knowing Peter was always in the stable. He'd been a steady part of it for her entire life.

"How's Sleipnir?" he asked, a strange hesitance in his tone. "His power feel okay?"

"Fine, yes." Sigrid pulled back, not wanting to get into that discussion.

"Sigrid," Mariam said sharply, coming over with her arms crossed.

Sigrid and Peter turned quickly, surprised by her abrupt appearance.

"I was just thinking—it doesn't make sense that the elves came to Borthorpe instead of Vanahalla."

"What do you mean?" Something twisted inside her at Mariam's tone.

"Why would they come to this village?"

Sigrid shrugged. "They ransack. That's what they do."

Mariam shook her head. "When I—when we met—Helena's army was in the stable yard, right? While all of the fighting was going on, it freed me to go get the Eye of Hnitbjorg."

Sigrid's insides plummeted. "A distraction," she said, barely audible.

Could this be true?

"But the Night Elves don't *trick*," Sigrid said with a note of desperation, thinking of General Eira's words. *Brute force and big weapons... They've never ventured into advanced tactics and trickery.*

Tóra sidled over and cleared her throat delicately, looking like she might be sick. "I received a message from Vala."

Sigrid shot to her feet. "What is it?"

"It said... Well, I don't know how else to put this." She looked terrified, her already colorless face appearing translucent in the moonlight. "Vanahalla is under attack."

CHAPTER FORTY-FIVE

CHOOSING
BETWEEN EVILS

Murmurs broke out as everyone relayed the news to each other across the camp. Footsteps pounded up as several people raced over to confirm.

"Did she just say *under attack*?"

"How did they reach Vanahalla so fast?"

"Oh, gods. What are we supposed to do?"

Sigrid grabbed Tóra's shoulders, making her flinch. "What did the message say, exactly?"

"N-not much, I'm afraid." Tóra drew a breath, her gaze shifting rapidly between all of the eyes upon her. "A couple hundred Night Elves reached Vanahalla. The senior valkyries are keeping them back, for now, but she wasn't sure for how long. She looked scared."

"Is the Svartalf King there? Did she say—"

Tóra shook her head. "I'm…not sure. She didn't say."

Sigrid huffed and let her go, not sure what to make of this. "Tóra, are you *sure* you saw this message from Vala?"

"Yes." She tilted her head in confusion. "Who else would I get it from?"

Mariam met Sigrid's gaze, no doubt thinking the same thing.

Tóra was new at her job, and while she was a great runes teacher, there was a chance she'd Seen something incorrectly. Or falsely. There was also the real possibility that Mariam's hunch was true—the Night Elves had tricked them.

A heavy silence fell over the group.

Sigrid looked to Mabil and Ragnarr, hoping they had more insight, but they both looked as uncertain as the rest of them. She pressed the heels of her hands to her forehead. "What if we go protect Vanahalla and it turns out this message isn't… No offense, but we need to be absolutely certain."

"I believe her," Fisk said gallantly.

"It's not about doubting what Tóra saw." Sigrid waved an impatient hand. "We don't know how real it is. Weren't you having trouble communicating before? Like something or someone was interfering?"

Tóra blanched, finally understanding the problem.

Mariam settled a hand on the Seer's arm. "Tóra, can you show us what you saw when Vala sent you the message? Can you do that thing where you…?" She mimed throwing a vision into the air.

"I would," Tóra said glumly, making the same motion, "but I don't remember how I did it."

Ylva stomped forward. "Last time, you tripped and did it by accident. Can't you do that again?"

Tears glistened in Tóra's large eyes.

"Quiet," Sigrid snapped. "There's no need for that."

Ylva shrugged. "Well, it's true."

Gunni stepped past Ylva, a wicked smile on her lips. "Maybe we just need to…" Before anyone could react, she shoved Tóra.

Everyone gasped. Sigrid and Mariam shouted several different curses as Fisk jumped forward to catch Tóra before she fell.

But then light burst from Tóra's flailing hand, and the camp fell silent.

Vala's study appeared, followed by the old woman's wrinkled, age-spotted face. The whites of her eyes and her white hair glistened, abnormally bright. She was breathing fast. "Vanahalla…" she said, barely audible.

The light flickered and died like a smothered flame.

It was nowhere near clear enough to hear the message—but it was all they needed to see. Vala had really sent a message to Tóra.

Ylva stepped forward, her expression stony now. "We have to go help."

For once, Sigrid agreed with her.

"Our job is to stay here and protect Borthorpe," Edith said, and several valkyries voiced their agreement.

"Our job," Mariam said, "is to do what the crown wants us to do."

All eyes fell upon Sigrid.

For some reason, she didn't flush and get the urge to crawl into the nearest foxhole. Maybe she was getting used to her title, or maybe she was too exhausted to be self-conscious. Whatever the reason, she was sure of how to lead them all.

"We go to Vanahalla."

Unsurprisingly, a dozen protests went up.

"Vanahalla is our priority." She had to shout to be heard over them. "What's Vanaheim without it? Villages, houses, and barns can be rebuilt. But the royal hall? Those golden towers, everything the sorcerers have worked on, the books and relics in the Seer's tower—you think those came about in just a few months?"

They were listening, so she steadied her breath and continued. "If the Night Elves get their hands on those treasures, all of Vanaheim's magic will belong to them. There's no telling what they'll do with it. But there's enough celestial magic in the hall that it could help them turn Vanaheim into a realm of darkness."

Everyone was silent, either debating arguing further or considering if she'd made a fair point. Both Mariam and Peter were unreadable—hopefully respecting her decision.

Her heart pulled toward Peter, who had dreams of marrying Leah and living in the village. For his future, and for the futures of everybody else here, she had to get the Night Elves out of Vanaheim.

"Anyone who doesn't want Vanaheim to become a world of night, get on your mares and come with me to protect it." She hurried off to fetch Sleipnir.

Edith caught up to her. "What about the other divisions?"

Good question.

"And what about the village?" Runa exclaimed, matching their pace. "There could be hostages in there."

Sigrid lobbed her reins over Sleipnir's head. *No clear choices, only lesser evils.*

Facing the junior valkyries and finding them waiting for orders was a strange sight. "We have to prioritize," she said. "This is my call, and I'm choosing Vanahalla over Borthorpe. The other divisions need to make their own choices about whether to stay where they are or come to Vanahalla. All we can do is tell them what we're doing."

There was a brief, tense pause.

Runa raised her hand. "How are we going to tell them?"

Sigrid hesitated. Stopping at several villages to tell the other divisions would delay them by way too long. But on the chance that any of the generals agreed with her that protecting Vanahalla was the priority, she had to tell them about Vala's message.

"I can ride to tell them," Tóra said, staying far from where Ylva and Gunni stood. "It's my job to communicate what I saw."

"No, I'll go," Gunni said, surprising Sigrid and apparently everyone else, because all heads turned. "I'll be way faster on a winged mare than you'll be on that pony, and my leg hasn't exactly made me fight well."

Sigrid nodded. Sending a valkyrie would accomplish the job

in half the time. "Okay. Thanks for volunteering, Gunni. Ylva, pick other riders to spread the word."

Pretending she didn't notice all the mumbles and shifty glances, Sigrid found a boulder to help her mount Sleipnir, too tired to vault onto his eighteen hands.

"Are we in agreement?" she asked with a foot in the stirrup.

"Yes, Your Highness," Runa said.

Edith echoed, and then more valkyries joined in.

Okay, maybe Sigrid wasn't *that* used to her title. Willing her cheeks to cool down, she settled into the saddle, breathing into the wonderful sensation that bled from Sleipnir into her veins. Pain and exhaustion became an afterthought, giving her the mental clarity she needed to continue to lead and fight.

Yes, this was the right decision. Atop Sleipnir, it was easier to push down the needling doubt in the back of her mind.

With a last look at the dark valley where the ransacked village of Borthorpe sat, Sigrid, the valkyries, and the stable hands left to protect Vanahalla.

CHAPTER FORTY-SIX

SORTING
OUT PRIORITIES

With the junior valkyries at Sigrid's back and Sleipnir beneath her, charging out of Myrkviðr toward Vanahalla brought back the feeling of thundering through the gates of Hel all those weeks ago. The thrill pumped through her veins as Sleipnir's hooves carved chunks out of the ground, pushing her to fight with every drop of remaining energy. This version of the valkyrie army—the formation with Sleipnir tearing up the ground and the *V* behind them in the sky—was the most fearsome and unstoppable of all.

Sleipnir was made for this, and his heir was meant to lead with him.

The sun peeked over the horizon as they climbed the grassy hill leading to the palace, bringing back the advantage of daylight. Sleipnir put in a burst of speed as the enemy came within sight—a swarm of about two hundred Night Elves. They pressed against the stone wall encircling Vanahalla, and above it, a fleet of twelve reserve valkyries fought to block them from climbing over or breaking through the gate.

Sigrid's lip curled as the sun bathed the hillside. The Night Elves might have enjoyed the advantage of a few hours of darkness, but their time was up.

"Fire!" she shouted.

Sigrid and the junior valkyries slammed into the horde of elves, pinching them against the stone wall. Under a shower of spears and Sleipnir's boulder-like hooves, the elves scattered with all the dignity of a flock of pigeons.

Several elves raced toward her, and she cued Sleipnir to rear. While she took care of the elves rushing in from the sides, Sleipnir advanced on his hind legs, his front hooves knocking out half a dozen elves in seconds.

Sigrid threw and recalled her spear as fast as she could, the surge of victory dizzying.

"Good, Sleipnir!" She let out a whoop, which was echoed by a few valkyries. She scanned for signs of elves with bows or fearsome beast masks as Mariam had said, but there was nothing.

No hint of antlers and an iron crown, either.

Where is he?

Nerves rampaged inside her. Was this another decoy? Was the Svartalf King waiting somewhere, forcing the valkyries to deplete their energy by fighting weaker, smaller divisions?

Dozens of elves lay dead in the grass while others fled like shadows across the brightening landscape, down the hill to the safety of Myrkviðr.

"They're getting away," Ylva shouted.

A cluster of breakaways moved across the field.

"On it!" Sigrid and Sleipnir followed, refusing to let them go.

A few juniors came to help, swooping into *V* formation behind her. She plowed through the fleeing elves, knocking them over with Sleipnir's breastplate and crushing them beneath his hooves. While she used her spear, he gnashed and bit and reached for them, forcing them to the ground with the agility of a cat chasing a mouse.

There were too many elves to manage, so despite Sleipnir's strength and the barrage of spears, the shadows disappeared into the woods.

"What if we steered them into the stable hands?" Runa asked, her voice high.

Sigrid swore, her insides twisting as she scanned the darkness. They were infuriatingly outnumbered. Should she keep pursuing? Sleipnir danced sideways, raring to go as she forced him to slow down.

"It's okay! They're here!" Ylva pointed at a spot near the main road.

Branches snapped and shadows appeared. Peter, Roland, Hestur, Tóra and Disa, Fisk and the captives, the other stable hands, and the sorcerers pushed through the bushes. The people sagged with exhaustion but the horses were peppy, their eyes bright and their ears facing home.

Relief washed over Sigrid, cooling off her desire to let Sleipnir run after the enemy. *Thank the gods.*

Hestur arched his neck and pranced like a colt, maybe proud for pulling a cart to the edge of the world and back, or maybe just excited to get home and eat hay. A pang went through her heart at not being able to ride him in battle.

"Good job pulling, buddy," she said, and the way he nickered back at her brought a smile to her lips. Even the best horse in the nine worlds couldn't compete with his spirit or replace the connection she had with him.

Sigrid and the juniors escorted the caravan up the hill, where the rest of the valkyries stood guard among a sea of dead Night Elves.

Sleipnir tossed his head, eager to keep fighting.

"I know." Her fingers trembled over the reins. They had to find the elves who'd escaped. They couldn't let that scum run loose in Vanaheim.

More importantly, they had to find the Svartalf King.

An elder valkyrie flew toward her. Sigrid had never met her, so she'd probably retired long ago and had been living a leisurely life in Vindabek. Her long white hair swung in a thin braid down her back, and despite the fact that she looked as old as Vala and her mare had a sway back, her fierce demeanor put little doubt in her ability to fight a battle. "They'll be back. They've been coming in waves."

"We'll be ready." Sigrid scowled at the place where the elves had escaped. "I sent riders to the other villages, asking them to come defend Vanahalla. Hopefully they'll heed the call."

"Excellent. Thank you for coming home, Princess." She nodded. "I'm Frida."

Sigrid nodded back, recognizing the name from her studies on war heroes. "Thank you for defending our home."

Frida studied Sigrid closely, a deep crease between her eyebrows. "We heard about General Eira. I'm so sorry."

A flash of her body plummeting through the air had Sigrid flinching. "She died in battle, like all great warriors."

"We will honor her." Frida nodded. "Queen Kaia asks all of you to come up to Vanahalla. You need to rest and recover before you can help fight."

Sigrid didn't move. "But the Night Elves—"

"Don't worry. We can keep watch while you eat and rest. We'll work on shifts guarding the wall later."

Sigrid scanned the hillside, where more than a hundred Night Elves lay dead, and the forest, where the rest had disappeared. She raised an arm to get the attention of the juniors and stable hands. "We have a few hours to rest. Meet in the royal hall for a meal."

It was also time to work on a plan.

CHAPTER FORTY-SEVEN

LIVING IN
SLEIPNIR'S SHADOW

Sigrid arrived last, letting the valkyries and the stable hands settle in first. Their tack was strewn about the courtyard, leaning against the marble-and-gold walls and transforming the pristine place into a disaster. The mares had taken off to graze and presumably roll in the dirt while their riders funneled through the enormous double doors.

The royal stable hands rushed over to take Sleipnir from her when she dismounted, his muzzle ready. But the stallion behaved for once and went placidly with them.

Delicious smells came from the hall where food was no doubt aplenty, but she had to talk to Aunt Kaia first. Luckily, she didn't have to get far to find her.

In the entrance hall, Aunt Kaia pulled Sigrid into a tight hug. She wore a dark blue robe, her hair in a bejeweled braid, and more gold than usual, setting her apart from everyone else in the hall. But beneath it all, she was pale and had dark pockets under her eyes, like she hadn't slept since the valkyries left for battle. "The sorcerers told us you were coming. I asked my chefs to prepare a meal."

"Thank you." Sigrid pulled back. "I'm sorry it took us so long to get here. We had to leave the villages—"

"That was such a good decision, Sigrid. They can easily rebuild, but Vanahalla can't."

Sigrid let out a breath, once again tamping down that needling doubt. "That's what I thought." The decision still weighed on her, like she wasn't entirely convinced she'd made the right choice. Had Sleipnir influenced her, or had she made it from her heart?

Either way, it was the right one.

Through the doors to the dining hall, a smörgåsbord covered the serving tables around the perimeter. Everyone gasped and moaned with longing as they grabbed plates and stacked them to overflowing. Maybe this was what the royal hall was supposed to look like on an ordinary day—full of people and feasts, instead of just the queen and princess sitting alone in a vast dining hall.

"How did your plan to bring the stable hands go?" Aunt Kaia asked.

Sigrid let out a breath. "We built a palisade, but it didn't hold, and the Night Elves got through. We did capture two of them for questioning."

"Excellent thinking, Sigrid." Aunt Kaia clasped her shoulders, holding her at arm's length. A faint smile tugged the corners of her lips. "You seem different. Sure of yourself. Like a leader. Battle looks good on you."

"Thanks?" Sigrid had never received so much praise in her life, and she wasn't sure what to do with it. Especially when she wasn't sure she agreed with all of it.

Different. Was she acting *that* different?

"And Sleipnir?"

Sigrid smiled. "He's amazing. Like a division of his own, for all the kills we made."

"Wonderful."

If Sigrid hadn't been paying attention, she would've missed the excited and calculated glint in her aunt's eyes. Maybe it was just relief. "Did Harald make progress with the iron arrows while we were gone?"

Aunt Kaia tilted her head. "In a way. They've figured out a rune that performs a similar curse, but it's not quite the same."

"It won't be. Fisk talks about siphoning magic from nature—it's not the same as runes."

"Really? Well, we can discuss that shortly." Aunt Kaia walked with her. "For now, you need to eat. You're trembling from hunger."

Sigrid shook her head. "We have to come up with a plan to defend Vanahalla and also figure out where the Svartalf King—"

"Eat, Sigrid. I'll manage the stable hands." Aunt Kaia clasped her hands and peered into the messy dining hall. "We can't have them lingering in here when there's work to be done. Now, you wait here and I'll have a better meal prepared and brought to you in a drawing room."

"No, this food is fine." Before her aunt could insist otherwise, Sigrid left her behind to grab a few sandwich fixings and sit at an empty table. Her knee bounced as she stuffed food in her mouth as quickly as she could.

Locating the Svartalf King wasn't the only concern. What should they do about the iron arrows? With the sorcerers making no progress and Fisk having no idea what they used to make it, they'd reached a dead end.

Unless the two Night Elf captives knew something.

The pair sat in the corner under the watch of two royal guards. They looked unlikely to try and make a break for it. Their masks tilted and swiveled as they took in the dining hall, pointing out its features to each other.

Fisk stood nearby, talking to Mariam and Peter as the latter two ate.

Sigrid frowned. They should be asking the captives about the weapons right now. Did Fisk make progress with gaining their allegiances, or should they move on to demanding information rather than trying to make friends?

Aunt Kaia was gathering the stable hands from around the

dining room and sending them out to work when Tóra ran inside, knocking into a few people. She spotted Fisk and gave a cry.

Something happened.

Sigrid shoved the rest of her sandwich in her mouth and dashed over to her friends.

Fisk patted Tóra on the back as she sobbed. Mariam and Peter had twin looks of horror at whatever she was saying.

"What is it?" Sigrid asked, reaching their side. "What's wrong?"

Tóra wiped her tears. "I'm sorry. I-I saw…they destroyed the village. It's…it's gone."

All the breath left her lungs. "How?"

"It wasn't clear, but…" She accepted a piece of cloth from Fisk and blew her nose. "They did something. Everything got covered in darkness."

"What?" Sigrid said through her teeth, something fierce snapping at her insides like the jaws of a wolf.

"Like the arrows?" Mariam asked.

Tóra nodded.

How had they done it on such a large scale? New questions piled on top of old. They still didn't know how the arrows worked, and now the elves had come up with a more destructive version.

They couldn't waste any more time.

"Have you made progress with our captives?" she snapped at Fisk, pointing toward the two elves.

Fisk drew back. "I'm working on them. They're not opposed to the idea of allying with us, but they are sort of scared. I think we need to give them a bit of time to realize that we won't hurt them, you know?"

"I bloody will hurt them if they don't hurry up." A rush of energy coursed through her the same way it had in the saddle, urging her into action. "The elves are turning our land to darkness as we speak. We need information. *Now.*"

"Calm down. We can figure this out," Mariam said, looking at her strangely. "They were just talking to me. So, I'll handle them, all right?"

Sigrid swallowed back her rage. "Fine. You do that. Fisk, let's get you back to Harald. Both of you can keep figuring out the iron arrows."

"But I already told them all I know—"

She growled. "Maybe you missed something. They're on the wrong track with runes, and we *cannot* lose another valkyrie or another *entire village*." Her chest tightened at those losses, and she huffed to get rid of it. "I'll work on figuring out where the Svartalf King is hiding. The sooner we find him, the sooner we end things."

Peter stepped closer. "Sigrid, I know you're under a lot of pressure, and we all want this to be over, but..." He looked around the room before setting his gaze back on her. "We've been at this for hours. Didn't you order us to rest before getting back out there?"

"A short rest, not waste-the-day-away rest." The words came out of her harsher than she'd intended, but she didn't take them back. A village had just been obliterated. Didn't they understand that war took no breaks? "Vanaheim is under attack, valkyries are dying, they're turning our land to darkness...and you want *more* rest time? Is that it?"

Peter frowned. "Yes. How can anyone fight if they have no strength?"

She rolled her eyes and turned away. Across the dining hall, Mabil and Ragnarr were leaving, the tails of their cloaks disappearing through the open door.

"Part of being a leader is checking on how your troops are doing," Peter called after her, as if Sigrid was still a kid and needed a lesson reminder.

She rounded on him. "I'm trying to stop the Night Elves from turning Vanaheim into a realm of darkness. I'm doing this for *all* of us. We can't afford to lose any time now." She snapped her fingers. "Fisk, come on."

Both Fisk and Tóra jumped at her order.

She hurried out of the dining hall, following in the wake of the two sorcerers.

Fisk rushed to keep up with her strides. "I just wondered if I could eat something before we—"

"Not now, Fisk." She walked faster, her mind a storm of thoughts and emotion. This was urgent. With Aunt Kaia busy, she had a chance to bring Fisk to the Sorcerers' Tower without being stopped. She needed Fisk to work where he was the most useful, and she was done waiting for her aunt's permission.

As they neared the Sorcerers' Tower, the crackle of its magic grew stronger, playing across her arms. They caught up to the two sorcerers, who were strides away from the dark wooden door.

"Mabil. Ragnarr," she called, and they turned around. "I need you to bring Fisk to Harald."

They exchanged a glance.

"I'm not sure if a Night Elf—" Ragnarr began.

"This is urgent. Harald is expecting him." It was a bit of a lie, but this needed to be done.

There was a pause. Mabil shrugged. "Come on, then."

Ragnarr opened the door, apparently not needing a key.

Sigrid nodded curtly. The power to make Vanaheim's troops, including the sorcerers, listen to her was immensely satisfying. Sleipnir had brewed this confidence in her, turning her into a leader.

Fisk hesitated to follow them.

Sigrid waved him on. "Go!"

Fisk swept after the sorcerers but turned at the last moment. "You said you wouldn't do it again."

The door clicked shut.

In the back of her mind, a piece of her cried out, but it was soon eclipsed by the need to eliminate the enemy. It was as if Sleipnir called to her, making her eager to get back to him and out onto the battlefield once more.

CHAPTER FORTY-EIGHT

ADMITTEDLY GRUESOME

Tracking all of the plans and battles was like trying to lead a dozen mares to their pastures at once, everything pulling in its own direction and demanding Sigrid's attention. Night and day, she and the valkyries took shifts fighting the hordes of Night Elves battering the stone wall like gusts of wind in a storm. The elves refused to back down, and the frustration of the stagnant battle weighed on everyone.

Between fights, the valkyries rested and ate in the dining hall, and Sigrid met with Aunt Kaia to strategize, study, and learn more about cosmic affairs with Svartalfheim. Things were not looking good on any front. Yggdrasil looked worse every day, which meant Loki was gaining ground faster than they could fight back. The sorcerers had tried a few new enchantments and runes, but none had worked in neutralizing iron arrows or pushing back the Night Elf army.

Sigrid struggled against the incessant buzz beneath her skin, which tried to pull her out to the battlefield when she was supposed to be in Vanahalla. Only visiting Sleipnir in the stables allowed her a moment to take a breath and calm her racing heart. But the urge to get back out there remained.

Meanwhile, her friends treated her oddly. Mariam kept asking if she was okay and if she wanted to talk. Peter opted to look disappointed anytime they were in the same room. And Fisk gave her terse daily reports about the progress of the sorcerers' research.

One morning, she was getting Sleipnir ready to meet the junior valkyries when Fisk appeared on the other side of his stall door.

"There's a deep well in Svartalfheim where darkness resides like a living thing," he reported in his driest tone. "The elves must have siphoned from there to create the iron arrows and whatever they used on Borthorpe. The sorcerers are exploring how to counteract it."

Sigrid's heart leaped. "How long until they have something ready?"

Fisk considered. "Mabil, Ragnarr, and a few others will be helping. So, not long."

"Excellent." She had a new weapon to test, and now that the iron arrows had been figured out, they had just gained a huge advantage. "Good job. You should be pro—"

"Is that all, Your Highness?"

Sigrid hesitated, then nodded once, an unnamed feeling stirring inside her. But she didn't have time to entertain it. She had a war to win.

As Fisk left, she grabbed Sleipnir's reins and headed outside to meet the juniors, where Gunni had just returned from her two-day journey from village to village to spread the word about Vanahalla.

"What happened?" Sigrid asked the moment she stepped into their midst, and they all broke off their conversations to face her.

"All of the senior divisions opted to keep protecting the villages." Gunni's normally pink face was drained of color. "I can't blame them. You should see it out there. The villages need all the help they can get. We found two more covered in darkness."

Sigrid ground her teeth, her stomach roiling. More Night

Elves than they thought must have invaded, moving undetected like swarms of mites. The fact that they kept attacking villages and forcing the need to protect them as much as the royal hall sent a ripple of dread down her spine.

They're being strategic. They're thinning our troops. This is the king's doing.

"Are the seniors holding up?" Edith asked.

Gunni swallowed hard. "Three more were hit with iron arrows."

Whispers rose around her.

"Nothing fatal," Gunni added quickly, "but the generals have been holding back their troops a little for fear of being hit."

Sigrid sucked in a breath. It was time to end these attacks before another valkyrie was killed or another village lost. If the sorcerers hadn't figured anything out by nightfall, then she'd go out there herself and take down every single elf until she found the Svartalf King.

Then she'd finish him off, too.

"Head up for a quick rest and a meal, Gunni. Tell the seniors we'll need to send more food and supplies to the valkyries defending the villages." Sigrid waited until Gunni took off before addressing the others. "Now, listen up. Fire is a Night Elf's biggest weakness. Hitting them with spears isn't doing enough, and we need to eradicate them. Mabil and Ragnarr worked all night to make these, and they've enchanted it with volcanic properties so it burns hotter than a normal fire. Runa?" She held out her hand, and Runa handed over the torch and saddle bag she'd requested earlier.

Everyone seemed to stop breathing as Sigrid secured the bag to the front of the saddle and lit the torch.

"The saddle bags on your mares are filled with straw that has been soaked in a flammable sulfur mix." She drew her golden spear and dipped it into the saddle bag, twisting a clump of straw around the point. "You'll wrap the end of your spear in the straw—

and light it up." She touched the straw to her torch, and it ignited with a *whoosh*.

Several valkyries gasped, and their mares shied.

Sigrid threw the flaming spear at a hay bale on the hillside. It caught fire dramatically, decimating the bale in seconds and leaving a smoldering hole in the grass.

She expected grins and appreciative nods, but no one met her eye. A grain of doubt rolled over her mind before she gritted her teeth. What was wrong with them? Were they tired of the fight or afraid of using fire?

Even Mariam fidgeted with her torch, not saying a word.

"Why don't we scare them away with fire instead of hitting them with it?" Ylva asked. "Enchanted fire could ruin everything if it goes amiss."

"Yeah," Edith said. "Burning them is dangerous."

"And gross," Mariam added.

Sigrid shook her head. "We can't be soft with them anymore. We have to show them there will be no mercy, all right?"

The valkyries exchanged glances, which sent a spark of frustration through Sigrid's middle.

"Sigrid," Runa said, a tremor in her voice. She pointed down the hill.

Without looking, Sigrid knew another swarm of Night Elves must be rushing toward them. It was the same tactic over and over again—regrouping, attacking, falling back.

Sigrid readied her spear and torch. "Let's go!"

They flew to meet the attack, new weapons in hand, Sigrid and Sleipnir tearing up the ground beneath them. The moment they were within throwing distance, Sigrid was the first to throw her flaming spear.

The effect was extraordinary but admittedly gruesome. The elf ignited, screaming, and fell to the ground before she'd even summoned back her spear.

"It works!" She raised a fist, basking in the energy surging from Sleipnir. "Valkyries, burn them to ashes!"

A hesitation passed over the airborne valkyries.

Then Ylva threw hers, and the others followed.

"Flank turn, left-right," Sigrid shouted, drawing on her evening spent studying maneuvers. The valkyries responded to the command, pivoting in formation and aiming a new attack. A thrill raced through her chest at the power she wielded.

The swirling fires in the sky were a fearsome sight. From the ground, Sigrid and Sleipnir broke the elves' formation like a ship cutting through the water's surface. Within minutes, the acrid smell of smoke coated Sigrid's nostrils and crept down the back of her throat, making her cough. The horses tossed their heads, agitated.

A group of elves made a break for Myrkviðr, apparently deciding this fight wasn't worth it.

With a rush of victory, Sigrid galloped after them, the chase sending a wild sensation through her middle. Sleipnir's rattling eight-beat stride tore divots in the meadow, his nostrils bellowing. They caught up to the slowest elf, and she leaned out of the saddle with her spear. Though he moved like a flitting shadow, Sleipnir was fast enough that she managed to hook the tip of her spear beneath his bovine mask.

He screamed, stumbling to a halt.

"Where is the Svartalf King?" she shouted, determined to use this opportunity to get information.

The elf swatted away her weapon and tried to keep running.

Sleipnir used his front hooves to knock him over, and Sigrid sprang out of the saddle as he hit the grass. She landed on her feet and grabbed him by the mask.

"Tell me where he is, elf."

"No!"

She hooked her fingers under his mask, giving him one last chance. "You get to choose how you want to die."

"I'll die keeping my king's secrets." He kicked her shin.

With a growl of frustration, Sigrid tugged upward.

"Don't!" he screamed.

The elf would burn to death the moment daylight touched him. But what would that look like? Was she willing to find out?

"Last chance."

His grip tightened on the mask, but he didn't speak.

Sigrid gritted her teeth. She was so close to finding the Svartalf King, and yet this elf dared to stand in her way. Frustration surged like boiling water, making her vision darken at the edges. The muscles in her arms contracted, wanting to pull the mask off, but the screaming in her head kept telling her otherwise.

A voice that sounded like Mariam's told her to *stop*.

She tried to let go. Her fingers wouldn't cooperate.

Let go, Mariam's voice said. *You don't want to do this. You're not Helena.*

Sigrid released the elf, falling back with a gasp.

The elf scrambled away on all fours, breathing fast. His mask clattered as his whole body trembled, and then he got his feet under him and ran off.

Ice coated her insides, making it hard to breathe. Her mouth dried up like she was going to vomit, and she held onto her stomach.

What did I almost do?

"Sleipnir," she called out, her voice breaking.

He trotted over to her side.

I'm not Helena. I'm not cruel.

Shaking, she vaulted on and galloped back to the others. Her balance waned as she tried to blink away the sight of the elf scrambling away in the grass.

What's happening to me?

CHAPTER FORTY-NINE

MARIAM'S WARNING

Later, in the quiet of the royal stable, Sigrid untacked and groomed Sleipnir. Her hands trembled, remnants of adrenaline and his power wreaking havoc in her. She tried to feel where the stallion's influence ended and her own feelings began, but the line was hazy to the point where she didn't know how much she could trust herself. Was this white-hot anger toward the enemy normal, or was it all Sleipnir?

The saddle had always given her a feeling of completeness, but what she'd experienced over the last few days was…new. Whereas Hestur felt like an extension of her limbs, her connection with Sleipnir had grown far beyond that.

Setting the brush aside, she ran her hand over his neck. Their pulses synchronized the moment she touched his steel-gray coat. He was calm, so no other emotions tugged at her. But in the middle of battle, his state was one of overconfidence, violence, and recklessness.

Even after riding him, the dangerous energy had stayed in her, making her all those things and more. *That isn't right, is it?*

Sigrid shook her head and grabbed the brush again. "All I feel is chaos."

Sleipnir snorted and pawed the hay-covered floor.

"You're a good boy, Sleipnir," she said, brushing him. "But

together, we're…."

A door clanked open, and footsteps came down the barn aisle, all of it amplified under her heightened senses. A moment later, Mariam appeared over the stall door. She opened it and let herself inside.

"Hi," Sigrid said, running a brush down the stallion's legs.

Even if Mariam hadn't been at her side earlier, her voice in Sigrid's head had been the only thing to pull her back from doing something horrifying. She couldn't face Mariam after that. She couldn't think about shameful actions, or pulling back, or doubting what she had to do—not when a war needed to be won and difficult choices made.

"Sigrid," Mariam said.

Focus on the war. There were so many moving pieces.

The other divisions needed to help defend Vanahalla. Yes, they were all at risk, but what was the use of defending villages if Vanahalla fell?

Mariam stepped closer. "We need to talk."

Sigrid had to get out there and find the Svartalf King. An alliance with him was no longer an option, but they could still get more Night Elf hostages and turn them. There had to be many more who would agree to turn coat. Fisk needed to be out there finding allies.

Mariam grabbed Sigrid's arm, her grip gentle. "Sigrid."

Sigrid swallowed back a surge of annoyance but didn't move her hands off Sleipnir. "Yes?"

They stared at each other, the silence stretching on. Mariam had deep lines in her forehead, her dark eyes searching Sigrid's face. The war had toned everyone's muscles and made them stronger, but Mariam looked gaunt, like she hadn't eaten enough to make up for it.

"You need to stop riding Sleipnir."

Anger sparked at the brazen command.

Mariam tightened her grip and pulled Sigrid away from the stallion. The brush fell from Sigrid's hand and clattered to the floor. "You've changed since deciding to ride him again. I'm beginning to think I was wrong before, when I said nothing can make someone—" She cut herself off, swallowing hard.

"Evil," Sigrid said, finishing the sentence. Her pulse thundered in her ears as she struggled to control her words. "You said nothing can make someone evil."

"I didn't take into account who Sleipnir is and where he came from," Mariam said, calm but clearly unwilling to back down. "Sigrid, something cosmic is at play here. Don't tell me you haven't thought about it."

"Of course something cosmic is at play!" Sigrid wrenched her arm back and stepped away. "This is my destiny. It was written in the beginning that Sleipnir's heir would—"

"Beside the point." Mariam stepped closer. "Don't you feel what he does to you?"

Sigrid's heart flipped.

It was hard to believe some of the things she'd done and the feelings that coursed through her, keeping her up at night—but she couldn't step back from it.

The worlds were in chaos. Vanaheim was at war. She and Sleipnir had excelled in battle, killing and blocking more Night Elves than any other valkyrie. If riding him meant she had to surrender to the violence of battle, then she'd do it. To stop now could make them lose.

Vanaheim needed her to fulfill her purpose as Sleipnir's heir, even if she was uncomfortable with what that meant.

Sigrid shook her head firmly. "He makes me a better warrior, Mariam. Have you seen what I can do in battle?"

"I've seen the things you've done," Mariam said, sounding disappointed, "and I wish you would talk to me about what you're feeling."

"I'm fine." The words sounded hollow, even to Sigrid. She

patted Sleipnir, glad for the way it settled her doubts.

"You're fine about your decision to abandon Borthorpe?"

"A strategic decision. What about it?"

Mariam's eyes widened. "You were completely indifferent about leaving all of those people while the Night Elves ransacked their homes. And they ended up getting destroyed by darkness. Do you see anything wrong with that?"

"Being a princess and a lieutenant comes with tough decisions. I chose to protect the royal hall over Borthorpe, yes. The town was already ruined, we got out as many as we could—"

"Are you saying you always would have made the decision to abandon a town full of innocent people in favor of protecting some marble-and-gold towers?"

"Yes," she snapped without pausing to consider.

Mariam turned her gaze to Sleipnir and shook her head. "You can't even step away from him, can you?" When she looked at Sigrid again, her expression was cold and held none of the tenderness Sigrid had grown used to seeing.

Sigrid squared her shoulders. "What?"

Mariam's eyes grew stormier. "What about General Eira?"

Something twisted hard in Sigrid's chest, but she ignored it. "There hasn't been time for mourning—"

"Everyone else seems to have found a minute for it!" Mariam's yell made Sleipnir snort in agitation. "All you've been able to think about is how to light some elves on fire. General Eira was—" She huffed. "She was one of few people who supported me when I said I wanted to bring my mom home to Vanaheim. Now she's gone, and probably so is my chance of bringing my family here. And you don't even care."

Sigrid's cheeks burned. A mix of emotions ricocheted through her body, making her tremble. She let anger win, clenching her fists as she shouted back. "We're at war! It's hard to focus on personal things when Vanahalla is under attack!"

"What good is it saving the world when you don't even care if the people live or die?"

The words sliced at Sigrid's heart.

Mariam shook her head and started pacing, crossing and un-crossing her arms. "You've changed, Sigrid. You've been acting completely heartless." Her expression twisted, and with her hair pulled into a tight braid and her fitted white uniform, she looked more valkyrie-like than ever. "And as far as I can tell, it's got something to do with your fancy new *royal title* and Sleipnir."

"You have no idea…" Sigrid's voice broke. "No idea what it's like to be in this position, Mariam."

"A princess? Sleipnir's heir? No, I don't, and I'm glad of it. Because it's turned you into the type of person you used to hate."

Sigrid pressed closer to Sleipnir, embracing the way he numbed her against all the hurt. "If that's how you feel, then you don't know anything about me."

Sleipnir pinned his ears and gnashed his teeth, which Mariam took as a cue to back out of the stall with her hands raised. *Good boy.*

"Tell the valkyries to get ready," Sigrid ordered. "We're hunting down the Svartalf King."

"Yes, *Your Highness*," Mariam said on her way out of the stables.

Sigrid removed her hand from Sleipnir, the heat lingering in her palm. She drew a breath, suddenly lightheaded. Guilt burned inside her. Why had she said all those things? She didn't mean or believe half of them. The words just came out, like someone else was speaking for her.

Mariam might have had a point. Would Sigrid have done and said these things if not for Sleipnir's influence? Did it matter? Embracing Sleipnir's power meant winning against the Night Elves. But at what cost? The people of Vanaheim? Her friends? Mariam?

Sigrid gripped the front of her tunic and leaned back against the wall of Sleipnir's stall. Her breaths sawed in and out. Then her knees gave out as the weight of her decisions settled over her.

CHAPTER FIFTY

YGGDRASIL'S BRANCHES

Sigrid ate with Aunt Kaia in one of the many drawing rooms, away from everyone else and so far removed from the frontlines that it felt like a world away. The waitstaff had piled her plate high with slow-roasted lamb, buttery potato dumplings with sour cream, pickled red cabbage, and raisin bread.

She tasted none of it.

Aunt Kaia was oblivious to Sigrid's spiraling mood, talking at length about how the stable hands ought to help make weapons, and the juniors ought to fetch the villagers so they could join the fight, and *someone* ought to go find the nearest untouched farming town and bring in more food before they ran out. Sigrid was too busy going over her argument with Mariam to chime in.

Her own name snagged her attention.

"...thanks to your brilliant idea to use fire," Aunt Kaia said, "we can finally move everyone back down to the valkyrie stable instead of having them clutter up the courtyard. You've done such great work. We've hurt the elves' morale and they're falling back."

Sigrid stared into her red wine. *Not so sure about our own morale.*

She couldn't forget the resigned looks on the juniors' faces as she handed them the torches and told them to gruesomely light the elves on fire. They'd clearly been uncomfortable with torturing the enemy by burning them to death instead of shooting them cleanly from a distance, and Sigrid hadn't paused to notice or think.

I should've been uncomfortable with it, too.

"I can't believe we didn't know the Svartalf King was assembling an army…" Beneath a thick layer of powder, the creases in Aunt Kaia's face were deeper than ever, aging her by years. She looked bony beneath her blue robe, and even her normally lustrous hair looked flat and dull. She shook her head and sighed. "He's been building one all this time, and we had no idea. I *knew* Óleifr was mistaken to trust that the other worlds were behaving."

"You think we should have monitored them?" Sigrid pushed her plate away, signaling she was done. A young man gave a small bow and took it.

"Absolutely. Once we push them back into their hole, we'll plan to check on them regularly to make sure they aren't building an army or doing anything else suspicious." She nodded as if it were settled. "It's our job as a high-ranking world to tame them."

Sigrid frowned. This sounded a lot like trying to make Vanaheim reign over the other worlds. She grabbed her wine cup but quickly set it down. Everything Mariam had said mixed poorly with what Aunt Kaia was saying now.

Could the decisions Sigrid made under Aunt Kaia's counsel have been wrong? She'd trusted her aunt, but her ideas and opinions often sat uneasy in Sigrid's gut.

Aunt Kaia's views of Yggdrasil—including Vanaheim's place next to Asgard, the elves' place near the bottom, and the need to enforce everyone's rank—were definitely skewed. After all, she'd known only a privileged life in Vanahalla. She had little concept of the world beyond these marble-and-gold towers, never mind worlds beyond Vanaheim.

Everything from the jewel-encrusted seat beneath Sigrid to

the gold bands on her aunt's wrist spoke of Vanaheim's endless wealth. The portrait behind Aunt Kaia showed the beautiful Vanir goddess Nerthus rising from a shimmering pool. The books on the shelves around them told tale after tale of Vanaheim's history and greatness.

It must be easy for Aunt Kaia and anyone else in this hall to think that other worlds were below them, that other worlds weren't as good or as worthy of a place near Asgard, when she'd never been there nor met their people. She'd grown up hearing tales of Vanaheim's greatness, never once considering that other worlds might be great, too.

"Tame them?" Sigrid asked casually, trying not to betray the storm of doubts raging inside her. "Because humans are a higher class than elves, right?"

"Exactly."

Sigrid's food threatened to come back up. "How do you think we should monitor and tame Svartalfheim, then?"

"We'll need to control the spring of Hvergelmir. I want to stop the elves from using it. Leave them in Svartalfheim. They shouldn't be coming this high up Yggdrasil. Don't you think?" She shifted, tapping her fingers on the wooden table. "Of course, I need to consult the council once everyone is here."

"Control the spring?" Sigrid's heart beat faster. Her aunt hadn't hesitated. How long had she been thinking of this?

"We'll have to get Ratatosk on our side—bribe him, or—"

"Capture him?" Sigrid clenched the armrests on her seat. "Aunt Kaia, that's what the Night Elves were trying to do. I thought we agreed that the spring is a neutral place and not for one world to control."

Aunt Kaia tapped her fingers faster, not meeting Sigrid's gaze. "This is different."

"How? It's not our responsibility to rule over the other worlds. It's our responsibility to help keep peace and balance."

"And that means maintaining our place in Yggdrasil. We're in a situation where we have to fight for our position at the top, or we'll be pushed to the bottom." Aunt Kaia fidgeted with the collar of her robe, which hung looser than usual so the embroidered boar's head sagged. "I just don't know what else I'm supposed to do…"

"We can fight for Vanaheim without being so hostile." Sigrid leaned forward. "It's not too late to try and reason with the Night Elves. Not all of them agree with their king. I'm sure we can sway them to our side."

Aunt Kaia studied her, then leaned back in her chair and heaved a sigh. She rubbed her face with trembling hands. "It's so hard, being in this position. All the decisions…"

"You're not alone in this, Aunt Kaia. We've got the council—Harald and Vala and the generals. You can trust them, lean on them. And you've got me."

She could understand fear clouding her aunt's mind, but this wasn't the way. If she couldn't make her see reason, then Vala or General Ulfhilda would be able to bring some sense to Aunt Kaia. They had to.

"Even with the council, our choices come with such consequences." Aunt Kaia held her gaze, her dark eyes wide as if pleading with her to understand. "After you and me, there's nobody higher up telling us *yea* or *nay*. We're it. We're the top, and we have the final say. I don't like it."

Sigrid considered her own decisions lately, how she'd been certain they were right until Mariam shouted at her. "Decisions can have big consequences, sure."

"I'm glad you agree, because I think we need more help," Aunt Kaia said. "You and I have limited experience. We need to bring in someone who knows what they're doing."

Sigrid frowned. What was she getting at? Hadn't Sigrid done a decent job leading the junior division? Sigrid had managed the entire battlefront since their return to Vanahalla, and they were doing fine. It stung that her aunt thought they were struggling.

"Aunt Kaia, I have the sorcerers working on countering the iron arrows, three valkyries patrolling for signs of the Svartalf King, two Night Elf captives willing to turn to our side, and the valkyries are flawlessly rotating shifts defending Vanahalla. How am I not doing enough?"

"It's magnificent what you have accomplished, but for how long can you keep it up? What we need is a strategy to end this. We need expert guidance." She cleared her throat and reached out to place a cold, clammy hand over Sigrid's.

Sigrid wanted to pull away. "From who?"

"Sigrid…" She drew a shaky breath. "I think it's time we bring my sister back from Helheim."

CHAPTER FIFTY-ONE

A WOLF
LYING IDLE

Aunt Kaia's words hung in the drawing room like smoke, coiling around them, making it hard to breathe.

"My…my mother?" Sigrid asked numbly.

Aunt Kaia squeezed her hand. "I know you had a big disagreement with Lena while you were there, but she isn't all bad. Please trust me."

A disagreement?

"She wanted to kill Óleifr and take over Vanaheim's throne, and then work on ruling over other worlds." The volume of Sigrid's words rose uncontrollably. "She tried to use me like a weapon!"

Aunt Kaia's lips pressed into a tremulous almost-smile. "Her methods might not have been great, but she had the right idea. We need someone like her to guide us through this dark time. We have no idea what we're doing, Sigrid."

"We'll be in an even bigger mess if we bring her into it!" Sigrid wrenched her hand out of her aunt's cold grasp. Helena was the most heartless person Sigrid had ever met. Nothing good could come of allying with someone like that. "She wanted to unleash Hel's army on the nine worlds. I don't think that qualifies as *having the right idea.*"

"Maybe Hel's army wasn't the right answer, but we need to

assert our position over the lower realms or else the Night Elves will take over Vanaheim. Everything in this hall will be lost to them—dangerous runes, prophetic power, valkyrie weapons, all of the wealth and priceless relics our family has earned since the beginning. We'll lose all of it."

Mariam's words echoed in Sigrid's mind. *What good is it saving the world when you don't even care if the people live or die?*

Aunt Kaia was worried about material wealth and status. But what about Vanaheim's people?

"I know we need to protect Vanaheim and our people," Sigrid said pointedly. "But do you really think launching an invasion is the right way to do this?"

"I want to discuss the possibility."

Sigrid shook her head, her heart beating faster. All of the lives that would be lost, the stress of battle on the people and lands, the injuries, wasted efforts, broken relationships—none of that was worth it. She might have agreed to assume her role as a princess, and she would gladly defend Vanaheim against an invasion, but nowhere did she agree to use her position to launch a war. She'd seen what battle did. She'd experienced it coming out of Helheim and Svartalfheim, and now here.

Fighting to defend her home was one thing, but she couldn't support an invasion that aimed to dominate other worlds.

"We can make peace without using war as a means to get there," she said firmly. "If we invade the lower realms, we're no better than the Night Elves. We'll tip everything into further imbalance. This is the mayhem Loki wants."

Aunt Kaia's eyebrows pulled down, making her look as sad as the day Sigrid met her. "The gods wrote, *A wolf who lies idle wins little meat.* If we idle, we risk losing the status our family has worked hard to build. Every book I've studied talks about how there has always been war, and there will always be war. It's the nature of the cosmos."

She was wrong. She had to be. Maybe their gods and ancestors had resolved problems with violence, but that didn't mean things had to continue this way.

"War brings death," Sigrid said, hoping to make her aunt see sense. "Valkyries will die, civilians will die, and more villages will be destroyed. Is that what you want?"

Aunt Kaia said nothing, her eyes brimming. "I thought you would understand."

Shock rolled through Sigrid like thunder. History was repeating itself, but instead of her mother, now it was her aunt who'd hidden behind a welcoming face, plotting all the while. "Is this what you've been working toward this whole time? You want what my mother wanted?"

"No," Aunt Kaia said quickly. "I never wanted to use you to raise the dead. That was heartless."

"But you want to invade other worlds and rule over them."

"And in doing so, restore balance."

"This isn't balance! This is a conquest!"

Aunt Kaia wrapped her fingers in her hair. "I'm not explaining this right. This isn't about deaths and conquests, it's... Sigrid, if we go together to get Lena from Helheim, she can explain it better than I can."

Aunt Kaia's affectionate nickname for Helena sparked a flame in Sigrid.

"No!" Sigrid leaped out of her chair, almost toppling it back. "My mother is in the underworld where she belongs. She's stuck there of her own selfish volition. I won't help you go get her."

Aunt Kaia gave a failed attempt at a laugh. "You're blowing this out of proportion. Where is the valkyrie princess who was ready to do whatever it takes to save Vanaheim?"

Mariam's words swam forward again. *You've changed.*

Sigrid's insides churned.

Maybe Aunt Kaia had reason to believe she had warmed up

to Helena and would go along with a conquest. Sigrid had given every indication that she enjoyed battle, that she would go any length to win this invasion, and would have welcomed an ongoing war with the Night Elves.

If Aunt Kaia hadn't made the mistake of bringing up Helena, what would have happened? Would Sigrid have agreed to hunt down every Night Elf from here to Svartalfheim?

With Sleipnir's power driving her, Yggdrasil would've been bathed in blood.

I would never… I will not.

Sigrid shook her head and stepped away from the table. "Does anyone else know about your plans? Vala? Everyone on the council?"

Aunt Kaia fluttered her hands as if to dismiss the idea. "We haven't discussed this yet. I was hoping to convince you first."

"And you have my answer."

"Please, let's talk—"

"I'm done here." A tremor seized Sigrid's voice. "I'm not helping you, and that's my final decision."

Pulse ticking in her neck, she stormed from the drawing room.

"You forget who your queen is," Aunt Kaia called after her. "When the time is right, the valkyries will leave for Svartalfheim. You should give them forewarning."

Sigrid stopped and looked back over her shoulder. Was that a threat?

Her aunt's expression shifted—challenging, haughty, spiteful. Where she'd seemed helpless and frail a moment ago, she suddenly came to Sigrid in a new light.

She was the queen, and if she wanted a conquest, then it would happen.

Not if I can help it.

Sigrid set her jaw and continued on without a word. The air prickled, the sensation more than just magic. The whole hall was tainted with betrayal.

She walked faster, taking a spiral staircase two steps at a time. Vanahalla was quiet, with the valkyries who normally filled the entrance and dining halls below having been moved back to their stable. It left the place hollow.

I should have seen through Aunt Kaia's deception.

All the small moments of doubt coalesced into a clear picture. Like when Aunt Kaia said King Óleifr never should have sent the senior valkyries to help Jotunheim and that helping other worlds was a waste of resources. She'd never cared about other worlds and only wanted Vanaheim on top. Why hadn't Sigrid seen it then?

And then there was the way she'd wanted to rank Sigrid next to General Eira, to make her a leader despite being underqualified, to force a royal into the valkyrie ranks. What about the praise she'd given Sigrid for deciding to leave Borthorpe? She only worried about royalty, precious items, and the palace being protected, but not about Vanaheim's people.

I believed the wrong person again.

A lump formed in Sigrid's throat as she stormed past the rooms Aunt Kaia had shown her and the many closed doors they hadn't gone through, heading for one room in particular. She had to see Yggdrasil. She had to see the states of Vanaheim, Svartalfheim, Helheim, and Asgard.

She made it to the woodsy room depicting Yggdrasil and slipped inside, shutting the door behind her. The humid air coated her skin, the ash tree's aroma soothing.

Asgard fluttered at the top as before, sturdy and unchanging. But below it, nothing made sense. Leaves sprouted and shrank back into the wall rapidly, the worlds changing places and tipping every few seconds. Vanaheim and Svartalfheim had become one, a large clump of leaves bearing two labels that fought for space.

How many of my decisions helped this along?

She touched the roots representing Helheim, wishing she could see what was going on in that world. Did her mother have any idea what was happening out here? And what about Asgard? If this was all Loki's doing, what was happening between him and the other gods?

A draft curled around her, raising the hairs on the back of her neck.

She looked around the circular room, her brow furrowed. The door was shut, so where was the breeze coming from? Then she noticed a vertical crack in the right wall where a beam of white light filtered in — a door, open slightly as if someone had passed through it.

Bracing for whatever might be on the other side, she pushed it open.

It was another circular room, open and bright because of a large window to the left. An enormous tree took up the rest of the wall, this one a tapestry with thousands of branches. The whole thing looked like it had been painstakingly sewn, each branch woven with great care. The bottom was more faded and frayed than the top, like it was much older.

Symbols flecked the tapestry like leaves, and as she stepped into the room, it became clear that they were names.

The royal family tree. So many names stretched across it that she wouldn't be able to count them all. The branches were tangled, the tree growing and ending and leaning every which way.

Would she find her own name at the top?

"Every new generation, another layer is woven."

Sigrid spun around, her heart hammering in her chest. Vala stood there, as ethereal as always with her white hair draped around her shoulders and a gnarled hand clutching a walking stick.

CHAPTER FIFTY-TWO

ANOTHER
CURSED TREE

S igrid stepped back. "Sorry. The door was open and—"
"No need to apologize for wandering around your own hall."
Vala smiled kindly, as if to remind Sigrid she was a friend.

A wave of relief passed over Sigrid at the old Seer's presence.
It seemed like a lifetime had passed since they'd spoken alone in
her tower all those weeks ago.

"Congratulations on officially becoming a royal, Princess
Sigrid. I don't think I've said that yet."

Sigrid pursed her lips. *Congratulations* was not the right
sentiment. "I'd rather you call me just Sigrid."

Vala inclined her head, raising her gaze back to the wall.
"It's quite a job, maintaining this tree. Every so often, the whole
tapestry needs to be shifted lower to accommodate more
generations."

Sigrid glanced at the names. Did this mean she had distant
cousins somewhere? Hopefully there was nobody else with a
thirst for ruling the nine worlds by force.

Vala's walking stick made a *thump, thump, thump* as she
hobbled to stand beside Sigrid. She used it to point to a cluster
of names at the top. "I believe this is what you're looking for?"

Sigrid's heart jumped. *Helena. Óleifr. Kaia.*

No children grew from any of them. Unsurprising. Her

existence had been a secret for sixteen years. It was an odd relief not to see her name woven into the walls of Vanahalla.

Unfortunately, Vala said, "Your name will be added as soon as we have a moment to breathe, I think."

"No need to rush it." Sigrid scowled. She didn't want to see any proof of her relation to Princess Helena and Aunt Kaia. Was it naive to hope they were the only bad apples on her family tree?

The rest of the names blurred before her, the hundreds of branches and letters indistinguishable. Her family was massive, and yet she'd grown up knowing none of them—a fact that would have been upsetting at one time. Now, after getting to know her mother and aunt, gratitude flooded her thoughts. She had no interest in this family.

"Fascinating, the way the throne has passed along these branches," Vala said. "Always to the firstborn male."

"Senseless tradition," Sigrid mumbled.

On that one point, she agreed with her mother. Would Helena have been as terrible a person if she'd been made queen? Maybe she would have been less set on vengeance. Or maybe that was her personality.

"This is unprecedented." Vala tapped the end of her stick on various names across the topmost branches. "No male heir is alive to take the throne. So where does that leave us?"

"It leaves us with Aunt Kaia," Sigrid said bitterly.

Vala hummed. "Is that the correct hierarchy, though? Or does the firstborn's firstborn have the claim?" She sighed, waving a hand as if to swat away the question. "This is where we've ended up, and now there's a war on our hands."

Sigrid stared at the place where her name should be embroidered, then traced her gaze downward, following the past connections until she got to the trunk, where the word "Óðinn" appeared. *Odin.*

Of all these people on the tree, she'd been the one to become

Sleipnir's heir—not her mother, aunt, uncle, grandparents, or any of her distant relatives. Nobody had been the stallion's rightful rider since Odin. After all this time, she still didn't understand why. What made her so special?

"Why do I have Sleipnir?" Maybe there'd been a mistake. Sigrid couldn't even manage him without turning into chaos herself.

"I think only the Norns can answer that," Vala said slowly. Disappointment must have shown on Sigrid's face, because the old woman added, "But…if I had to guess, I would say it's because you're different from everyone else on this tapestry."

At one time, she would have considered "different" to be an insult. But this put a hopeful bubble in her chest, because she desperately wanted to be different from the family she'd met.

"I don't want the same things as Aunt Kaia or my mother, if that's what you mean."

Vala's icy blue eyes searched her face. "No?"

"My mother wanted to raise Hel's army and rule over the other worlds, and Aunt Kaia thinks we should go get her from Helheim. She agrees that Vanaheim should have the highest place in Yggdrasil, next to Asgard. They're willing to launch a conquest to make it happen."

Vala sighed. "The positions of Yggdrasil's branches have been a point of contention since the beginning, and it's complete nonsense. It's based on a misunderstanding of what it means to be close to the gods."

Sigrid tilted her head, considering her words. "What's the right way of looking at it?"

"Well, being close with Njord, for example, means respecting and cherishing his domain—the sea. It doesn't mean one has to go destroying every other world so that their world can exist on a branch closer to Asgard." She huffed. "These royals are so fixated on asserting power that they fail to see what a true relationship with a god looks like."

Sigrid furrowed her brow. This made more sense than how her aunt approached it.

"No royal has truly understood this." Vala exhaled, sounding more tired than ever. "Vanahalla has suffered from a woeful lack of compassion. Even King Óleifr had his faults."

Sigrid shifted on her feet, knowing full well all of her own faults. "Maybe I'm not that different from them."

Vala leaned on her walking stick, fixing Sigrid with her penetrating gaze. "Why do you say that?"

"Sometimes, I'm scared that I—" Her voice broke, so she tried again. "On Sleipnir, it's like this power overcomes me, and…I've made choices I'm not proud of." Her throat seemed to close. She shook her head. She couldn't admit how much influence Sleipnir had over her and how much she feared she was like her mother— as if saying it out loud made the fear more likely to be true.

Vala nodded slowly, as if examining each word Sigrid had voiced. "How much do you know about the concept of *balance*, Sigrid?"

She'd heard too much about it recently. Thinking back to what Ratatosk had told her, she said, "Order and chaos. Good and evil."

"This kind of equilibrium also applies to family trees. There are a lot of branches in front of you, and Odin's name is the most prominent and celebrated in this whole tree. But two people are needed to make a baby." Vala pointed with her stick. "Odin came from one side of your tree. Who is on the other?"

"My mother said my father was a nobody—"

"Not him. I mean further back on your mother's side."

With trepidation cinching her insides, Sigrid traced her gaze down the branch labeled *Helena*. Each name she passed frayed the thread connecting her to the royal family. She'd never heard of any of these people.

A name near the ground made her stop breathing.

Vala must have noticed, because she said, "Tangled within

your roots, we find the goddess Hel. And do you know who Hel's father was?"

All the blood drained from Sigrid's face, leaving her cold and dizzy. *No.*

She shook her head. "I'm not. I can't be."

But there it was, snaking down the branches connecting Helena to the rest of the tree—Loki.

"Loki is in your blood, Sigrid." Vala's voice seemed to come from a long way away. "You are the descendant of Odin and the heir to Sleipnir—but you are also the descendant of chaos, and you have those forces running through your veins."

Everything Ratatosk had said about Loki was a part of her. Mischief. Chaos. Obscenity. Lies.

Evil.

This was the missing link—Helena, Aunt Kaia, and Sigrid's own erratic emotions whenever she rode Sleipnir. Of course Aunt Kaia was in allegiance with Helena. The forces of mischief and imbalance ran in her family. The tapestry in front of her proved it. And with Loki's blood in both Sleipnir's and her veins, they embodied far too much of the god of chaos.

Everything Sigrid had done, her affinity for Kaia and Helena, Sleipnir's hold over her—it all made sense. Sleipnir's hold on her was not so much an influence, but a conduit to Loki.

"Sigrid?" Vala's tone softened with worry. "Are you okay?"

Sigrid's breaths came fast, making her lightheaded. "I—I have to go."

The Seer's eyebrows arched with concern. "I hoped that understanding your family tree would help—"

"It's fine. I just need to think." She swept from the room.

Vala called out after her.

But Sigrid kept going, a hand over her mouth to stifle her panic.

Sleipnir wasn't making her evil—he was bringing out the evil that was already inside her.

CHAPTER FIFTY-THREE

GOOD HORSES
AND BAD HORSES

All this time, Sigrid had thought she'd chosen to let Sleipnir in and struggled to control his impulses—but after talking to Vala, she understood what was going on better than ever.

The impulses were *hers*.

Sigrid ran down the corridor, her chest tightening until she could barely breathe. The god of mayhem was a part of her. How was she supposed to keep fighting, knowing this? As soon as she rode out on Sleipnir, her clouded judgment would put everyone in danger.

Her feet took her to the royal stable, where she stopped in the doorway and drew a few deep breaths. The truth bounced around in her brain, drowning out all other thoughts, like the inside of a bell.

I'm descended from Loki.

Hestur nickered in greeting.

Sigrid raced over, tears burning her eyes, and threw her arms around his neck. She held on, breathing deeply until the suffocating feeling in her chest loosened. He'd always been there for her, a reminder of who she was. Now, he stood still with his chin on her shoulder, seeming to know that she needed a hug.

"Thanks, buddy," she said, hearing the tiredness in her voice.

Am I destined to fail?

If Loki was part of her, she might never be able to choose good over evil. Aunt Kaia, Princess Helena, and the Svartalf King were all on the wrong side of the cosmic scale, and maybe she was, too. This wasn't a war of order fighting chaos, or of good fighting evil—this was chaos fighting more chaos. She'd planned to rise above it, but maybe that was impossible. Fate had its own plans for her.

She let go of Hestur and continued on to Sleipnir's stall. He nickered in greeting, too, just like Hestur had.

When she entered the stall and rested a hand on the stallion's wide forehead, his power tried to secure its hold on her, like a bodice tightening around her middle. But working against it, her sadness at having failed Mariam and Fisk bubbled up, loosening the invisible laces.

I don't want war. I want to settle this peacefully.

That counted for something, right? Maybe Sigrid could break free from Loki's influence if she focused on that wish.

Or maybe Sleipnir would keep bringing out the evil inside her, and she was doomed to succumb to it no matter how much she resisted.

The stallion nuzzled her, like the way Hestur asked to have his ears rubbed.

Sigrid frowned. Was Sleipnir inherently evil, or was his connection to Loki to blame? After growing up around horses and gleaning generations of knowledge from the older stable hands, she had come to understand that there was no such thing as a bad horse. There were only poorly trained horses and ones who acted defensively after being mistreated.

Sleipnir was no exception. A horse existed somewhere inside this wild, eight-legged shell, and he wasn't a bad one. She just hadn't figured out how to access the good part of him.

She kissed the stallion's nose, his heat passing from her lips to the rest of her. "It's not your fault you were born with this power."

Riding Sleipnir before figuring out how to work with him had been the wrong decision. In trying to do the best thing for Vanaheim, she'd rushed it and failed.

"I'm going to ride Hestur and keep you here for some rest, okay?" Her voice cracked. He bobbed his head like Hestur did when she talked to him. "You've earned a break."

Mariam's pained words echoed in her mind. *You don't even care.*

She'd been asking the real Sigrid to come back—the Sigrid who let compassion guide her. That Sigrid would have made sure her friends were okay after the battles. She would have filled Vanahalla's empty rooms with stable hands and valkyries to ensure they were well rested and safe. She would have questioned why Aunt Kaia forced the stable hands to work past exhaustion, and why she spent Vanaheim's wealth on robes and jewelry, and why she invited Sigrid to lavish meals while everyone else crammed into the dining hall and ate stale sandwiches.

The real Sigrid wouldn't have shouted at Fisk, or left people defenseless, or done any of the other horribly callous things she'd done in the name of getting ahead in this war.

And she would have apologized and kissed Mariam instead of shouting at her.

All the energy drained from Sigrid, weakening her legs as she leaned against the wall of Sleipnir's stall. A sob contracted her ribs. Her shoulders shook and warm tears ran down her cheeks, unstoppable. The stallion sniffed her face, his warm breath washing over her cheeks.

Mariam was right. Sigrid had surrendered to the way Sleipnir and her royal title made her feel—powerful, invincible, driven by the gods of war. Leaving the people of Borthorpe had been too easy, and all of the kills she made in battle came without hesitation. The valkyries had every right to question her decisions. No wonder they were reluctant when she told them to burn the enemy to ashes.

General Eira and Drifa...

General Eira had spent years stopping Sigrid from reaching her potential, but she'd also given Sigrid a job and let her ride with the valkyries to Svartalfheim. Beneath her harsh exterior, she'd been someone who'd dedicated her life to defending Vanaheim. And Drifa was sweet and gentle and always happy to see Sigrid. Now they were both gone, lost in a war that seemed impossible to end.

The *click-clack* of wood-soled shoes on marble approached, and Sigrid straightened up, sucking in a breath.

She wiped her face quickly, dropping her hand just in time for Aunt Kaia to appear on the other side of the stall door.

Sigrid ground her teeth, tasting bile.

"Sorry to interrupt." The queen's tone sent a ripple up Sigrid's spine. She sounded so much like Helena.

Sigrid squared her shoulders. "We have nothing more to discuss."

Aunt Kaia raised an eyebrow. "I thought you might want to know that one of your valkyries returned from patrolling Myrkviðr. She says she found the Svartalf King."

CHAPTER FIFTY-FOUR

A NEW PLAN

Sigrid froze. "We *found* him?"

"He's a half hour away." Aunt Kaia held out a map, watching Sigrid closely. "He has a large division with him and they're moving in this direction."

Sigrid took the map, numb. A freshly inked, black *X* marked a place next to a ravine in Myrkviðr. "Coming to attack?"

"Maybe. Or he might wait in Myrkviðr until he feels the time is right."

Sigrid's pulse raced. Her plan to send valkyries on patrol had *worked*. "Looks like we're handling the invasion just fine without Helena."

Aunt Kaia's eyes narrowed, her expression cold. "Don't mistake luck for brilliance."

This wasn't luck. Sigrid made a plan and it paid off.

Or had it?

Was this too easy?

Her heart flipped. The only way to find out was to ride out to find him.

"Where are the juniors now?" Getting the information firsthand was better than trusting her aunt to deliver all the facts.

"Back at the valkyrie stable with the others."

Sigrid opened the stall door, forcing her aunt to back up.

"We'll head out to meet him. The reserve valkyries will stay and defend the hall."

Without waiting for a response, she strode to the tack room so she could saddle up Hestur. But a sudden question had her rushing back out to the aisle. "Aunt Kaia."

The queen turned, dropping her hand from the stable door and letting it close again. Her eyes widened and her brow lifted almost imperceptibly. "Yes?"

"Why did you want me to learn about runes so I could communicate with Loki?"

The idea had only made sense when the plan was to use the link to try and stop Loki. But knowing there was a connection already between her and the god of mischief, strengthening it seemed reckless.

Aunt Kaia searched her face, her shoulders dropping ever so slightly, as if this wasn't what she'd hoped Sigrid would say. "I thought you might be the most successful at opening a conduit with him."

Sigrid nodded, nausea rising all over again. "I see."

Aunt Kaia had kept the full details of their lineage from her on purpose.

Sigrid had the strongest connection to Loki out of anyone. If she'd used runes to open a direct conduit to the god of mischief, who knew what kind of havoc would've been unleashed?

Her frown deepened as she held her aunt's gaze. *I will never write the runes to call on him.*

"May you bring the Svartalf King everything he deserves, Princess." With a swish of her robe, Aunt Kaia left the stable.

Sigrid let out a breath, hurrying to saddle up.

My family is the worst.

Queen Kaia and Princess Helena had turned out to be the same—royals with no experience outside these golden towers, failing to understand what Vanaheim's people needed and what the nine worlds needed from Vanaheim.

Sigrid was different. If she reached beneath whatever hold Loki had over her, she was still a stable hand who knew what it was like to live at the bottom. She was just an orphan girl with a Midgard horse who happened to be linked to the gods.

Ranking and lineage were no indication of greatness. She had plenty of proof of that, having been stuck serving the "nobler" valkyries her whole life. Low-ranking stable hand or royal, they were all people of Vanaheim, and Sigrid would fight to protect them all. She would also fight to protect the nine worlds from her own family.

"I *will* succeed," she told Hestur as she put on her armor. "I've fought, strategized, and made successful plans. I can keep learning. Be better. And I have friends who have my back." Or she would again, once she apologized. "Nothing can stop us, right, buddy?"

Hestur snorted.

They had to find the Svartalf King and drive the Night Elves out, but Sigrid wouldn't allow Aunt Kaia to launch a conquest and throw the cosmos further out of balance.

As she mounted up, the thought of becoming a traitor to the crown sent a spike of panic through her, which she tried to calm with a few deep breaths.

Opposing the crown was exactly what her mother had done before fleeing to Helheim. It was the very thing that got Mariam's mother banished to Niflheim. If Sigrid tried to oppose Aunt Kaia, what would happen? Would she be killed for treason?

I have to accept that risk.

Vanaheim needed her.

Sigrid urged Hestur into a gallop, heading down to the valkyrie stables.

As she entered the yard, all twenty-one juniors and a few stable hands were finishing getting ready, every valkyrie in her armor and every mare tacked up. They all stopped and stood at attention, their gazes flicking between Sigrid's face and Hestur.

Edith, Runa, and Roland walked closer, followed by the others.

Edith spoke first. "Why aren't you riding—"

Sigrid raised a hand. "Everyone, listen up. There's been a slight change of plans."

CHAPTER FIFTY-FIVE

MEETING
IN THE FOREST

Everyone in the stable yard seemed to draw a breath at Sigrid's proclamation, their postures tense—like they expected her to start barking orders and demanding violence and bloodshed. How much had they noticed the change in her while she rode Sleipnir?

She kept her voice steady, meeting their wide eyes. "The key to ending this invasion is the Svartalf King. You've done the impossible and found him. Good work." In the thick silence, she held up the map from Aunt Kaia. "He's a half hour away in Myrkviðr. This is our chance to surround and trap him so I can talk to him one-on-one."

"Talk to him, or kill him?" Edith asked.

Sigrid held back a wince. "Talk."

Their expressions said they didn't quite believe her.

"Look, I know Queen Kaia's intent is to kill him, but that's not what we're going to do," she said. "We're going to end this war without more bloodshed, and negotiate peace. That's the whole point of the valkyries, isn't it? To keep peace? Killing him would just incite his army and make everything worse."

There was a pause, and then one by one, the valkyries nodded. Their shoulders relaxed, the strain on their faces melting away.

Sigrid's heart lifted.

"He had a small army with him," Runa said. She must've been part of the patrol that discovered the king's location. "We might not be able to hold them off for long while you talk."

"That's okay. We'll do the best we can."

All of the juniors nodded and murmured, "Yes, Your Highness," which made Sigrid squirm in the saddle.

Mariam stood at the back of the group, not meeting her eyes.

"Bring your torches to surround them, but *don't* light them up," Sigrid said. They had to fight with everything they had, but she was done with the gruesome kills.

In the hot evening sun, the stable hands quickly checked over the mares, and the valkyries finished getting ready. None of them spoke to her, not even to note she was on Hestur instead of Sleipnir.

Fisk was there, and to Sigrid's surprise, the two Night Elf captives were helping tend the horses.

She nudged Hestur closer. "They've decided to help?"

"Yes, Your Highness."

Okay, I deserve that. "Have you found other allies?"

He checked the buckles on Mjöll's bridle. "Are you going to shout at me if I haven't?"

Sigrid swallowed. "No. Fisk, I'm sorry—"

"I'm working on it. Is that all?"

"Let me explain."

"I don't want explanations." He stomped past to help with the next mare. "Now please stay out of my way."

Her chest squeezed. Clearly, she would have to work harder on her apologies.

As the twenty-one junior valkyries mounted up and began the ride down to Myrkviðr, Sigrid trotted closer to Mariam. "I'm sorry—"

Mariam took off into the sky.

Caught in the whirl of dust, Sigrid shouted after her, nudging

Hestur to keep up. "You were right! I was a jerk. Please, Mariam. I need you."

Far from melting at the apology, Mariam cast her a stern look from up high. "Words aren't enough, Sigrid."

"I'm riding Hestur, aren't I?"

When Mariam looked unconvinced, Sigrid considered explaining what she'd seen in her family tree. But if Mariam found out Loki was in her blood, she might want nothing to do with her.

"This is who I am," Sigrid said, dizzy from looking up while Hestur was moving. "If you don't like it, then…" A lump in her throat stopped her from finishing the sentence.

"It's not who you are! It's who you've turned into because of whatever's going on—but I know you. The *real* you. I remember a Sigrid who cared deeply about others, who could make me smile when I needed it, who showed me what trust means."

"I don't know if the old Sigrid is here anymore, Mariam." It hurt to say it, but she couldn't lie and say she was exactly like she used to be. She didn't know who she was anymore, and after everything she'd been through, she might have changed forever. Mariam needed to know that.

A pained expression crossed Mariam's face. "That's really too bad. Because I liked her."

She steered Aesa away, leaving Sigrid dizzy and blinking away the burning in her eyes. The others riding with them pretended not to have heard, nor to see when she wiped her cheeks.

Sigrid struggled to keep her breathing steady and her attention focused as she galloped Hestur toward Myrkviðr with the valkyries overhead. Confidence was hard to summon. Mariam and Fisk were angry at her, the valkyries resented her as much as ever, she'd left her war horse in the barn, and the path ahead involved treachery.

But Hestur powered onward beneath her, his ears forward,

ready to face whatever she put him up against—and maybe that was all she needed. Hestur had always been, and would always be, her rock and her ally.

A little like the way she channeled Sleipnir's power to help her fight, she channeled Hestur's fearlessness to help her face whatever was coming. For him and for the land they galloped over, she would fight her hardest.

They plunged into the woods, where thick trees smothered the daylight and the temperature dropped. In place of the hot sun, mist clung to Sigrid's cheeks.

"Runa, lead the way," Sigrid said, trusting her directions more than the map from Aunt Kaia.

Overhead, Runa swooped in front of the *V* formation, and everyone else adjusted their positions. They rushed over Myrkviðr in a direction Sigrid had never been, Hestur's nimble body weaving between the thick brush to take her quickly along a deer path.

Trusting him to place his feet, she clamped her legs tighter and held his mane, scrunching her face against the branches sweeping by. She'd gotten used to Sleipnir flattening everything in his path, whereas Hestur used his slender build and agility to dodge obstacles.

Beneath the sound of Hestur's pounding hooves, a stream burbled nearby.

"Up ahead!" Runa shouted.

Sigrid shortened her reins and adjusted her grip on her spear. "Valkyries, flank!"

The valkyries swooped lower to flank Sigrid below the treetops. Sigrid's ears filled with whooshing wings, cracking branches, and Hestur's thumping hooves.

Ahead, shadows filled the dark forest. Eclipsing the mossy floor, bushes, and vast tree trunks, the Night Elves shouted and raised their weapons as the valkyries charged.

Maybe Sigrid had spent so long dwelling on the Svartalf King, or maybe something about him made him stand out, but her gaze instantly locked onto his antlers, bear mask, and iron crown—bringing with it a rush of satisfaction.

Finally.

"Center, split!" she shouted over the roaring army, launching her spear into the nearest elf.

The valkyries burst into the moving shadows and split the army down the middle. Mariam kept formation on the right, flying tightly behind Edith. The trees were hard for the mares to navigate, and they had to make way for the enormous trunks and low branches. The mares folded their wings and pitched and rolled expertly, feathers grazing branches and sending pinecones raining down as they circled back.

Sigrid summoned back her spear. "Split quarters! Light up!"

The valkyries divided again. Their torches flared to life, the moving flames creating rings of fire around four clusters of Night Elves.

With the opposition divided and surrounded, elves hit the forest floor rapidly—but the low canopy made it easier for them to retaliate, and between shots, the valkyries had to dodge arrows, spears, and lances.

Sigrid bent closer to Hestur's neck. "Circle tight!"

The Svartalf King fought in the center of Mariam and Edith's circle, flashes of his antlers visible between the moving shadows of Night Elves.

If they could take down those elves, she could get to him.

Gunni shrieked as Oda crashed into a tree. Cracks filled the air as they fought out of the branches and rejoined the formation.

"Sorry!" Ylva shouted.

The elves in their circle made a break for it, flitting like moving darkness.

"Round them up," Sigrid shouted. "Everyone else, stay put!"

Gunni and Ylva swerved and pitched through the trees, stopping the group from scattering.

"Isolate the king," Sigrid shouted, and Mariam and the four others surrounding him expertly worked to take down the elves trapped in their circle.

Sigrid's heart pumped with the speed of a hummingbird's wings. The combination of adrenaline and the whirling flames in the darkness left her dizzy and struggling to keep track of the king.

Three Night Elves were left with him.

"I'm coming in!" Sigrid steered Hestur close to the swirling mares. "Keep circling low."

If they paused to let her in, they would lose momentum.

While the five mares circled, Sigrid galloped alongside them. She nudged Hestur over and merged into their formation.

With the king in sight, she threw her spear at the elves, knocking out one. Two more golden spears found their targets, and a third knocked the bow from the Svartalf King's hand. It fell to the forest floor, leaving him clutching his wrist.

And then he was alone, surrounded.

Every spear whooshed back to its owner.

Sigrid's heart pounded. They'd done it. They'd trapped the Svartalf King.

Inside the dizzying circle of white mares and trailing flames, she drew Hestur to a halt. They faced each other as they'd done in Svartalfheim. Screams and roars surrounded them as the valkyries contained the army.

"I want you to order everyone to leave Vanaheim immediately," Sigrid said. "Whatever grievances you have against my world, we can resolve them by talking, not fighting. Do you agree?"

The Svartalf King shifted, the moving fire casting shadows over his expressionless mask. "And if I don't? You'll kill me?"

His voice was less deep and smooth than she remembered it. Was he scared?

"I'd rather avoid that." She lowered her spear, hoping the action would show the truth of her words.

"Come on!" His roar was like the snarl of a dire wolf. "Get off that horse and fight me hand-to-hand. Prove how much of a valkyrie you are."

As he taunted her, a warning tingled in the back of her mind.

The king stepped closer, turning his mask to take in the surrounding mares and torches.

Her heart thumped faster. When he'd stood from his throne in Svartalfheim, hadn't his antlers been so big that the tops had been cast into shadow?

She traced her gaze along the mask's canine teeth. *One had a broken tip.*

It wasn't there. Each tooth was flawless.

And it hit her, in a chilling, nauseating realization—this was not the Svartalf King.

CHAPTER FIFTY-SIX

WORTHY
OF THE VALKYRIES

"Valkyries, back to Vanahalla, now!" Sigrid spun Hestur around, cursing at herself. *Tricked again.*

"What?" Runa cried.

"It's a trap! We have to get back to the wall!"

The valkyries scattered.

Behind her, the elf who wasn't the Svartalf King roared. "Stop them!"

Sigrid didn't even have to signal Hestur. He burst into a gallop, taking them fast away from the false king. Loud thumps blasted all around as weapons buried into the surrounding trees. Sigrid gasped as one clipped her, a white-hot sting tearing open near her elbow.

Overhead, someone screamed.

"Up! Up!" Ylva shouted, and the mares' wings rustled the trees as they took their riders higher.

Hestur galloped faster, moving at lightning speed through the woods, jumping over enormous logs, darting around ferns, and ducking under branches. She stayed close to his neck, trusting him to pick the best path.

The elves swept through the woods behind her, the snapping branches and crunching rocks much too close. A spear thumped into a tree to her right, and Hestur dodged left, taking her away from it.

They burst out of the forest and into the meadow.

In the distance, a horde of elves was at the stone wall, flooding over it and making their way up the hill toward Vanahalla. Valkyries fought them back, but they were so outnumbered that clusters of elves got past unimpeded.

An army was racing toward the golden towers.

Sigrid cursed. "Valkyries, charge!"

She was about to nudge Hestur faster when he skittered sideways, and she gasped as she lost her balance.

Something hit her helmet hard.

She separated from Hestur, disoriented, and saw the ground slam into her before she felt its slap against her cheek and shoulder.

Sigrid groaned and tried to get her feet under her, but the world tilted. Cool grass pressed against her hands and knees as she tried to get her bearings.

Hestur snorted in fright, his hooves pounding away.

She had to call him back…had to go help the others…

A hand closed over her arm and threw her onto her back. She screamed in pain and kicked out at the figure looming over her—and froze at the familiar rasp of laughter.

The real Svartalf King looked down at her. The iron crown on his head, the antlers, the bear mask, the very visible chip on the mask's tooth—all of it strikingly familiar, making her furious that she hadn't recognized the fake right away.

"This fight is beyond your understanding, orphan girl." He strode closer and kicked her in the ribs. "Don't you realize that it would be a mistake to kill me?"

She scrambled back on her hands and heels, gasping for air. "I—I wasn't. I just want to talk. Tell me what Loki told you. Whatever he said, it's a lie."

The king tilted his head, his antlers leaning to the side. "What do you know about the god of mischief?"

"I know he has plans that serve him and no other." Sigrid

dragged herself further back, trying to see where the juniors went. "Vanaheim wants peace. We can work together and reach an agreement."

When the king didn't come after her, she stood, ready to defend herself against his next move. Hestur's breaths and hooves sounded nearby, but she didn't dare look over or call him to her.

The king stood squarely, a chilling sight even with his short stature. "Loki agrees that Svartalfheim has spent too long near the bottom of Yggdrasil. A completely unfair position, given all that we've done for Asgard."

Sigrid didn't know enough about Svartalfheim to say whether his words were true, but stories of the magnificent craftmanship of Night Elves were widely known. How much had they helped the other worlds with their inventions?

She reached for her spear, feeling vulnerable without it, but the king reached behind him to where a quiver would be.

She froze, and so did he.

"Loki told me what Vanahalla has inside those shiny gold towers," he continued calmly, waving a hand toward Vanahalla, "and how much Vanaheim relies on that stolen bit of Hnitbjorg. Odin has such a weakness for prophetic knowledge—you know how the poems go. How could Odin resist keeping Vanaheim close when you possess such a useful rock?"

"Our position is about more than the relics we've accumulated." Sigrid tried not to sound indignant, but he had to understand that Vanaheim deserved its status. "Vanaheim was home to the Vanir gods, and today it's home to the valkyries. We spend our lives serving and protecting the nine worlds, and that gives us our position—"

"Protecting the nine worlds, are you?" the Svartalf King said venomously. "Where's my protection? Where were the valkyries when Alfheim invaded us years ago? Where were they when we needed help rebuilding after the volcanic eruption a year before that? Don't feed me lies about serving the nine worlds when all you serve is yourselves."

Sigrid clenched her jaw. She hadn't known about these events, nor had they been mentioned in any of her history classes. Vanaheim had obviously decided not to send the valkyries to help them.

A jolt of uncertainty shot through her chest.

Valkyries were for protecting the upper worlds, weren't they? When the gods created them, had they meant for them to protect *all* worlds, not just the upper ones? Who decided only the upper worlds were worthy of the valkyries' service?

The Svartalf King laughed, his shoulders shaking. "You finally understand what I'm saying, orphan girl."

She studied him. He was calling her that for a reason. After spending her life as an orphan and a stable hand, the idea that only a certain class of people had the valkyries' protection suddenly seemed all wrong.

If Aunt Kaia has her way, the valkyries will protect nobody but Vanaheim.

Nausea rose in Sigrid's gut. By refusing to help Svartalfheim, the valkyries had ignored their responsibility.

"This is why we're here." The Svartalf King advanced with his arms spread. "Vanaheim has failed us, and we need to set the cosmic balance right. You brought light to our world, and now it's time for us to bring darkness to yours."

A chill rippled over Sigrid, and she backed up. Her fingers tingled, wanting to grab her spear. But talking was better than throwing weapons at each other. "If we promised to serve Svartalfheim with equal dedication as we serve Alfheim and Jotunheim, would you retreat?"

The Svartalf King tilted his head as if considering. "Perhaps. But your word means nothing. We both know the powers that matter would never make such an agreement."

He reached for his weapon, and Sigrid reached for hers.

His was an iron arrow—and with a rush of dread, Sigrid saw it was unlike the ones they'd seen before. The arrowhead was entirely black.

"These have come in handy for your villages." The king twirled it across his gloved fingers. "I wonder how Vanahalla will look covered in darkness."

"Wait," Sigrid said loudly, her pulse frantic. If he unleashed one of those here, how far would it reach? Were these arrows powerful enough to engulf the entire royal hall?

A treaty. We have to make a treaty and we can end this.

"Let me bring this to the council. We'll negotiate."

"Who are you to make such an offer?"

"I'm the prin—"

"Sigrid, run!" Mariam shouted. A gust of wind blew against Sigrid, and a winged mare swooped down so fast that a wing slammed into the king, knocking him off his feet.

Around her, the junior valkyries came to her rescue, swarming the Svartalf King in a blur of white wings.

"Don't kill him!" Sigrid shouted automatically, holding up her hands as if to block them.

But she hadn't gotten the words out when Mariam shouted, "No!"

The king threw the arrow, and Sigrid had no time to react. The sharp tip embedded in her shoulder, the force of the throw knocking her onto her back. Pain burst through her whole body, and a scream tore from her lips.

Darkness exploded around her and obstructed her vision. An icy sensation squeezed her chest until she couldn't breathe. The cold snaked over her arms, around her ribs, and crawled into her mouth and nose. It went inside her, suffocating, freezing…

The trees and the meadow spun, becoming a blur. Her eyelids fluttered, everything blurring into a haze of winged mares and shadows darker than the night.

CHAPTER FIFTY-SEVEN

A VALKYRIE'S PURPOSE

Sigrid awoke with a gasp, the pain in her shoulder so strong it made her stomach queasy. She groaned and tried to roll over, but the nausea got worse.

"Sigrid," Mariam said over and over, her hands blissfully warm on Sigrid's face. Her face was swollen from crying, her eyes wide with panic.

Sigrid blinked, looking past her to the ceiling.

She was in the valkyrie barn.

Someone had removed her breastplate and winged helmet and placed them beside her, along with the iron arrow. The breastplate was completely black, as if it couldn't be saved from the webs of darkness that had engulfed her.

Her pulse spiked, sending shards of pain through her temples. She touched her face, running her fingers over her skin. What had the weapon done to her?

"You're okay. We pulled it out in time." Mariam's cheeks were streaked with tears, and she sat back, wiping them away with a shaking hand.

Several valkyries and stable hands looked down at her with concern, including Peter, Roland, Runa, and Edith.

Sigrid sat up, her heart thumping, swaying from a wave of dizziness. "Is everyone okay?" Her voice barely came out. "Did anyone else get hit?"

"No," Runa said, "the darkness exploded outward, but then…"

"Mariam grabbed you and pulled out the spear," Edith chimed in. "You should've seen it. There were webs of darkness all over her and Aesa, like—" She flailed her arms, miming something Sigrid had no idea how to interpret.

"Then Ylva threw her torch at it—" Runa said.

"And the webs totally shriveled up and made this sound like *eeeeee*." Edith mimed this, too, making claws with her hands. "And Mariam took you right out of the flames."

"It was incredible," Runa said.

They were both breathless, their eyes huge as they looked at Mariam in awe.

Mariam flushed modestly. "It was nothing."

"Thank you for saving me." Sigrid's eyes welled. She could have thrown herself at Mariam right there in front of everyone. Instead, she croaked out, "How's Hestur?"

"I checked him over for injuries," Peter said. "He's fine."

Of course he was. He was always fine.

Sigrid rubbed her forehead, letting out a breath. Fresh pain spread through her body and amplified the bruise already aching below her collarbone. A bandage was on her shoulder where the king's arrow had gotten her.

Fire. Fire was their only hope against the darkness.

Past all the faces and the tips of Hestur's brown ears, the sky turned pink as the sun crossed the horizon.

"We stopped the elves from making it to Vanahalla, but…" Edith said hesitantly, as if wondering how ready Sigrid was to talk about it.

Sigrid nodded at her to continue.

Edith cleared her throat. "We lost the Svartalf King. He got away while we were trying to save you."

Sigrid swore under her breath. But as their conversation

drifted from her hazy memory, carrying some interesting details, hope sparked in her chest. Now that she knew what the Night Elves were fighting for, she could work on an agreement that would serve everyone.

The valkyries had to protect all nine worlds, regardless of status. There was no doubt about that. Could the council be convinced of the same? Aunt Kaia wouldn't consider it, but maybe the others would.

The reserve valkyries still guarded the hall, leaving the juniors and stable hands around Sigrid—familiar faces of people who, to some extent, trusted her.

While determination coursed through her, giving her strength, she got to her feet and waved everyone closer. "Come on. I've got things to say."

They surrounded her, solemn and attentive.

"I want to apologize for the way I've been acting. It's been… bad." She winced at how feeble that sounded. She probably should have rehearsed this. "I've been making decisions according to what's best for the crown instead of what's best for the people."

No one said anything, which both encouraged Sigrid to continue and confirmed that she did have a lot to apologize for.

"I haven't been fully honest about…what happens when I ride Sleipnir." She looked tentatively at Mariam, whose expression was solemn. "He's not a normal horse, right?"

Peter snorted, which made a couple of others smile.

Sigrid was grateful for his attempt to ease the tension. "Sleipnir comes from the gods, and the influence of Loki and Odin sort of pass from him into me. It's why I've been so…"

"Chaotic?" Mariam supplied, bitterness in her tone.

Sigrid nodded. She tried to convey in a glance how sorry she was, but Mariam looked away.

"But I'm going to do better. Starting with honesty." She addressed everyone, her heartbeat quickening as the truth rose to the surface. "Queen Kaia told me she plans to send everyone to invade Svartalfheim once we push the Night Elves out—"

Murmurs broke out, some valkyries looking scared, others angry.

"—but I'm not going to let that happen. It's not worth risking our lives for revenge. In fact, I...I disagree with the queen in a few ways."

She sucked in a breath at the wave of pain in her head, a cold sweat breaking out beneath her uniform. Everyone stared at her, hardly breathing.

"Queen Kaia wants to bring Princess Helena out of Helheim and use the valkyries for a conquest."

Several valkyries and stable hands gasped. Others stared in silence, their mouths open. Ylva and Gunni exchanged a look, as if checking whether the other believed her.

"Their plan is to subjugate the lower realms," Sigrid said, "but I'm sure you agree that this isn't our purpose. Valkyries are supposed to protect the nine worlds. *All* worlds. And we've already failed."

She told them what the Svartalf King had told her, of the disasters in his world and how the valkyries had not answered their call for help.

"A conquest is not what the gods intended for us, and if we follow Queen Kaia's plans to put ourselves above the other worlds, we're causing unrest, imbalance, and hostility. We're pushing Yggdrasil into chaos, which is exactly what we're fighting against. The Vanaheim I know is better than that."

She swallowed hard, unsure if her words had made an impact. But the juniors and stable hands relaxed their postures, their expressions interested. Mariam was looking at her now, her brow pinched as she processed Sigrid's words.

Roland crossed his arms and huffed. "I never liked Kaia. You saw it, Sig. The way she's treated the stable hands. We've had to eat and sleep in secret."

Shame sent heat into her cheeks, because she hadn't seen it. She'd spent her time absorbed in her royal life with her aunt and her war horse, oblivious to everyone else. But she believed him. She'd heard firsthand what Aunt Kaia thought of elves and statuses.

"We've been noticing how Queen Kaia has been…uncertain." Runa's voice was so low that Sigrid almost missed it. "She doesn't seem comfortable with being queen, and her decisions haven't been the best for the valkyries. Asking us to waste time rounding up commoners to help fight, for one. What do you think we should do?"

We. The simple word lifted Sigrid higher.

"As princess, are you able to talk to her and tell her what the Svartalf King told you?" Edith asked.

Ylva and Gunni both looked sour at the word *princess*, but said nothing.

Sigrid chewed her lip. Would they side with her when she told them what she wanted to do? "Queen Kaia is determined to stomp Svartalfheim to the bottom of Yggdrasil. Meanwhile, the Svartalf King wants us to suffer for treating them this way. Both are acting out of vengeance and both want to destroy the other world. Neither is right. Attacking each other will get us nowhere."

Edith nodded vigorously. "This war has to stop."

A few others nodded and murmured in approval.

Sigrid stood taller, bolstered by their support. "We don't need to go on like this. There's room for both worlds near the gods. We just need to make a treaty—if the Night Elves return home, we'll vow to serve Svartalfheim like we serve Alfheim and Jotunheim. Do you agree?"

The stable hands, Edith, Runa, and a few other valkyries nodded. Ylva, Gunni, and the rest looked to their friends.

"The first step—" Sigrid swallowed, unable to stop a twinge

of fear that Aunt Kaia was listening from behind a manure pile. She drew a breath and lowered her voice. "We have to find the Svartalf King again so I can talk to him. I'll propose a treaty, and he'll have my word as Princess of Vanaheim that the valkyries will follow through."

Ylva raised a hand. "And what happens when the queen finds out we're making a truce instead of launching a conquest?"

"She won't approve," Sigrid admitted. "But we have to do it. Before Vanaheim ends up in ruin or another valkyrie gets killed."

Gunni scrunched her face. "This would make us traitors to the crown."

Sigrid nodded once. She couldn't ask them to do this without making it clear what allying with her could mean. "I don't expect any of you to follow my plan if you don't want to. You can do what the queen says and go on a conquest to Svartalfheim. I'm just letting you know what I'm doing, because I don't think her plan is right for any of us."

"Sigrid's right." Edith turned, addressing everyone. "Queen Kaia is going to get us killed. We've lost so many already. Do any of you honestly want to go back into Svartalfheim on an invasion?"

Sigrid's heart leaped as others voiced their agreement.

"I joined the ranks to serve the nine worlds, not to kill Night Elves," Runa said. "We have to end this war and get back to the valkyries' real purpose."

Others nodded.

After a moment, Ylva drew herself up like a swan ready to take flight. "Okay. I can get behind putting an end to this war."

Sigrid's heart beat faster as she scanned everyone's determined faces. Having them as allies meant more than she could express.

"When do we go find the king?" Ylva tossed back her braid. "It's our turn to go on duty, like, right now. The reserve valkyries are probably wondering where we are."

"We can ride out at dawn. I'm not exactly feeling up to it right now." Sigrid touched her head, still feeling out of sorts. *Understatement.* She might throw up from pain and dizziness if she didn't sit or lie down soon.

"We can be ready at sunrise." Edith looked to the others for confirmation.

The energy in the barn rose, everyone twirling their spears and adjusting their armor as if preparing to fight.

"Sunrise, it is," Gunni said.

CHAPTER FIFTY-EIGHT

TAPESTRIES

The valkyries left to get ready for their turn protecting Vanahalla, and the stable hands dispersed to help. Sigrid remained where she stood, working through her aches and wondering if she could take one more hit to her heart.

Her insides twisted as she contemplated going after Mariam. They needed to talk, but what if Mariam was still furious with her? What else could she say to show how truly sorry she was?

Peter stopped beside her. "She was a wreck before you opened your eyes."

"She was?" A bubble of hope formed in her chest—not that she was happy Mariam cried, but that she cared.

Peter shrugged. "I don't know what's going on between the two of you, but I thought you'd want to know."

Sigrid cast him a grateful smile, and he pulled her into a careful hug.

"Peter, I'm sorry—"

"Don't worry. What you said made sense, in a weird way." He pulled back and looked at her with that proud brotherly smile. "I'm glad you're back, Sigrid."

She could only nod as her eyes watered.

Fisk and Tóra walked by to help the stable hands, working together to check Roskva's tack. Tóra had taken on some stable hand duties, apparently—or maybe she just wanted to be close to Fisk.

Fisk reached out a gloved hand and gave Tóra's a squeeze. A deep red flush crept into her pale cheeks, and when she walked away, she practically skipped.

Sigrid couldn't help smiling. He deserved this. Later, when she had a moment with him, she would have to apologize properly.

"I saw Tóra kiss his mask the other day," Mariam said, coming to stand beside her.

Sigrid's heart flipped. She clasped her hands to keep from reaching out and tried not to smile too widely as she took in Mariam's features—bright eyes, smooth skin, lips, cheeks, every part of her perfect. "Cute. I was wondering if the mask would complicate things for them. If they wanted to be…physical…that is."

"Hm…" Mariam tapped a finger to her lips. "I guess if it's pitch black in the room, Fisk could take off the mask."

Sigrid tilted her head, watching Fisk flit around the barn. "What do Night Elves look like, though? Does Fisk even have a physical form or is he made up of, like, darkness?"

"I think they have a physical form…" Mariam chewed her lip. "You know what? I'm not sure."

They were silent as the juniors began taking flight out the barn doors and the reserve valkyries landed outside.

"Anyway." Mariam turned her gaze back to Sigrid. "Let's stop thinking about what Fisk looks like naked and figure out how to find the Svartalf King. This plan of yours better work."

"Mariam, I…" Sigrid faced her. "I should've trusted you. My mind was clouded and I tried to resist, to work through it, but… it didn't work. I'm sorry I didn't tell you. And I'm sorry I didn't listen when you tried to help me."

Mariam's shoulders sagged, and she stepped closer, searching Sigrid's face. "You're not alone. You have me. And Fisk, and Peter, and Roland, and more. You know you can depend on us."

Sigrid could barely get any words past the knot in her throat. "I know. And I will from now on. We can talk all the time. I have *so* much to tell you."

Mariam exhaled, and the corners of her lips curved into a small smile. "You're forgiven. But next time, we will kick your ass."

A laugh burst out of Sigrid, and she brushed away the drops that had gathered at the corners of her eyes. "I'll keep that in mind."

Mariam looked past Sigrid to where Hestur waited like a gentleman. "Where's Sleipnir?"

"In the royal stable."

Sigrid hesitated. What would happen when she told Mariam about having Loki in her blood? Mariam had to live in Niflheim through no fault of her own, so maybe she would forgive circumstances outside of Sigrid's control. But what if she looked at Sigrid differently? There would be no coming back from that.

The juniors finished vacating the barn, and in their place, the reserve valkyries trickled in.

"I'm late," Mariam said. "Come with me while I tack up?"

Sigrid swallowed hard and nodded. If she didn't tell Mariam about her family tree, she could let her believe—as Sigrid had believed earlier—that her behavior started and ended with Sleipnir. But hiding who she was had only brought pain. She had to be honest, even if Mariam didn't want her anymore because of it.

They walked down the barn aisle toward her old stall, now Mariam's. Homesickness cinched her insides at the familiarity. "You've got it set up the same as I had it, except for the tapestry."

The art hanging on the back wall had threads of gold woven intricately through the black and red wool, giving the illusion of a shimmering pool. It was a symbol—a rune, maybe. "What does it mean?"

"It means *fire*." Mariam hesitated. "Well, fire and death, actually. I bought it in a market with my first valkyrie wages."

Sigrid raised her eyebrows, a little startled by the meaning.

"It's nice, isn't it?" Mariam motioned to it with a hopeful expression.

"It is. But why fire and death?"

"Because it reminds me of…" Mariam averted her gaze, blushing. "Of us. Of what we went through, I mean. Garmr and Helheim."

Sigrid's heart expanded in her chest, like there wasn't enough room in there for all her feelings. She took Mariam's hand. "Let me show you something."

Mariam followed her out of the stall.

They walked down the silent aisle, fingers entwined, boots scuffing on the clay floor.

Sigrid led her around the corner to the hay room and pointed to the window. "I was here when I first saw you. You were just through there on Aesa with a couple of Night Elves. So I guess this is my tapestry. I think of you whenever I look at this window."

Mariam gave no response. Was she unimpressed? Or feeling awkward?

The stable was quiet, the reserve valkyries too tired to talk at a volume above a murmur. No mares were in their stalls to snort and stomp. The chickens had holed up somewhere, maybe sensing the air of danger. Here in the hay room, it was just her, Mariam, and the shadows of hay bales turning gray in the fading daylight.

Mariam's perfect eyebrows pinched together. Her black hair was fanned out, her toned shoulders peeking through.

Sigrid gently pushed the locks back so she could see her better. Beneath the rich smell of hay, Mariam's sweet scent was soothing, giving Sigrid a sense of home. "How did I get so lucky?"

She wasn't aware of moving, but Mariam's breath tickled her face, and the warmth of her body was closer than before. Sigrid could count each freckle dusting her nose. Her deep brown eyes carried a past that Sigrid wanted to know more about. She wanted to spend hours, days, years with Mariam, hearing about everything she'd been through and everything she dreamed of.

Mariam let out a soft breath that brushed Sigrid's lips.

Sigrid closed her eyes, lingering in this moment.

I can't keep my family tree a secret. Mariam was born in Niflheim and knew evil better than anyone. How would she feel to learn that Sigrid was descended from the god responsible for all of the suffering she'd been through?

I have to tell her.

If she'd learned anything since meeting Helena and claiming Sleipnir, it was that she couldn't hide who she was. She had to share the truth with the girl she cared most about in the nine worlds.

Summoning all the strength she had, Sigrid swallowed around the tightness in her throat. "Mariam, in Vanahalla, I—I saw my family tree."

Mariam's eyebrows pulled down, as if she was thrown by the sudden shift. "And?"

"Loki—" Sigrid's tongue failed her. She tried again. "Loki is in my blood. That's why Sleipnir affects me so much. It—the god of chaos—is part of me."

A silence passed that seemed to last forever. Sigrid's pulse beat in her throat.

Mariam's expression was unreadable. "You're descended from Loki?"

"I—I just needed you to know what you're getting into," Sigrid said, her lips numb.

Voices rose in the aisle, and Ylva called out, "Mariam! We're waiting. Hurry up."

Mariam let go of Sigrid's hand, and the sudden emptiness in Sigrid's palm sent a rush of coldness up her arm. Her chest constricted, making her breaths shallow.

Sigrid searched for something to say, her throat too tight to make a sound. *Don't go.*

"I should get out there and join the others. Let's talk later, yeah?" Mariam looked back and simply nodded.

Stay. Talk to me now.

Mariam left the hay room, leaving an ache in Sigrid's heart like nothing she'd experienced.

Forget what I said, and forget the battle.

She couldn't, of course. Mariam's job as a valkyrie was more important than Sigrid's feelings.

Sigrid wiped an arm across her burning eyes.

Not important.

With Yggdrasil in this state, her feelings were an afterthought, a tangent, something she could maybe resolve when this was all over.

If they were lucky enough to survive this war.

CHAPTER FIFTY-NINE

MOMENTS ALONE

After tersely letting Aunt Kaia know the Svartalf King had escaped and the junior valkyries were on wall duty, Sigrid retreated to her chambers and locked the door.

A chill settled over her as she paced the chambers. How many would agree with the queen's conquest? The god of chaos was everywhere, bleeding through every world and all of the people in them. Loki could be acting from within Vanahalla, too, encouraging the people in these walls to be selfish, seek power, and wage wars on lower worlds—giving her aunt all the supporters she needed to carry out her vision.

The urge to take Hestur and Sleipnir and spend the night in the tree fort sounded great, but this wasn't the moment to raise her aunt's guard with a midnight escape. She had to get through the night like normal.

It wasn't like Aunt Kaia would hurt her. Sigrid was the only person in the nine worlds with the power to bring Helena out of Helheim.

Reassuring as that was, her plan to oppose the queen left her jittery. She sat on the edge of her bed, a prickle of cold sweat under her tunic.

This is reckless. The last thing we need is a civil war on top of everything else.

She shook loose her braid and worked her fingers through the waves, frustration growing each time she hit a knot.

Was this all a horrible idea?

No, this was about saving the valkyries from a dangerous conquest and providing the lower realms with equal protection. For this, she would fight until her last breath.

Besides, Vala told Sigrid she had just as much of a say in the fate of Vanaheim. The firstborn's firstborn. She had no desire to challenge Aunt Kaia for the throne, but if her aunt wasn't the right leader for their world, maybe it was time for someone new.

I'm doing what's best for Vanaheim—and for all of Yggdrasil.

The window rattled, and Sigrid jumped to her feet. A shadow moved on the other side. She summoned her spear from the corner of her room, ready to use it.

Wait. Her chambers were several stories up. Night Elves wouldn't be able to get this high. Which meant…

A flash of white wings caught her eye.

Sigrid dropped her spear, raced to the window, and flung it open.

Mariam hovered on Aesa's back, smiling, the feathered tip of the mare's wing brushing the window ledge. "Can I come in?"

Sigrid's heart jumped into her throat. "Of—of course."

Mariam backed Aesa against the window and crawled over her rump to Sigrid, who extended a hand to help her climb in.

As Aesa flew away, her wings silent, Sigrid shut the window.

"Hi." Mariam had put dark makeup around her eyes and combed her hair, which fluttered over her shoulders like silk. In the room's candlelight, she looked more beautiful than ever.

"Hi." Sigrid's throat ran dry. *Mariam. Is here. In my bed chambers.*

"Now that we have a minute…" Mariam's lips quirked into a little smile that accentuated the perfect apples of her cheeks. "I don't care who's in your family tree, Sigrid Helenadottir."

Sigrid could have melted into the floor. "You don't?"

Mariam shook her head.

A surge of victory hit her, like while riding across the meadow to find the Svartalf King—but better. Much better.

Sinking into the lure of Mariam's dark eyes, Sigrid stepped closer. "So…"

Why is Mariam here? asked the most naive part of her.

You know why, said another.

Nerves hadn't made her tremble this much since she was about to ride alone into Svartalfheim. But that ride hadn't given her this underlying excitement. Her insides swooped with anticipation, a joy like nothing else.

Mariam closed the remaining distance, tucking a lock of hair behind Sigrid's ear. "So… Nothing has ever been ours before. Neither of us has had a proper home, a normal upbringing, an easy life that has space for someone else in it."

Her breath brushed lightly over Sigrid's lips, more tantalizing than any of the extravagant desserts this royal hall had to offer.

"Or time," Sigrid whispered, "or moments alone."

She caught Mariam's hand, their fingers entwining.

"That's why I thought, maybe, we could have this one night." Mariam's head tilted, the candlelight glinting in her dark eyes as she scanned the room. "Nice chambers, Princess."

Sigrid's breath caught as their lips brushed. "It gets a little lonely."

Their lips met in a kiss so gentle, so teasing, that she couldn't help a moan escaping.

The noise seemed to ignite a fire in Mariam. She put a hand on Sigrid's neck and pulled her closer.

Sigrid shivered, lifting her hands to tangle in Mariam's hair. They moved against each other, their breaths coming faster. Warm fingers trailed down Sigrid's arms, around her waist, to the hem of her tunic.

There was no one to interrupt or stop them, so she grasped Mariam's hands and brought them underneath, against her bare skin.

The movement was bold and automatic, something instinctive taking over and guiding her—but unlike whatever came over her in battle, this bloomed from a place of joy instead of anger, adoration instead of hatred. She wanted to give Mariam every bit of happiness and pleasure the worlds had to offer.

Mariam's breath hitched, the noise sending a rush of heat through Sigrid's middle. She kissed harder, and Mariam reacted by pressing closer, her hands tracing over her skin.

Sigrid trembled from exhilaration and nerves as Mariam's fingers roamed over her body, softly but confidently. She tugged Mariam's tunic upward, asking a silent question. Mariam responded by pausing to pull it over her head and toss it aside. Her white chest band was knotted in the middle, drawing Sigrid's gaze down, following the lines in her toned midsection.

Then Mariam was on her, pushing her back. She fell on the bed with a soft laugh and the weight of Mariam on top of her, a dizzying thrill racing through her head.

"Are you okay?" Mariam whispered, glancing to the bruise on her collarbone.

Sigrid hummed. "I'm great."

Mariam kissed her neck, rocking against her, their bodies moving in an intoxicating rhythm.

Pinned beneath her, Sigrid explored the smooth curves and dips of Mariam's body with her free hands.

"Sigrid…" Her breath tickled Sigrid's lips.

This made up for everything—all of the waiting, all of the missed opportunities. They had a room to themselves, the nicest room in all of Vanaheim, and it was theirs for as long as they wanted. Nobody was there to hear them or interrupt them, freeing them to get lost in each other.

Everything outside of her quarters disappeared from Sigrid's mind, as her entire focus centered on Mariam's body and the way it pressed against hers. Their breaths became the only sound in this world. Sweat dampened their skin, and bedsheets tangled at their feet as pillows fell to the floor.

Something in Mariam's eyes changed, softening.

"Are you happy in Vanaheim?" Sigrid whispered into her lips, a desperate wish that tightened her throat.

"I'm happy with you, wherever we are," Mariam said before kissing her deeply.

The night dissolved into sensations beyond anything Sigrid had ever known. And when the sun began to rise and they drifted off, too exhausted for anything but sleep, she forced her mind to stay in the moment, in this bed, with this girl, because dwelling on what might happen in the coming days was too much to bear.

CHAPTER SIXTY

OVER PANCAKES

Sigrid startled awake at the loud banging on the door of her chambers. The sky outside was still dark.

"Sigrid! Open up, quick!"

Mariam sat up beside her with a gasp, her dark eyes wide with surprise.

Sigrid paused before throwing the blankets off, distracted by the sight of Mariam beside her. "Uhh…"

Another frantic knock.

"Sigrid!"

Mariam blinked. "Is that—"

"Tóra." What could the Seer want at this hour?

Sigrid pulled her tunic back on hastily—her skin tingled, a reminder of Mariam's touch—and ran to open the door a sliver. She peeked through to find Tóra's pale, panic-stricken face. "What happened?"

"Queen Kaia's seen what yer planning. She's rallying the reserve valkyries."

Sigrid gripped the door frame. "Seen? Like, in the Eye? Wait, did she see me succeeding?"

"I don't know exactly… She demanded that Vala bring the Eye to her last night, and it must've shown a vision. She was furious. I guess she saw me with ye because she shouted at me to tell her what I knew. I didn't, of course," she added quickly. "Vala supported me. It's not our place to meddle. It's better for a Seer to withdraw than to share too much and do harm."

Anger sparked inside Sigrid—toward her aunt, and even toward the Eye for showing Aunt Kaia what she was up to. Were there no secrets around here?

"Is Mariam with ye?" Tóra tried to lean around her to see.

Nope, no secrets.

Sigrid sighed. "Yes. She is."

"She needs to fly down and tell the juniors before the other valkyries get to them."

"Thank you, Tóra. Please stay safe."

After the Seer ran off, Sigrid closed the door, her heart pounding.

She had to find Aunt Kaia before she did anything drastic, like unleash the reserve valkyries on her.

Mariam was already dressed and opening the window. "Aesa!"

"I'll talk to her. It'll be okay," Sigrid said, not sure if she believed it.

"Come with me?" Mariam put one leg out the window. "You can sit behind me on Aesa. We can get the juniors first. Might be better than facing your aunt alone."

Sigrid shook her head. "She'll get defensive. I need to talk this through with her on my own. She has to understand what we have to gain by making a treaty."

Mariam held her gaze, looking like she wanted to say more.

Sigrid raced across the room and grabbed her for one more kiss. "Wish we could stay here forever."

Mariam smiled against her lips. "Me too."

They kissed for the time it took Aesa to back up beneath the window, Sigrid's heart so full it ached, and then Mariam jumped out and flew away.

With the sun preparing to rise, the land was shadowy blue.

Patches of singed grass flecked the hillside, as if balls of fire had fallen from the sky. The world was eerily still and quiet, the air damp against Sigrid's cheeks.

The Svartalf King wouldn't wait long to attack again. And she had to stop her aunt before that happened.

Sigrid got dressed and braided her hair, nerves making her fingers fumble. She sheathed her spear across her back. There was no need to set the reserve valkyries on the juniors. They could talk about what needed to be done without resorting to violence.

As she speed-walked down the corridor, a door swung open, and she nearly crashed into the cleaning staff exiting with a cart.

"Oh—sorry!" the man said, looking mortified at nearly running down the princess.

Sigrid skirted around the cart—and the inside of the room caught her eye. It was bright, open, everything sky blue and yellow. Sigrid paused, searching her memory, an unpleasant sensation coiling inside her.

This suite used to be your mother's, Aunt Kaia had said when she gave Sigrid a tour.

In Sigrid's imagination, Princess Helena's old room had a blanket of dust over everything and cobwebs connecting all of the furniture. But this room was spotless, bright, and smelled like a garden.

Aunt Kaia was obviously making it ready for her sister, even though Sigrid had already refused to get her.

The man closed the door gently behind him, casting Sigrid a quizzical look.

Was it odd that Princess Helena's chambers had stayed intact for seventeen years while King Óleifr's had been vacated right after his death to make room for Sigrid?

A thought tingled at the back of her brain—a truth that had maybe been lingering there for some time.

Pulse beating in her throat, she crossed the entrance hall,

dread building inside her like a boiling kettle. Mariam was right. It was better not to meet with her aunt alone. She switched directions and headed toward the royal stable, ready to make a break for it—when wood-soled shoes clicked behind her.

Aunt Kaia stepped out of the dining hall looking more energetic than she had in days. Her large eyes glinted, her posture straight and sure. She wore her sky-blue robe with the boar's head near the collar, dark hair falling loose around her shoulders, the amber crown glinting on her head.

"Aren't you joining me for pancakes?" Aunt Kaia motioned behind her with a smile that was too calm.

Sigrid didn't move. Should she play along as if she didn't know that Aunt Kaia found out about her plan?

She won't kill me. I'm the only possible way to get her sister out of Helheim.

Squaring her shoulders, she summoned courage. Vanaheim needed her to protect its land and people, and right now, the queen striving to launch a deadly conquest was as much a threat as the Svartalf King. If she couldn't make her aunt see sense, she had to stop her.

Sigrid strode back toward the dining room. "Yes, sorry. My mind was on the battle." She slipped past Aunt Kaia, a chill on the back of her neck, and took her usual seat at the table.

Aunt Kaia shut the door.

That's different. The door usually stayed open while they ate.

Aunt Kaia sat across the table, her smile failing to reach her eyes. "What's on your mind, Sigrid?"

The waitstaff came to load their plates with pancakes.

Sigrid had no intention of eating, and apparently, neither did Aunt Kaia. They stared at each other across the absurdly large table while steam rose from their plates.

She cleared her throat. "I hoped to convince you to change your mind about sending the valkyries to invade Svartalfheim.

I've spoken to the Svartalf King, and I think we should be trying to reach a peaceful understanding with the other worlds instead of asserting our dominance."

Aunt Kaia let her shoulders drop with an exaggerated sigh. "Sigrid, we've talked about this. We're opening ourselves to invasions if we show weakness and shake everyone's hands."

"The valkyries are supposed to protect *all* worlds, not just those we declare worthy."

"A mistaken point of view that led us to this position."

"No, our failure to protect Svartalfheim led us to this position," Sigrid countered, her voice rising. "If we'd treated them with the same kindness and respect as we treat all the other worlds, they wouldn't hate us."

So much for staying calm.

Aunt Kaia tilted her head and quirked her lips, like she was watching a kitten take its first steps. "That's a sweet thought, love. If only the worlds worked that way."

"Aunt Kaia, we have the opportunity to form an alliance with Svartalfheim. If we promise to serve them the same way we serve the upper worlds, the Svartalf King *will* back off. I'm sure of it. It's all they want, to be treated equally."

The queen smiled. "When we get Helena, you can present this idea to her."

Sigrid ground her teeth. There was no making her understand. She'd already made up her mind. "I will never bring my mother back from Helheim. And I won't stand by your side if you want to launch a conquest."

Aunt Kaia's expression flickered. She sighed. "Sigrid, are you going to let my brother's death go to waste? What's the point of him being gone if we aren't going to take advantage of it?"

They stared at each other for a long moment. The smell of pancakes filled the room, while dawn brightened the sky and songbirds chirped beyond the window. The waitstaff lingered at the back of the room, seeming afraid to breathe.

The lingering truth took shape, and into the stalemate silence, Sigrid asked, "What illness did King Óleifr die from?"

Color rose in Aunt Kaia's pale cheeks, and she blinked rapidly, breaking Sigrid's gaze for a fraction of time.

The reaction told Sigrid everything.

Icy dread filled her, chilling her bones, as she and Aunt Kaia stared at each other across the table, the lie unraveling between them.

CHAPTER SIXTY-ONE

KING ÓLEIFR'S LEGACY

"D id—" Sigrid swallowed hard, struggling to get the words out. "Did you do it so you could put your sister on the throne?"

Aunt Kaia covered her mouth with a trembling hand, taking several deep breaths. She stayed like that for a moment, steadying herself, before pulling her hand down and making a fist on the table. "I always believed Lena would return. We used to talk about making her queen someday, before she disappeared. When that army attacked from Helheim and stole the Eye of Hnitbjorg, I knew it was her doing. She was going to come back. So…"

Silence stretched between them.

Sweat glistened on Aunt Kaia's face. "With him gone, the throne would fall to my sister. He was the only thing in the way."

Thing. Like he was a boulder that needed moving.

"He was never sick," Sigrid said—a statement, not a question.

"I thought if I poisoned him slowly and made it look like a progressing illness, no one would be suspicious when the day came for me to finish the job." Her aunt's voice trembled as the truth trickled out.

"So when I came back from Helheim," Sigrid said, clenching her fists to try and stop shaking, "and I confirmed that Princess Helena was trying to return…you took this as your cue. You finished the job and intended to use me to bring her back."

"Not *use* you, Sigrid. Never *use* you. Work with you. An ally."

"But this is why you invited me up to the hall. You planned to ask me to get Helena since the day you found out I have Sleipnir."

"You don't understand." Aunt Kaia shook her head, an apologetic, watery look in her eyes. "I hoped we could come to the conclusion together."

Sigrid let out a growl of frustration. *This cursed family.* She'd been right to doubt her the moment she got the invitation up to the hall. "You're just like her."

"Please give her a chance—"

"Is this also why you were so upset by the Night Elves' attack? You didn't plan to deal with something like this before putting your sister back on the throne. You hoped for a smooth transition from Óleifr to Helena without having to take on any responsibilities in the meantime." Sigrid gave her a mocking smile. "Well, it didn't work out that way, did it? A war is happening, and you're responsible for leading this world."

Aunt Kaia's expression clouded, a mix of anger and hurt.

"You honestly killed your own brother," Sigrid said, "the only decent person in this family, in order to help your deranged sister return to these towers." She tried and failed to get her breath.

She looked down at her pancakes, not touching them. *What if they're poisoned? How angry and desperate is she?* "What happens to me, now that you've told me what you've done?"

Aunt Kaia's fists were clenched on the table, her knuckles white—but her voice was calm. "I expect you to keep serving Vanaheim on Sleipnir like we agreed."

Sigrid raised an eyebrow, challenging. Inside, her heart slammed against her ribs. "And if I tell people what you did?"

Aunt Kaia nodded toward the door to the kitchen, where the waitstaff were. "Those who found out what I was doing have been handsomely compensated. Most agreed even that he was a spineless king who was hurting Vanaheim. I'm not concerned."

Sigrid's pulse raced faster. Could nobody in the royal hall be trusted?

Aunt Kaia leaned over the table with a pleading expression. "You have no idea what went on behind Óleifr's perfect exterior. When he was given the throne, he knew how much it hurt Helena, and he didn't so much as talk to her about it. He accepted his privilege as the firstborn male, no questions, no conversations. He took what was his and ignored how much it hurt his sister."

"So you think he should have refused the throne?"

"Not necessarily, but would it have been so hard to acknowledge the situation and talk to my sister about it?"

Sigrid said nothing. She agreed, but that was no reason to kill him.

"And don't get me started on his diplomacy," Aunt Kaia said. "That spineless *boy* would sooner have seen Vanaheim fall to Yggdrasil's roots than stand up for this world. Other worlds treated him like a well-bred dog. He was a coward."

"Leading a world is hard," Sigrid said. "You know this."

"Oh, his cowardice went way beyond leading a world." A storm passed over Aunt Kaia's face, and she took a moment to get her next words out. "There were several occasions when your mother and I were pushed out of our positions, stepped on, manipulated by his advisors. He had a lifetime of opportunity to defend us. He watched his own sisters be humiliated and disrespected again and again, and he did nothing."

Sigrid scoffed. "You think I believe that Vala and the generals stepped on and humiliated you?"

"Not them. You think I kept those other fools around once he died? They're long gone."

Sigrid clenched her jaw, nauseous. If this was true, then yes, maybe Óleifr was a coward, a boy born into a life of privilege who never understood the needs of the people he ruled—but Sigrid had also seen him be kind, and for his whole reign, he'd chosen peace over greed.

Maybe, in the end, nobody in this family was fit to rule. None of them understood life beyond these walls, and they'd all failed Vanaheim in some way.

"If you're hoping for sympathy, I'm sorry to disappoint you," Sigrid said coldly. "None of this changes the fact that you're Helena's ally. You're just like her—jealous, manipulative, a murderer."

Aunt Kaia sighed. She reached to the seat beside her, the jangling gold bands she always wore filling the silence, and placed a bow and arrow on the table. The arrow was dark, polished, with an unfamiliar rune etched on the hilt.

CHAPTER SIXTY-TWO

ACTS OF TREASON

"Harald was able to make something that holds a similar curse to the one the Night Elves harnessed." Aunt Kaia thumbed the bowstring, which made a low reverberation that sent a ripple up Sigrid's back. "Just one, mind you, but it's a start. It doesn't match the iron arrows that the Night Elves have, but it serves a similar purpose."

"Oh?" Sigrid's mouth went dry.

"I'd planned to give it to you to use on the Svartalf King, but I'm prepared to use it on whoever poses the biggest threat to Vanaheim." Aunt Kaia brushed a hand along the arrow, and the room was so quiet that Sigrid heard her skin scrape against the iron. "I wonder… Is Svartalfheim's army the biggest threat, or is treason?"

Sigrid pushed her chair back and stood, a motion that made Aunt Kaia seize the bow.

"Treason?" Sigrid spat. "The woman who poisoned the king is talking to me about treason?"

"Your opposition to the crown is no better than what I did. It's no better than what my sister did before she ran away." Aunt Kaia sneered. "Don't act above it."

The comparison stung, but Sigrid lifted her chin. "My plan doesn't involve murder. I'm doing what's best for Vanaheim."

"So am I," Aunt Kaia snapped. "Don't you see that Vanaheim

needs Helena back on the throne? Óleifr was ruining our world by wasting our line of defense, sending them to protect the lower worlds when we had nothing to gain."

"Nothing to gain? What about morality? Balance?"

Aunt Kaia said nothing, and Sigrid stepped back. They would never agree on how the worlds should coexist. Aunt Kaia might have been uncertain about leadership since the beginning, but she'd made one decision that was irrevocable—to follow Helena's plan.

Sigrid crossed the room and laid a hand on the doorknob when Aunt Kaia spoke.

"Remember your status in this family, Sigrid. We might disagree, but in the end, it's your duty to obey your queen."

Even though she wasn't ready to claim any of it, the words came to her strong and true. "That's just it, Aunt Kaia. There's nothing written to say that you have the right to the crown. Does the role fall to the youngest sibling, or to the firstborn's child?"

The flash of shock on her aunt's face was glorious.

Aunt Kaia regained her composure and raised the bow. "Enough. If you don't bend your knees for your queen, I *will* fire this."

Sigrid raised an eyebrow, aiming for calm defiance.

Except she'd seen the same look on her mother's face while trying to get out of Helheim, and she still had a mark on her arm where her mother's spear had sliced her.

I should've gone with Mariam to the junior valkyries. I would've had better luck convincing the Svartalf King to an agreement than convincing Aunt Kaia to change her mind.

"You are not to set foot out of this hall," Aunt Kaia said. "I sent for the other divisions last night. They've just returned to Vanahalla and have been given orders to stop you at all costs. Unlike some, they are ready to follow their queen and do their jobs without question."

Sigrid struggled to find words. If the senior valkyries were home, were they in a quarrel with the juniors right now? Had they already disobeyed their orders? Had she incited a civil war among the valkyries?

She did her best to look contemptuous, even though her heart had started a racing, anxious beat. "I guess family doesn't mean as much to you as you say it does."

Footsteps pounded somewhere distant.

"Sigrid!"

Peter? Why had he come all the way up here from the valkyrie stables? What was going on?

Sigrid and Aunt Kaia exchanged a look of confusion before the door flew open with such force that it smacked Sigrid in the back and knocked her on her face.

She stumbled to her feet. "Peter, don't come in here!"

Totally disregarding the warning, Peter, Roland, and several stable hands shoved through the door, grabbing her and pulling her back.

Aunt Kaia's aim faltered, her eyes widening in surprise. "What are you all doing in here? Get out of my hall!"

One of the tall windows shattered, and she screamed, dropping the bow.

A golden spear struck the opposite wall, then shot back out the window. A flash of wings flew past, and Sigrid caught a familiar blood marking on the mare's shoulder.

Aunt Kaia cursed, clutching her forearm. A line of blood oozed where the spear had sliced her, coating her gold bands. "Treason! Guards!"

"What are you doing?" Sigrid asked as Peter pulled her into the entrance hall. They were going to get killed.

"We need to get you out of here," Roland said.

"Why—?"

The royal guards surrounded them, raising their weapons and

shouting for everyone to surrender. Fortunately, the stable hands had the foresight to arm themselves, and they blocked the attack. Shouts and clashing weapons echoed in the vast entrance hall, an indistinguishable roar that sent Sigrid's pulse racing.

"What's—going—on?" Sigrid used her spear like a sword to help keep the guards away from the stable hands. "Guards, stand down!"

A couple of guards faltered at her command, but only for a moment—their duty was to protect the queen, even if that meant going up against the princess.

"The seniors came back," Peter said, panting. Sweat dripped down his face, like he'd just run all the way here. "They know the juniors were planning to oppose the queen, and they all got into a shouting match."

Sigrid cursed. "Is everyone safe?"

"I think so. The juniors were trying to tell them about the queen's plan for a conquest so they'd understand. But Queen Kaia got to them first, so I don't know if they'll be swayed."

All around them, the stable hands fought the royal guards valiantly, and Sigrid's heart swelled that her brothers had come to save her.

Shouts erupted outside.

The double doors had been left open, and a winged mare swooped through and landed noisily on the marble floor.

It was Leah, her eyes wide with panic. "Your Majesty, the Night Elves broke the drawbridge."

"Drawbridge?" Aunt Kaia snapped. "They're here?"

Everyone turned toward the open doors.

An army of Night Elves poured through the courtyard like a flash flood.

Sigrid's stomach sank. While the valkyries were preoccupied with her and Aunt Kaia, the Svartalf King's army had broken through their defenses.

CHAPTER SIXTY-THREE

PROTECTING
THE TOWERS

Night Elves filled the courtyard, flitting in all directions like leaves in a windstorm. Though valkyries swooped in after them, there were too many to contain. They slashed limbs off the gold statues, tore up gardens, and destroyed everything in their path.

"Leah!" Sigrid stopped her before she left the hall to join the fight. "Fly up and get Vala and Tóra out of the Seer's Tower."

Leah raised her spear. "They're safe with me."

She flew back out, her mare angling up and away. The royal guards and stable hands rushed to shut the double doors behind her. Just in time, too, as the elves slammed into them as they groaned closed, jamming axes and swords through the gap to try and wedge it open.

For a moment, she feared they would push through, but the closing doors sliced the weapons like they were made of butter. The lock fell heavily into place, its noise echoing through the hall.

Sigrid blinked at the severed metal weapons. *Magic?*

While everyone leaned on the door, panting and wide-eyed, she scanned the hall for weak points. Aunt Kaia stood at the back of the crowd with guards surrounding her, holding the bow and arrow with a trembling hand.

"Aunt Kaia, are the windows guarded with magic like the door?"

"I—I don't think so."

Great. Whose brilliant idea was that?

"Barricade the windows," Sigrid shouted. "Leave the door. It's sealed."

The stable hands and guards rushed to obey her, covering as many windows as possible with anything they could find—chairs, tables, vases, paintings. It wouldn't completely stop them from getting in, but it was a deterrent.

War cries and crashes outside became louder. The Night Elves were never supposed to make it this far. If they got inside Vanahalla—inside the *Sorcerers' Tower*—the result would be cataclysmic.

Sigrid's heart pounded, panic threatening to cloud her mind. How many elves had made it into the courtyard? And how long could they sit inside these walls defending their position?

We need the sorcerers. We need to use runes.

And I need to find the Svartalf King.

"If anyone sees the Svartalf King, tell me at once!" She paced the hall, her energy not permitting her to stay still. "And somebody get the sorcerers!"

"I'll find them," Roland shouted, running in a little circle. "Which way?"

Sigrid pointed. "Be careful!"

He ran off, Peter following close behind.

"Hey," Durinn interrupted, "your *elf* friend disappeared earlier along with the two captives. Now they're all attacking the hall, and—"

"And what? His loyalty is not in doubt." Sigrid rounded on him with her teeth gritted, tired of people hating her friends for how they looked or where they came from. This was not the time to distrust each other. "Focus on your duties and help defend this hall."

The nearby stable hands looked between her and Durinn,

uncertainty clouding their expressions.

Sigrid was about to tell them off, too, when the echo of clip-clops came from somewhere close—from *inside* the hall? She spun around, searching for the source.

Hestur trotted out of a corridor, followed by Sleipnir, the goats, Disa, and the other royal horses.

Sigrid's jaw fell slack. "How…?"

"*Maa!*" a goat said, munching the leaves of a potted plant.

One of the royal stable hands sprinted up behind the herd, panting, holding a bunch of halters and lead ropes. "I had to bring them in." He dropped the halters in a tangled heap on the marble floor and clutched his ribs. "The Night Elves surrounded Vanahalla."

The intensifying sound of battle confirmed his words. While the entrance hall was secure for now, the long connecting corridors leading to the towers were not. The elves would no doubt take advantage of the many unprotected windows.

Vala would be in Leah's care by now, so that left the Sorcerers' Tower and the corridor leading to it—and she'd just sent Roland and Peter there.

Gods, she should've gone with them. She couldn't stay here and do nothing.

"Good work. Keep them safe," Sigrid said to the harried stable hand while putting on Hestur's halter and lead rope. "Guards, make sure all the courtiers are accounted for. Keep this hall secure. Any free hands, with me!"

She vaulted up, feeling naked without armor, and nudged Hestur down the corridor leading to the Sorcerers' Tower—the one housing their most dangerous magic and relics.

Footsteps pounded after her as a couple of stable hands followed.

All around her, doors flew open, and Vanahalla's staff rushed out in a panic. They wielded anything they could get their hands on—a kitchen knife, a marble bust, a wooden chair.

She maneuvered Hestur around them. "Head to the entrance hall! You'll be safe there." Or at least *safer*.

Weapons and stones cracked against the corridor windows as the elves tried to get in and valkyries worked from the outside to keep them out. The ominous dark shapes ignited a heavy dread in Sigrid.

Is this what the villagers felt right before…

She shook her head. *Focus.*

The elves wouldn't use their arrows to destroy Vanahalla, at least not yet, because the Svartalf King was after the relics inside the hall. They'd be looking for the weakest place to break in, pushing against the hall's defenses until they broke.

They wouldn't be able to hold off the army forever, so the question wasn't whether they would break in, but when.

Sigrid leaned into Hestur's neck, and he plowed on with urgency, not letting the corridor's unfamiliar marble floor slow him down. Her skin prickled as they sighted the dark, wooden door of the Sorcerers' Tower. The energy from beyond it pulsed along the hallway as strongly as ever.

Peter and Roland were already there, banging on the door to try and get the sorcerers' attention.

Her relief at seeing them safe was short-lived. A Night Elf squeezed through one of the open rectangular windows, and Hestur balked, nearly unseating Sigrid.

The elf reeled and fell back when he saw people on both sides of him, cracking his mask against the wall.

Sigrid raised her spear and took aim. "Stop!"

The elf snarled and leaped to his feet, racing toward Peter and Roland as fluidly as a shadow. She threw her spear and it drove into his neck, killing him—but more elves climbed through after him. They flooded the corridor like nightfall, blocking her way.

"Attack!" Sigrid shouted at the guards and stable hands that had followed her. She recalled her spear as Hestur's strides gained on the elves. "Don't let them into the Sorcerers' Tower!"

Peter and Roland had stopped banging on the door to face the incoming elves. Without valkyrie spears to throw and recall, they could only fight hand-to-hand.

Sigrid threw her spear again, urgency making her throw sloppy. She couldn't let her friends be pinned, defenseless. Another bad throw made her scream.

As if hearing her desperation, the tower's door cracked open, and two sorcerers burst out—Mabil and Ragnarr. They slammed it closed behind them, the lock engaging on its own.

Mabil, holding a fistful of golden valkyrie spears, passed one each to Peter and Roland, whose eyes widened at being given permission to use a valkyrie weapon. Ragnarr sprinted past them, making a strange motion with his hand as if drawing a rune in midair. A cold wind swept through the corridor, buffeting the elves so hard that they were knocked off their feet.

Sigrid held onto Hestur and took the opportunity to fire a few more shots. Her friends and Mabil helped from the other side, driving spear after spear into the elves. Slowly but surely, surrounded on both sides, the group of elves thinned.

The wind stopped abruptly.

Sigrid's breath caught, dread surging before she turned her gaze.

Ragnarr stumbled, looking down at the arrow protruding from his gut.

"Ragnarr!"

Sigrid and Mabil's shouts blended together as he fell.

Mabil raced over—and a second arrow caught her in the leg. She fell to the floor, crying out.

"No!" Sigrid's insides turned to ice, her mind spinning in disbelief.

Just as she'd thought they gained ground, a second stream of elves climbed through the window and raced toward the tower door. They swarmed the fallen sorcerers and pushed past Peter and Roland as if they weren't even worthy of a fight.

Sigrid nudged Hestur onward, refusing to give up. Hestur was less confident than Sleipnir about trampling the enemy, but he obeyed her commands, holding his head high as they plowed into the intruders.

Shouts rose behind her from the guards and stable hands following. She dared not look. If the elves found another window to break through, they would have to manage on their own. She had to keep pushing ahead, closer to protecting Peter and Roland, closer to the tower door.

A commotion rose, and a cry of pain rose above the fight.

Peter fell on all fours, roaring in pain and gripping his shoulder.

"Peter!" Sigrid's chest constricted as she fought harder to reach him. *I won't lose him.*

Roland cursed. With a roar, he stabbed an elf in the chest, then hurried over to help.

Sigrid reached their side and made to dismount.

"I'm fine," Peter shouted, his strained voice indicating otherwise. "Keep going, Sigrid."

She wanted to disregard his order. She wanted to stay and help. But the group of elves that reached the door had taken axes and were trying to smash their way in.

Sigrid cursed and pushed Hestur to gallop on.

At the end of the corridor, the Sorcerers' Tower door was imposing, thick, and full of magic, none of which deterred the elves from throwing themselves at it to get it open.

With a battle cry, Sigrid attacked. An elf at the back spun around, ready to use his axe on her, but her spear was already flying toward him. He collapsed to the marble floor, the commotion alerting the others. While she summoned her weapon back, they faced her, forming a wall between her and the door.

At the door, one elf rose his arm for another blow—but it wasn't an axe.

It was an iron arrow, and the arrowhead was black.

Sigrid gasped, throwing her spear, but it was too late.

The elf embedded the arrow into the wooden door, and dark tendrils exploded all over it, crawling up the sides and into the wood grain itself. As Sigrid's spear thunked into the center, the door broke apart, falling to pieces along with the darkness.

Sigrid couldn't breathe. Dizziness overcame her, making her sway in the saddle.

I failed.

Night Elves flooded into the dark corridor of the sorcerers' domain, breaching Vanahalla's most dangerous tower.

CHAPTER SIXTY-FOUR

INSIDE THE
SORCERERS' TOWER

The magic beyond the broken door reached for Sigrid, a prickly sensation tingling across her skin. As the weight of protecting the Sorcerers' Tower pressed down on her, she drew an unsteady breath, struggling to contain her panic.

The fight continued behind her, with more enemies spilling in through the windows. The urge to go back to check on Peter competed with the need to stop the elves that had broken into the tower.

He'll be okay. Roland and the others are with him.

Sigrid adjusted her spear and the lead rope with trembling hands, her heart ready to explode out of her chest. This wasn't the way she'd planned on exploring the Sorcerers' Tower.

Hestur snorted, eyeing the narrow corridor beyond the broken door and its dank, underground feel.

"Just like when we were in Svartalfheim, buddy," she said, rolling her shoulders.

He tossed his head, and they galloped after the elves, plunging into the dark passage.

If she thought the tower's magic was tangible before, that sensation had nothing on how it changed the air on the inside. Her skin prickled so much it was uncomfortable, like sweating in a thick wool tunic. She wanted to shake it off, to back away and leave it behind.

The passage opened up to an area at the base of the tower, like a gathering place with bookshelves, a crackling fire, and furniture—all of it destroyed after the elves had passed through. Open arches to the left and right led to hallways that curved around the tower, and one led right through.

Footsteps and cries echoed from the middle, and Sigrid nudged Hestur down it.

"Against the walls, sorcerers!" an elf yelled from beyond an open door.

Sigrid drew Hestur to a halt outside it. The dim room looked like the inside of a cave, with runes scraped into the walls, ceiling, and floor. A long wooden table took up the center, scattered in all manner of items—sand, gemstones, bones, hair… *Wait, are those severed fingers?*

The three sorcerers in the room refused the elf's order, fighting back with swords in hand. Gold runes caught the light on the blades, which explained why they sliced through the elves' chainmail as if the blades were molten. Two elves collapsed, gasping their last breaths, while the rest rifled through everything on the table, sending most of it crashing to the floor and pocketing several items.

A sorcerer shrieked in outrage. "Get away from that!"

Sigrid threw her spear at the nearest elf, hitting her in the back. As she fell, the sorcerers seized the opportunity to jump on the rest. The room filled with shouts and thumps.

"Go, Princess!" A female sorcerer waved her off. "We've got them!"

Hestur snorted and pranced as shadows flitted behind them, more elves coming from the main corridor. Worry for her friends and those who stayed behind threatened to freeze her up again, but Hestur didn't give her a chance. He surged after them.

They followed the horde, Sigrid taking down as many as she could along the way. An elf dropped a sword, and she leaped off Hestur to get it, running alongside him for a few steps before vaulting back on and continuing at a gallop.

When the hallway split in two at the tower's outer curved wall, Sigrid continued her chase to the right. She embedded the sword in the chest of the next elf and released her spear into the one behind him, sending both crashing to the floor. Something metallic spilled from their arms. They'd been coming from a room full of spears and armor—unfinished valkyrie gear. The metal had been forged but not yet coated in enchanted gold. Another elf was inside with an armful, and she threw her spear at him.

We're failing. Her chest tightened as she tried to get air. The Svartalf King had built an army so big that it couldn't be stopped by the best warriors in the nine worlds—and they were about to steal everything Vanaheim had acquired since the beginning of time.

"Princess Sigrid!" Harald boomed from down the hallway. Two sorcerers behind him lifted tables and chairs, making a barricade.

Sigrid finished off another elf and hurried over, the sorcerers closing the gap behind her. "How can I help?"

"I've sent sorcerers to guard the entrance hall, and we've sealed the door leading to the Seer's Tower, but…" Harald grunted, setting down an enormous desk and tipping it over. He carved a rune on it with a trembling hand. It had better be a rune for strength, or the elves would make short work of this barricade. "There are artifacts and research in the upper levels— the celestial magic. We must not let them have it. But we need time. This barricade isn't impenetrable."

Sigrid looked back toward the noise, wheezing. "I can hold them off for a while." When he hesitated, she set her jaw and pointed to the stairs behind him. "It's an order, Harald. I will buy you the time."

Harald bowed his head and left with his sorcerers, racing up to protect Vanaheim's most powerful and dangerous relics.

Sigrid turned Hestur so they could face the barricade and the curving hallway beyond. It remained empty, but the rising sound of footsteps was like a herd of horses galloping over the fields. Her arms trembled, but she held her spear in a secure grip.

Hestur danced in place, agitated.

"It's okay. We're okay," Sigrid said, reassuring them both. "We'll stop—"

A horde of elves charged at her, their shadows obscuring the hallway like an incoming storm. The moment they got close enough, Sigrid roared, throwing her spear and recalling it as fast as she could.

There was no slowing them down.

Too many, too many, too many.

The barricade didn't last. The Night Elves were on them before she could think to flee.

Sigrid gasped as hands closed over her arms and hauled her off Hestur. She yelled, fighting to pull free of the elves as she hit the floor. An elf yanked her spear away. She thrashed, throwing punches and kicks until she broke free from her captors' grips for the fraction of time she needed. She summoned her spear back and used it like a dagger on one, thrust a knee into the other's groin, and made a break for it, running fast down the hallway.

"Hestur, come!"

Hestur aimed a well-placed kick, sending an elf crashing into the wall, then barreled after her, lead rope trailing, keen to get away from the mob.

Sigrid hurtled through the nearest door, pulling Hestur inside, and bolted the door behind them, wheezing for breath. She needed a moment to figure out—

Something seized her wrist, and she shrieked, ready to stab with her spear again. "Get off—Vala?"

"Listen." The old woman had a surprisingly firm hold as she locked Sigrid with a fierce gaze. "We *cannot* let them take the relics in this hall."

"I know. Harald is protecting the celestial magic. We won't let them turn Vanaheim into a realm of darkness, Vala." Sigrid looked around wildly. They were in a small, dim room with shelves full of books, glass bottles, stones with runes etched on them, and trinkets.

Vala shook her head firmly. "There's no time. He will fail."

Sigrid swallowed, her hands turning icy. "Did the Eye show—"

"Don't concern yourself with that, Sigrid. I have a plan."

Sigrid was about to insist when it struck her that Vala shouldn't even be here. "Wait, why aren't you with Leah? She came to get you."

"She took Tóra to safety. Don't worry." She pulled Sigrid back a step, further into the darkness. "Now, do you trust me?"

"Of—of course," Sigrid said, panting. Why hadn't Vala seized the opportunity to get away from here? She was too old to fight. She could barely run, no less throw a punch.

"The main corridor has been sealed, but behind that tapestry is a door leading to my tower." She pointed to the back of the room, where a large, gray tapestry woven with hundreds of runes took up the whole wall. "Go through there—your Hestur is small enough to fit—and back to the entrance hall. Round up everyone in Vanahalla. Get outside. Take yourselves far from here, down to the valkyrie stable."

Sigrid didn't move. "Why?"

"I will use a rune that has never been used before, a rune we dared not name for fear others would find out. It's dangerous magic." She clutched Sigrid's hands, her blue eyes full of warmth. "Please, Sigrid. You're the only one who can keep everyone safe."

Sigrid's heart jumped. "What about you?"

"I'm stronger than you think, Princess." She pushed Sigrid gently toward the tapestry. "Go."

"But you're coming, too, right? After you've done this?" Sigrid grabbed Hestur's lead rope. "Promise me."

"I promise, Sigrid," Vala said without hesitation. She unlocked the door. "Now go!"

Sigrid nodded, panic tightening around her throat. She

wanted to ask what Vala was going to do, but this wasn't the moment for lengthy explanations.

With a dark feeling churning inside her, Sigrid obeyed and entered the secret passage. It was barely big enough for Hestur to get through. She clucked to him, inviting him to follow. He eyed the passage, then dipped his head and squeezed through quickly, as if afraid it was a set of jaws that might close over him if he lingered.

"Good, Hestur." She vaulted onto his back.

Beyond the tapestry was a room mirroring the one she'd left. They passed through it and emerged in a dark corridor. She galloped down it and came to another door, which she leaned down from the saddle to open. Beyond it was the familiar ground floor of the Seer's tower, which she rode through without a second glance before slipping through the opposite door to get back to the entrance hall.

The clamor of battle rose as she neared it, and she readied herself for whatever she would find. When she burst into the hall...

A maelstrom of chaos.

Royal guards and stable hands faced a horde of Night Elves who'd managed to get in through the windows. Where Harald's sorcerers joined the fight, explosions knocked elves off their feet, strong winds stopped their advance, and torches of enchanted flame roared to life. The horses and goats lingered near the walls, agitated, along with the poor stable hand who'd brought them in.

Despite the barrier on the door remaining intact and the windows not providing much space for elves to break inside in large groups, their defenses were failing, the number of Night Elves already inside steadily pushing them back.

Bodies and blood tainted the once-pristine marble and gold surfaces—Night Elves and a few royal guards.

Sigrid's chest tightened as she scanned for her friends. Peter, Roland, and the others fought hard alongside the guards. Blood stained Peter's tunic, but at least his arm had been bandaged. A few other stable hands were wounded as well, but none critical.

Vala was right. Staying inside to defend this place was hopeless, and now she was about to unleash some unnamed power. They *had* to leave.

"Everyone out," Sigrid shouted, nudging Hestur forward. "Stable hands, guards, leave the elves and come with me!"

A few looked at her, but they stayed put, fighting hard.

"We need to clear out of this hall right now," she shouted. "Vala—"

A thump came from overhead.

Sigrid winced, ready to launch her spear.

Aunt Kaia raced along the second-floor balcony, her blue gown whipping behind her. Several sorcerers followed in her wake, the one in the lead holding a bow and arrow.

Aunt Kaia leaned over the railing and pointed at someone in the crowd. The sorcerer stood beside her and raised the bow.

Sigrid followed his aim, her breaths coming fast. Who were they targeting?

Night Elves kept up the fight, their crude weapons making serious damage wherever they hit. Deer mask, bears, wolves, and so many more...but amid the confusion, one elf made Sigrid's heart stop.

Tall antlers, a bear mask, and an iron crown.

The Svartalf King fought at the far side of the mob, ready to push through to the corridor that led to the Sorcerers' Tower. He'd not seen the danger.

"Aunt Kaia, don't!"

Killing him would ruin any hope of making a truce with Svartalfheim. Their world would never forgive Vanaheim.

Aunt Kaia looked right at her, and Sigrid saw her lips form the word, "Fire."

The sorcerer released the bowstring, the arrow flying true and finding its target in the time it took Sigrid to blink. It buried in his chest, pushing him back a step. With a shudder, it melted into ropes, which coiled around the king and bound him tightly, the same way the webs of darkness spread out from the iron arrows.

The Svartalf King fell, pierced through and tied in ropes that twisted around him like snakes. He disappeared beneath the scramble.

"No!" Sigrid galloped over, keeping her eyes on the king as he writhed and shouted.

Behind her, footsteps thumped as Aunt Kaia and the sorcerers followed. More arrows hit the elves nearest him, binding them and keeping them from reaching their king.

Sigrid reached him first, leaping off Hestur. She dropped to her knees, grabbing the ropes as they tightened around his neck. The king gripped the strands as well, and together they pulled, but the ropes kept tightening. "No, no, no—"

Aunt Kaia caught up. She gripped Sigrid's shoulder and shoved her out of the way.

Sigrid fell sideways, letting out a sharp breath before scrambling upright. "We can't kill him, Aunt Kaia! This is not the way to peace!"

"Don't be ridiculous, Sigrid." Aunt Kaia seized the Svartalf King's mask, a sneer curling her upper lip. "Let's have a look at the face beneath all of this chaos, shall we?"

The king snarled, gripping the base of his mask tightly. "Finally, the queen shows her face. It won't be long until we see what Hel makes of such a coward, *Your Majesty*."

The queen's expression hardened, her teeth bared, a glint of rage in her eyes.

Sigrid scrambled forward on her hands and knees, reaching for her aunt, desperate to stop her. "Please, don't—"

Aunt Kaia yanked the king's mask off.

CHAPTER SIXTY-FIVE

VALA'S PLAN

The Svartalf King shrieked loudly enough to sting Sigrid's eardrums, the tone so chilling that bile rose in her throat. Fire roared to life before they could see his face, and the blast of heat and brightness knocked all of them off their feet.

Sigrid hit the marble floor on her side, coughing, a flash of panic shooting through her. *Am I on fire?* She sat up, gasping for breath and running her hands over her prickling face.

Hooves clattered as Hestur skittered back.

Sigrid stared at the remains of the Svartalf King. Where his face and neck would be, there was nothing. The fire had extinguished as quickly as it had come, leaving an empty shell of leather and chainmail. A bear mask with broken antlers and burn marks lay steps away next to Aunt Kaia. His iron crown rested nearby. Not even charred skeletal remains littered the floor, and not a fleck of ash floated into the ceiling.

Sigrid's breaths came fast, her chest tight.

Beneath her horror, fury rose like bubbling lava.

Aunt Kaia was a monster. Beyond killing, beyond greed and ruthlessness, she had ruined all hope of stopping this war. How was she supposed to get the Night Elves to retreat with their leader dead? They would never stop fighting.

Sigrid turned to her aunt, who backed away, her face gleaming with victory. The sorcerers looked alarmed and unsettled as they followed, waiting for her orders.

"You've ruined *everything*."

Aunt Kaia laughed. "No, darling. We've won."

Go after her. Punish her.

The urge overcame Sigrid, like when riding Sleipnir—but this was not the time. Vala was about to use dangerous runes. Right now, she had to get everyone in the hall outside.

Sigrid jumped on Hestur and stood in the stirrups. "Ground troops, we need to get out of the hall. Follow me!"

Peter and Roland raced to her side, followed by a few others.

"If we leave, the Night Elves will get into the tower," Peter said. He had a fierce expression, but he was clearly losing energy.

"Vala will take care of it." Sigrid kept her voice low enough for his ears only. "She's using a powerful rune, and if we don't get out of here, we'll all get in the way of whatever she's about to unleash."

Peter hesitated, then obeyed, turning to the other stable hands. "Everybody outside! We need to clear out of here. Help those who are injured. Let's go!"

The royal guards looked conflicted—but with their allies leaving and the Night Elves vastly outnumbering them, they had little choice.

"The princess is trying to save your hides," Roland snapped. "Now move!"

This helped urge everyone to follow quickly.

Unopposed, the elves flooded past and into the corridor.

Peter opened the double doors, and everyone spilled into the courtyard. The royal horses and goats shot past in their midst, Sleipnir in the lead, Disa close behind.

"Sigrid!" Aunt Kaia hurried toward her, her expression twisted in rage. She carried the Svartalf King's mask like a trophy. "What are you doing? The fight isn't over. We have to eliminate these creatures invading our home."

"I'm leaving," Sigrid said. "You should, too. Vala said so."

Aunt Kaia stepped back, like the words had smacked her in the face. "What? You can't just—" She gritted her teeth. "Where is she? Where's Vala?"

Sigrid ignored her, standing guard as everyone rushed past to get outside.

Aunt Kaia threw the mask at Sigrid's feet with a screech and then stormed down the corridor toward the Seer's Tower, followed by a few guards and sorcerers too loyal to abandon their queen.

The lobby emptied, leaving the elves to rampage through the hall unhindered.

Sigrid took in the destruction, numb. But the moment her gaze dropped, she found the bear mask—broken antlers, singed black, a distinctive chipped tooth…with no life inside.

"We will do better."

The valkyries would protect all worlds equally.

Sigrid shortened her reins, ready to join the others in the courtyard, when a mare swooped down and blocked her exit.

"Traitor!" Frida shouted. She was the elder valkyrie who'd met Sigrid at the wall when they returned to Vanahalla. Her face twisted in anger. "How dare you go up against our queen. You were nothing until she invited you into the hall. You have no right—"

"Get away from her!"

Sigrid's heart jumped as Runa wedged herself close so Tobia bumped the other mare's shoulder.

The valkyrie pointed her spear at Runa. "Don't interrupt me—"

"Hey!" Edith flew beside Runa, joining her in hovering between Sigrid and the older valkyrie.

Several valkyries flew closer—juniors, seniors, elders, the remaining generals—shouting at each other, the mares bumping dangerously in the sky.

"Hey! Stop it!" Someone was going to get hurt, and it would be her fault.

"Where's the proof that this girl is even Princess Helena's daughter?" a senior valkyrie asked, inciting more shouts all around.

"Stop wasting time!" Sigrid shouted, but her words drowned beneath the arguments. Her pulse raced as she sat below them on Hestur. Had they ever been so divided? "Listen to me! You need to fly up to the Sorcerers' Tower and see if anyone needs—"

"The tower!" Roland shouted.

Outside, several valkyries and stable hands gasped and pointed, echoing his same cry. Sigrid looked back at the corridors, but other than Night Elves still breaking in, nothing was amiss.

Abruptly, Hestur scooted forward, snorting in fright, and Sigrid gasped as she lost her balance.

An ear-splitting noise filled the air, drowning out all else. A wave of heat prickled her skin as if she'd stepped too close to a fire. The air that entered her lungs was so hot and dry that she coughed, gagging on nothing. A rumble rose from every direction, the entire hall seeming to shake, and then everything vanished in a whirl of dust that exploded outward from the corridors.

Hestur spun, trying to get away from the explosion and out into the courtyard.

Sigrid hit the ground hard, the breath leaving her as she rolled. A blur of sky and cobblestones turned in her vision until she came to a stop outside. Smoke filled her nose. Her skin prickled.

She coughed until her throated ached, struggling to get her feet under her. The dusty haze in the air made it impossible to see. "Mariam?" she shouted, the first name to her mind, the first one past her lips.

Hestur stood beside her, snorting and looking around. He whinnied, calling to his friends. Nearby, several of them replied.

People shouted to each other, confused and afraid.

The dust dissipated enough for Sigrid to notice the blue sky seemed to have changed color, and she blinked to check if her eyes were deceiving her. A tinge of purple bled across her vision.

Hooves clattered, and boots thumped onto the cobblestones. A face swam into Sigrid's vision, making her heart miss a beat.

"Sigrid, what's happening?" Mariam grabbed her arms. "Where did that eruption come from?"

Sigrid blinked, the sight of Mariam grounding her in reality. It took a moment before she could get words out. "I—I don't—"

A blast of heat roared out from the hall, and screams echoed from down a corridor.

The Sorcerers' Tower.

"Fire!" someone shouted, and then more voices rose.

"Fire in the Sorcerers' Tower!"

"There's smoke coming from the windows!"

"I can see the flames!"

Fire? Why would Night Elves light a fire when they feared it so much?

"Valkyries, with me!" General Ulfhilda shouted, and all of them took off into the sky, rising above the golden towers and out of Sigrid's sight.

Mariam looked back at Sigrid, a desperate expression pulling down her eyebrows. "Sigrid, is this fire the work of elves or one of us?"

Sigrid shook her head, at a loss.

And then it hit her, and she swayed as the truth washed over her.

We cannot let them take the relics in this hall, Vala had said.

Her meaning became clear, as obvious as the scent of smoke wafting under her nose.

Sigrid met Mariam's gaze, her lips numb. "Vala's going to destroy the entire hall to stop the Night Elves from taking it."

CHAPTER SIXTY-SIX

THRONES BURN TOO

Smoke crept out of the Sorcerers' Tower, rolling up like a dark beast emerging from slumber. Another explosion rumbled the ground, and a purple glow tinted the sky.

I left her behind. She pushed me to leave.

Vala must have known the risk. She wasn't fit enough to run from the flames, and still she'd chosen this path.

Mariam cursed. "What do we do?"

"I...I don't—"

"Sigrid!" Mariam grabbed her shoulders. "You have to lead us, Princess."

The faces in the courtyard ranged from shocked to angry to devastated. Their home was in flames, their queen focused on revenge. It was not the time for the princess of Vanaheim to lose her composure.

Swallowing to wet her throat, she gave Mariam a sharp nod. "We have to make sure anyone left in the Sorcerers' Tower gets to safety. Lead the junior valkyries down the hill. I'll take care of the people here."

Mariam stepped in and kissed Sigrid, and Sigrid slid a hand around her neck to hold her there. In this moment when everything she knew was turned upside down, she wanted— *needed*—this time to memorize Mariam's taste and feel before they broke apart.

Too soon, the kiss was over, and the horror of the moment rushed back.

"Please be safe." Sigrid couldn't stop the desperation in her tone.

"You too, Princess." Mariam jumped on Aesa's back, a flash of fear in her eyes. "See you soon."

Mariam flew off, leaving Sigrid in a gust of wind. The valkyries followed her without question.

Sigrid moved toward those gathered in the courtyard. "We need to control the flames until the valkyries make sure everyone is out. Any sorcerers that can manage it, please redirect the water." She pointed at the moat.

A group of sorcerers ran toward the moat.

Sigrid found Peter and passed Hestur's lead rope to him. "Take him, and bring everyone to the valkyrie stable. Do *not* let him try to follow me, whatever you do."

She placed her hands on either side of her gelding's face. "Hestur, I'm trusting you to lead these people to safety, all right?"

He nickered.

"Stay safe, Sigrid." Peter called out orders to the other stable hands, leading Hestur away.

Ignoring the twist in her gut, Sigrid ran inside the hall, across the lobby, and into the corridor to the Sorcerers' Tower. She retraced her steps to where she'd raced with Hestur to reach the locked door and been ambushed by Night Elves.

Their bodies lay scattered along the corridor—among them, Mabil and Ragnarr. They'd fought like warriors until the very end.

Outside the windows, the valkyries swooped close to the tower, checking the windows for anyone who needed rescuing. The clash of battle rang out as other valkyries took out swarms of Night Elves who tried to flee back out to the courtyard.

The air thickened with smoke, making Sigrid cough and

wheeze as she crossed over into the Sorcerers' Tower.

She promised to follow me out.

She lied.

Eyes burning, Sigrid followed the dark and hazy hallway. The walls rumbled, threatening to collapse on her.

Her heart beat faster. It was too hard to breathe.

Calm down.

Where could Vala have gone to unleash the rune?

The hallway brightened up ahead, where a patter of footsteps raced closer.

"Hello? Is someone—"

A blast of heat made her gasp, along with the terrifying memory of her encounter with Garmr. Screams reached her before a group of elves appeared around the corner and barreled toward her at full speed, a fire roaring after them in a wave. It consumed everything, wisps of blue and purple licking the walls as it ate magic and relics. An elf tripped and hit the ground, screaming as she caught fire.

Cursing, Sigrid turned and ran, the fleeing Night Elves at her heels.

This was not a normal fire. Fire wouldn't burn through everything this quickly, not when these walls were made of stone.

Structures cracked and crumbled, the fire eating every wall, portrait, tapestry, table, shelf, and anything else in its path with terrifying speed.

I need to get out of here.

Sigrid put on a burst of speed down the long corridor, jumping over cracked stones and chunks of wall that kept falling in her path. The moment she emerged in the entrance hall, she darted left behind a column. Fire exploded out, shooting some of the Night Elves across the hall. Those that survived fled past, screaming, out into the courtyard.

Fire stuck to the columns and stairs, devouring the place. *I can't leave yet. I have to find Vala.*

Sigrid coughed and looked around the hall for another way. The closest spiral stairs were engulfed in flames, the potted plants beside it smoldering. At the far end of the hall, the three marble-and-gold thrones had caught fire—and the significance of it made her chest tighten.

This whole hall...all of its magic, all of its history...

Vanahalla has fallen.

A whisper of her name came so quietly that she might have missed it if her senses hadn't been so heightened. With the hall still burning, the smell of smoke, and the heat of the magic fire... *Is my mind playing tricks?*

"Sigrid."

She followed the call and looked up.

On one of the spiral staircases, Vala appeared like a vision out of a wall of smoke. The Eye of Hnitbjorg hung around her neck on its long chain, strangely illuminated in the wild flames.

Sigrid rushed to the stairs, but the moment her foot touched the first step, the entire structure groaned. It wouldn't hold her weight—and it might not hold the wispy old Seer's for much longer. She stepped back and reached up in vain. "Come with me. The sorcerers are working to redirect the moat, and we'll get the valkyries to dump buckets of water onto—"

"It can't be extinguished." Vala's voice was clear and calm. "This is the only way to stop them from taking everything. If they use the magic in these towers, all of Vanaheim will be in ruins. The cosmic scales will be irreparable."

"But we're still fighting, and we won't give up." Sigrid's voice broke. Losing another person to this war was unacceptable. Losing Vala was—

She stepped as close as she could, braving the heat of the flames crawling closer from the sides.—as if she could catch Vala if she jumped. "Please. You have to hurry."

Vala tapped her walking stick on the floor, which creaked. She smiled down at Sigrid. "Starting over isn't so bad, Princess."

Sigrid nodded, still holding out her hand. "We can start over together."

Vala stared at her for a beat or two, then inclined her head. She started hobbling down the steps, moving so slowly on her walking stick that Sigrid could have screamed. The stairs held under the Seer's weight, but the flames crawled closer.

Wisps of fire from the walls licked dangerously close to Vala, threatening to ignite the furs around her shoulders. Sweat rolled down her age-spotted face.

"Do you remember my words to Tóra during the Seer's ceremony, before we were interrupted by the Eye?" Vala asked, wheezing.

Sigrid searched her memory. "You told her she was a messenger who transfers knowledge from the Norns."

Vala coughed hard. "The Norns…are the goddesses who weave fate, and they…send messages to us through the Eye of Hnitbjorg." She cleared her throat. "They created the Eye, and they can create another."

Create a new Eye?

It was getting harder to speak with the smoke closing in around them, but Vala continued. "Trust Tóra. She knows what to do…to restore balance to Yggdrasil. You can get back what we're about to lose."

"You said it was impossible to make a new Eye of Hnitbjorg!"

"I tried, and I failed—" A hole opened in the steps in front of Vala, the edges crumbling away and disappearing into the fire below. Smoke billowed up like a black steam column.

"Vala!" Sigrid's heart was in her throat.

The Seer regained her balance, then slowly skirted it, squeezing between the hole and the flames on her other side. "As I've come to see what you can do, I think you could be the one to do it. It's our only hope of restoring Vanaheim's place in the cosmos."

Sigrid wanted to scream. How could she be talking about future plans at a moment like this? "Vala, please. Hurry."

Vala had at least twenty steps to go when a tongue of fire licked across the remaining steps, crumbling two of them. She couldn't make it.

Sigrid's eyes burned. "No…"

Instead of panic, the most serene expression crossed the Seer's face. "Sigrid… You were afraid that you were like your mother and your aunt, but you are *not them*. You were raised in a barn and learned about the rewards of hard work. You…view obstacles as a challenge to overcome, and you don't give up. You also don't judge people, no matter what world…they come from." The Seer coughed, a horrible sound that hurt to hear. "Your struggles make you compassionate… That is your strength. You understand life and balance in a way your family never could."

Sigrid shook her head, both at her words and as a refusal to give up right now. "I still carry his blood. I am still tempted to do bad things." She pressed her foot on the first step, the heat agonizing on her exposed skin.

"Princess, we all have temptations. You just have to work at ignoring them a little harder than the rest of us."

I have to run to her.

Despite the risk of the stairs crumbling beneath them, the fire closing on both sides, and the ceiling alight overhead, Sigrid started forward.

A shout and pounding footsteps rose beside them. Aunt Kaia hobbled out of a corridor, wheezing for breath, clutching a raw spot on her arm. "What did you do?" she shouted, the words coming as a sob.

She shoved past Sigrid on her way up the spiral stairs, knocking her off her feet. The marble slammed into her back, stinging hot and covered in debris.

Vala waited calmly, one hand clutching the Eye of Hnitbjorg dangling from her neck and the other on her walking stick. Sweat poured down her temples, and her chest heaved as she struggled for breath. "It's the only way…to stop the Night Elves…from taking everything, Your Majesty."

Aunt Kaia wiped an arm across her reddened face, a mix of fury and grief twisting her expression. "I knew you'd lost your mind," she shouted, crying in earnest. "We should have replaced you years ago. You destroyed *everything* my family worked for. Give me the Eye."

Sigrid heaved to her feet, dizzy, her lungs burning. Seeing her aunt crying without restraint made her chest ache. The queen had reason to mourn her hall as it burned to the ground—but wasn't she the reason this was all happening in the first place? If she and her family hadn't tried to subjugate the lower realms, would the Night Elves have been angry enough to attack?

Or it's my fault. The thought came unbidden, sending a tremor through Sigrid. *If I'd followed the path of my family, like fate intended, I wouldn't have divided the valkyries at a crucial moment. We could have stopped the elves from getting past the wall.*

She had opened a fissure in their defenses, determined to do this her way instead of Aunt Kaia's way, and that had been enough to break them.

Aunt Kaia stretched out her hand over the break in the stairs, dangerously close to the flames. Her airy blue robe flapped around her ankles, smoke rising from the hem.

Vala wrapped a gnarled hand tighter around the pink stone, backing up a step.

When Aunt Kaia jumped the break, tearing her dress and landing on her knees, the stairs shuddered.

"Both of you, stop!" Sigrid moved forward, but a shower

of embers rained in front of her and she backed away from it, coughing.

Aunt Kaia resumed her climb, and for every step she took, Vala retreated further up and closer to the fire behind her. The smoke obscured them, turning their figures into a haze. Another shudder.

"Aunt Kaia, the steps! Come back!"

The queen didn't listen, focused on the stubborn Seer backing into the smoke with Vanaheim's most important relic around her neck. With everything obscured, the two of them seemed to float over the inferno. Standing helplessly below, Sigrid coughed and wiped her streaming eyes, backing away from the agonizing heat.

"Vala, throw the Eye to me right now," Aunt Kaia said. "As your queen, I order you to—"

With a deafening groan and a crack, the stairs gave way.

CHAPTER SIXTY-SEVEN

NOTHING
TO FIGHT FOR

Sigrid screamed as she stumbled back from the explosion of debris and landed hard on the marble floor, cracking her shoulder against it. Her vision blurred as she tried to make sense of what was going on around her.

Aunt Kaia and Vala, two of Vanaheim's most powerful people, had just disappeared into the inferno consuming Vanahalla.

The flames roared their victory like Garmr at those he stopped from crossing his domain. There was nothing left of the stairs, and just like them, the rest of the hall would crumble into itself soon enough.

Sigrid coughed, her lungs spasming as they filled with ash. Everything burned—eyes, tongue, throat, skin. The smoke darkened everything, obscuring any speck of marble and gold in the surrounding space.

I need to get out.

The fire was deafening as it hissed, spat, split wood, and toppled structures. The whirling embers seared her skin and charred her white uniform.

She lost all sense of direction, groping about on hands and knees. Sickeningly dizzy, she fell flat, each gasp agonizing as the air seared her lungs.

"Help…" The word barely came out, her throat too raw to work.

A high-pitched sound pierced her eardrums. In all the destruction, it could have been anything—a scream, a pillar giving one last groan before falling, a dying relic.

It came again—a whinny.

A rhythmic clatter grew louder.

Was this what death did? Make her remember familiar noises?

Hoofbeats?

In her delirium, they moved sporadically, unevenly, like an echo.

Something bumped her in the ribs. She rolled on her side, unable to pull herself up in the whirl of smoke. It hit her again.

A pair of large nostrils blew in her ear.

An enormous, steel-gray head nudged her persistently, nickering, growing more frantic.

"Sleipnir?" she said, the word barely a croak.

His shape became the most solid thing in her line of sight, the only constant in the shifting smoke and flames.

She reached up, her muscles struggling to cooperate, and wrapped a fist in his black mane. He lowered his neck, doing everything to help. As she leaned into him, he dropped his four front legs, getting to his knees so she could mount up.

Fighting the tunnel closing around her vision, like she was going to lose consciousness, she swung a leg over his back.

Sleipnir got up and lunged forward, nearly unseating her. She grabbed his mane and held on with her only shred of remaining strength.

Riding him without a saddle, his energy bled into her, keeping her awake.

I'm alive.

She sat up, moving with his eight-beat stride as he galloped through the inferno. Her legs stuck to his sweaty sides, her fingers wrapped in his mane. Their surroundings had no walls left, no doors, no stairs.

Vanahalla was all but gone.

In a few long strides, clear brightness opened in front of them. *Outside.*

A massive pillar crossed their path, flames rising to eye level. Sleipnir didn't slow down. Sigrid cinched her legs around his ribs as he rocked back and gathered his hindquarters.

They jumped over the smoldering pillar, soaring over the flames and bursting out into daylight.

As they landed, Sigrid coughed, the smoke in her lungs agonizing.

The stallion kept going, taking her far away from the burning hall. The fire's heat washed over her back for a long moment as they galloped through the courtyard, over the bridge, and down the hill.

A sob escaped her lips, her cheeks damp from a flood of tears.

Vala was dead. Aunt Kaia was dead. This couldn't be real. Why did Vala have to take such a drastic measure to protect Vanahalla's relics? Wasn't there another way?

I should have run up the stairs and carried her down.

I should have refused to leave her side in the first place.

I should have stopped Aunt Kaia.

She could have done so many things differently, but she hadn't, and now they were dead, and Vanahalla was burning to the ground.

Vala had stopped the Night Elves from getting Vanaheim's relics, but they'd lost all of Vanahalla in the process. All of Vanaheim's magic was gone, including its books and records, the tapestry of her family tree, the room with Yggdrasil on the wall, enchantments that had taken thousands of years to develop, and the Eye of Hnitbjorg. The sorcerers' efforts to replicate the Night Elves' iron arrows had been wasted.

What about new valkyrie weapons and armor? Were the spears in the valkyries' hands the only ones left? *How are we supposed to defend Vanaheim?*

Her body hurt, her mind struggled, and her heart…

Across the expansive meadow, shadows raced away from the burning hall. With their king dead and the relics destroyed, the Night Elves were in retreat—whether back to Svartalfheim or sheltering in an abandoned village, it wasn't clear. Did they meet their goal when Vanahalla fell, or did they still plan to claim the land as theirs?

It didn't matter. Vanaheim had nothing left to fight for.

The valkyries and stable hands gathered in the valkyries' stable yard, along with more than a hundred courtiers and sorcerers from the royal hall. All of them gazed up at the flaming towers, their faces contorted with grief, while embers fell around them. Peter's arm was bandaged, and he looked drained as Leah kissed him repeatedly. Many others were bandaged and limping, and several sorcerers had bubbling burns.

"Sigrid!" Mariam leaped off Aesa and ran over, reaching up to take Sigrid's hand and help her dismount.

"V-Vala is dead," Sigrid said, her chest constricting in panic. "Aunt Kaia, too. The ceiling collapsed. I—" She gasped, unable to catch her breath.

Murmurs and gasps spread over the group like a windstorm through the forest, destroying any last bit of hope they'd harbored. Their homes were destroyed, their land ravaged, and there was one royal left to lead them. What would they expect of her?

It was suddenly getting harder and harder to—

"Breathe," Mariam whispered, wrapping her strong arms around Sigrid. "It's okay."

Sigrid allowed herself to be held and broke down in Mariam's arms, unable to hold back all the fear and emotions any longer.

It wasn't okay.

They'd failed to save Vanaheim.

CHAPTER SIXTY-EIGHT

INTO MYRKVIÐR

Sigrid and Mariam decided to lead the valkyries, stable hands, courtiers, and sorcerers to the secret tree fort in Myrkviðr—the only place they could think of that any remaining Night Elf groups wouldn't know about. Everyone agreed that they needed to convene somewhere hidden, because between their exhaustion and the rock-bottom morale, they would fail if anyone attacked them now.

Ash fell from the sky like snow, covering the hillside and muting the green grass as they left the smoldering remains of Vanahalla behind. The fire continued to burn even after every last pillar crumbled to the ground.

By nightfall, not even the stars were visible under the forest's thick canopy. Everyone settled into the clearing around the tree fort and, as tired as they all were, began unpacking. Farm animals went into Sleipnir's old corral, which had grown sturdier than ever. All of the equipment the stable hands had grabbed from the tack room, along with the veterinary supplies, were heaped in a pile until they could build a new structure.

Sigrid moved automatically, unloading carts and tending the horses without paying attention to what she was doing. The familiar actions from her days as a stable hand were comforting.

"Impressive craftsmanship!" Harald boomed, clapping a hand

on the fort's ladder. His family was with him, his kids standing on his feet and clinging to his legs the same way they had when Sigrid first met him. He seemed unhindered by them as he walked forward, holding a lantern up to inspect Fisk's handiwork from all angles.

Sigrid's eyes burned. *Fisk, where are you?* She hadn't seen him since yesterday, and nobody seemed to know where he'd gone. Was he hurt? Did he run away?

Durinn kept looking at her with an eyebrow raised and an *I-told-you-so* air about him, which made hot anger flare in her chest.

Several other glares burned the side of her face and prickled the back of her neck as she moved about. It wasn't hard to guess why. The same valkyries who'd accused her of treason must be convinced that she killed Queen Kaia. The juniors believed her because they knew her better, but besides them, nobody saw what'd happened, so they had to take her word for it.

Sigrid didn't spare them a thought. She hadn't stopped crying over Vala since leaving the hall. Every time she thought she was done, she would hear a sob from Tóra, and the tears started anew.

"I understand why she did it," Tóra said through her blotchy, swollen face, "but I wish there'd been another way."

"Me too," Sigrid said, not wanting to share her fear that Vala had lost her mind.

Aunt Kaia shouted as much at her before they'd both fallen. Others might have felt the same, talking about Vala's decision in hushed tones, words like "detached" and "reclusive" drifting to Sigrid's ears.

Many in the crowd grabbed lanterns and lit fires, giving the clearing a flickering warm glow. Though it might be safer to be in the dark and extinguish any flames that could reveal their location to the Night Elves, Sigrid didn't have the heart to tell everyone to smother their only source of comfort.

Nearby, Mariam helped Leah and her friends get their mares settled.

"Wow, is it dark there?" Leah asked. "Are there trees?"

Mariam bent to wrap bandages around Leah's mare's legs. "There's day and night, and huge forests, but it's really cold and misty. Not a lot of sun. I can't believe how clear and dry it is here."

"Wait until we get our rainy season," Leah said with a small laugh. "You'll regret using the word *dry*."

Mariam seemed more relaxed than she'd ever been around the juniors as they chatted. When she finished bandaging the mare's legs, Leah put an arm around her shoulders and gave her a squeeze. The sight lifted Sigrid's heart. Maybe Mariam would find a few friends among the valkyries, after all.

While Sigrid pried open a crate of emergency rations for everyone to eat, General Ulfhilda came over and extended one of her painful handshakes. "I'm sorry for your losses, Princess Sigrid."

Sigrid nodded, her throat too tight to speak.

"Although we're all in mourning and there is much to discuss," the general said, "please know you have my support."

"T-Thank you, General." The solidarity gave her hope that at least some senior valkyries didn't assume the worst of her. But her words brought another complication to mind.

How long would *Princess Sigrid* continue to be her title? As she was the only royal left in her family line, would they expect her to become queen?

The weight of this choice, and the loneliness in it, were too much to bear.

General Ulfhilda rubbed her side, wincing in pain. "I'll work with the others to come up with a plan for the Night Elves. We need to check if they've all left and decide whether to retaliate. Please join us when you're ready."

Retaliate. As if we haven't fought enough.

What would General Eira have done? Would she have fought for an alliance or sided with her queen? Had she known about Aunt Kaia's plans?

It doesn't matter. General Eira was not among them anymore.

With more tears threatening to fall, Sigrid retreated to a stump, wiping an arm across her puffy face, while others came over to take their rations.

"Want to join us?" Edith asked, motioning to where the juniors were gathered. They sat around a fire along with Roland and a couple of other stable hands, leaning on each other for warmth and comfort. All of them looked beaten up and exhausted, the valkyries' white uniforms dirty, bloody, and singed.

Sigrid shook her head, grateful for the invitation but not up for their company. "Thanks, Edith. Maybe another time."

As Edith walked away, Sigrid swallowed hard, unable to get rid of the lump in her throat. In truth, some of her grief was for Aunt Kaia—if in an agonizing, conflicting way. She'd grown to like her aunt. But the woman's beliefs about the lower realms, her loyalty to Helena, and what she'd done to King Óleifr couldn't be ignored. *Or forgiven.*

Mariam came to sit beside her, draping an arm across her shoulders. She was in no better shape than the rest of them, with a bloody wound on her arm, mud on her face, and white ash coating her tangled hair. But underneath all of it, she was as bright a presence as ever.

Sigrid leaned into her, closing her eyes and sinking into the comfort of having her there. She'd told her that Aunt Kaia had confessed to killing King Óleifr, but they both agreed there was no point in trying to convince everybody of the late queen's crime. Why should they believe her word?

"I'm sorry you had to lose your aunt," Mariam whispered into her hair.

Sigrid considered raising a shield, like, *She deserved what she got,* or, *I always knew I couldn't trust her.* But this was Mariam, one of few people she wanted to be fully open with. "It's hard to know how to feel. Aunt Kaia… She knew no other way. She thought she was doing the right thing."

Mariam nodded. "She was taught that Vanaheim belonged next to the gods at the top of Yggdrasil, and so she acted accordingly. She did everything she could to secure that place."

"Yeah," Sigrid whispered. "It's twisted, but…she did it all to protect Vanaheim — and for Helena."

Maybe it'd been impossible to ask Aunt Kaia to break her loyalty to her sister. It was about facing life together, no matter what. Would she be inclined to sink with Peter's ship, if she knew it was doomed? Probably.

Sigrid exhaled hard.

Mariam kissed her hair again, pulling her closer. "If you think of Kaia's actions as being motivated by love for Helena, does it feel better?"

Sigrid nodded. "It makes me hate her less."

"Then that's the story you should go with. She wasn't purely evil. You trusted her because she cared about you."

"Did she, though?"

Mariam's gentle fingers traced up and down Sigrid's arm. "I think she did. You're Helena's daughter. If she cared about Helena, then she cared about — well, she cared about half of you."

Sigrid cracked a smile, which faded when the image of her family tree came to mind. "Any possibility that the other half of me is less horrible?"

Maybe everyone embodied shades of both good and evil — Aunt Kaia, the Svartalf King, and herself.

Mariam leaned down, locking her gaze. "Sigrid, you might have layers of evil in your family tree, but you also have layers of good. I think it's obvious which parts you're choosing."

The tightness in Sigrid's shoulders relaxed a little. She

shivered as the cold night air bit her skin through the torn and singed uniform, but she was too tired to rummage for a cloak, so she nestled deeper into Mariam's arms.

There must have been some truth to Mariam's words, because one fact stood out above all others—*Sleipnir saved my life.*

In disbelief, she watched the mythical stallion chew strips of bark off a tree with Hestur. He was wild, unruly, full of chaos, and still… A horse who saved her life couldn't be all bad.

"There's a trick to riding Sleipnir," Sigrid said. "I just haven't found it yet."

"I believe you. And you *will* figure him out." Mariam squeezed her. "You know, he won me over when he galloped into cursed fire to save you."

He'll be getting all the treats from now until forever for that.

Sigrid got up and walked over to the stallion. She rested a hand on his neck, focusing on the hot sensation in her palm. Though his power seeped into her veins, she was too overwhelmed and grief-stricken to let it overtake her.

I will learn to tame it someday. I just have to let the right parts of me guide my actions.

Mariam came up behind her and scratched Sleipnir's neck. He leaned into it and twisted his head, wiggling his lip like the way Hestur did when Sigrid massaged him with the curry comb.

"Clearly not evil," Mariam said with a little smile. "Look at this dork."

Sigrid smiled. "But still a menace."

He tried to nip the hem of Mariam's tunic, and she swatted him away. "At least there's only one of him."

"There's always that." Sigrid went to bury her face in Hestur's mane, breathing deeply. "General Ulfhilda asked me to come discuss what to do about the Night Elves. But fighting a war with them isn't going to restore Vanaheim's place in the cosmos. We lost."

"We didn't lose, Sigrid," Mariam said fiercely. "We saved Vanaheim from becoming a world of darkness. The royal hall is gone, but the world is still here. *We're* here."

True, Vanaheim had been saved from a worse fate—but even without a living map of Yggdrasil, it was clear this world had fallen as low as Hel's domain. They had no magic, no relics, no prophetic power offered by the Eye of Hnitbjorg, and not even a royal family.

"I'm sorry you didn't have enough time to experience Vanaheim for what it was," Sigrid said, her heart aching.

Mariam shook her head. "I got to experience enough of this world to know that I want to fight for it. I got to see where my mom grew up, and that was pretty great. I get why she misses it so much."

Sigrid drew a breath, ready to do whatever was necessary. "We have to—"

Abruptly, the horses lifted their heads and snorted at some rustling in the woods.

Everyone turned, their weapons ready.

In the flickering light from the fires and lanterns, a dozen or so Night Elves emerged between the dark trees. The one in front had a wooden sword in his belt, and a familiar, ridiculously large dire wolf mask.

CHAPTER SIXTY-NINE

CHOOSING SIDES

"Just me! Don't shoot!" Fisk held his hands up. "Wow, to think I'd meet all of you here. What luck."

"Fisk?" Sigrid whispered, her heart lighter than it'd been in a long while.

Tóra squeaked nearby and ran over, throwing her willowy limbs around him. Holding her in one arm, he swept the other behind him. "At your service, Princess Sigrid."

The silence snapped like the explosion that'd destroyed Vanahalla, followed by the rumble of accusations and threats. Then several valkyries raised their spears.

Sigrid reacted before her brain caught up, sprinting over to Fisk. It was probably Tóra who saved him from being immediately shot. Sigrid threw herself in front of them with her hands up. "Everybody quiet!"

To her surprise, the noise calmed, until a hush fell over the group.

"We've not been betrayed. I asked Fisk to get allies for us—"

"How are we expected to trust the same elves who just burned down everything Vanaheim had?" Frida snarled, and several voices rose in agreement.

Sigrid wasn't surprised to find the elder valkyrie arguing against her once again. She kept her hands up. "Because these are not the same elves. They've come to help us."

"How do you know they won't betray us?" Durinn asked.

Sigrid glared at the persistently distrustful stable hand. "Because I trust Fisk. He helped me get the Eye of Hnitbjorg back when Princess Helena stole it. He's saved my life. He's fought and risked his own life for Vanaheim." She turned her gaze to everyone gathered. "If we want to create peace, this is where we start. We start by trusting each other. Working together."

Sigrid's words were met with murmurs of agreement. Mariam came to stand beside her. So did Peter, Roland, Runa, Edith, Gunni, Ylva, and then nearly all of the stable hands and junior valkyries. The crowd was divided, two sides facing off in the dark woods.

"You're prepared to trust them without even knowing who they are?" another valkyrie asked, still holding up her spear.

A valid point. Perhaps it was time for some introductions.

Someone cleared their throat behind Sigrid, and she turned to see an elf in a deer mask step forward. Across his forehead were three black stones.

Sigrid blinked, a rush of recognition shooting through her chest. "It's you! In the underground cells. You...helped us."

The elf inclined his head. "I am Nýr, youngest son of the late king of Svartalfheim. And I would like to help once more."

A prince? Sigrid looked at Fisk in disbelief, and he gave her a tiny nod.

"After my father's death, my world is in a state of anarchy," Nýr said. "My siblings will be warring for the throne, but I hope to convince them to withdraw from Vanaheim. Some of us agreed with our father more than others. I would say I agreed with him... the least."

A hush fell over the crowd.

"Thank you," Sigrid said, breathless. Having him on their side, a direct connection to his siblings, would give them some time to figure out the rest.

"Fisk has told me of your dreams, Princess. Of restoring balance to the worlds." Nýr placed a fist over his heart. "I would like to help you achieve this."

"I welcome your help." She looked to each elf and nodded, and then back to the valkyries. "We've experienced unimaginable losses, and I know for many, right now it looks impossible to find a bright spot in all the darkness. But I think..."

Mariam gave her an encouraging nod.

"I *know* this is where we start—by setting aside our differences and making allies. These Night Elves are willing to talk and even work with us as we rebuild our home. We would be foolish to turn away a helping hand."

An uneven *thumpa-thumpa* rose beside her, and everyone watched Sleipnir walk over to Sigrid and stand at her shoulder. She stared up at him, his massive form as intimidating as ever.

Did he sense that she needed his strength? There was so much about their connection that she didn't understand.

"Princess Sigrid," Harald said at the front of the crowd, sounding breathless. "Sleipnir's Heir, descended from Odin. I am at your service, and I hope we can restore Vanaheim to its place at the top of Yggdrasil."

A wild sensation fluttered through her chest as the crowd fell silent, and Harald came to stand beside her. When General Ulfhilda followed, the valkyries who still looked uncertain and angry lowered their weapons, soft gasps emitting from several of them.

It wasn't a unanimous agreement—but under the circumstances, it was the best Sigrid could hope for.

CHAPTER SEVENTY

MOUNT HNITBJORG'S CALL

Sigrid's heart still raced as she looked around their camp, playing out how many different ways the encounter with their Night Elf allies could have gone. With the majority in her favor and the elves declared not a threat, the crowd had dissipated to continue settling in.

Prince Nýr and the others remained nearby, waiting on her.

She stepped closer to Fisk. "Do you think with the extra help, you could expand the tree fort? We're going to need a place to live."

Fisk turned to them for confirmation, and when several of them nodded, he faced Sigrid. "Sure can do!"

She stood at a loss for words as he gave them instructions for materials and they jumped into action. Even the prince gave a little wave and left with them.

When they were gone, leaving Sigrid, Mariam, Fisk, and Tóra staring at each other, Mariam took Sigrid's hand and gave her a nudge. Her heart couldn't help but soar.

Fisk cleared his throat. "Tóra and I are courting," he announced, holding Tóra close. She hung from his shoulder, looking up at his mask with a gooey expression.

Sigrid and Mariam glanced at each other.

"I see that," Mariam said.

"Congratulations." Sigrid grinned, happy for the two oddballs.

His mask turned between her and Mariam. "Are you two finally courting?"

Heat rushed into Sigrid's face. "What do you mean *finally*?" she asked at the same time as Mariam said, "How long have you known?"

"Well, I figured it out that day I returned to Sleipnir's corral and the two of you had been kissing. You both had heat coming from your lips."

"Excuse me?" Mariam said, aghast.

He pointed to his mask's eye holes. "Heat, not light. And both of your faces look a little hot right now."

"That is so creepy," Sigrid whispered.

Fisk chuckled. "I'm glad you're back to yourself."

"Me too. And I'm sorry about...all of it."

"All is forgiven. We're starting over, right?" Fisk motioned to the camp, at the people of Vanaheim building their temporary homes with the help of Night Elves. Never before had this happened, but they were slowly changing things.

"Anyway, I'll get to work on the tree fort. See you all later!" He walked off with Tóra on his arm, standing taller than Sigrid had ever seen him.

Face still burning, Sigrid swallowed hard. "Are we?" she asked Mariam.

"Courting?" Mariam cast a smile that weakened Sigrid's knees.

Sigrid smiled back, the battalion of wings in her belly as wild as ever. She took Mariam's face gently between her hands and kissed her, savoring her soft lips and smooth skin.

"My *girlfriend* is a princess," Mariam whispered, as if tasting the concept.

Those words on Mariam's lips sent a ripple of pleasure through Sigrid. She pressed closer, kissing her harder, her head spinning from the feel of Mariam's body against hers—thighs, hips, stomach, lips, palms…

The murmuring and shuffling people around them forced them to break apart before things became too heated.

"Gods, I could kiss you for days," Sigrid whispered, grateful this world still had her slice of perfection in it.

"We can do that." Mariam pecked her lips. "But there's a fort to build, animals to take care of, and a whole lot more."

Sigrid groaned.

Mariam laughed, attracting Aesa's attention. The mare came over and nuzzled her gently, as if checking on her.

Tap, tap, tap.

Sigrid and Mariam pulled apart, exchanging a quizzical look.

Behind them on a loaded cart, slow tapping came from one of the crates.

"Did…one of the chickens get misplaced?" Mariam asked.

Sigrid walked closer. "That doesn't sound like a chicken scratching."

She reached for the lid.

"Careful," Mariam said, rushing to her side.

"Why? It's nothing dangerous."

"Still, we don't know what it is, do we?"

Slowly, Sigrid removed the lid. When nothing erupted, they leaned over.

Inside was a jumble of tiny halters, blankets, gloves, a stethoscope…

"This came from the foaling barn," Sigrid said, digging through everything.

Near the bottom, her hands closed around a metal rod. She pulled it out. The uteroscope was active, turning in her hand.

At Mariam's confused look, Sigrid said, "It's enchanted with a fertility rune. It tells the vet if a mare is—"

The rod pulled to the right, where Aesa stood.

"Um."

"What?" Mariam asked sharply, looking between Sigrid and Aesa.

Sigrid couldn't finish the sentence.

"The foaling barn?" Mariam asked sharply. "This tells the vet if a mare's pregnant?"

There was a long pause. Sigrid moved her hand, watching the end of the rod lean toward Aesa. "Yep."

"Give me that." Mariam snatched it. She moved the uteroscope purposefully around Aesa, watching the end pull in the mare's direction. She shook it. "It has to be broken."

Sigrid looked to Hestur, who'd spent a lot of time with Aesa. But Hestur was a gelding, so that would have been impossible.

"Maybe it is. We don't even keep stallions in the valkyrie stable," Sigrid said, struggling to sound calm for Mariam's sake. But her heart pounded, because something told her the device wasn't broken.

Mariam froze. The muscles in her fingers must have failed, because the uteroscope slipped from her hand and clattered to the ground, where she left it.

Sigrid's heart thumped so hard that it pulsed outside her chest.

In unison, she and Mariam turned around.

Sleipnir stood there, his ears perked, a strip of bark hanging from his mouth. He chewed and swallowed, an unmistakably smug look on his face.

At least there's only one of him, Mariam had said moments ago.

"Gods, help us," Mariam whispered.

"J-Just what we need—another descendant of Loki," Sigrid said, stammering.

A *foal*. An eight-legged, *winged* foal.

Loki's tricks knew no end.

They looked at each other in horror, and the expression on Mariam's face was so stunned that Sigrid couldn't stop a small laugh from bubbling up.

Mariam stared at her for another moment, then smiled in spite of herself.

The dim glow brought to mind the way she'd looked in the darkness of Sigrid's chambers, a perfect silhouette in the moonlight. The fires cast just enough light to see the freckles across her nose.

Standing between Mariam and her favorite horses, surrounded by the stable hands—her family—the knot in Sigrid's belly loosened a little. No matter what came next, her heart was full of love, and that gave her all the strength she needed.

They would work to restore Vanaheim to the way it was—a world of prosperity and abundance. Vala had told her where to start, and although Sigrid wasn't convinced she could achieve something that Vala herself had failed at…she owed it to her world to try.

"There's a way to restore Vanaheim's place in Yggdrasil—and if we can do that, we'll be able to fix the cosmic balance."

Mariam nodded, her breath catching, looking like she was ready for whatever Sigrid was about to say.

Sigrid took her hand. "I have to make a new Eye of Hnitbjorg. Will you help me?"

ACKNOWLEDGEMENTS

I wouldn't have been able to write this book without the people who cheer me on every step of the way. Thank you, Toshi, Stephanie, Ben, Mom, Dad, Alex, and my personal hype crew, Sandy, Ada, and Amanda. Special thanks to my emotional support group and critique partners, Lindsay, Deana, Ashley, Kelly, and Bee. To Amy and the rest of the Entangled team, thank you for helping me to bring Sigrid's story to life.

Let's be friends!

🐦 @EntangledTeen

📷 @EntangledTeen

f @EntangledTeen

♪ @EntangledTeen

📰 bit.ly/TeenNewsletter

entangled teen

an imprint of Entangled Publishing LLC